THE WIDOWER'S SON

Alan Sillitoe

STAR

A STAR BOOK
published by
the Paperback Division of
W. H. ALLEN &. Co Ltd

A Star Book
Published in 1977
by the Paperback Division of
W. H. Allen & Co. Ltd
A Howard and Wyndham Company
44 Hill Street, London W1X 8LB

First published in Great Britain by
W. H. Allen & Co Ltd, 1976

Copyright © Alan Sillitoe, 1976

Printed in Great Britain by
Richard Clay (The Chaucer Press), Ltd.,
Bungay, Suffolk

ISBN 0 352 39514 1

ACKNOWLEDGEMENTS

I would like to express my thanks to Brigadier Shelford Bidwell (author of *Gunners at War* and *Modern Warfare*, etc.) for his comments and suggestions on the early part of this novel especially Chapter Five. Any errors in gunnery and artillery procedure that might remain are entirely my own.

My appreciation also to Major R. G. Bartelot of the Royal Artillery Institution, Woolwich, for allowing me to see battery records from the 1940 campaign in France and Flanders.

Also to Doctor Philip Towle, for kindly supplying notes on the education of Boy Soldiers before the Second World War.

THE WIDOWER'S SON

Also by Alan Sillitoe

FICTION
Saturday Night and Sunday Morning
Loneliness of the Long Distance Runner
The General
Key to the Door
The Ragman's Daughter
The Death of William Posters
A Tree on Fire
Guzman, Go Home
A Start in Life
Travels in Nihilon
Raw Material
Men, Women and Children
The Flame of Life

POETRY
The Rats and Other Poems
A Falling out of Love and Other Poems
Love in the Environs of Vorenezh
Storm and Other Poems

TRAVEL
Road to Volgograd

PLAY
All Citizens are Soldiers
(with Ruth Fainlight)

ESSAYS
Mountains and Caverns

Part One

CHAPTER ONE

After his best friend had been killed by his side at the pitface Charlie Scorton decided to join the army. When he told his father that he was 'going for a soldier' he was ordered never to come back through that door wearing a uniform. It was a common enough shout in those days.

Standing six-feet tall in the tiny kitchen, Charlie demanded to know what was wrong with the army and its uniform. His father was a small ageing forty-year-old, bald and bearded, with lively eyes whose blue glitter had been put there by splitting coal for nearly three decades down the mine. He sprang at his son and belaboured his face with such violence that Charlie staggered under the shock. He locked his fists at his side and turned to go, ears stopped to his mother's craven weeping.

He went into the depot at Nottingham with a bruised face and two raw eyes. The sergeant laughed as he handed him the Queen's shilling, but was almost respectful when he signed his name in the finest copperplate.

He knew in his heart that his father had said the service of the dead over him, which could not matter anymore because his mind was dulled by the marching and countermarching at Aldershot, the turning and wheeling, musketry and guard duties, fatigues and parades, which soothed him no matter how hard and prolonged they were. To be tired was insubordination. To be slow on the uptake was insolence. It was criminal to be slack. Everyone was in a blinding rage; everything must be done at the double, or you joined the Jankers Men. He had to bend his nature to a higher will, and little else could get into his mind.

Being tall, and finding a sudden preternatural smartness in

himself – due as much to the coldness of spirit that came over him, as to inborn qualities – he was picked out for battalion marker. Before a regimental review, and after the intense and meticulous bulling-up of accoutrements in the barrack room, four of his mates had to carry him to the required spot on the parade ground so that not a speck of dust or a wrinkle would be picked up on boots or trousers or belt or rifle while walking there himself. If any such blemish caught the eye of the inspecting officer he was for it. This initiation into the torment of being something special only increased his taciturnity. A thousand men used him as a post on which to form their ranks.

As months went by and life slipped into a routine, he came from under the cloud of his disaster. He made friends, discarded a fraction of his silence, but retained the frozen image of his father's rage that had been stamped on him during the argument before leaving home. He learned to bite so hard on the bullet of his heart that it took little effort never to think of the old man again.

When he could, he met his mother at an aunt's place in Retford, a convenient point on the railway while stationed at York. He'd give her presents, or the few shillings he'd saved up, but never mentioned his father though she always hoped he would. She died and got buried while he was six thousand miles away.

Those locked fists that hadn't smashed into his father were used eagerly enough in many hand-to-hands on the North West Frontier. He was glad to get to India, hot as it was, having realised early that England was no place for a soldier. He loved it because he'd been born there and spoke the language, and missed it at all times, but a soldier had to be where the sun and action were, otherwise he might just as well have stayed down the pit – which place he likened to clawing at the walls of a dungeon with no possibility of ever getting out.

After five years in India he served in Natal, later in Gibraltar and Egypt, and during the Great War in France. More than half his army life was spent out of England, and he ended his time in Mesopotamia – or Messpot, as he called it.

His travels made him into a smart and knowledgeable sergeant, barely affable but indispensable to the famous regiment he belonged to. In the mess it was sometimes jokingly said that sergeants were a sight better at the pursuit of warfare than their officers. When the beer flowed many hinted that if given it as an exercise they could run the army any day. While he never said as much, Charlie often thought it possible.

He was once offered a commission, but turned it down because a ranker from the so-called lower-classes with a sub-altern's pip on his shoulder had a hard time for want of money. He preferred the good life of three plain stripes, with just enough pay and not too much responsibility.

After twenty-four years he left the army, and came back to live in Ashfield because he thought it might be easier to land a job – and that living would be cheaper – where he'd been born and brought up. The pension, on top of his wages as a post-man, made him a few bob a week better off than most people round about. A good soldier never looks back, was one of his sayings, but on that occasion he had to, because by then an-other factor was that he had a wife and son in Ashfield, as well as his sister living a few streets away.

When he'd been home a while he discovered that a score-and-four in the army hadn't been such a long stint after all, that people remembered him as clearly as if he'd only been away a short time. The friends of his youth were in their middle forties and easily recognisable, though most looked older and certainly walked less upright. His years as a soldier had not erased his past as much as he'd hoped they would. When he recalled it he hated it, and was piqued that he could no longer shun by distance all that had set him off in life. He looked on his time with the army as the making of him, only regretting that he had been forced into it by circumstances, and not by his own free decision.

When it looked as if his humdrum and not unhappy life was set in for good, his wife caught influenza one winter. It was weird and awful, because she was tall and well-built, with hardly an illness in her life. Such people often packed in at the first blow. He'd known it happen. Yet the day she was in bed giving birth to William, she'd insisted, between the pains, on

9

plucking a fowl for their dinners that night. And then when the 'flu struck she went out like at matchlight in the Hindu Kush, no word or smile through the choking that carried her off. He'd seen people die even quicker, and had grieved almost as much over some. By his wife's coffin he called back the first time: 'Dig, you bastards, dig!' the sergeant screamed in that first Afghan venture. There was a sound like a stone hitting a cushion when Leonard didn't get down fast enough, and so his bosom pal folded and was gone.

'It was the beer-gut gave it a noise like that,' said Oxo, and Charlie half-killed the swivel-eyed ingot for not keeping his remarks to himself, pummelled him by the *nullah* when the pair of them had been told off for the rearguard. Nearly lost his lance-jack's stripe over it. But the pain began to withdraw from his bones and veins at the fusillade over the grave by that remote sangar in the hills of Waziristan, and later after other short scuffles in half-eyed dumps where he had lost friends with a bitterness and bewilderment that could hardly be borne.

Here was a pain no battle would ease. He had to look, listen, talk, work and sometimes sleep for the rest of his life when even to live another minute hardly seemed on the cards. Yet he'd been trained to keep moving whenever he felt the black dog's weight, and the fact that he did so now was one more item to thank the army for.

The big diversion came in looking after his son William, and of finding some means to launch him in a career. And when he'd go away, as all male offspring must, there'd be nobody to account for but himself, which would be no trouble at all. He could be his own man again then. For all his suffering, sense of loss and anxiety in case his son too should be carried inexplicably off, he was not a man who looked oppressed by melancholy. His eyes alone might have showed it, but the curve of his lips would too often give it the lie.

Nevertheless there wasn't much room in the strait-jacket of life to move your limbs about, he told his sister Doris grimly after the funeral, adding – and she believed him – that if there wasn't young Billy to bring up he'd have hanged himself without thinking twice.

But he soon lost that narrow-eyed look of death that seemed too much out of place with his mouth and the habitual straightness of his back. People wondered when he'd be getting wed again, and the more familiar teased him on his rounds. He'd only smile, and say that married life was not for him.

His secret heart, treacherously, as he thought, had indeed caused him to wonder why he shouldn't find someone. But who'd want a man near fifty? A young girl looking for a gran-dad maybe, or a widow searching for somebody else to poison. Most of the personable and bonny girls were set up already, and if they weren't he wondered why not, and what was wrong with them. He made a faint approach to thirty-year-old Alice Brown who lived next-door-but-one, but was just as gently pushed off when he talked to her outside the chapel in which he'd been married a dozen years before.

Doris saw it all. 'Never mind, Charlie, there are plenty of other women.'

'Aye,' he answered, resenting her outspokenness, 'for other men' – a retort heard often in the mess when somebody had been jilted and you tried to hand them a flake of comfort.

But he wasn't disappointed. He had only been able to make the attempt because he hadn't really wanted to get married again. He stamped on it. Wedlock was another of those com-plete and finished lives he'd have to put behind. And what he got on the side would be his own affair. There was always a bit of that knocking around for an ex-soldier in Nottingham, fourteen miles away.

Charlie's son William was born in a street where, if the curtains of a house weren't open by half past six in the morn-ing, it was thought that somebody had died during the night. An old woman might call and ask whether there was laying-out to be done, or an undertaker's scout would knock and wonder – with eyes agleam – about business.

At woodwork classes in school the boys made book-racks and took them to homes where there weren't any books. They sweated and felt pride over fancy rollers to hold lavatory paper where only newsprint was used. But it kept them busy, and that, the teacher swore, was next door to happiness.

His mother died when he was seven, so from then on he was brought up by his father, a rare happening that set William apart in the eyes of others and therefore his own. School pals thought him lucky to be singled out for an adventure so different from theirs, whereas women who lived in the same street looked at him as if he'd had an arm off.

A few boys in his class were left with only a mother because the father had died in the 'War to end Wars'. Some had flitted. Others had never turned up in the first place, but he was the only one to be lumbered with nothing but a father. The inside horizons had crumbled when his mother died, but he soon got used to his father waking him up in the morning. The earth revolved at night in his deepest dreams. The mist of living clung to him, and he learned to see through it.

Every Saturday afternoon Doris came over to sweep, scrub floors, change bedding, iron a shirt and tie for them each, and blow dust off the row of a dozen books. She pressed the trousers of their suits only once a month, because Charlie kept his creases in by laying them neatly between the mattress and the springs of the bed he slept on. He taught William to do the same, because a soldier often had no other way.

While Doris worked, Charlie and his son were out at the market buying the week's provisions. He would do a swift reconnaissance, then go back to the stalls he'd chosen to trade with. They went from one to another, Charlie seeming parsimonious and slow; fussy almost at getting what was marked on his list at the right price.

William noticed traits in his father that were in his aunt Doris when it came to shopping. If he stopped at the same couple of stalls week after week instead of chopping and changing about they would have got to know him and given him a better deal to keep his custom. But he couldn't tell him this, and in any case his father enjoyed doing 'the commissariat' in his own way.

While they were shopping Doris lit a fire under the scullery copper and filled the bath with hot water in front of the living-room fire so that Charlie could have his tub the minute he got back. When his father had finished and gone upstairs with a towel around his middle, William sat in the same water, but with a bucket of fresh and a scoop standing on the hearth rug so that he could swill himself down and get properly clean.

He was glad to pull off his weekday clothes and feel the fire's heat before stepping over the rim. His father took only five minutes to get scrubbed, so the bath was still hot and he sat down slowly, ladling the soap-bubbles and water up to cool before he was totally in. He wondered when he'd ever get a first bath all to himself, yet wasn't too bothered because it was comforting to use his father's. The bucket of fresh was almost cold, and he shuddered as it poured over, glad to stride out and reach for the fire-warmed clean towel that was his alone.

Doris stayed to cook dinner. It was Charlie's luxury of the week, and maybe reminded him of life in India when he'd had his own servant. He dressed for it in a dark suit, white shirt, black thin tie, high collar and a gold watch at his waistcoat. He sat at the table in the tiny parlour, and barely glanced at Doris as she came in with the various platters. His hair was short and dark, almost shaved, no parting showing. After the meal he would stay at the table with a cup of milky coffee, smoking his weekly cigar.

William was spruced up in his best short-trousered suit, a parting like a knife blade down his sandy hair. He'd hardly seen his father before the age of seven. When Charlie came back from the War – a tall soldier in a khaki overcoat and laden with kit – he was a stranger, except for a shadowy picture far back in his mind, matched to the framed photo on the sideboard. He'd wondered when he would go off for good and leave him once more with his mother. But she died after a year, and the man stayed because he was his father.

He was always aware of his father trying to teach him something, couldn't remember when he hadn't known how many inches there were to a mile. The number was repeated at him till he knew it – 63,360 – as if it were the primal quantity in life. He wrote it out a hundred times without knowing its importance, a magical cypher he then had to parrot on demand in order to please his father.

Charlie went on to teach him other more interesting facts, and behind the laying out of signs and sketches William sensed that his father wanted to tell him something absolutely profound – but wasn't really able to. This made him more eager to learn as if, should he take in everything now, his father might eventually reach those revelations which were of vital importance to them both. But his father constantly replenished his knowledge from books when he seemed at the end of his supply, and whatever he had to say, that William thought would be so important, he was never quite able to dig up.

During the week they'd eat by gaslight, but on Saturday Charlie set two brass candlesticks on the parlour table, took candles from the dresser drawer, and lit them before the meal began. He frowned once when Doris, thinking he'd forgotten, herself placed them on the cloth. He used the nearest candle to light his cigar from after dessert, and only he knew how close it had to be.

The platter was brought in with the first course of Yorkshire pudding and jam: 'If a compass bearing on a distant windmill is 260 degrees, what angle would you draw on the map?'

'Is it near Nottingham?'

'Closer to Worksop, I'd say.'

A coal fire burned in the grate. William contrived to make the answer appear a more difficult problem than it was, knowing it pleased his father if he puzzled a few moments over it. He taught him all he knew, but never hit him when he made a mistake. If he stumbled over the answer, Charlie would only frown, then patiently explain how it might be done, so that next time he would do it quicker.

When meat, potatoes and vegetables were set down for his father to serve, the questions were relatively slow. Charlie ate quickly, and didn't need to consider them because they took a mere second to formulate. William too had his world, but it was less placid because he had to be ready for pulling the next answer out of his brain. He couldn't mull too much on a coming cricket match at school, or wonder how he'd do in next term's tests, or hope he could add to his chemistry set at Christmas. Charlie wouldn't allow it. He had to be alert when he was with other people at table.

Knowing that the local magnetic variation was sixteen

degrees west, he subtracted it from the bearing to give the answer. It was basic stuff, but he was still young, and Charlie knew what he was doing by sharpening his brain to mental quickness. His idea was to train him, make him malleable and eternally curious for the time when he would be sent out into the world.

On one Saturday evening a month the training was curtailed, and Charlie ate hurriedly before leaving for a night out in Nottingham. He left the table half an hour early to catch his train, the cigar only half smoked as he put on his stetson-type hat, said good night to Doris, and went out by the scullery door.

At chapel on Sunday morning, William's back had to be as straight in his seat as it had been at table the evening before. 'Always keep your back straight,' Charlie dinned into him. 'People will respect you then, even if you haven't more than a shilling in your pocket. And if they respect you, you'll be all right. You can always go on from there.'

They'd walk home from chapel to a meal of stew and vegetables which Doris had cooked the night before, so that Charlie had only to warm it up on the stove. The afternoon was for walking a few miles towards Shireoaks, or into the Dukeries, taking Sheet 46 of the one-inch map and Charlie's prismatic compass in its leather case. He'd show him how to march on a bearing, and count the paces by putting a pebble into his pocket at the end of every hundred, and give an example of how to find their position from two (or three) conspicuous landmarks whose angles they'd take by the compass. He'd coach him on dividing the Horizontal Equivalent by the Vertical Interval in order to get the gradient of the slope, and then they'd sort out problems of Intervisibility through a series of contour lines plotted on the map.

William's feeling for landscape was accurate but easy going, almost a love of it, so that later it became so much part of him that he didn't know whether or not he'd been born from the leaves and rolling grass itself. At ten he could recognise the ground called 'dead' on which, from a seeming vantage point, you could not see an enemy advancing. It was a dip of the land in which they were invisible and safe from your fire, and the name 'dead ground' was a sinister label for a place wherein all sorts of secret forces could assemble before destroying you, and after the unequal fight you ended up in that other piece of 'dead ground' called the cemetery.

But the more he saw what it actually looked like, the more it was obvious how to deal with it – if you had the power and equipment. 'Always watch it though,' his father emphasised. 'Detect it early so's you know it's there. Keep it in mind. A good soldier never neglects dead ground. No matter how well you deploy your platoon, there's always bound to be some.'

It was not by pure chance that he was fascinated by what his father had to teach. He also sensed its necessity. And perhaps Charlie recognised early on a foolproof device for keeping them close as father and son.

While rambling into a deep part of the Dukeries, where keepers no longer thought they were up to mischief, gun-shots leapt through trees and down from the sky at the same time, and his father asked how far off the firing was, and from what direction it came: 'One day you might have to take a bearing on it,' he said, 'and if somebody else does from a mile away, you can fix the devils, once and for all.' After a pause he added: 'As soon as your enemy fires, you'll know where he is. And if you're still alive, you've got 'im!'

William wanted to ask how many men he had killed during all his time in the army, but couldn't bring his question out. He imagined his father lying alone among scorching boulders, looking from behind cover in such a way that no one could see him, rifle loaded and cocked, ready for the slightest movement in front. He saw him as cool, rapid, and unkillable, always running forward, never back, moving on his belly like a snake, edging mile by mile nearer to that golden city of Baghdad, which he said was so filthy once you got inside it.

Another imparted skill was how to judge distance. 'You'll never regret knowing it,' his father said, one clear day at a junction of straight avenues in Clumber Park, 'whatever you do in life. When you come to fire a rifle or a gun you'll know its value. Any sharp-eyed chap can fire at a target whose range he knows, but it takes real salt in the eye to pick a man out of the landscape and know how far off he is without being told. You've got to see him before he sees you, get the range, adjust your sight and fire.'

He knocked out his pipe: 'I'm going to walk a hundred and twenty paces into those fir trees, so's you'll learn to know what a hundred yards looks like. Then I'll do another hundred – two hundred altogether, see? You'll know what *that* looks like as well.'

William stood, cap in hand, as his father strode scientifically away, a derby-hatted figure who maybe imagined he had a whole platoon under instruction. He wondered what it was all about. Bemusement lay under his surface fascination, but he learned nevertheless to register the distance, and carry that two hundred yards vividly in his head.

Returning home through town the training went on:

'How many windows did that house have?'

'Which one?'

'The one we've just passed. DON'T turn round.'

He hesitated. He hadn't really noticed.

'Come on, look sharp! Your eyes took a picture as they went by. They allus do. Like one o' them cameras. Law o' nature!'

William's backsight turned somersaults inside him. He was right: they had. 'Eight?'

'Ten – but you were close. See what I mean?'

'Yes. I do.'

'How far off is that bridge?'

'Four hundred yards.'

'Four-fifty. A fair guess. How wide was it?'

'Twelve feet?'

'Damned good!'

He felt real happiness when he scored a hit, but his father's keenness at times embarrassed him.

'You've got to train your powers of observation,' Charlie went on. 'Don't just look at things. Describe 'em to yourself. Write it down, if it'll help. Always carry a little notebook with you. Use the King's English. If you know what things look like, you'll twig how far off they are. It'll mek a smart soldier out of you, as well as an intelligent man. Most people see nothing. They don't want to. Don't have to, I suppose. But if

17

you train yourself to see as well as look, you'll be better than most. And the joy is – it's all dead simple. A matter of training – nowt else. Costs nothing. Nobody's born with it. At least none that I ever knew of.'

So William was taught how to judge distance and, what went with it, to *keep* his distance as well. Charlie passed on to his son what he had learned in the army: that you can't keep your distance unless you know it, and then you must do it so well that people don't even notice it. You appear to be your own man, an isolated individual who can move and do as he likes with himself – even though he wears a uniform and has nearly every hour of the day circumscribed. The more you educate yourself in the army, he implied, the more you're able to keep sane, clean and look after yourself. He was given to understand that keeping yourself to yourself made you a better soldier.

Hearing such tales about Aldershot and Shorncliffe, of his travels and of his time during the Great War, he knew early on that his father was no mere postman, but a man of the world, who for some reason had now to earn his living like anybody else. Not that he made this apparent to his mates at school and during the two hours a week he was allowed to play in the street. It was only in his daydreams that both worlds mixed and it struck him how much out of the ordinary his father was. Many years passed before he realised that maybe he wasn't such a rare person after all, and that most boys thought the same about their fathers.

They went every fortnight in wind, rain, sun or snow to tidy up his mother's grave and leave a few flowers there.

His father never talked of her during these visits and, climbing the curving leafy lane to the plateau, William liked this chance to grit his teeth and push any thoughts of her deeper back into the swirling powder of his mind.

Between school, work, chapel and study there was no spare time. It may have been true, as Charlie said, that the Devil made work for idle hands. Yet William had a feeling that talk was the enemy, not time. By packing every minute with activity they were saved from speaking to each other, which developed the habit in him of only opening his mouth at

18

home when there was something to say, so that he looked forward to the noise and chatter of school.

He sometimes talked with Doris about his mother after his father had gone out on one of his Saturday nights. 'She wasn't a saint – nobody is. Don't think *that* – just because she's dead and was your mother,' she told him. 'She was a funny sort – hard and soft at the same time.'

He poked at the fire, and waited for her to go on.

'She was hard because a woman had to be who married our Charlie. And she was soft because she wouldn't say boo to a goose – especially to your father. Maybe *her* father had hammered her a bit. People in the street took her for an all-hard woman, even though they knew her. A tartar, in fact. But they didn't know her as I did. She was like a lot of women, especially after they get married. I'm glad I never did, though I had my chances. It never did a woman any good as far as I can see. It's a good job I've got eyes in my body, though, or I might have dropped into it!'

The suspicion that she and his father talked about his mother when he wasn't there made him feel more alone in the world than if he'd been in an orphanage. He felt fundamentally left out, standing in the cold while his father stared at the grave with jonquils in his hand. But then he imagined Doris forcing Charlie into it 'for his own sake', and his mood lightened, though the sober way in which they kept silent showed how important his mother still was to all of them. Knowing there was no need to talk helped him to keep the tears back from his eyes.

His father carried a haversack, and after they had duly laid the flowers he took the prismatic compass from its leather case and sighted it on a corner of the chapel. It had rained much of the night, and water-puddles glistened along the radiating paths. William shivered, and fastened the top button of his overcoat.

His father brought the compass down: 'We're going to do a survey of the cemetery. Draw a map of it.'

He wanted to get out of the wind, and back home. 'Is it hard to do?'

'Not very. As long as you're logical, and take pains. I'll

show you. Patience is what you need, though – patience, neatness and knowledge.'

'What are we going to do it for?'

Charlie looked down at him. It was obvious he'd thought about it a long time. 'Practice. It'll test our draughtsmanship. If it looks nice, we'll frame it. Hang it on the wall.' He handed him the compass: 'What's the bearing of that big elm over there?'

William lined it up with the middle of the trunk, looked into the prism till the degree card steadied and stopped. His greatest fear was, not that he might call the wrong bearing, but that he should drop his father's compass. It had been on many hard marches, and with his half-hunter, short telescope, pocket barometer and stop-watch completed his few treasures.

'To the nearest half-degree,' he was cautioned.

A woman came by with a spoutless watering can in one hand, and a huge bundle of daffodils under the other arm as if they were a load of firewood. He thought she would bump into him, and the number shifted.

'Imagine you're being sniped at!'

He re-aligned it. 'Hundred and forty five and a half.'

Charlie turned from looking at her. 'That's what I made it.'

He was pleased, so William was worried that he wouldn't do as well next time. All he wanted was to get away from these gloomy headstones. He once thought that when you were buried the body turned into a solid tongue of stone that poked itself for ever above the soil, with your name and the date of death inscribed on it. He shivered at the idea, but was glad that some memories were already fading.

Huge cold white clouds left little of the squally blue in the vast yonder behind. In one far corner a grave was being dug, and he could hear the spade hitting the soil. He wanted to run away, but felt tired and weak. He couldn't tell his father that he'd like to knock all the stones flat. Some were grey and some were black, perhaps to tell you who had done good and who had been evil.

Charlie took a bagful of penny cakes from his haversack. 'We'll eat these before we start.'

The sight of the cream buns made him feel better. Things often turned up at such times if you said nothing. He ate the first two quickly. The cemetery always made him feel clambed.

'My guy,' Charlie laughed, 'you must have been as hungry as a hunter! If you don't steady on you'll have them indigestion-rats chewing at your vitals.'

His energy was coming back, and he found the picture funny. 'That wain't do me much good, will it?'

'It won't,' he answered sternly. If he laughed at the same time it often took his father's humour away.

'We'll make a start then,' Charlie said.

He paced from a corner of the chapel to the large elm, a deliberate gait so as to make his steps exact. The long overcoat flapped against his legs, and he looked dead ahead, and came on in a straight line for the tree.

The grave-digger observed a man whom nothing could stop in a walk towards the remaining memorial of his grief. He shook his head, and thrust his spade back into the tough soil.

William turned from his own glance at the grave-digger as his father approached. 'Two hundred. That'll be our base line.'

'How many base lines do we need?'

'Only one. Write it in the notebook: base-line and bearing.'

He drew the pencil twice down the centre of the page, from which to mark off angles and measurements. 'You do it bit by bit. It comes together like a jigsaw puzzle when you make the fair copy on a big sheet of paper at home.'

Using both ends of the base-line, they linked up the main points: church, caretaker's hut, fountain, each bend of the walls – tramping through wet grass till William knew that even his father was numb and cold. 'We'll feature her grave in red,' he said casually, 'when we come to draw the map. Then we'll see it clear.'

He packed the book and compass into the haversack. 'In a fortnight we'll come back, to put in what we've forgotten.'

'Is there much?'

'There shouldn't be, by rights, but I've never known a case where you've remembered everything. Usually it's no skin off your snout, because all the *vital* things are there, and that's

21

what matters.'

They walked home for tea, before going out again to do the shopping.

When his mother was alive his parents had had little to say to one another, as if they'd got through all the talking to be done before he was born. He also noticed that his father only took an interest in his school work after she had died. There'd been enough time for him to start before, but nobody had seemed bothered about it then. Now that he was coming on for eleven his father went to the headmaster every few weeks and talked about his prospects. Charlie, as a postman, was also well known to the teachers, and he arranged for William to sit for the grammar school scholarship. He announced it one Saturday evening, after Doris had been in with the steamed-pudding and treacle, breaking a long silence that had led William to expect something unusual.

'I don't know what we'll make of you, but I do know that the first thing is to get you to a proper school.'

'Aren't I at a proper one now?'

'A better one,' he told him, his back straight, and forearm at an angle of ninety degrees as his hand dug at the pudding with his spoon. Early in his army life Charlie had been a waiter for six months in the officers' mess, a job he'd disliked, but he'd made his observations all the same on how to eat at table. When you had something to forget, you became a dab hand at imitating the ways of others. 'I want 'em to teach you French, and trigonometry. You'll happen need trigonometry one day.

A bit of pudding fell from his spoon.

'You don't need to be so quick at it,' Charlie snapped, as if slopping the pudding was a way of arguing against him. 'You'll get it into your mouth even quicker if you take it steady.'

He wondered why he wanted him to learn all about angles. 'Do *you* know trigonometry?'

'Not enough to teach you. I'm a bit rusty on it. But you'll need trigonometry to be an engineer. Or a gunner.'

He was more careful with his pudding. 'Why have I got to learn French?'

Charlie looked hard. 'You'll need that to be a gentleman.'

One of his heart-beats hiccuped. So that was it. He dropped another piece of pudding, but his father, having got rid of what had been on his mind, said nothing. French wouldn't make him any gentler. To be a gentleman, all he had to do was get taller and older. The word had an attractive sound. In a book called *The Smugglers* he had read about gentlemen. They were brave, but they led easy lives.

With such a suddenly clear horizon, and precise orders for pursuing it, it was no wonder that he failed the first hurdle of the scholarship test. Being honest, Charlie didn't know who to blame, but being intelligent he thought it best to devise a plan. If you couldn't take a Mahsud sangar in Waziristan at the first charge you didn't sit down and cry about it, but calmly made better dispositions and tried again. Instead of going at it head on, you put your brainbox to some use – a few men here, a section there, a battery hidden, crown the heights with a machine-gun and get others in from the rear. You had to be as sly and ruthless as them buggers, finish 'em off with the queen of weapons.

He arranged for William to take the examinations again a year later, but this time the preparation was better. The months between were hard to live through. His father's manner changed, his resentment becoming a powerhouse of push and persuasion. William could not avoid the keen expression continually turned on him. He felt almost as if he was being blamed for having killed his mother, but he took it without bitterness, almost with pride, and if his father didn't seem harsh, it was only because he had judged his son well.

'Speed is of the essence,' Charlie said.

'Yes.'

'And accuracy. That's of the essence, as well.'

'Yes, dad.'

He hammered it in: 'Speed without accuracy isn't speed. See what I mean?'

He did.

'It's a disaster. There are things in life, son, that we can't do without: speed, accuracy, knowledge and energy.'

William wondered whether he ought not to write the words

down in his notebook, but thought he'd remember them right enough.

'We'd better throw in love as well,' his father added. 'As the preacher says. We mustn't forget that.'

What a lovely hypocrite, Doris thought, hearing him from the scullery.

Charlie got up at half past five, and left an hour later to go on the morning delivery – after wakening William with some tea and putting his tin plate of bacon in the oven to sizzle.

From seven to half past eight he'd plough into mental arithmetic, shuffle through sheets of simple conundrums, rubbing his eyes and yawning, but gradually getting clearer in the brain. He quickened his speed. It seemed as if nothing were beyond his understanding, that he could master all the tricky depths in the world. When it was a matter of mechanics, it was almost as if there were no depths, that he had only to spread his intelligence to answer all questions.

After a few weeks he'd leave his mates at the school gate and come straight back in the afternoon, get the door key from Mrs Towle and go in to swot for an hour, even before cutting a doorstep of bread and jam. If his father was home, after the barest greeting he'd go into the parlour – that smelled of stale pipe smoke from the previous night – and lay his papers on the round table covered with a red plush cloth.

Nearer exam time Charlie, leaving nothing to chance, got a master to come in once a week from the grammar school and coach him. William never worked so hard. Nor did his father forget to keep him up on map-reading during the more than necessary walks at the weekend. He became strong in the head and body, though in more human moments his father wasn't sure: 'Are you all right, Bill?'

He was irritated at the question, as if it were one more small weight piled onto that of his swotting. 'Of course I am.'

'It's not too much for you?'

The touch of anxiety in his father's voice made him smile, because he was already used to life's overloaded programme. 'I'm all right, dad. I *like* studying.'

Charlie held a hand towards him, a theatrical shift of the shoulder, and when William took the two fingers, as he was meant to, it was merely an excuse for him to stand up and stretch his legs. The hours at school were easy compared to this stunning régime.

He couldn't understand why he liked it, especially in spring when his pals went to the ponds for tadpoles, and into the woods for birds' eggs after school. But the bigger part of him did enjoy the rigorous time-schedule worked out like an artillery fire-plan that his father forced him to keep to. 'The poor lad's nowt but a dog chained up at home,' a neighbour said, who saw what was going on. But it gave him a feeling of importance, and of being cared for.

Charlie had some cash put by to pay for tuition, and for the books he'd bought on a special trip to Nottingham. The idea and the sacrifice went hand in hand. When William sat at the parlour table in the bitterest weather without a fire his father said it would 'harden him'. In fact it didn't bother him much because doing the dozens of English and arithmetic exercises with a stop-watch by his side gave enough warmth. Nothing in this line would floor him anymore. He'd be able to solve any problem that fate was likely to throw at him, his father said, though William was often kept warmer by nervousness at the thought of the coming exam than by cockyness at what he could do.

His father seemed to live in his skin. When William was sipping cocoa by the fire before going to bed he said: 'You're doing well, Bill, but don't get too cock-a-hoop about it.'

This advice felt like a blow between the eyes.

'I'm not.'

The gas-mantle flared on its bracket coming out from the wall above the shelf. He got up to adjust it.

'I mean – not so's it stops you passing.'

'I'll try not to.'

'You'll have to keep cool, calm and collected on the day. Then it's a matter of up and at 'em. That's the long and the short of it. Provided you've practised, and know your stuff, you'll get through.'

'I hope so.'

'Course you will! You've got to get used to examinations and tests. Life's full of 'em. Even I've done a few in my time, so don't be frightened of it.'

'I shan't be.'

'It's your baptism of fire – as far as exams go.'

'All right, dad.'

'Don't forget: speed is of the essence!'

So many words added up to a bonus, but they also disturbed him. The facts of life made him momentarily afraid. He wondered, as if he'd asked the question in a day dream years ago and the memory had just come back, whether he was really his father's son. He thought somebody else must be, and the idea of going through a baptism of fire triggered it off with more than bleak reality.

He felt as if a dragon were breathing over his shoulder, and that if he didn't work he'd be eaten. The harder he worked, the less he noticed the dragon. Halfway through the evening his father opened the door to make sure he was hard at it. Seeing that he was, Charlie brushed a finger along his moustache as if slightly embarrassed at having thought he might not be, and, knowing William sensed his purpose – which was unmistakable – retreated without a word. William felt sorrow, without knowing why, for his father, for himself, for the world, for the fact that the evenings would get short again. He felt like crying, but fought it off and laughed at himself before getting his head back to paper. But something was missing, and he didn't know what it was.

He remembered, and again didn't know why, that when his mother was alive there'd been a framed photograph of his father in full-dress regimentals dated 1905 on the sideboard. Now only a biscuit barrel stood there, as if to stop the top white runner blowing away in a wind. After the funeral was over, his father had put the photograph away, and he hadn't seen it since. Had Doris got it? Had he smashed it and thrown it in the dustbin? His belly ached because he didn't know. A photograph of his mother had not taken its place. The absence of a face puzzled him. He wanted to fill the desert, even with one of himself.

He won his scholarship and the headmaster told his father that it was one of the best results in the whole of Nottinghamshire. A paper he took home gave the news, and when Charlie read it he got up from his fireside chair and held out a hand. William felt slightly foolish taking it, and must have held it overlong, or unthinkingly squeezed too hard.

Charlie stood with his back to the fire, hands in the 'at ease' poisition behind. 'I'm proud of you. Nobody 'ud deny it. I must give credit where it's due. But you must never do more than *touch* a hand when given it to shake.'

He winced at this admonition – good-natured though it was, judging by the smile in his father's blue eyes. But it was also typical, and he felt it strange the way he accepted everything from him as the normal way of dealing with people. There was a feeling that his time at home was almost over, that even if he stayed another few years he was no longer a proper part of it. Not that he thought his father was trying to get rid of him, but it was plain that he had 'ideas' for his future, and that all his efforts in that direction had been his one and only way of showing affection.

He watched him washing supper dishes in the shadow of the scullery, an ordinary chore considering the way they lived. Charlie stood by the sink calmly drying the plates and stacking them on the shelf behind, and William wondered, from his seat by the fire, what other notions he might have for him.

Around his waist, to protect his trousers from the splashing, his father had tied one of his mother's old aprons which was little more now than a piece of thin flowered rag. In spite of his unshakeable calm the clatter of knives and forks was intense. I'll never wash pots, William thought with a fierceness that surprised him, angry at not knowing what was inside his father's mind. At such times he wished for a mother, but it was difficult to remember her face.

Charlie Scorton had been more unnerved by the death of his wife than he knew. If she'd been called so suddenly by the God of Israel, as it were, so could he. A bus or cart could flatten him on his rounds, or some terrible quick plague strangle his vitals. And then what would happen to the apple of his eye ? He shook with disapproval at the thought of Doris taking his son over.

A boy could be brought up by a man alone – and that was bad enough – but to be reared by a woman, there was nothing but peril in it. That was why he'd come early to the idea that William's future was too precious to be left to chance, and that something had to be done – soon.

CHAPTER TWO

William felt the old familiar world flood in as he stepped beyond the gates of the Military College of Science that sunny Saturday morning on his way home for a bit of Bank Holiday furlough. The humid estuary heat wafting over Woolwich made him sweat as he hurried downhill and got into the train for Charing Cross, *en route* for Nottinghamshire.

He looked every inch the soldier in his well-pressed khaki, wearing a flat cap with its Royal Artillery badge, a white lanyard at the shoulder, his tunic clipped at the throat with brass buttons shining below like a row of guns, a small green flash on the bottom of his trousers, and puttees, spurs and shining boots to finish.

The earth seemed familiar and intense as the train drew out and went along the squalid warrens by the Thames, the difference in army and civvy worlds giving extra zest to moving from one into the other. He thought back to the ritual of first donning khaki and cap and webbing – everything from top-coat to bootlaces – which made him forever different from those ordinary people he'd been reared with. The barrier next to his flesh gave him a strangely conspicuous pride in knowing he could never feel the same as before. Even his father was one of these people he had left outside.

The first things got from the army on his arrival as a boy soldier of fourteen had been a knife, a fork, a spoon and a hair-cut; and after that vital issue they had filed into the mess to be given a huge slice of bread spread thickly with margarine and apricot jam. He would never forget the delicious and satis-fying taste after his long trip down and the exhaustion of getting over the first hurdle of his change. He'd been almost wild with happiness, though as Charlie's son he kept it well

29

hidden, thinking that if it stayed like this, he was going to love it here.

Even before the train stopped at Ashfield he spotted his father standing at ease by the station exit so as not to miss him when he came through. Charlie wore his best suit, and clip-on medal ribbons. He hadn't seen William for three months, and wondering how he'd been getting on was his method of being pleased to have him close for a week.

William felt a different person as he walked up, offering his hand:

'Hello, dad!'

Though pleased by what he saw, Charlie thought the time had come to clear up the finer points of his behaviour: 'We don't need any handshaking. You haven't been absent all that long. Another thing is that you ought to call me 'Sir' now in public.'

William was amused, and saw that after all, as far as his father was concerned, the College and home were much the same thing.

They faced each other.

'Yes, sir.'

'Haven't they taught you that much yet?'

William's back went up. I'm trained to kill, that's what I'm taught. I do survey at Larkhill, and gunnery with twenty-five pounders, and I can take a horse over the jumps.

'Don't look so hard done by,' Charlie said. 'Let's get back to the house and see that magnificent spread Doris's laid for us.'

They made their way between carts and motors outside the station, and strode down the road. 'How are you getting on down there?'

'All right. I like maths and physics.'

'Your exams, though?'

William smiled as they went along in step. 'I mostly do well. We're using theodolites. I like that, too.' As good as a university, with the technical education you get, the C.O. had said at his pep-talk. What better upbringing could a youth have than to be trained as a British gunner? was his message. William was pleased to tell all this, because he was doing what his father had never done.

They walked down the street, a fish-and-chip shop on the corner and a beer-off opposite. You could smell both, but the sky was so blue it didn't matter. Colliers' wives talked to each other outside their houses. One woman was scrubbing her doorstep as if speed indeed was of the essence.

'Years ago,' Charlie said, 'when they got the Sankey Award, you'd see the odd motorbike propped against a wall, but after the Strike the poor beggers were put down lower than animals. It's a crying shame men can't be properly treated, especially when a good few were in the Trenches. There's no sign of things getting better though, either.'

A cut-glass bowl laden with pineapple chunks was on the table, flanked by plates of bread and butter, vanguarded by a basin of salmon, a fruit cake at the rear. Charlie expected him to sit to it in his tunic, but William took it off and stood in his shirt. When he reached over to pick a piece of pineapple from the juice as if he hadn't eaten for a week he wondered whether his son was getting the right sort of domestic training.

'Can't you wait for the tea to be made?' he rapped out. 'It's not a borstal you're in.'

Behind William's head the enlarged and framed photograph of his father in full regimentals had returned to the wall, its eyes boring into his brain. Must have put it back since sending me to be a soldier. He met his father's actual eyes in front. 'I was hungry.'

'Never show it. It does no good. A soldier always gets fed. But often he has to wait.'

'I know that.'

He put the kettle on the fire. 'Didn't you get something at a station?'

'I had a cup of tea.' He could have had more, but he'd forgotten. You can eat sandwiches on a train or bus, but never fish-and-chips from a piece of paper. It had gone around that a boy had been thrown out of College for breaking that simple rule. He noticed the wireless. A good one. Must have cost three or four pounds. He switched it on.

'Like it?'

'Nice set, dad.' A dance band was playing, but didn't come

31

through either loud or clear. Its small lit-up arc glowed a few hours a week when Charlie listened to it in the dark to save the gas. He enjoyed the news, and the music of brass and military bands. He sometimes regretted not having got one years ago to brighten William's life up a bit. Nowadays it drew Doris more to the house.

'The accumulator wants recharging,' William said.

'I know. We'll take it in after tea.' He liked showing his son off in the district.

William disconnected the terminals. 'Next time I'll bring you a volt-meter, then you can test it. Tells you how much life is left.'

Charlie was amused at him throwing his knowledge around, and expected there'd be a lot of that from now on. Have to get used to it.

'I'll fix an aerial on a pole and set it out the bedroom window,' William said. He saw a short length of wire trailing up the wall. 'Have you earthed it?'

'I have.'

'You'll get good reception with a proper aerial.'

Charlie poked the fire and steadied the kettle: 'Wash your hands and face in the scullery sink. Then put your tunic on, comb your hair, and come back so's we can get stuck in.'

William knew that he was the soldier now, and at sixteen felt the master of his fate. If you don't feel it at that age you certainly won't go far in life, Charlie mused. But he thought William was being deceived, like everyone else in the same grip. He was too young and optimistic to notice that he'd been cooped up for life. What was he so cocky about? He'd have despised him though if he hadn't been. We're all locked up one way or another, because that's what civilisation is: hemmed in by family and hooked by a job, though being in the army holds you in every way, which might be just as well with a youngster like him.

'The army's everything from now on,' Sergeant Jones said to William and his class. 'It's mammy, daddy, teacher, boss: a brand-new pearly-buttoned strait-jacket you'll never get out of – nor ever want to if you've got any sense and know what's good for you. Don't ever forget: you're soldiers, and wherever you piss, daffodils come up.'

Sergeant Jones spouted his customary diatribe to make them feel they belonged and were safe, so perhaps it was the army's collective all-caring spirit that made him appear so cocky to his father, who recognised it only too well.

While helping himself to a potted-meat sandwich he caught his father looking at him in a way he'd never done before. He was to remember this cool appraising gaze from eyes that wondered whether it had done the right thing in sending him away. William's confidence told Charlie that because it was too late to know, he might as well make up his mind that he'd done the right thing. Yet his speculation was mixed with a regret he couldn't control, asking what life would have been like if William had stayed at home. Having moulded him towards becoming a better version of himself, he felt he had lost him for ever. You give and you lose at the same time.

That distinct yet puzzling gaze led William to wonder what his father's life had really been like as a soldier. Charlie never said much, but William gathered that from being a sparky young man he had joined up on impulse from a sea of misery, to forget losing his best pal down the pit in a sudden terrible splitting of props so far underground that they were beyond all sight of the stars. A slab of rock had crushed his friend only a few feet away. Why him, and not me? Charlie had said in anguish. It was a question that drove him to the madness of enlisting, where such questions might become so frequent that they would lose their relevance.

William had lost no one yet, except his mother. His father's stare over that summer tea-table, with sunlight blossoming through the window from the backyard, across the huge tin bath on the wall and the rusting mangle below, was a scrutiny that made William's soul uneasy, causing him to move his eyes and twist his mouth with annoyance because his father, who had pushed him out of the house and into the army, was still trying to get at him.

He reached to pour more tea, feeling that he didn't belong here anymore. His father had finished providing for him, as far as he was concerned. He liked coming home, but only as long as he was left alone.

33

After tea Charlie took out his pipe. William belched for the second time, and his father pulled him up again for lack of manners: 'You sound like an Arab,' he said. 'They're the ones who belch. An Englishman farts – if he has to!'

He didn't know whether to laugh or get mad, so said nothing. His father cleaned his pipe as if he were going over his Lee Enfield before small-arms inspection, then settled down to smoke it. The smell of tobacco made him feel sick. Pipe smokers, Sergeant Jones quipped, go ga-gar sooner than fag-puffers. But Sergeant Jones didn't know everything.

Facing his father across the table, he took out a Woodbine and held it to his lips, waiting to tell him to go to hell if he was ordered to put it back. But Charlie came near to a smile: he's defying me. He's growing up. He'll look after himself, all right. William was disappointed and surprised that his last chance of an open quarrel had gone, and when Charlie smiled again to show he knew what he was thinking, William saw that the army had made the old man subtle as well, though it could be, he conceded, that he had been born that way, and being a soldier had nothing to do with it. If you were a good soldier, the army only makes you more like yourself.

It was lucky he'd left home when he had, however it had come about, for he sensed he was getting more and more like himself as he grew older. Maybe his father had known after all what he was doing by pushing him out before he could show his real self and make life awkward for them both.

He looked at the various army manuals and map-reading books on the single shelf nailed between the fireplace and the wall. There was also a small red vest-pocket thing called NOTES ON VISUAL TRAINING AND JUDGING DISTANCE IN RELATION TO MUSKETRY by Quartermaster Sergeant J. Bostock, as well as the Field Service Pocket Book for 1913, a score of old maps, a tattered red dictionary, a ready reckoner, a Bible which had 'Officers' Club, Calcutta' stamped on the inside but not well enough crossed out, plus a small copy of *David Copperfield* which Charlie had carried around during the War, whose page-borders were almost as brown at the edges as the nicotine-stained right thumb which he held over the bowl of his pipe.

He stood up also, as if uneasy sitting down while William

was on his feet, seeing his son as now properly set up in life, a strong one right enough who had already ridden him down and was on his way to doing the same to others. 'You've started shaving,' he said approvingly.

'We have to,' William laughed, as if it were something to be shy about, 'whether we need to or not.'

'The Army'll make a man of you, I'm sure o' that. It's well calculated. It's tradition.'

'I'm a man already!'

'You're not far off,' Charlie answered, 'and that's a fact. But they'll make more of a man of you than if you'd stayed at home with me pampering you all your life!'

CHAPTER THREE

He walked out of the Station like a fully-grown soldier, head up as if he were the only person alive in the world. There was a homely smell of horseshit and petrol-fumes while crossing Parliament Street, and two girls turned from a frock-shop window to give him a passing glance. They looked pale but pretty, set at the spice of life, maybe on short time from the slumping lace trade.

They laughed loudly – at him he was sure. Nottingham tarts, he told himself, in a manly way. The inside of his left thigh twitched. All pink and healthy, his hair was ready to spring up under his cap at the thought of soft breasts knocking their blouses.

'He's a boy-soldier!' one of them shouted. 'Quick march – quick march! Hey!' – she called across the street, 'got two ha'pennies for a penny, mate?'

They laughed again, and he walked into Clumber Street to get his photo taken so that he could give one to his Aunt Doris as he'd promised faithfully when last in Ashfield. He used it as an excuse to stop off in Nottingham, up that morning from Woolwich on his way home for Christmas. As for not having two ha'pennies for a penny, those trollops were a long way from right, because out of his pay, he'd saved a bob a week since summer, and Doris sent a half-a-crown postal order now and again, and his father had put a pound note in his birthday card. At eighteen he'd remuster as a man, and get twenty-one shillings a week – which would really be corn in Egypt. Later on there'd be all sorts of extras for passing at this and that – emoluments unto death, was how Sergeant Jones had put it. You'll be rich beyond the dreams of avarice, he screamed, which is more than I'll ever be.

36

He smiled under his blushing at being riled as if he were a man already, instead of only seventeen, though what else could you expect in a place like Nottingham ? He had well over two quid in his pocket, which was as much as a man's full wage, so he could spend the night here if he wanted.

There was a slight frost in the air, though a ray of midday sun got through. Under his greatcoat he was warm, always dead set on a vector after his first foot went forward, though he felt that the girls' jibes had put a spoke in his wheel. He was glad the arrow pointed up some stairs to the photographer's studio because he could decide in the half dark ascent whether to have three for one-and-six or five for two-and-three, as it advertised outside.

He'd come down later and see if the two dollies were still there. If he got off with them and they all went into the Flying Horse or Yates's Wine Lodge for a drink, they wouldn't mock him. And then ? Skin you dry. Take you for all you'd got. They looked good though, especially the one who hadn't shouted after him.

A bloke with black wavy hair sat at a small table with a plant pot on it: 'How many do you want, sir ?'

'Five.' He could give one to a girl if he clicked.

'Do you want to keep your hat on ?'

'I'll hold it.' With the cheese-cutter you only saw two eyes, nose, mouth and chin, while without it there was a forehead and hair as well, which gave more for your money.

The man slid the plates in: 'On furlough ?'

'Yes. Seven days.'

'Nice place to spend it.' He took William's shoulders and edged him towards a chair so that he could rest his hand on the back. Aspidistras curved in from behind. 'That's fine, if you keep it there.'

He didn't like being touched, but he supposed it was part of the job. He held the hat against his middle, and stuck out his chin. 'This all right ?'

He wasn't satisfied. 'Why don't you sit down, and look a bit more easy ?'

He let some of the stiffness out of his muscles. 'I want to stand.'

'Look a bit better if you smile.'

For God's sake get on with it, slow-coach. The girls would be halfway to Mansfield before he got back.

'Watch my finger, then. Quite still!'

He lifted his chin, looked fearless and bright, well-combed and washed, a smile about to break as if the plant leaf had got him at the neck. The stare in his grey eyes was preoccupied with some problem other than that of the girls who had known him straight away for what he was. Hair grew short and thick above his middling forehead, on which there were lines due perhaps more to the stiffness which he hadn't finally been able to get out of his pose than from experiences which had put them there. Anxiety was a way of life that, long since buried and no longer noticed, only made him look alert.

'You can pick 'em up in the morning. That's two shillings and thre'pence.'

He stood by the mirror to fix his cap, then put on his great-coat. Some people had time to burn, but not him. Minutes were precious. You had to go somewhere, do something. Why should he look for those girls? They'd gone home, or back to their factory. Plenty more pebbles on the beach. He'd buy a football paper in the Market Square, then walk to Wheeler Gate and find a place for lunch. Afterwards he'd go up to the Castle. Might see a girl or two there.

He got change from his florins and went downstairs. They were looking in the window of a gramophone shop. He walked across the street and stood between them, heart beating fast and eyes-a-glitter. They saw his image reflected in the glass. 'Look what the wind's just blown at our feet!'

On the train he'd felt the thrill of green countryside, a mixture of frost and sunshine, mist and pools of water from heavy rain, an exhilarating scene that launched him into this flirtation, gave him the blind courage to sail in without being put off. On previous traipses around Nottingham he'd been too shy to say boo to a goose.

They were both brunettes, and smelled of scent won at the Goose Fair. He liked the taller one who was his size, but it was the other who'd shouted after him, and he stared into her brown eyes, though only for a second: 'Anybody can look in a shop window.'

She jerked her head away. 'Nobody's stopping yer.'

'Let's go, our Helen,' her sister said.

'I fancy that nicky little portable at fifty-seven-and-six,' he smiled.

'Cheapskate,' Helen grinned back. 'That one at five quid's the best. Or the de Luxe one at ten.'

'That's eight weeks' wages,' he said, 'with overtime an' all! The littlest would have to do for me.'

'Ugh! Who'd be a sowjer? A tramp in uniform.'

Money jingled in his pocket. Let 'em know you've got some, the corporal told them in the pub when they bought him a pint. They understand. All the old advice and rules were coming back, quips and maxims he'd heard for years. Bloody amazing how they slotted in so naturally. Never be without a brace of French letters. If ever you were, make sure you shoved half-a-crown into her hand afterwards in case you left her with a bun in the oven.

A score of other such gems touched his guts, and didn't now seem so senseless and rotten. 'A soldier's free,' he said. 'Footloose and fancy free!'

The other one spoke her mind for the first time. 'Not wi 'me.'

'A link o' muck wi' a rope round his middle,' Helen retorted. 'That's what a sowjer is, in't it, our Jane?'

This definition saddened him and, because of it, made him sharp and angry. But pride stopped him speaking.

'Leave 'im alone,' said Jane. 'Let's go onto the Arboretum.'

She'd moved to his defence, but he fancied the one with the foul mouth. He strolled down the street, and they came with him. 'There's nowt on the Arboretum except old men and parrots,' Helen said.

Little John boomed half past twelve from the new Council House. He felt like smoking, but had been told never to take out a cigarette on the street. 'Where do you work?'

'Hollins's mill.'

'When they let us,' said Jane. 'There ain't much work for anybody. I should think yer'r well off as a sowjer, ain't yer?'

'All right,' he answered, knowing he wasn't in it for the money. 'I thought all Nottingham girls worked at Players, making fags.'

'We did, but we got locked out one morning. It was on'y two minutes after eight, but they bleddy well wouldn't let us in. So we got our cards. Can't stand the pong at Players. It's like dates and cake, but it makes you heave. You get consumption if you're there long. Worked at Raleigh for a bit, but that's worse. It was clean at Players, though, but they sack you fer nowt. One woman got her cards for teking fags out in her bloomers. They were on'y rejects, an' all.'

'That worn't for nowt, was it?' Jane said. 'She did nick summat didn't she, eh?'

He passed a newspaper-man and forgot to buy one. 'It was a wonder she didn't go up in smoke!'

Jane pulled her coat around her and walked with arms folded across her chest. 'Ain't it cowd?'

With one on either side he felt a man of the world in more ways than one, a change in him that wasn't totally due to sergeants and teachers but equally because of those he barracked, billeted and bivouacked with. Some boys at the College were sons of soldiers serving abroad; or they had only one parent because the other was dead or divorced. Most came from normal homes however, and he occasionally went to a friend's house in Croydon where he spoke his neutral English and observed what social graces went on. But back in Ashfield or Nottingham his voice could slip easily into the old accent when there seemed some advantage in it.

'I could do wi' a bite t' eat,' he said, wondering how they'd answer.

They turned into Long Row and walked towards Market Square.

'Let's go into Yates's,' Helen cried. 'I'm that bleddy snatched.'

'I'll buy you something.' He felt warm and comfortable enough with vest, shirt, pullover, tunic and greatcoat between skin and the raw air. The bits of flimsy and feather covering their thin blouses wouldn't keep a cat warm, though it made both bodies so much closer to him, and he hoped for a kiss out of Helen at least before the day was out.

Yates's was well filled with noise and smoke.

Helen pushed through to find a table. 'It's like Billy Balls's taproom.'

He put a hand in his pocket to prove the sky was the limit. 'What do you want, then?'

'Gin,' she said. 'I'm perished, as well as clambed to death.' He looked at Jane.

'Stout.'

He only wanted half a pint, but got a full one because anything less would seem too mingy in front of them. When he bought crisps and cheese cobs he was surprised that no one thanked him. Not that he'd done much, and it was only money, though thanks was thanks, after all.

'We're looking for a job,' Jane said. 'Dad chucked us out after breakfast because he'd read in the paper that hands was wanted at Adams's. But he was lying as usual. He'd say owt to get us looking for work while he stays bone-idle at home.'

William took a first sip of his cold pint. 'What's his trade, then?'

Helen drank her gin, which put colour back in her cheeks. He saw her delicate neck and white throat, when she had pulled her coat open on sitting down. 'He ain't got a trade. Never did have. He's as idle as the rest of 'em. Loves it on the dole. Sends *us* out to bring money in.'

'Not too much, though.' Jane was also warmed – or fed, rather – by her drink. He noticed how thin she was compared to her younger sister. 'If we earn too much they cut his dole. He don't know where he is. Nearly took him to prison once because he didn't tell 'em we'd got work. He did get a job on the new Council House heaving bricks, but that's all finished now. He got laid off, and then they tried to send him down the pit, but he towd 'em to chuck it. "What do you think I am?" he said, "A mole? I can't see in the dark." So they stopped his dole, and we had to live on relief. That was a right ta-tar, worn't it?'

Helen nodded to her empty glass. 'It bleddy was.'

He ordered the same drinks, as well as more cobs and crisps. They'd polished off the first consignment, but he hoped to get a share of the next one.

'Things aren't as bad in Nottingham,' he said, 'as they are

41

in some places.'

Helen reached over and held his hand. 'They are for us, though.' His flesh jumped, as if an electric shock had gone through it. 'You'll look after us, wain't yer?'

He recovered, and laughed as he was meant to, then squeezed her hand. 'You know I will! I look after a lot of people, all over the country. The army smothers me with money. On pay parade this morning the captain said: "Here you are, William, five quid! Now go off to Nottingham and look after somebody with it – a couple o' nice girls, if you can find 'em!"'

When the plates of cobs came he managed to get one before their hands descended. Helen opened her mouth even wider over the bread roll. 'They're lovely. Nearly as good as tripe supper. Ever been to Pepper's, Bill? New taters, and tripe in milk sauce?'

'I've never had that.'

'I like black pudding, and Nelson Squares after it, as well. And lots of tea to swill it down.'

Jane didn't want to be left out: 'Chitterlings is good, though, and cow heel and pork scratchings and poloney and faggots and fritters and potted meat. Fish and chips and a barm loaf as well as mashed-spuds and fatty chips, Yorkshire pudding, strawberry jam, cream-buns, corned-beef, fried bread – with pints o' shandy. That'd suit me. I wish I could eat as much as I liked.'

'You'd be as fat as a pig.'

'I wouldn't mind a leg o' pork, as well. Breast of mutton, steak and onions, bread and butter, rabbit stew. Nice!'

'You like all that stuff?' William thought she'd be as sick as a dog.

'Puts lead in your pencil,' Helen laughed.

Jane gave her a mean look.

'Well, he's got to have summat to write with ain't he?'

'You didn't mean that though did yer?'

'Oh shurrup! Can't you stand a bit o' fun?'

'I can take a hint.' He was flushed with his beer, and ordered more crisps, cobs and drinks.

After another round he promised to take them to the

pictures.

'We'll go to the Ritz and hear Jack Hellier on the organ,' Helen cooed.

They stepped into a thin and bitter drizzle. Clouds were low and grey and, though not yet two, it was prematurely dark. He put both arms out and steered them across the road between the trams and vans.

'You'll ruin yourself,' Jane said, when he got three one-and-nines and a packet of Gold Flake.

They walked up the foyer. 'I'm not a skinflint.'

'You're only a sowjer, though,' she said.

He handed the tickets to the girl at the door. 'I've still got a quid left.' His railway warrant would take him on to Ashfield, and back to Woolwich after his leave. At home he might borrow something from his father, though he'd be groused at for a spendthrift. Or he could tap his Aunt Doris, and get a caution that money didn't grow on trees as she handed it over. He'd never thought it did, but a soldier had to enjoy himself now and again, and that was a fact.

Only a score of people sat in the balcony, but it was warm and perfumed. The arm he put around Helen's shoulders was more welcome than the one across Jane's.

A tail of coloured lights fanned up over the screen curtains, and the ponderous echoes of an invisible organ filled the large cinema with 'All the nice girls love a sailor . . .' A great music battery ascended slowly from the pit and, at the keyboard, which swayed slightly as the chords crashed out, with his back to them, was the famous Jack Hellier pounding his popular tunes; the talk of all Nottingham for wonder and skill.

'In't it marvellous?' Helen exclaimed. 'Wish I could come here every week.'

'You'll have to get a job as an usherette,' he said. 'See it three times a day, then.'

'A what-erette?'

'An usherette.'

She nudged him in the ribs: 'Clever bogger!'

'Shurrup,' said Jane. '*I* want to hear, if yo' don't.'

The more they shut up and listened the closer he'd get his face to Helen's warm cheek, and when he did she didn't mind

43

at all. The song changed to 'Roses are blooming in Picardy,' and went on through half a dozen old clap-trap favourites till, to a spatter of applause, both man and organ descended slowly out of sight.

Helen said that he played lovely: 'Better than most of them on the wireless if you ask me.'

'Sandy MacPherson's good, though.' Jane leaned across William to make sure her sister heard.

'Noisy lot,' a man shouted from two rows back.

'Tell 'im to bollocks,' Helen bawled across to her sister, the vile word shattering its wicked way over a ziz-zag of empty seats. William choked so as not to laugh, wondering how he'd ever met up with these two. He didn't fancy getting into a fight, for they'd been warned about brawling. A sound mind in a fit body didn't scrap unless the honour of the regiment was at stake, and then it was better to have a couple of mates with you, either to prove that it had been, or to chip in if it got out of hand. A silent hugger-mugger in a darkened itchy-koo picture-house over a couple of bints wasn't the sort of thing to be on the carpet for. Life wasn't your own anymore, and he knew it most when away from the barracks and his mates.

Not satisfied with her plain retort, Helen kept snapping her head round in the man's direction, all through the news, a cartoon, and 'Coming Attractions'. Noah Beery grinning on the screen finally settled her eyes. William lacked interest in the twisting ropebeams of light. His hand went into Helen's lap but she pushed it away, so he rested it on her thigh, where it stayed, while his other arm drew Jane closer – who tut-tutted sharply and pushed him off. So he concentrated on Helen.

To get his hand out of the danger zone her hot fingers pressed it against *his* thigh so that hers might be safe. Though she seemed so engrossed in the North-West-Passage Mounted-Police chaps chasing the crooks, the fight to keep him off was efficient and successful. He couldn't be as bent on the pictures as she and her sister, but thought only of the cloying sweet seas of *her* northwest passage, fixed in the hope of a little bit of midnight sugar that an old soldier in a pub once told them had often been his lot in India from the black and buxom nukkywomen of the bazaars. 'A white man wants 'is slit, my lads, even if he gets covered in you-know-what to get it!' His humorous senile cackle hadn't really fixed the meaning of it, and they laughed because somehow it only seemed funny.

Helen shoved his hand aside when it edged too far in again, as if she might like it but couldn't let herself go in case they not only discovered afterwards that they didn't care for each other but that she'd got her belly up and he was to blame, as her mother had bellowed time and again, and even slapping her face once when she didn't take a blind bit of notice.

He put his hand on her blouse, undid a button and found the soft fleshy warmth. She moved that hand too, because she wanted to scratch, and then wouldn't let him come back to it, so he cursed the flea that had started the itch. The beer from Yates's caused him to stand up.

'Where yer going?'

He pushed along the row: 'Shan't be a minute.'

'Don't be long duck.'

She thought he might not come back.

'You'll miss the picture,' Jane jeered, as he knocked her thin legs.

'He'll miss summat else, as well,' the same gruff and knowing voice shouted from behind.

William glared in its direction, wanting to dive in from the gangway with fists flying. The hot-aches of humiliation made actual pain in his limbs. 'Do you want to come outside, then?' he demanded, 'because if you do' – encouraged by the silence – 'let's get it over with.'

He waited a few more seconds, for a response to his manly challenge, but the longer he looked the dafter he felt, and so more ready to take savage offence again, till it seemed best to break the matter off and go on his way, because people were turning at the disturbance, and the manager's flashlight shone at the curtains.

He walked up the gangway, still far from his urgently needed relief, to be stunned before reaching the exit by a loud raspberry from the same man. But he had the sense to ignore it, happy enough at having got off with Helen.

Looking in the toilet mirror as he washed his hands, he felt

45

he didn't know where he belonged. His normal life as a soldier was in another world, not this one, beyond Nottingham and the comfort he felt, behind some tough fabric he'd never be able to fight through. Even his father and Aunt Doris at Ashfield, who expected him home already, weren't part of his life when on this sort of caper.

He smiled at his own smile, knowing he belonged only to himself. The barracks was a walled-up island, but this was beer-and velvet country, and home was a honey and pineapple pot, and all three places were made for him alone.

He didn't like being where he was, washing his hands and thinking in this lit-up stepping stone between all three and too far off from any good cheer. So he bought some ice-creams from the girl in the entrance and went back into the one-and-nines, and walked half a dozen times up and down the gangways with the melting ices in his hand before he realised that Helen and Jane had gone.

Bang went his midnight sugar, both lumps. Bless 'em all. He buttoned his coat against the cold and foggy dew and walked through the darkness towards Parliament Street. The long and the short and the tall. The song sang under his breath as he puffed at his Gold Flake. You'll get no promotion this side of the ocean. He threw it down, and a young kid dived from a doorway, snatched it up, put it straight into his mouth, and swaggered away coughing but happy at his find. So cheer up, my lads, fuck 'em all.

He bought a newspaper outside the theatre, where people were going in for the evening house. Things weren't so bad that he wanted cheering up, but he missed his three meals a day, so went into the Empire Café. Up at the counter he ordered a plate of sausages, two fried eggs, bread and butter, a mug of tea and some chocolate cake.

It was good to be off the street, in the smoke and food smells of the crowded low-ceilinged room. He ate, and read that the Japs were fighting in Manchuria, and tried to get some idea of their tactics from the sketch map, but both it and the reports were too skimpy to make him much wiser. Be nice to find a war somewhere, get into a good battery and pound the others to bits. Unlimber the old twenty-five pounders and smack 'em spot on every time. But it's too good to hope for.

A football match in the mud might serve just as well, though he wouldn't get that till back off furlough after Christmas. The old man and Aunt Doris would have a leg of pork and plenty of apple sauce at home, as well as a bottle of port and a barrel of Shipstones. But it could wait for tonight because he didn't want to miss staying in this electric town while he'd got the price of lodgings in his pocket.

An old man selling matches and bootlaces stood by his table as he shoved the last half-sausage into his mouth. He shook his head. The man was about to move on, but said: 'Got tuppence for a cup o' tea, soldier?'

He wasn't old, younger than his own father in fact, but dressed in a holed overcoat pulled tight round the middle with a piece of rope. He'd said 'soldier' instead of 'sowjer' and William looked closer than he might otherwise have done. He had a week's grey stubble on his chin, and water coming from one of his grey eyes. But he gazed at William, straightening himself: 'Sherwood Foresters. Fifth Battalion. Gommecourt. Then Arras. Third Wipers. It's a rare life, ain't it?' He smiled, holding up his cardboard tray. 'Ain't had a bite since morning, soldier. You look rosy enough, though.'

The stare made him uneasy because there were too many questions in it. He had nothing to say, being mixed up and sorry, as well as mad at him and knowing he should either hand over all his cash or tell him to clear-off and leave him be. He felt into his pockets, let a couple of pennies slip through, and came up with a threepenny bit. But it was sixpence.

The man took it: 'Merry Christmas, mate' – and marched to the counter.

William stirred his tea, hoping the poor sod wouldn't come and sit near him. He observed how straight his back was by the tea urn; then he turned with a plate of bread and butter and two mugs of tea and walked back in his direction. He hid behind the sports page, the last of the cake in his mouth. The man marched by and sat at a table where a fat old woman was already parked. She reached for a slice of bread and butter even before the plate was down. He set one of the mugs before her, and reached out to caress her other hand before lifting his own to drink.

'Bloody old cadgers,' William grumbled, as the man took off his vendor's tray to reach the food before his woman gobbled it all. 'I seem to be feeding half Nottingham.'

He finished his tea and walked out, ready again to face the freezing fog. The town's excitement was still in his veins as he went through Trinity Square, passed the Mechanics Institute, and crossed to the station.

Not wanting to stay the night now in this dismal town, he collected his pack from the left-luggage, but the train didn't leave for an hour, so he went up the road to the first pub.

Someone rushed through the exit while his hand was still on the door knob. The huge body fell against him so he braced his legs at the stepping-out pace of thirty inches, held it for a moment, and then, when the man could no longer bear him down, let him crash against the door before pushing through to the bar for a pint.

Pipe and cigar smoke knocked him back, so he lit his third fag that day – from a packet which often lasted a fortnight.

'A glass of bitter, please.'

He tried to pull clear strands from the talk and make sense of it, as if some stray phrase upchucked out of a drunken and addled mind would give answers to questions he hadn't yet thought to ask. And with a bit of luck it might lead him along a pleasure trail to some place where he really belonged, and would recognise from the bottom of his heart if ever he got there.

Lifting the glass, he hoped he was having a good time. A girl over the way with a lovely chest was being tanked up by an air-force warrant-officer. She was only his age, but there were bags under her eyes, worlds of rouge and red hair and hidden promise. Maybe she appeared so tired because she was out of work. 'What's that bleddy sowjer lookin' at me for?' she called.

He felt angry and ready enough to fight those who continually brought their spiky thoughts into the open. You couldn't even look at anybody without them shouting to all and sundry that you were after summat precious which none of them had got.

48

But nobody took notice, though the warrant-officer was forced into sparing him a flash of the eyes before she'd turn her head away. If anybody interested you enough to look at them you had to make your glances crafty and sparing, otherwise you might end up spitting blood and teeth onto the stones outside. There'll be somebody to keep me company if that happens: he hadn't boxed twice a week for the last three years to be put down as easy as that. He wasn't used to glancing slyly at people as if afraid of them. His father had told him to always look people in the eyes, and a soldier wasn't given to much less than that.

There was a tap on his shoulder and he tensed himself, clenched his fists before turning. To be safe in this pub you needed all-round vision like the pigeons. A good thing to have, as that master-gunner said when he took them on the range at Shoeburyness.

'Did you think you could find somebody better?' he said, not eager to show his pleasure, and thinking of the three ice-creams dumped in the rubbish tin.

'If I did I wouldn't have come up to you. Would we, Jane?' Helen demanded, but with a smile, which made his anger flow away. 'Aren't you glad to see us?'

'Never felt happier.'

'I can see it written all over your clock. But I said we'd find him in the Rose of England, didn't I?'

'Don't ask me,' Jane said wearily. 'It's time we went home, I'll tell you that.'

He picked half-a-crown from his pocket. 'Have a drink first.'

Helen took his hand and looked at his eyes. 'You know *my* favourite.' He got two gins and more beer for himself. Things had turned very bright after thundery showers. They even found a table to sit at.

Coming out later into a cold fog of iron filings, he needed the sharp crude air more than at any other time in his life. He walked straight because Jane and Helen took his arms, but his head was so big and empty that the compass inside, having nothing to grip on, spun madly, a sensation which had advantages because it made him feel like singing, though as a boy-

49

soldier he kept such rhythmical impulses from his lips. The pack seemed lighter now, but Helen offered to carry it.

'It'd double you up.'

She thumped him. 'I've worked at places lifting bigger loads than that.'

He didn't know where to go: 'The cafe's still open. Do you want some tea?'

'Let's go home.' She squeezed on to his arm. 'It's only down Old Radford. We'll get a tram.'

'What about your mam and dad?' But he was game for anything.

'They won't mind. Call in a beer-off and get 'em a few quarts o' Shippoes, and they'll adopt you for ever!'

'Skin him alive.' Jane squeezed his arm in case her words frightened him. He tripped on a kerbstone.

'Oops, duck!' Helen roared. 'Don't let the devil get you or he might keep you, especially if you fall down that fevergrate.'

'I'm not that thin. Feel!' He pulled them close, kissing each in turn: Helen smelt of perfume and beer, and Jane of pepper and sweat.

They jumped on a tram at Chapel Bar, climbing steps to the top deck. 'Hey,' the conductor called. 'You can't take that pack up. Leave it down 'ere, duck.'

He grumbled, unlooping it, and passed it back via Helen. 'Don't let me forget it.'

'It'd be the sack for me, duck,' the conductor said amiably, 'if you took it on top.'

'Fancy being frightened o' losing your job.'

'So would you be,' said a woman coming up behind, 'if you had one to lose.'

Everyone's against a soldier, he thought glumly, except when there's a war on. 'I've got my life, like everybody else,' he said to the woman, after he'd decided to ignore her.

'So had my old man' she said, 'but he got done in as a sowjer. November the bleddy tenth, 1918.'

'I'm sorry.' He thought not a few must have got it the next day as well, before eleven o'clock.

'Oh it's all right, duck,' she answered cheerfully. 'I got married again. Often wish I hadn't. I go charring offices till all hours of the night to keep the idle bogger. Gets up at ten, and expects his tea steaming on the table, as well as bacon and tomatoes and a fag. Then he goes to the Labour Exchange, and they send him to look at a job. He looks at it, right enough. That's all he does do. They look at him as well. Have a bloody good look all round, they do, and see he ain't good enough. Then he comes home spitting and cursing till his dinner's ready. Has a doze by the fire in the afternoon. Scrounges money for a pint in the evening. Wonders why I get on at him. Good job I'm fit and strong, that's all I can say!'

The tram rattled its bones up the hill and shook around Canning Circus like a rogue elephant after its mate, the driver banging his bell to get the road clear, which was empty anyway.

'I sometimes wonder why I did join the army.' William was talkative on such a night.

'Why don't you desert then, duck? A bloke in our yard did.'

'They caught him, though,' Jane said from across the gangway.

He kissed her lightly on the cheek. 'I'm not that sort. I've done three years already, and I'll sign on for twenty-one when I'm eighteen.'

'He knows which side his bread's buttered on,' the cleaning woman said.

Do I? he wondered. Reveille at six-fifteen meant straight out of bed and padding by the cold coal stove to dip in icy water at the ablutions for a few minutes, and then to slop back under a towel and dress while still wet so as not to be late for parade at six-forty. After breakfast came four hours of science and maths and sport and survey, and then the same in the afternoon of engineering in the workshops, and drill and draughtsmanship, with English and French thrown in, and what with a dozen other topics you didn't have much spare time till lights-out at half past ten.

'I'm on the go from six in the morning till ten at night,' he told her. 'I like it, though.'

'Bloody fool,' she said before getting off.

They filed down at Hartley Road, Helen collecting his pack on the way out and making him fix the straps in the right places so that she could carry it: 'I'm a sowjer now. Ha ha ha! Not bleddy likely.'

They bought fish and chips, and a quart of ale at a beer-off, wending towards St Peter's Street. The sharp angles of the school loomed and Helen spat in its direction: 'I'd like to gob on the windows. The head teacher's a real swine. Mr Curtin's his name. Used to hit me with a strap every day.'

They passed the church opposite. 'Everybody got it from him,' Jane said. 'Still do. That's all he knows.'

'My teachers were OK,' William said, glad at the colourless life he'd led.

The mildewed pungent water of the Leen just out of Radford pit was hard at the nostrils. A lamp post draped its coal-gas glow over the pavement. Old Mr Lancaster shuffled in after his evening walk, gross and diabetic, rubber lips from which a slender pipe stuck. 'People say he's worth a thousand quid,' Helen said, 'but I don't think so, because who'd live round here with all that in his pillow? He's a dirty old sod, though; I do know that much.'

He didn't ask why. I'll kill him if she tells me to. Jane clutched the bundle of fish and chips, and he gripped the bottle. They went up a dark entry leading to Peveril Yard. It was a closed in court, a high wall and a row of lavatories facing houses left and right, lights glowing through variously-coloured curtains.

They walked across, and Jane pushed the door open. 'Can we come in?'

'Who the 'ell's "we"?' a gruff voice demanded.

'Helen, and her fancy man,' he heard Jane say, as Helen nudged him in before her.

'You might as well let the whole bleddy neighbourhood in while you're at it, especially if he's got some ale,' he added, seeing the bottle in William's hand. 'Well, I'll be boggered if it ain't a sowjer! He's a young sowjer though, and that's summat. None o' your old sweats here. The bleeders made my life 'ell in the War, they did. I got to be a corporal though in the Machine Gun Corps. I mowed a few down at Meteren. But I can't stand owd sowjers. If I saw an owd sowjer I'd knife the bleeder.' He picked up a wicked looking carving knife from the table. 'I would. But come on in, lad, then, come into the booby hutch and sit down if you can find a box to put your bum on.'

William was dazzled by the gas mantle turned up full. The place stank of beef-fat and coal smoke, stew and tea. A thin black and white dog lay in a box by the blazing fire. An iron kettle steamed on the hob. A woman was knitting a scarf whose ends were at her feet. She was fat, wore a piece of sacking as an apron, and looked not too unkindly at William through wire-framed spectacles. Her face was lined but she had short and wrinkled black hair as if she'd spent an afternoon at the curling irons.

The table had a half loaf of bread on it, a jar of pickled onions, a large black teapot, and several cracked cups with 'Players Canteen' painted on them. As was his nature, and as he had been trained to do, he took everything in. There was no cloth on the table. The rug on the floor made from rag clippings and laid in front of the fireplace had been so much trampled on it was as colourless as a piece of ancient dish-mop. A small Christmas tree with its few strands of tinsel stood by the stairfoot door. He took in the geography, and fixed his line of retreat. It wasn't the sort of place he felt at home in.

'This is my dad and mam,' Helen said.

'Where the hell have you two bin all day?' her mother asked.

'Looking for work, but nobody 'ud set us on,' Jane said. 'We'll try again tomorrer.'

'If somebody don't get a job soon,' the mother said, but without much anxiety in her voice, 'we'll be on the parish.'

Helen put William's pack down by the door, while Jane spread the fish and chips over the table. The father, without moving from his chair – though he had to let his newspaper fall – reached up to a wall-cupboard behind and drew out a large pewter tankard which he thrust forward.

'Fill it up with some ale. I'm very grateful to you, sowjer.'

'His name's William,' Helen snapped, as half the beer sped into the mug.

'Well, sit down, Bill. And pass some fish and chips, you idle twosome. You'd see me starve, while you stuff your own rotten guts.'

'There's plenty for everybody,' Helen snapped. 'He got half-a-crown's worth.'

William observed him, a short-statured man wearing a collarless shirt and pale corduroy trousers held up by a wide belt. His boots and socks were under the table, toes well in towards the fire. He looked as if he'd smiled and suffered and felt the world only through his eyes, and had lived in violent sunlight all his life, for he squinted either as though expecting trouble, or as if he wanted to laugh as he'd sometimes been able to but didn't dare anymore in case somebody came up and hit him around those all-feeling eyes. William had a sensation of awe on looking at him, as if he himself, had he been born in a different family, might have grown up to be like him. He was careful not to stare, but took it in quickly enough to realise, before turning away, that neither daughter looked like the father.

Jane cut up the loaf and shared it out, so that with fish and chips, tea and beer, they had a good supper. Even the dog was fed, on crusts and scraps of batter.

The gas suddenly dimmed to an orange glow. 'Have we got any candles?' the father asked.

'They went last night.'

'Even the devil can't see in the dark,' he belched. 'Not a bit o' candle-end in that pack o' yourn, is there, William? We used to carry one in us packs in the trenches, but I expect it's different now. You've all got traction engines for electricity.' He moaned belligerently, 'Anybody got a penny then to put in the gas meter? Or an old button the same size? The rats'll come out o' their cubby-holes and eat us if we don't get a light on soon.'

Helen nudged William, so he took the hint and sorted out five pennies from his pocket, handing them to the father, who passed them to Jane: 'Put 'em in, then. You'd sit there all night if I didn't tell you.' He winked at William. 'Got to sergeant-major 'em a bit.'

'Do it your bloody-self,' she snapped.

'Oh, give 'em here,' said Helen, taking them to the meter under the stairs. William heard three pennies drop heavily in,

54

and supposed they were saving the other two for tomorrow night.

When the light came on the father reached for the beer bottle and poured what remained into his capacious mug: 'Finished,' he complained. 'A good drop of stomach-tea, but it's like all the best things in life: you'd better not get used to 'em because they're bound to come to an end. You young 'uns are a bit too green to know that yet, but I expect you will, one day.'

His wife was back at her knitting: 'You blab too much.'

'Aye. I suppose you'd like to hear the last o' me.' He turned to William: 'Can you see your way to getting us another quart or two of that brown bevvy, sowjer? We might as well make a night of it.'

He didn't mind. He could just about do it.

'There's a beer-off at the next corner. Tek that jug. If they're closed, go to the back door. Trade's bad, so they'll let you have it. Crawl on their bellies to sell a pint of ale.'

Helen stood: 'I'll show him where it is.'

'They clothe you well.' The father watched him button his overcoat. 'If I worn't too owd I'd go for a sowjer tomorrer. It's good cloth, that is.' He ran his fingers over the tunic.

'Join up then,' said his wife. 'Get some peace, I would.'

Helen picked up a white wash-stand jug from the scullery, and he followed her into the foggy dark. 'You can't see a hand before you,' she said, 'being so near the Leen. That's why Jane's got a bad chest.'

He slid a hand around her waist, felt the sway of her hips as they crossed the yard. In the cover of the entry, he stopped for a kiss, pressing her to him. Her knee went against him, lips over his mouth and cheek: 'You're ever so good, duck. Lovely.'

Someone walked up the entry shining a flashlight. 'Well, if it ain't a bloody sowjer! I don't know what next.'

William stiffened, and moved back from her.

'Don't mind him, duck'

His mood of love was broken. 'Let's fetch that ale.'

At the shop he told her to go in on her own, handing her half-a-crown. He didn't want any more remarks about bloody soldiers, or he might smash somebody. A soldier had his pride among all this riff-raff.

She soothed him on the way back. 'Don't take any notice. They don't mean it.'

Not much they don't. Yet he couldn't hold a grudge too long, especially when she put the laden jug on the pavement and held him for another kiss. 'I got five pints of ale,' she said. 'We'll let dad and mam drink it so's they'll sleep well. When they've gone to bed you can come up to our room.'

The limits of his world were pleasurably vanishing, though he was still unable to believe he'd ever reach the unknown compound of what she'd got. 'They'll kick me out when the booze is gone.'

They crossed the yard: 'We aren't like that.'

The old man held up his tankard as soon as they closed the door. 'What a good sowjer! It's like my birthday!'

'I wish I was young again,' her mother said, taking a pot mug from the table, 'I know what I'd do! I wish I knew what I know now!'

Her husband laughed. 'You're still young, my owd duck!'

Jane tut-tutted: 'You say owt when you've got a drop of ale inside yer.'

'You forget' – her father's dignity was bruised – 'that we're just as human as you young boggers.' He can't be a day above forty, William thought. 'I was a bleddy good machine-gunner, I was: I had good hands, good eyes, and a good arse to sit on. Once I sat down it took more than the Germans to make me stand up. Bleddy rocks bumping on my helmet, but I didn't shift. I can work hard as well. They wouldn't a built that new Council House if it worn't for fellers like me.'

William poured him another pot full.

'That's it, my owd lad. Wish I had a son like yo'.'

'You've got two good daughers,' Helen nudged him.

'Ah!' he winked at William, 'but they don't go and get a job though, when you tell 'em to get out to work. Not on your life they don't.'

'We'll manage,' his wife said. Helen filled her mug. 'We'll get through.'

'Yes, I do wish I had a son like William who appreciated a

56

good father like me, a lad as went out and made his way in the world, then came back and saw me right – like I deserved. That's what a son's for.'

'He's got nowhere to stay tonight,' Helen said.

'Eh? How's that?'

'Can he sleep down here in the kitchen?'

He hunched over the fire, as if the problem weighed too heavily. 'I don't see no feather bed.'

'He can sleep on two chairs,' she explained loudly.

Three, he thought, noting their existence.

The mother missed a stitch of her knitting. 'He'll be all right with that topcoat over him.'

Father came back to life: 'He's a good son, though. He's welcome to kip down. He can have the dog to rest his head on. Can't he, Pissy?'

Helen poured hot water in the pot. They had more tea, while the beer went to the parents. 'I told you we'd put you up,' she said. 'You've spent enough on us, so you won't have to pay for lodgings.'

He was sorry he hadn't brought in twice as much beer so that the parents would have gone upstairs too blindoe to notice anything. The seven pints seemed a drop in the ocean. But at half past ten the old man stretched himself. 'Climb that wooden hill, you two,' he said sharply, 'or you'll not get out early in the morning to find a job. I'll walk downtown with you, and see if I can't land summat,' he added nobly, staggering towards the door with his shoes and socks, as if the only place he wore them was in bed.

The round of goodnights lasted ten minutes, but they finally went, a wink from Helen which he hoped her father, who appeared far from tiddly, hadn't seen.

Left alone, he pushed the table back from the fire, for 'a soldier always knows how to make himself comfortable', and placed one straight-backed chair for his head, one for his feet, and the third in the middle as a bridge. It wasn't the best billet he'd ever had, but he could imagine worse. The dog scratched itself as if it owned the place. He wondered how he'd got into this house, and whether he'd ever get back to his real life. He screwed a fist into his eyes, and laughed at the idea that this *was* real. He was here to have a good time, so he'd give it till eleven before making his way up to Helen.

Lying on the three chairs became an ordeal. The middle one was unsafe and started to crack, which at least gave him an excuse to stand up. He opened the old man's newspaper and, fetching a pencil from his tunic pocket, did a few clues of the crossword. Why am I dossing in this old den, when I could be kipping nicely in some bed-and-breakfast place down town?

Sharp and regular knocks at the back of the fireplace startled him, as if someone were walled-up and signalling to be let out. It came again. He felt his hair shift and itch, but at the sound of a man's heavy cough he realised it was from another house backing on to this.

The dog stirred and stood up, shook itself and, as must have been its habit, scratched at the embers in the fireplace, cocked a hind leg, and pissed against the still hot bars, a steady gaze of accomplishment and pleasure at the opposite wall. The stench of the steam made a pungent ricochet into the room, as if some foul and ancient boiler had burst. Satisfied with its performance, and relieved of a certain weight and pressure, it settled back comfortably in its box. He wanted to aim his boot at it, but was afraid of the yelp being heard in the bedrooms.

When the gas began to die he made a rapid survey of the room, splitting it into north and east co-ordinates so as to know the right way to steer when it turned pitch black. The compass he'd been trained to carry in his forehead gave an accurate bearing on which to tread to the stairfoot door.

He threw his fag into the fireplace and stood up, facing the last spark of the fire. He took off his boots, and set them under the table to keep each other company while he was away. Calculating forty degrees, and the five paces necessary to get him to the stairfoot door, he walked slowly, holding his arms full out as a vanguard.

His two hands steadied and softened the latch, and the door opened towards him, so that he had to draw back a pace. The smell of sleeping bodies and stale air was like going off guard and back into the crowded tent near to dawn on gunnery practice.

He took the first two wooden stairs without a sound, but the

58

higher he got the more they creaked, and he slowed so much that he counted five before each step and willed himself into weighing only half of what he did. He suspended the beating of his heart, but the ball of it thumped in his stomach instead. He closed his eyes, as if even the act of trying to see in the dark put on a few more stone. Then he placed his feet as close to the wall as possible, which improved things. He was pleasantly surprised at how quickly one learned in an emergency. The training manuals were right, he smiled, though not too wide in case that weighed something as well.

She'd said the door to the left. At the top was a latch on either hand, and he prayed she knew her left from her right as he slowly lifted the appropriate one to its fullest angle.

'Come on in, then,' she whispered.

Jane coughed, asking sleepily: 'Who's that?'

'It's on'y my young man. Shut the door, and be quiet about it!'

She couldn't see his smile, though much of it was for himself at having succeeded in his perilous ascent. She placed a stump of candle on a saucer by the bedside, its feeble light showing her as more soft and mysterious than she'd appeared during the day. Her bare arm came towards him, and she had only a white cotton shimmy on. Jane was sleeping near the wall in the same bed, her back to them, shifting now and again as if his alien presence were keeping her from real dreams. He knelt by the bed and put his arms around Helen.

'I thought you'd packed up your troubles in your old kitbag, and hopped-it,' she said. 'Don't stay there all night or you'll catch cold. You're not at Sunday School, you know!'

He took off tunic and shirt, socks, trousers, underwear, and with nothing but his identity disc swinging like a third bollock from a bit of string around his neck, got under the clothes.

She blew the candle out: 'Mustn't waste it.'

'Ain't you got a young man?'

She kissed him. 'I did have, but he went to Derby and started courting there. Now I've got you. I like to enjoy myself now and again.'

'I've never had a girl.' He placed one hand under her cheek,

59

and the other on her back.

'You have now, duck.'

They lay silent a few minutes.

'Are you asleep?'

'No,' he said.

'Don't you know what to do? I'll tek my shimmy off, if you like.'

His hand roamed and flattened her warm soft breasts. 'Go on, then.'

'You're smashing!' She touched his hard penis. Her hair tickled his faced and he laughed as his hand reached the lower hair and a finger was held between her legs. She drew him so that he went in easily: 'Not too quick. That's nice. Come on, I'll show yer.'

It's like shoving your cock into a tin of worms, Deakin had told him. But Deakin lied. Oh God, it was marvellous. He lay in without moving, happy to kiss her and feel the slight motion of her haunches, and the heat of her mouth against his cheek. All the foul phrases vanished. The bed creaked at his unavoidable thrusts, but she slowed him again, a hand around his neck.

Jane was wide awake: 'What are you doing?'

She must bloody know, he thought.

'What's he in our bed for?'

'Go to sleep,' Helen said, breathlessly, and he felt her tense beneath him. 'He's only staying for a minute.'

'I know what's going on,' she said in a resigned voice, and her head went down on the pillow, though she didn't turn to the wall as before.

It didn't put him off that she was in the same bed. He felt he knew her as much as Helen, having been with them both all day. Something bigger than embarrassment had him in its grip. He held himself up on one arm, and with the other smoothed Helen's breasts, then let his face down to kiss her lips.

'Oh, come on, duck,' she moaned. 'Do it proper. Fuck me honest!' She clutched and pulled to show that she meant, and soon he wondered whether she had, as the term had it, 'come', for he felt her squirming around him. He went more violently, going deep in, till all the world's honey burst its salvoes out of his impacted prick, and he kept going till both brain and body seemed empty.

She eased him on to his side: 'Was that nice?'

He breathed into her ear, his senses still full of the feel and smell of her. 'Yes. You?'

'Yes.'

He lay in a half sleep, tired to the marrow. Jane's bare leg was touching, and in moving nearer to the wall, he felt her thinner body burning with a greater heat than her sister's. She said something.

'What?' he whispered.

'Now me.'

She kissed him with dry lips, her arms over his shoulder, more than ready as his finger rubbed and went in. He felt too lazy, but she gripped him like iron and got him to move so that, in a sort of half sleep, stiffening again, he mated himself into her cloying tunnel. He slid slowly in and out, fixed by her so that he could barely move, using all his forces to keep going till he burst into her. There were tears on her hot cheek, and he wondered what he'd done to make her cry.

'Are you all right, duck?' he asked.

'Does it look like it?'

'I'm sorry I hurt you.'

'It won't you.'

He was puzzled: a rare way for things to turn. 'What's the matter, then?'

'Wish I knew.'

Her misery jerked him up on his elbow to see what he could of her thin face, hair swept back and hidden as if she had none. More beautiful than Helen. She must be older than me – and for some reason he felt glad of this. But if she don't know what hurt her, how am I expected to fathom it? The idea that he ought to know stopped him asking her again what was the matter.

She tried to tell him: 'I suppose I liked it so much that I'm fed up now it's over. But I'm all right, so don't worry about me.'

He kissed her softly, arms not touching, as if afraid of her, or as if they were in love. It was hard to believe Helen was asleep, though she stirred just enough to be so. He stroked Jane's face. 'You'll be all right, I know you will.' He didn't know why he said this, because he had a sudden stricken feeling that even he would never be all right, that out of the darkness in this sleep-filled small bedroom had come a shadow following his joy, sneaking into the best time he'd had so far. He wondered if he'd ever get to be old, ever reach thirty, feeling that one day a war would come and he'd be splintered by his gun, with horse flesh and petrol and buckled steel swirling through the last bit of earth and sky.

There was no such thing as absolute blackness. The thin window-covering reflected enough light on them to distinguish the shadows by. The weather had cleared and let moonbeams in. He put a hand on her belly: the flesh was firm, her muscles taut as she moved to the wall to give him more room and asked: 'Can you do it again?'

Something had been knocked out of him, but he moved over and found that, after a while, in a loving trance, with only the softest of kisses, he could. He loved her as long as his energy lasted. He hoped Helen wouldn't wake up, for he felt a deeper peace with her sister.

His bladder was full of sand. 'I want to go to the lavatory.'

'There's a po under the bed. Go on, we all use it.'

He felt his way across Helen, reached the floor and crouched on his haunches, half circling an arm under the bed till he touched a cold handle.

The draining away of his piss let in a kind of sanity. He didn't want to be cast into the wilderness, away from this all-embracing world of living flesh, but he thought it a good idea to get back downstairs to his allotted place in the house – on three chairs in the company of a scratching dog.

He pushed the pot back. Cold, naked and wondering, he gave a smile no one could see. Going downstairs with his clothes in his arms he didn't worry about the noise, only knew he was a soldier who wanted in many ways to stay in this house. But he didn't belong here, nor in any other. He knew it properly for the first time.

The dog, as if forgetting they had a guest, barked as he opened the stairfoot door. 'Be quiet,' he said roughly, sending it back to the stone-cold embers.

He got dressed and pulled his greatcoat over, sorry it wasn't long enough to cover his feet. Every minute of sleep was paid for by swift grey dreams, so chopped up that even in his sleep he knew they were dreams. When grey light pushed at his lids he saw it was half past eight. He thanked God, and stood up to stretch some life back into himself. There was no stirring from above. Feeling in his pack he fetched out his shaving tackle, and got the stubble off with cold water at the scullery sink, the smell of mildewed bricks and plaster sharp at his nose.

The dog scratched by the door. He let it out, and followed it. He thought of leaving before anybody got up. The courtyard was empty, sky clear, air keen below his folded shirt-sleeves. The dog scrambled into the almost shut door, and ran back to its box.

It was as if he lived here. He put on his tunic and walked out through the entry. A motor lorry full of builders' rammel drove along St Peter's Street. Life wasn't easy to think about. A boy and girl without coats came out of a doorway and went hand in hand to school, one wearing plimsolls, the other wellingtons.

At the corner shop, with almost the last of his money, he bought a pound of bacon, six eggs and a loaf. The lardy-faced woman wearing curlers and a primrose apron looked as if she wanted to ask him a question or two, but didn't think it right. She smiled on giving the change.

Jane stood with arms folded after lighting a few sticks in the fireplace that crackled into flame and sound. 'What have you got there, duck?'

He put it on the table. 'Something for breakfast. How do you feel?'

'Same as I do every morning. Wondering what's going to happen today.'

He sat by the fire. 'Yesterday wasn't too bad.'

'Thanks to you. But you're going soon.'

'I'll call on my next furlough, at Easter.'

She opened the packet of bacon and ran her finger along the top slice. 'Shall you?'

'As long as you don't shut the door in my face.'

'I shan't do that.' She separated the slices. 'We can have a good breakfast. Be summat in our bellies for when we go downtown.'

'Maybe you'll get a job today.'

Her smile cut into him. 'If I do I shan't hold it long. I'm not fit for work.'

The doorlatch rattled and Helen came in, hair all tangled. 'Is *she* moaning again? Allus on about her rotten life. As if nobody else's got owt to put up with.'

'I wasn't *moaning*,' Jane put lumps of coal on the fire from a bucket.

William felt part of the family, especially when the dog came across and rubbed against his leg. 'We were saying what a nice day it is outside.'

Helen pushed her hair straight, but it sprang back. 'I heard you,' she cried. 'Especially last night.'

'What did you 'ear?' Her father stepped in, carrying his boots, and sat straight in his chair by the fire as if he had no intention of putting them on. He groaned: it had tired him getting from a prone position in bed to his headquarters seat downstairs. 'Where's my bloddy tea?' he demanded, king of the fireplace. He turned to William. 'Yo' still 'ere?'

'He's bin in our bed all night,' Helen blurted tearfully, pointing to Jane, 'with *her*. I heard 'em going at it, but I daren't say owt in case they mobbed me!'

William was appalled. He looked to Jane for a bit of help, but she stood pale, tearful and thin. The old man stood up, threateningly: 'What the 'ell's bin going on in my house? I give shelter to a bleddy sowjer, and what happens?' He appealed to a massed imaginary audience: 'And then what happened, eh? What bleddy happens?' He was so upset, William noticed, that he was even sounding his aitches.

'Nothing that nobody wanted to,' William told him. 'Did it, Helen?'

She gritted her teeth. 'He's blaming me, now, the rotten effing gett.'

'He brought us some breakfast,' Jane said in his defence.

He put his cap on, and picked up his pack. 'Enjoy it. I'm off.'

The father came close: 'You'd better be. Let's see the back o' you. I'll never have another bleddy sowjer in my house. Gerrout, see?' He lifted his hand, as if William might turn wild again, and not only go for his highborn daughters but scramble upstairs for the wife as well.

'Keep your fists down,' William warned. The dog barked, but whether in anger at its master being treated in such a way, or in agreement with William's attitude, William couldn't say, because it was a half-hearted sort of yap, and he didn't wait for another but backed out of the door and went across the yard.

Before he reached the entry someone shrieked: 'Effing sowjer thief!'

He wished for a grenade to hurl and blow them to kingdom come. But he saw Helen in the doorway, smiling and secretly waving. To get to the bottom of that mad house would have meant going back to strangle somebody, or to do 'em both again till next All Souls came round, so he made his way on to the street, wondering how he'd tell about his exploits at college after Christmas so as to keep 'em roaring for a couple of hours. There'd be nobody in Ashfield to relate it to, neither friends, family, nor undertakers, though he'd have a good time there, all the same, he thought, getting on a tram to the station, and knowing he'd broken the ice at last in good-old rotten-old Nottingham.

Raddled and tired, he sat on top to watch the clouds. With one last sixpence in his pocket, he visualised them, while he felt starved, tucking into his pound of bacon, six eggs, and a loaf. Even the dog would get a crust and rinds. He laughed and swore in the same breath, but felt an ache in his stomach at the thought of Jane.

After a cup of tea and a bun, he got on his train. When it drew up at Ashfield Station William realised he'd not been back for the photographs taken in Nottingham only yesterday morning, five hundred years ago.

Part Two

CHAPTER FOUR

Coming out of Ashfield Station he gave back a smart salute to
a young soldier who smashed his boots to attention as if his
greatest ambition was to crumble macadam all by himself.

His valise was heavy, but he decided to walk. The high
street looked narrower, the red-bricked building dirtier,
almost black. There was the old rooty smell of fog and soot and
stale gas, broken biscuits and mildewed fruit which reminded
him of days gone so far by that he wished to God the whole
place would go up in smoke and vanish from his life for ever.

People queued at a grocery shop to buy what they could and
stock up a bit of sugar before proper rationing began. A young
woman with a sallow face and a cigarette in her mouth stared as
if she'd seen him somewhere before. Maybe she had, but you
couldn't remember them all, especially one like that. He felt
sorry for the poor buggers who had to stand in line, but the
people of this country didn't know what they were in for.
They'd be lucky if that was all they had to do in the next few
years.

He hadn't let Charlie know he was coming, so there'd been
no welcome at the station. He liked it better that way. Things
moved too quickly for such ceremony. As far as the old man
knew he was pottering about on Salisbury plain, after his four
years in Palestine, where he'd spent some time when a
sergeant attached to Wingate's Special Night Squads, way-
laying the waylayers. The trace of suntan from Galilee and
Haifa had soon gone, though he squinted at the memory, and
remembered Jerusalem in winter, almost wishing he were
back.

He'd skipped rapidly up the ladder of promotion since then,
and had gone through a crash course at OCTU to get his com-

mission earlier in the year. His father didn't yet know that he'd just put up his third pip after one typewritten line of regimental orders.

There was a touch of December snow in the air, though he didn't suppose it'd drop till gone Christmas, by which time, with a bit of luck, he'd be on his way to France where he belonged. The Gaiety picture-house was open for Saturday afternoon, and people were going in – mostly kids. A soldier in the queue made as if he hadn't seen him so as not to salute. He gave him the benefit of the doubt.

People looked down on a swaddie, a mud-crusher, a bloody-back, a die-hard, a footslogger, a howitzer's pullthrough – remembering Sergeant Jones's deadbeat expletives collected into a penny notebook. But he now had the pleasure of discovering that, while such soldier-labels had been accurate enough, people made way for a commissioned officer. Gunners and private soldiers either feared you or kept their distance, often both, while the respect of sergeants had to be won. The common people tried to ignore you, though in most, there was that split through the eye that separated the world into yours and theirs. He swore blind he felt it, but was able to ignore it, while the professional people, who'd be officers anyway if they were in the army, took you as an equal at seeing three pips on your shoulder.

He pictured the disapproval on his father's face when he turned up unexpectedly. Maybe he'd smile at a captain walking into the house, a fair rank to reach by the age of twenty-seven, though not surprising now that millions would be brought to the colours, and that such gunners as he were as scarce as new peas at Christmas.

He changed his valise to the other arm. The country was in for a bad time, but he wasn't downhearted at the prospect. It exhilarated him. The wide horizon which he carried in his mind had smoke on it. The ground vibrated. There'd be no end to the war as far as he could see, especially now that Hitler and Russia had teamed up, as one might have known they would. It was hard to imagine this country getting out in one piece, with so many lead-swingers all over the place. Luckily, the type of soldier who'd saluted at the station was more common that the sort who turned the other cheek in the picture queue.

His father answered the door, glasses on and holding the *Daily Telegraph*. William felt a stranger to him and, smiling to cover such heartlessness, wondered whether the feeling was mutual. He wanted to say hello, mention how cold the weather was, then say sorry and walk off because he'd got the wrong house.

Charlie's hand reached out, and his puckering lips under the grey moustache turned to a smile of delight: 'You'd never fool me in a disguise like that!'

A joke, a sense of humour! It was marvellous indeed, but made him stranger still. He laughed all the same because it brought them closer as equals, something he'd never thought would happen. 'I'd almost expected it,' his father went on. 'I've got my dreams and expectations, you know! When I opened my paper this morning to see how the war was getting on – war! Blimey! – I thought to myself: William will be promoted again soon. He's got more than it takes to make whatever he wants to be! A captain, though?'

'You guessed right.'

'I wish you'd have let me know.'

'It happened so fast. You know how it is.'

'Aye, I do.'

'I wanted to surprise you.' He'd done it, he supposed, to show him that he now had a man's independence.

In the kitchen there was a smell of mould, but the place had only been up six months, lived in for just four. His father had complained in his letter that the bungalow was damp, but William had written that a few coal fires ought to cure it. It was good nevertheless that Charlie had got out of the old house. He was a year off retiring, though he might go on working now the war was on. Doris had left her place and moved in with him, so they'd have company if bombs began dropping.

Charlie's face was a bit pale, his sit-down job at the post office not so much to the taste of his constitution as the one in all weathers had been. Ought to get a few walks in when he retires. His grey hair was close-cropped, his back as straight as ever. Once that ramrod aspect started to go he wouldn't last ten minutes, which was all right because he couldn't ever see him living without it.

He filled a kettle and put it on the fire: 'I still save the gas when I can.'

William took off his cap and laid it with gloves and stick on the sideboard. 'You love using an open fire. Reminds you of the old days in bivvy street.'

'I suppose so.' He stood by the mirror to put on his collar and tie. 'Well, how are you in yourself?'

'Fit as old Nick. We had a boxing match last week. I can still beat the young 'uns at twenty! You don't look a day above fifty yourself.'

'I don't feel it, and that's straight. It wouldn't hurt *me* to be back in the army now there's a war on. I expect they'll need me before it's over.'

William saw the glint in his eyes. There was nothing his father would like more than to be posted near the edge of some wood with a good old Vickers machine-gun, no dead ground and a fine sweep of fire so that only a direct hit would get him out of it. And in between fire-fights he'd be crouched in the shelter of a bank of earth, brewing tea and swapping yarns with his half-section. I suppose that's all most of us want. Maybe one day the world will grow up and we won't be children anymore. The direct hit would come when the mess tin of hot char was half an inch from his mouth, and who could wish for a better way to go at sixty-odd? Ashes to ashes and dust to dust, if God won't do it, the Germans must, as long as you're not alive to see your bits and pieces chucked all over the place.

Charlie took a half-bottle of rum from the cupboard. 'We'll have a drop o' this in our tea. Or do you prefer coffee?'

'Tea'll do. I won't know the difference with that matelot's grog in it. They use it for getting paint off walls in the mess.' He felt none of the previous heaviness. A dozen more years in the army, and his own moustache would be touching grey, if he grew one.

'Doris will be surprised when she comes back with the shopping. It's a wonder you didn't bump into her on the street.' He tipped four spoons of tea into the small pot: I shan't sleep for a week, William thought. 'She's been a fine sister to me,' his father said. 'I realise it more and more.'

She'd kept a sharp and generous eye on him for twenty years, and only now would he say how good she'd been. But maybe he said it to himself often enough. William thought how nice it would be if he had a sister, but he'd been brought up to realise that you couldn't have everything. A father and an aunt were enough to think himself lucky about. He felt strange to be back, and put the fact down to war, absence, age, temperament, and the way your past comes to pieces in its silent and cunning way the further you get from where you once belonged. The more your eyes see – the more you travel, hear, feel, talk and meet other people – the more the soul inside you alters and sets you apart from what you were once rooted in, and so from yourself. Maybe this enables you to put up with all that life does to you. It certainly takes you so far away from where you started that you'll never get back to it. Or will you? And yet such soul-searching was, finally, soul destroying. It was safer that the present only existed in the future, which you re-created from there and called the past. While things were actually happening you were too busy to recognise them as the present. And things could never be less clear, or become more diminished, for taking a backward look at them.

He kicked such rubbish from his brain, for there was a war on, and work to be done. His father passed the cup. 'You seem in a cheerful mood.'

'Seventy-two hours in Ashfield's a prospect to warm any man's heart.'

'You're ironic,' he responded sternly, a touch of the old days. 'But I suppose it's the way with young people. I was never like that.'

You must have been, he wanted to say, when you were in your twenties blowing up Afghan villages and chasing people out at the point of the bayonet. The army is ninety percent efficiency (when you can manage it) and ten percent irony, and it's hard to get by unless those proportions are fixed in you. 'I'm serious though. I always look forward to coming back. It still means a lot to me.'

'Funny,' his father mused, 'I don't think I ever gave it a thought for years at a time.'

We're more different than both of us realise. 'You came back here.'

'There's a point in life when you can't do anything else.'

It won't be the same for me. When those two have gone there'll be nothing to claw me to this place. The town will be empty, birds fled and houses flat. I wouldn't be here now if it weren't for Doris and the old man. Joan wanted me to go for Christmas to her parents' house in Basingstoke, and I love her for asking me, but I wouldn't be able to stand lolling among strangers while the thought that I could be up here made me feel colder and colder. In any case there'd be no chance of jumping into her bed with that steely-eyed churchgoing architect father hovering around. Not to mention her mother, who doesn't think even a commissioned soldier would be the right sort of chap to make her daugher's life a misery. They'd talked of getting married, and to be in her house for Christmas might make the idea more definite. She knew that was why he'd gone to Ashfield, so maybe he'd queered his pitch already.

He'd turned down more than one chance of wedlock because he didn't want to lose the last freedom left to him, a fact which made him cautious if nothing else. Also important, though less so now, was that a gathered assembly of male and female at an army function was addressed in a speech common to all as 'Officers and their ladies, sergeants and their wives, soldiers and their women.'

Such blatant stratification had struck him in a very chilly way. The ordinary discipline, and the level of life of which he was so fixedly a part, where cogs and seams latched and sand-wiched more or less comfortably together, didn't worry him at all, for there was no harm or hardship in it once you'd accepted the fact that you were a soldier of the king for life. And being a gunner made it easier, but the phrase 'soldiers and their women' affected life beyond the barracks, and created a possibility of decay both in the outside world and in himself.

While in the ranks he stowed such thoughts below his consciousness and out of sight, and now that he had his commission his wife would be a lady as far as the army was concerned, so it wouldn't matter anymore if ever he thought to plunge in at the deep end.

'You look a bit thoughtful,' his father said. 'What's a young chap like you got problems for?'

He lit a cigarette. 'We've had a lot on our plates the last year or two.'

'You mean that re-organisation of the artillery? I read about it. Your letter told me enough.'

All he wanted to do was forget it, and get used to the new system. 'The old ones found it worse. Cursed them at Larkhill. We'd been trained to work six-gun batteries, with four batteries to a brigade. Now it's a four-gun troop with three troops to a battery, and two batteries to a regiment. Whoever made the new arrangement's not so cranky, because the guns'll be easier and quicker to concentrate. The only thing is we should have started ten years ago, practising day and night. Now we've got to train in front of the Gerries. Expensive way of doing it.'

'It is,' Charlie laughed.

'I saw what they had in mind, though, but these manual writers don't realise that you need to explain things a dozen times in the army, because that's what most of the chaps need, except a few of us gunners, of course! You should 'ave heard some of the old 'uns cursing. It would have frightened me if I hadn't got a sense of humour. Same thing when Hore-Belisha got blokes like me on the move up the ladder.'

His father looked at him after a long gaze into his tea and rum: 'I remember before the last war what the officers threatened to do to Haldane if they got their hands on him. And he was the best reformer the army ever had. Wouldn't even have got the BEF to France without him, though I expect there's a lot who think it wouldn't have been a bad thing, considering how many didn't come back.'

'I'll have a drop more o' that rum ration. I got cold walking from the station.' The damp gnawed through his tunic. The fire blazed, but couldn't have been made long because the coal hadn't burned into a solid bed that gave real heat, and what did come out didn't reach the right places.

'I don't go too far with these Tank theorists, either,' William went on. 'It's no good having tank masses unless

75

you've got supporting infantry moving at the same speed, and plenty of guns to go forward as and when they're needed. They'll never do anything without plenty of artillery. They realised that in the last war when they got stuck in the mud.'

'As long as you have more artillery than the other bloke,' his father smiled.

'You only need more in one place, then you can punch through. Nobody can have it everywhere. All you want is strength and mobility. We'll accept it that courage and skill are already there.'

'You'd better, I'm thinking.'

'Artillery's the God of War, but some would have it the cart-horse.'

'In my day,' his father said, 'they looked down on a soldier who read more than was good for him.'

William laughed. 'It's a bit different now. I'm always up front in the rugby team. And I'm good in the ring, so nobody bothers me when I want to be alone and read a bit of military history – Napoleon and Jomini, even Liddell Hart and Fuller. I read ordinary books as well; we were encouraged to at College.'

'It's good to hear you talk,' his father said. 'I don't get much of it from anybody round here.' He stood and looked at him: 'It's a happy man who brings his son up in the image of what he wanted to be but couldn't.'

William wished he would shut up, though knew there was no hope of it. His father had tried to help him, and deserved that much credit. The world was run by the triers, really, and those who worked, as well as those who had some kind of vision. It didn't matter about the rest, though they did have a right to as good a life as possible. Anybody could become a trier, and better himself, if he cared to. That's what we're fighting for, after all.

'You'll have a lot to face, now there's a war on,' said his father.

He thought so too, and everything about it was unknown, though the principles were simple. He had his duty and he had his job to do, like the rest of the people. 'I think I'll have a wash and brush up before Doris gets back from the market.'

The bathroom was even colder when he stripped to the waist. If he had time he'd dig a damp-course. Follow the engineering manual. He felt in his prime, saw himself spading the soil outside to make a start, and recalled his geology to decide what he would find underneath. Learning to read the earth was in his blood, having acquired a sympathetic feeling for it. We come from it, and we go back to it, so why not? Like every gunner he'd been trained to know it. The surface of the earth had the same number of variations as the human face, and to read one made the other more understandable. The 'scientific interpretation of scenery' meant looking at it from the geological-geographical-botanical-meteorological viewpoint, because they all interacted on each other to give a picture that was more than skin deep and for that reason could never be complete because it was far too complicated. But you could get near enough.

Whenever he went to an area the first thing he did was look up the geology. If he knew what the solid-and-drift was made of he could then observe the vegetation with a more understanding eye because it told you how people got a living from the land. He'd also know how hard the gunpits would be to dig, or shelters to excavate, whether it was grit or shale, sand or clay or chalk or marl or limestone or gravel; and how far under the soil to go before hitting rock or coal or finding water. Looking at the earth with such surface and tectonical knowledge in mind was like having your field-glasses turn into an X-ray machine.

Any man's profession that didn't branch out into a dozen different subjects must be a dullish one. Either that, or he hadn't much interest in life. He packed his shaving tackle back in its case. There were a lot of people like that nowadays.

Doris came home yoked down with two baskets, and set-to making one of the old dinners he'd been brought up on. She was stouter and greyer, and wearing spectacles made her look more relaxed, almost a person he hadn't known before, so that he realised how afraid he must have been of people as a child. Maybe things did turn easy as you grew up and got older. His father and aunt had been lonely and hardworking. Life had been meagre for them, and still was, and was for most people.

But it now seemed a world he'd never firmly belonged to, something he had merely walked through to become what he now was – an artillery captain. It was weird indeed to be back in that same atmosphere. Yet it wasn't the same, and never could be, thank God. Time was something you kept pushing behind you, digging up and slinging rearward where it piled up harmlessly, you hoped, out of sight and never to incommode you again.

He felt isolated, insecure, embarrassed, but kept his hard and customary grip, though knowing he wouldn't have felt any of these things if he were a real all-concrete man. And how much more of a man can you be than a gunner? He inwardly winked to himself. With their banter about the old days, they were trying to make him feel like the child he'd once been, but he put up with it because he thought they didn't know what they were doing, and if by any chance they did, it was only one of the simple pleasures of life to which they had long been entitled.

He saw that democracy and equality had dawned at last when Doris came in with the oxtail soup and sat with them to eat. He fetched a bottle of three-shilling Burgundy from his valise, which he'd bought on his way through London. 'We'll drink to you coming back safe and sound when the war's over,' his father said.

'Happen he'll be a general by then,' Doris laughed. 'I never thought there'd ever be a captain in our family.'

The rich soup was a meal in itself. Food in the mess was rarely like this. 'I'll never be a general.'

His father flashed: 'Robertson was. He started as a trooper. Haven't you read about *him*? Chief of the Imperial General Staff?'

'Who'll carve?' said Doris, bearing the platter.

'I shall, with a drop more wine.' Charlie picked up the knife and steel, clashing them together with the noise of two sabres.

'Robertson was a cavalryman. Gunners don't often get that far.' He felt a fool for taking his father seriously, and so dropped the matter. 'I expect you two'll be all right while I'm away.'

Charlie put a huge slice of meat on his plate, and Doris

served baked potatoes, and brussels sprouts.

'We will, unless *she* runs away wi' a black man, and I find a rich widow! We won't either of us go off the deep end. Not at our time of life.'

That wasn't what he meant, and they knew it. He loved them and, whatever else he felt, there was no one in his life who meant more. He tucked in, as each advised him to. 'There's a war on. You'll have to look after yourselves.'

His father sipped at the wine, before making a great cut across his meat. 'By the time this lot's over I'll be back in the army myself. See if I'm not right.' He winked: 'Doris as well.'

Maybe he knew, in his old soldier's brain, how bad it was going to be. He would doubtless welcome it. But there weren't many who would, and that was a fact. And if they didn't know, how could you tell them? In any case, why should they believe you, since their lives were hard enough already? It was always the common people who took the brunt of things – if only because there were more of them.

His father stood, full height, top strength, and William saw he still had a good deal of both, so that even at over sixty he was 'every inch a soldier' and didn't need worrying about. There might come a time though, and he felt sure it would, while still hoping he was wrong, when bombs fell and bullets flew. Whatever happened, he hoped that this life of his father and aunt would not be destroyed. He would carry the tableau with him – while seeming to forget it, as is the way with soldiers.

CHAPTER FIVE

If he went into the wood and let his head rest half an hour in the bracken he might wake up and find none of his four guns left. He might be miles away, but he was still down to earth. It was touch and go with so many dive-bombers screaming around. Or he could open his eyes to some Gerry swine levelling a Luger on him. He might come to and not even be there himself. Exhaustion gave you three lives, each like a dream. A couple of young gunners by the signals truck got their faces in the chalk, not wanting a double-six peppering from splinters – after the long, rushing never-to-be-forgotten whistle of a falling bomb.

Joan's letter had reached him a week ago, her final notice to quit crinkling in his battle dress pocket. His only regret was that he'd not made up his own mind and packed her in first. On the other hand he wondered why it had taken her so long. 'It's impossible to wait around and waste my life,' she wrote, and who could blame her for that?

Funny how you half fell in love again as soon as you got the boot. Most of his life he'd tackled every changing situation as if there was a war on, having a soul that unravelled chaos only to create dull order out of it. No wonder he'd turned into a soldier. So her blow was softened by pushing him back into a feeling of isolation, a state of single-mindedness that made him see things more clearly for the job in hand. He felt ten years younger, even with soil and chalk in his mouth.

For half a minute the sky was clear, then a trio of wailing banshee Stukas came out of low cloud from Armentières and did their stuff east of Messines. The dawn chorus, he supposed. It was awkward when they slid in behind, but there was no front or back any more. The Germans were trying to get through from Hazebrouck and Cassel, only twenty miles west, to meet up with others pounding from the reciprocal direction. We'll hold the corridor, he thought, till the lads have shifted to safety from further south at Lille, where the French must be having hell for us.

A box of four shells threw up the earth's guts, one lorry blazing, another on its side. If you didn't have a slit-trench you could lie flat. Flame ran by, and veered off. No more than hot air. The sky was mouldy and grey. On the canal the Gerries were over in places and trying to get up the valleys and spurs. The earth was rich, with brown and green patches. Dead cows in fields looked like old sacks spilling red gillivers.

'Troop-target!' called out the Gun Position Officer. 'H.E. 117, charge 2 . . .'

The Number One heard the order. His arm shot into the air. Thunderclaps began, that crude sharp boxing on the ears that charmed like music. A sort of music. He spat. Sweat dried so often he'd be safe from pneumonia for life. Two weeks ago it was peace and paradise on earth, with only the odd dose of ceremonials, and the work of organising Interdiv Rugby, training the lads to batter hell out of each other by way of waiting for the Germans to get cracking. It had been obvious they would, yet it only made it more of a shock when it came. But it wore off. We got their measure, weighed up every pint and quart.

Our guns were firing all along the line, and back almost as far as Kemmel and Mont des Cats. He wouldn't like to be Gerry's infantry coming up those spurs, peppered in the pea-fields and shallow valleys. It was no walk-through. We'd throw 'em back if we had equal stuff, but they've got an army corps against our bits and pieces.

Last night he hadn't fancied sleeping under the petrol tank of a gun-tractor, with so many shells and bombs roaming around. To be blown to bits is one thing, but to get burned to death is another matter entirely. Oxton said it was the most comfortable place, rain or no.

Stretcher bearers with heavy feet and rusty lungs carried a groaning man away from one of the guns, a three-cornered blue rip in his cheek. Shattering ripples of Bofors fire near

Ploegsteert Wood were trying to claw a couple of 87s out of the sky. One went gracefully towards Ypres with a smoke-plume at its arse. Die, you bastards. The only good German was a dead one. How often he'd heard it. The German Black Death was on Europe again. Yet he thought it half jokingly. Don't do to hate the enemy.

He hadn't felt like sleep, in spite of the rush from Arras to bolster the line, and all yesterday that seemed like a long year holding it. You didn't fear for life and limb, because this was too good to miss, a damned fine substitute for the arms of his lovely French telephonist in Arras. He uncorked the flask of brandy she'd given him, and pushed a gulp down to greet the new day.

Oxton brought a tin of shaving water from the radiator of a capsized lorry, and he scraped his face smooth in the half light, feeling fresher but wanting to change his filthy uniform, and get out of the boots he was afraid to take off.

'I hope you got some kip, sir.'

Trying to mammy me as usual. Oxton's false teeth rattled as he spoke. After the whine of a shell they felt the vibration. It took a bite of earth and spat it back from twenty feet up. Oxton's tin hat was at an angle, the lined face under it white as always. Bad diet. I'll get him a medical when we reach base, wherever that'll be. If he's A1, I'm Carnera. Can't have gunners looking like ragbags, but he tried not to sound too sharp: 'Put your hat straight.'

'Yes, sir.'

Oxton was over forty, and had been here in the last war, so thought that everything this time was a cushy billet as long as it wasn't six feet deep in mud. He couldn't have been more than a lad then, and he must think it funny to be back at one of the same places he'd slopped in.

'The Gerries had the ridge, sir, in 1917. But we blew it up, and then took it. Killed thousands. I saw 'em, all mangled. The other half went batchy. This is a picnic compared to what it was then, sir.'

'Anything to eat?'

'I'll go and see, sir.' He went through the hedge and onto the lane where the car was.

Watkins was out as Forward Observing Officer, and kept the battery busy. William walked into the wood, glad to feel energy still in his legs. Hadn't had a crap for a couple of days. No time, no will, no place. He went behind a bush and unloaded himself, happy to be among the birds and back with the shitless living. He gloried in his accomplished stink, till a shell whistled its workaday journey. He wiped himself and felt the draft of it bump at his flesh. Splinters came down like peas, a piece hitting his hat. Another like a bird ripped his shoulder-cloth but didn't reach skin.

A hundred guns on an eight-mile front. They seemed to pump all at once.

'Lot o' wounded coming back, sir,' Oxton said. 'I got this.' He carried a loaf of French bread like a shell he was about to slide into the breech. And this, sir' – a slab of pâté wrapped in greasy paper, and a flask of hot coffee. He sat on the steps of the 1914–1918 memorial. Those digging gunpits had found skulls, bits of rusting rifles, decayed helmets.

'You eaten, Oxton?'

'I'm all right, sir.'

He broke the bread. 'Sit down.' They shared the pâté and coffee.

'I never go without my scoff, sir. There's a farmhouse at the foot of the hill, and I got some bread and cheese, and a dose of cold coffee. There's snap for the taking in every place – eggs, butter, bread. They must a' left on the double.'

'A few of our fellows buried here from the last lot,' William observed.

'Sherwood Foresters, sir. Used to go down like ninepins. I was infantry in them days. Seven hundred of us went in at Third Wipers, and two hundred traipsed back to Pop a couple o' days later. But we drew rum for seven hundred. Drunk as lords. Tension, sir. We'd earned it. Up near Passchendaele we had to shelter in some o' their pillboxes. On my way in, it was so slippy wi' mud, I had to steady myself. I put my hand out and it closed on summat in the dark. Still got it in my maulers when we sat down. One of the lads lit a match. It was a full bottle of whisky. A few of us swigged the lot. Then we got rum. Merry as hell when we went over the bags. Six of us was blind drunk, and we never got touched.'

The food was good, and he was eating fast. Hungry without knowing it. A dozen shells hit the wood, throwing up stones and bones in the cemetery. Rusty marlin spikes and bits of wire spewed from the craters.

'Yes,' Oxton said between munching. 'Lot of our blokes dead in Belgium.'

'Be careful, or you'll lose your teeth.'

He didn't speak for five minutes. No sense of humour when it came to something like that. Before the war he'd been a builder's mate, stood in for a deaf mute at funerals to earn a few extra bob. But he'd stayed in the Territorials, relishing his booze and reminiscences after parades, and came up for more last year.

Oxton was the ugliest man he'd ever seen, but inside he was as good as gold, as Aunt Doris might have said if she'd known him, and if he hadn't been a man. He had big features, rubbery lips, puffy cheeks, a shapeless nose, narrow eyes, and was almost overbuilt, bulging and sloppy, which no amount of sergeant-majoring had cured. He had infinite stamina but, lacking a technical mind, had been an absolute menace at the guns, so was William's batman. A contented dogsbody, he had a certain amount of common sense which, combined with diligent foraging and blind loyalty, made him indispensable. Wispy baldness showed without his tin hat, and there were scars on his skull. He had big hands, and was the sort of man no woman could love but his mother, she having made him like that because she felt early on that that was the kind of man he would turn out to be. So he would live with her for the rest of his life, except when a war was in the offing and she sent him to join up (seeing he was chafing to) as she'd send a child out to play. She helped him to make up his mind, saying that his country needed even him, and so he'd gone happily enough, though his most basic thought, which no amount of army service could eradicate, was to get back as soon as we'd won, to find a job again and look after her. He'd lived all his life with her, and sent most of his pay home. He once said to William that at seventy she looked almost younger than he did himself, as if it was his greatest compliment.

'This is the second go we're having at the Gerries, sir, and there'll be a third time, believe you me.' He often spoke as if there wasn't much rank between them, though William hardly ever 'put him in his place' as he ought, suspecting that he'd heard the other officers saying he was only a sergeant's son – or some such thing – which led Oxton to believe that he could get away with being matey. William had known many like him in infants' school in Ashfield, scruffy do-nothings who might easily have grown into the same sort.

From the edge of the wood they looked across the shallow valley. 'That cottage down there was called Byron Farm in the last lot, sir. Smashed to bits it was. Getting thumped again now. It's terrible, ain't it?'

Along the roads and lanes going northwest towards Poperinghe and Bergues were lorries, scout cars, motorbikes, ambulances, Bren Carriers and men, men, men, walking through fields when they couldn't find space on the roads. They'd got an early start. They'd never stopped, in fact. You could hear the noises, but couldn't see much. He stood by the traces of an old dugout from the last war, an enormous slab of concrete with only a few inches of gap between it and the soil.

The land was lush and green in the early light, flat till it hit the range of hills a bit south of west from where they were, which must have been Mount Kemmel, the way to its slopes dotted and clotted with woods, clumps and single trees which seemed to give off smoke in the still air. The first sharp sunray glistened from behind low cloud and hit windows under the heavily wooded range. There were so many it looked like a château. He picked out Dickebusch church to the right. Behind and over his own hill, shots were echoing, merging, a continuous noise, drowned sometimes by incoming tremors, or by thunder claps sending stuff back. They were getting it from the west as well. The whole bloody compass has it in store for us today, he thought.

We hold these hills till everything's safely north, then pull out and follow. It'll be hard on the French, though. There wasn't much artillery in the choking flow. Either it stayed till the end, or enough of it was already in the next line. He saw the movement closer in his mind, felt its pace, congestion, numbers and attempted hurry, but when his binoculars didn't let him see the clear reality, he dropped them against his chest as if the sight would have burned his eyes anyway.

'Byron Farm? I wonder who named it that?'

'Don't know, sir. They called things funny names, last time.'

A Bofors battery, invisible to field glasses, opened up when the Junkers came again. They'll cop it soon. Bombs fell on a convoy crossing the Dickebusch road. The Bofors went after one of the planes: bum-bum-bum-begumm-begumm-bum-bum-bum – scores of shells seeing it off at ground level against the slopes of Mount Kemmel, where it sent up a cloud of steely smoke you could almost smell.

'That's a sight for sore eyes,' Oxton shouted. 'I can't see enough o' the bleeders go down. Young squarehead! I'll die happy now.'

'Don't talk like that,' William said.

'Oh, I don't mean that, sir. I mean I'll die happy when I'm an old man. We're a long-lived family, we are, sir.'

Byron Farm had no roof on. Bombed or shelled, he couldn't tell. But the wood was like magic, bringing back a bike ride to Newstead with his father at thirteen, speeding down the drive from the main road through the park to that big old house where Byron had lived, and then to the spot where he'd buried his dog.

The boom and clap of explosions was too much to reminisce by. You almost couldn't think at such a time. You relied on your training and instinct to do the right thing. When they walked, Oxton stopped as if to avoid the noise of the guns. In the lulls they heard deep distressful bellowings from un-milked cows in the fields and abandoned farms, an inhuman pathetic sound that got at the stomach nerves.

Oxton read his thoughts: 'In the last lot, sir, we found a cow once wandering between the trenches. Nobody could think how it got there. Chewing around as large as life. One of the lads had been a cowhand, and got it in. We kept it a week for its milk. Then we killed it for meat. We had the rosiest cheeks in the whole battalion, our platoon did. We even made some butter!'

It seemed like one long war to Oxton, and William wondered what had brought him back for this second round. It wasn't patriotism. Only a loudmouth would talk about that, and you never fought side by side with one if you could help it, because he'd either do something bloody silly at the wrong moment, or bore you to death. 'Oxton?'

He held a branch out of the way till he got by. 'Sir!'

The clatter of Bren and Lewis guns mingled with louder explosions. 'Why did you join up this time?'

'It's where I belong, sir. Can't have the Germans walking all over us. I love my mother, sir, so I suppose that's why I came back in.'

The wood had a homely smell about it, of damp bracken and greenery, and the sort of ease on the eyes found in any patch of trees. Eight-inch shells further south were lobbed over the ridge towards Zandvoorde and Tenebrielen. The earth under the trees trembled.

On the edge a score of dead lay in two lines as if on their last parade, blankets held down with stones at each corner. A few more would be pulped in the next day or so. In war you don't think, which might be all that's good about it. The dead were quickly cleared because there was nothing worse than those who'd caught a packet having to lie a long time while you were at the guns. Some of the poor chaps with guts up or legs gone screamed for God or mother to get them out of pain, which was soon done by a scientific needle. Why are we killing each other? But he stamped on that one. You didn't think that way when you had a job to do. Yet if you didn't think about that you didn't think about anything else, either. He scotched that one, as well. His father had told him for ever and ever that there were times when you just didn't let yourself think no matter what the cost.

A brigade from the 4th Division was filing up to Wijtschaete, where they were needed, though they didn't seem much more than a battalion. Could do with extra guns, he thought, watching them go forward to set up mortar positions. Can't have too many. Those things are only pea-shooters.

Groups of walking wounded, arm in arm and hand in hand, were looked over by a tall thin hawk-eyed Redcap. They hobbled and shuffled through the drizzle, then stood to get breath, and when they got moving again there were no smiles or thumbs up, but a silent urge forward, an inner grit to stay on their feet and get right out of it. When one fell, an RAMC orderly bent over the young man's features that had closed up like an old apple.

Laden stretchers were shunted along the edge of the wood by a sergeant-major. There but for God's grace go I and a few more of us. The leaden and rainy sky was full of cotton wool, paper brown, orange and white and green.

He walked to the command car. 'B' troop, five hundred yards away, opened up its twenty-five pounders, smashing over the intense strings of machine-gun fire and lesser thumps. Howitzers on a reverse slope further down the hogsback burst into life, then the whole circus packed up, and in the silence he heard his own footsteps, heartbeats less tight, till a sly shell spun over from the other side, copied by a score more breaking around them, and in the following lull came that guttish command for stretcher bearers that seemed worse than actual shells.

The staff car and lorry had been driven into a field. How they'd got them out of the lane he couldn't imagine, but it was well-covered by the two small woods. He saluted the major commanding the battery, an old RHA man, and forty if he was a day. The adjutant and he were eating scrambled eggs and grated bully beef out of mess tins near the signals' gharry. A map was mounted on two broomsticks and hung from a post, and the Intelligence Officer was marking the infantry positions with a chinograph pencil. William was offered some breakfast.

'Eyes still tired, Scorton?' the Battery Commander said.

'No, sir.'

'We'll be pulling out tonight. Without the guns. There's a bridgehead up north, so I hear. Meantime we'll give 'em hell on the Canal. They're over it this morning.'

He wanted to plead for the guns, but that sort of thing wasn't done. Maybe they'd get them out, because he'd seen a wink in the major's teasing eye, though if it came to the worst you slid one shell in the breech and another snout-first down the muzzle, which would do the trick all right when you fired.

He'd defy the Devil himself to get them going after that, but until such a time they'd go on firing like the beauties they were.

The BC was studying his 1:40,000 map of the Ypres Salient, a spin-off from the official map of twenty years ago, like too much of their equipment. The BC should feel quite at home with it, having spent a few months in France at the end of the last war. But there'd been a terrible shortage of maps, though it wouldn't have been the first time the army had fought without them. Happily, some bright spark (thank God there always is one) had raided the depot at Hazebrouck just before the Germans got there, and brought back enough to wrap fish-and-chips in.

'Glad you had some shut-eye, Scorton.'

'I rested well, sir.' He hadn't, but what's a bit of kip when the brain might suddenly be switched off for ever? He'd feel worse after a real rest, all ragged and shot at the eyes.

The BC looked at him: 'Get no shut-eye, and the kidneys go. All sorts of diseases come from no shut-eye. Don't want to lose a good rugger man like you. Who's going to train the team if you get cooked? We wouldn't have won that match at Amiens without your coaching. Good work you put in there.'

'Thank you, sir.'

'Master Gunners can be made,' the BC said. 'They're ten a penny, but rugger trainers are like gold.'

There was work to do, but the old bloke wanted to natter. He accepted a cigarette: 'A gunner don't like to lose his guns, sir.'

'I can't see us getting 'em back, though. Got to face it. We'll leave every nut and bolt behind. Be lucky to save our skins. Don't like losing a match, eh? Nobody does, Scorty. But you aren't like the others, I can see that.'

He'd heard this before, in the mess and out on the sports field, that he was different to those who'd gone through Eton and Sandhurst, or 'the Shop' at Woolwich. He'd pulled himself up by his own bootlaces, was what the BC hinted to all and sundry, and no doubt told them behind his back. But he hadn't. His commission had been handed to him on a platter because of technical skill, seniority and – the war. He'd begged for nothing, and all of them knew it. Thank God for the war. He was still more like them though than anybody else, and they knew that, too.

You weren't always favoured by those who'd been *born* to command – as they say. But if you were good at your profession it didn't much matter. In war such prejudices had to vanish, though you still got a whiff of them from people who thought you were different and wouldn't let you forget it with their needle-jabs. You didn't want them to forget it, either, because by God you *were* different and often enjoyed knowing that they realised it. And in their funny way they liked the fact that you were from a different background yet got on well together. They could talk about it to their friends at the Hunt. But the army looked after its own. Once in, never out. And if you were an engineer, or a gunner with brains, they couldn't afford to stop you getting on, and that was democracy enough for him. Long live Hore-Belisha, say I and a few others.

He thought of Section 133: procedure in case of retirement, and if his memory served him right – a bad one certainly did – it was one thing to remember it from a training manual, and another to be part of the backward track under shellfire and dive bombers. The CO at Regimental HQ would be working out details of the withdrawal. William enjoyed such tricky situations though, like on the Dyle and Escaut rivers two weeks ago, and since then each day had seemed a month, what with the amount of switching from one so-called front to another. 'This ain't a bleeding front,' he'd heard one gunner say. 'It's a bleeding back-to-front!'

The book laid down suggestions for the retirement, as it was modestly put, in which you formed a Brigade Commander's Group, a Brigade Reconnaissance Group, a Battery Reconnaissance Group, a Brigade Headquarters Group, then Battery Headquarters Groups, and Gun Groups, and First Line Groups, and Echelon Transport Groups, all in a well-ordered flowing fallback, so it was assumed, a far cry from the bloody scramble under fire down the hill when it did come. Still, the army had a knack of moving through chaos with order uppermost. Those fussily filled-in forms, those tenaciously coloured charts and zig-zag lines on maps did finally mean something when they had to pull out intact with enemy field-guns throwing steel-tipped shit about.

The machine worked. Everyone at his post. He took Joan's letter and tore it into small pieces that fluttered like snow behind a bush when he went for a piss. In a retreat everything had to go, even the stray thoughts in your innards.

'I want you to relieve Watkins at the Observation Post,' the BC said. 'He's at . . . tell him where it is, Jack.'

'470652, sir,' the Intelligence Officer said.

'It's a bit unhealthy, but it gives a good look down the Roozebeek. The situation's all right at the moment, but they're having a hard time. Got three divisions against us today. It's very ding-dong. They're trying to get through the woods. Oh, by the way, Scorton?'

'Sir?'

'Couldn't read your report last night. Writing had gone all quirky.'

'Sorry, sir.'

He smiled, sourly. 'Didn't know you were so knocked up, did you?'

'I thought it was the finest copperplate, sir.'

He got testy: 'It looked as if a drunken spider shat all over the place, then tried to plough its way out. Can't make battery records from that. Got to look neat. No pressure on us.'

'No, sir.'

Was it a sense of humour, or didn't he like to lose the guns, either?

      'Major Cole was a merry old soul
      A merry old soul was he,
      He called for his maps
      And he called for his booze
      And he called for his howitzers three . . .'

William picked up his map, Target Board Form, and protractor with a bit of knotted string hanging from it, then collected his sergeant and signallers. He went through the lines, noting the tired faces of his gun crews. There was a litter of boxes and tins, field dressings, bits of steel, wrecks, split trees, tangled bushes, a twisted motorbike, a couple of upturned lorries, and a scattering of craters. You got it cleared up, but in no time at all it was back to square one. Cable was strung around the place like tripwire, some of it snapped and no good. Bleeding pegs don't hold, sir. Maybe not. He'd tell the signals to put their house in order, except that there'd be no time. They'd be clearing out tonight.

The noise of small arms ruffled up from the canal. A couple of mortar bombs plopped. Half a dozen chaps stood cautiously smoking by the signals gharry but he said nothing, caught only the vegetable whiff of a French cigarette in the cold dawn air. When the Woodbines are gone they'll smoke anything.

He could do with less sleep than the young ones. Twenty-eight was a ripe old age. Life seemed so long, but he still felt young. He sipped at the brandy, then put the stopper back. He closed the wall of his fingers around a cigarette.

The signals sergeant pushed in a spare jack and let him hear the news from London. Desperate times were coming up. The Germans claimed that the British Army was surrounded near Ypres – meaning them. What was the point of such lies? There was talk at home of forming Local Defence Volunteers of men from sixteen to sixty-five. He wondered what difference that would make if the Germans landed a few hundred tanks. His father would be putting his name down already. What a blood bath if they got there. He couldn't believe it, but a few weeks ago nobody thought they'd get into France. Take note of what you don't believe is possible, because as sure as God exists, that's what's going to happen. And if you foresee it you might be able to put your foot in the spoke and stop it coming to pass. Otherwise you don't have the chance of a cinder in a snowstorm.

The Bren Carrier waited up the lane, its engine drowning other noises. It took them east beyond the Ypres–Messines road. It was quiet. Like going on a tractor through the late spring countryside. Locked into himself, he looked at thick grass and foliage peacefully growing. Soldiers mull on the world's tranquillity at this stage of the game. He hated such lulls, thought it better with hell flying loose. You hadn't time to wonder where you'd be next minute when a lot was going on. He felt glad the others couldn't know what was on his mind. Probably in theirs as well. Shells began bursting along the open lane. No cover. They can see us for miles. The driver swerved, smashed over a low fence into a field, and ran to-wards another bracket. Not far enough. The furrowing smell, uprising smoke and lethal pieces, spun the Carrier.

They cleared the injured before the petrol tank went up. The driver had a lolling semaphore flag for an arm that wouldn't signal yes or no for a while. They uncoiled the sergeant killed by a splinter, blood pumping out of his face. William was all right, told a signaller to care for the injured. He looked at the sergeant. Man like himself. Careless bastard to get killed, he'd thought, first time someone swung dead beside him on the Escaut. Another letter to write to the next of kin.

He went on foot towards the observation post a mile away, making east down the slope, and through fields by the corner of a wood from which smoke lifted as though it would shoot up wild flame at any moment. He always veered left down a gradual slope, and the opposite coming up. First noticed it in training, but soon scotched that deficiency in a gunner. Learn to *compensate*, as the old-sweat raged at Shoeburyness. It's as well to know the errors you've got in you. It's those you don't know about that get you in trouble.

A ruined farmhouse at the edge of a smaller wood was a battalion headquarters. Men outside were eating and smoking, laughing and talking, as if at a big larkabout. He turned angry as he walked close, ready to pounce if they didn't get up and salute. They did. Part of the real army. A short walk through trees brought him to the road, with a line of Brens along the culvert.

A sergeant-major was talking to a lieutenant. William lifted his stick when they turned. He climbed into the next field, looked at his compass and added a few degrees that took him between a farm and the lane, then went quickly on towards the Warneton–St Eloi road.

His signallers trotted to catch up. One was a thin youth, pale, too tall for his strength, hardly fit to be on a stunt like this. Been lounging around all winter wanking himself silly. They'd have been better playing three hours' football every morning and going on a route march in the afternoon. The army should have trained all the hours God sent. Have to look sharp if they wanted to get out of this lot in one piece. Stukas dived at the guns.

The threadle of Bofors seemed far away. Then the blast of a shell-ripple hit the main road down the slope in front. 'We'd better get a move on.'

Watkins held out a hand and pulled him into the culvert. 'Wondered when you'd get here.'

'The CO's dead hot on a cast-iron relief system for his FOO's!'

'Bloody good views, Scorty. I did a nice panorama. But it got a bit rained on.'

'I know. They're talking about it all over the regiment. A real artist, they said. Sending it to Woolwich for framing. Place of honour in the mess. Reckon you'll get the MC for it.' It was part of life to make your insults humorous. He'd long since learned to take them, and give as good as he got.

'You're a sarcastic gunner this morning!' Watkins' two almost rectangular front teeth were the first things you noticed when looking at him. A wide smile – a peculiarity of his – spread to the rest of his face, and entered his grey eyes as well. At the same time it cast up both points of his moustache and set lines creasing along his forehead. As it spread with such rapidity he seemed to be inwardly worried that his smile, which he knew to be his main charm because many women had told him so, should get out of hand.

There was a difference about him today, another layer superimposed. The eyes under his helmet were set firm as if, should he allow them to blink, they'd close into sleep and never open again. His face was filthy and chalk-grey, his uniform torn in a dozen places, a field-dressing around one hand because a tiny splinter had spun across and caught the lower part of his fingers. Blood had seeped through and dried.

He was a year or two younger, and craved his share of experience and action with a greed that never showed on his face. After the fight near Hazebrouck he'd said: 'I've nothing to do with Nazism or Fascism, Scorty. Know nothing about that. They're not English things, don't you see? Belong to Germans and such like. I just want to kill Germans. Don't

94

know why, really. Sport, I suppose. In my blood. My father nearly squeezed my hand to death when I said I'd go in the army. He got through the last war, and expects me to come through this one. Be one hell of a row if I don't!'

Tall, thin, almost brittle, he didn't look as if he could kill a fly. William knew different. An English fanatic – but human. The upper class version of his own father. He said goodbye, and took half the signallers with him.

The sappers had knocked up a sort of shelter, a few sandbags in front and a parados behind. A shallow dugout protected the equipment. A bit soggy underfoot, but duckboards were out in this war. Didn't stay in one place long enough. Not very well revetted, either. The low hedges angling away made good approaches for the infantry. Gunnery officers could fend for themselves, except when the foot-sloggers wanted blanket fire to wipe out every living thing.

Little concealment had been done, except with a couple of nets and a false bush. He hoped his equivalent on the German side hadn't pinpointed their cubby-hole, though he expected a low-flying Henschel wouldn't be too long about it. Gunners didn't like to overdo the camouflage. At least you might think so. It was all right for those who wanted to cover their own true selves from the world, but he didn't see the sense of it, thinking he didn't have much to conceal either from himself or others.

There was a good view down the gentle green decline towards Hollebeke, not steep at all on this side of the canal, but with enough dead ground to worry any FOO. Roozebeek stream was a sunken tongue to the right, with a dark wood on its southern rising flank. Have to watch that. He remembered his father's warning about dead ground, built-in almost from birth. They'd surely come up that way. It was common sense and intuition, as much as science. The subtle re-entrant widened as it went down.

Bring fire on Germans crossing the railway and canal near Hollebeke. There was no water in it, only mud, and a few tadpoles, and maybe a daisy patch here and there – though he couldn't see it. On the edge of Ravine Wood birds still whistled, in spite of shot and shell. Blackbirds chirp out their greedy hearts through anything. The 2nd Inniskillings were dug-in this side of the canal, and the 2nd Wilts were in the wood behind. Brandy tasted like hot water, but good for spots like this. A lovely touch of French reality when his girl-friend filled it in Arras.

A flat report and the slow whistle of a mortar bomb. Trees splintered behind. Soil rained. A map reference – 485659 – clipped up into his alert brain. Five regiments of artillery stocked the line. Shells from other troops threw up earth opposite the smashed roofs of Hollebeke Château.

Another brace of mortars ranged on him. They're after our reserves. Must have Daddy Bruchmuller down there. One shell came close. It's getting personal. A splinter scored the bakelite telephone like a piece of pork.

They'd hold them off, but could they go all day? No questions. Too much dead ground between the spurs of that gentle hill, so we have to keep 'em pinned to the canal, though they're well over it by now. Dead ground needs more troops to watch it, and our lot only come in penny packets. Get them with the guns, then. Spray their all-conquering heads with splinter. But where first? Out in the hot spots on the Dyle and Escaut rivers his real self had showed, the sergeant's son who had made it through the ranks. When the dozen guns began bellowing in anger he'd wallowed with an inner joy at finding that his true self was glad to be a gunner. None of *that*, either.

More slow whistling mortar bombs. He stared through his binoculars. We'll get you, my lovely. And there they were. Try, anyway. Thought they were hidden from my chiking eyes, did they? His reflexes got him working before he was conscious of any decision.

'Troop target. HE 117. Zero two-four degrees. Angle of sight . . .' Oh Christ, what's the angle of sight? Let's see – he placed his protractor on the map, pulled its bit of string. Laughed. Let's have a go, then: 'Fifteen minutes elevation . . . seven-four hundred, right ranging. Fire . . .'

Agony, agony, come on, come on, come on – while Signaller Brown from good old Leigh in Lancashire wrote it down with his scratchy pencil. Oh don't break the point, lad, or you'll have to sharpen it on a box of matches and the war will be over by then. Methodical, that's us. William told it again, and heard Brown's homely voice repeating it back.

'FIRE!'

'Shot one!' the earpiece quacked quite audibly.

'Shot one, sir,' Brown said calmly, as if on a bloodless stint at Larkhill.

'Where the hell is it, then!' – and bang! a plume of brown earth and black smoke. . . .

'Right two degrees. Seven-four hundred.'

Beautiful. Sergeant Levy had the ranging gun, and his layer was fast and dead accurate. 'Fire for effect. Add fifty, five rounds gunfire.'

Glory! Lovely scene! Better than Matlock on Sunday afternoon. The little doll-like figures were falling over. 'We got 'em!' he said to his signaller who, fag behind one ear, and a spare pencil (in any case) behind the other, looking like a funny aerial from Mars, stared at him 'gone-out'.

'Shoot effective,' Brown said into the mouthpiece.

'Shoot effective,' quacked his man back in the command post.

And: 'Troop, stand easy.'

But not for long. Glued to his map, then to the landscape calling for support onto a spreading rush of German infantry coming up the opposite spur towards a Bren post and slit trenches: 483649.

Machine-gunners were laying into them, but they ran, dropped, dodged, got up again, and moved on skilfully, a whole company plain in the glasses, a couple of flame-throwers up front. It was impossible to tell our guns from theirs with continual firing all along the ridge. Salvoes fell two hundred yards to the right.

He coaxed his own fire on target: 'Less two degrees three-o-minutes . . .'

A dozen bursts sprouted there. One of the flame-throwers went up. Serve the bastard right. He hated them. Everybody did. Even those who carried them. Fire and smoke. Kill 'im. I expect their mothers loved them. A Bren-gunner must have got the other, for a match flickered to his left eye, orange and black spinning from the ground. Grenades were coming over from the weapon pits. Between gun bursts he heard their peculiar cracking noise. They moved away, not running but fighting back step by step. The bastards are well-trained. Some fell. Some stayed there for good.

There was firing from Ravine Wood to the left. Pine, or coniferous of some sort. It looked too dense to use except along the rides. Taking a chance on it, weighing up the tactical situation, he called down fire on one half from 476662 to 478659. It was risky in case some of our chaps were caught, but he thought fast and guessed that the Germans had reached it. The CO of the infantry battalion gave him the all-clear. Groups were going forward with rifle and bayonet, and Lewis guns, to take the wood in flank and kick the Gerry arses out of it. He stood up from the culvert to see how his guns would help, when a tall infantryman rushed by shouting: 'Get down, mate!'

He smiled. Machine-gun bullets shattered the top of the culvert. The Germans went through the wood like grey mites. Must have stopped some in the shelling. He tried to help the counter attack, but it cracked up and the troops stayed just inside another belt of trees. Field of fire too short.

A company officer motioned them with his stick, setting up machine-guns for enfilade from the corners of the wood. My guns are for bloody good soldiers like you. Shells clapped and upchucked on open ground. The officer staggered, then pulled himself upright and walked slowly back.

It was front line stuff and no mistake, the only place for a Fire Observing Officer. A smouldering compost smell hung over the wood, the burning gardens of Babylon. The infantry wanted more rounds into the smoke in case the Germans re-grouped. Some of our blokes were walking away. Others were digging like rabbits. They wouldn't get far in this chalky stuff.

A distinct whistle told him that something close to his number was crayoned on the arse of it. His signalman was spreadeagled over the radio. A ball of black concrete pushed through like a maniac and crushed his dreams like a beetle. Shellshock, he thought, percussion, concussion, a pin-cushion, black flocks and mattresses bouncing and pressing out the light.

He shook himself, stunned. Sergeant Weaver had come back with a runner: 'Wait here.'

A hundred goods trains rumbled through a tunnel under the earth he was lying on. 'What happened to the guns?'

Gone a bit deaf. No, not yet. 'FOO to Command Post.' He heard his own voice to Brown. 'We'll try 476651. Should get 'em coming up the Roozebeek. Don't want to lose it.'

'Right three degrees . . .'

'Hold your nose and press, sir,' Sergeant Weaver said. Thank God you got flattened onto the phones, Brown. Wires still OK. Radio works, anyway.

'We put more juice in 'em at the charging-wagon, sir.'

'Miss! Oh my God, they're laying the guns with coat-hangers!'

You gave the wrong bearing.

Didn't. That's slander.

'Two degrees right. Fourteen minutes elevation. Seven-five hundred, right ranging. FIRE!'

'Fire.'

Shoot effective, you hope.

'Shoot effective!'

The violent crackling of noise suddenly shot back. They lay flat. The ground rocked. Heavy stuff. Disturbance to his ears affected his balance. The earth was still shifting. A sergeant and half a dozen men fired from the culvert and out of craters. 'You leapt on the phones like a cat on its breakfast,' he said to Brown. 'Our lifeline.'

A pebble in his boot was bothering him. Hadn't felt it when walking. Maybe it had blown in through the laceholes. A captain came over from the footsloggers: 'You lot had better fall back. They might get through at the next rush.'

'We've had no orders from the CRA.'

'You can observe just as well from the road.'

'You do your job: we'll do ours.'

'Die then! If you need anything, let us know.'

Sarcastic. Stand up to 'em. Pull rank, if you've got any. Help 'em, though. That's what we're here for. They need it, poor bastards. Swearing again: did anyone curse worse than a gunner? His head had been screwed off and put back on.

Loose wind whistled inside. Gunfire brought up the bile, dried it on your lips. His father would have a fit to hear him, but no doubt he'd done it in his time, though with him it'd be the grumbling sort of cursing in a normal working day when he was out where the guns couldn't help them.

A yellow and white butterfly came up slowly from the grass in front, then quickened away as if deciding to get out before the noise splintered its fragile wings. Brown tried to grab it.

'Get down, you bloody fool,' the sergeant said.

His body tensed, but he drew his hand back.

William laughed. 'What sort is it?'

'A Pale Clouded Yellow, sir. I collect 'em. At least, I did once.'

'Leave 'em alone for today.'

He changed batteries on his set. It was all right again. He stroked it like a cat, while drinking from his waterbottle. The butterfly came back and settled, visible but then forgotten. Half a battalion was going in rushes towards Ravine Wood, shells striking the trees. German four-point-twos scattered the khaki skirmishers. He felt an urge to run down and be with them. From the edge of their own wood they were sending 3-inch mortar shells in almost vertical trajectories, high up and fireworking down to thud-crack among the trees, more for moral effect than real damage. They moved with fixed bayonets, Bren-gunners foremost lying down to fire. Half the attackers were knocked out, or maybe just doggo, but some managed to inch up. Fire from the wood decreased, till some of our blokes were in.

He called all guns on the eastern and southern exits, and a lot of Gerries must have been caught as they scarpered. An attack from Hollebeke was swept in enfilade from the wood, and one was smashed halfway up the Roozebeek as the Germans tried outflanking from the south.

Their game was obvious, but you bled them white till there was no game left and they just made one bloody rush after another. They bled you white as well, but the longer you held the more they had to play it your way. They were getting ratty, impatient, unsubtle, losing their skill and therefore more men at each dud try. But we're losing a lot, and can afford it less.

Some attacks were stopped almost by the guns alone. More by luck than judgement, he grinned. Smoke drifted over the whole ridge. A fairground noise came from further south, without the music. It sounded worse there. A brilliant black and white magpie leapt into the air and clipped away, as if feeling the danger of the spot, maybe to warn other birds of what was impending, for a couple of shells intended for the swaddies in the wood landed near the bush it had been in, and set it ablaze.

There was no water left. Cracked voices shouted orders and map references, few words for each other in the occasional lull. The lowering sky sent sweeps of rain over them, bringing relief and discomfort at the same time. William felt a grey-faced ragbag, wanted to take his boots off, but there was no time for anything but observing the wood-patched, pitted, descending land in front. He covered it in the mind's eye by immediate close-squared co-ordinates in which to net every slight movement.

More Gerries were upping from the narrow cut and fanning this end of Hollebeke, hopefully invisible by lengths of hedge and ditch. They were unlucky, their presence guessed, battery fire called on them. Through glasses he saw a couple of Germans on a motorbike combination coming up the lane. The guns soon had it. One shell dropped close enough and sent them sprawling. Plumes of smoke and earth forced the rest to scatter. He couldn't help but marvel at how they came up the spur and again reached the wood. The crack of guns erupted from behind. The barrels must be about ready to split, with such rapid and continual fire. Maybe they were spending ammunition so as to save blowing up the dumps. If they ran out though before evening, everyone was in trouble.

The attack was a feint. Grey figures moved towards the crossroads a thousand yards south, the real one filtering up the spur on the right bank of the Roozebeek. He hoped to God, sweating his signallers, that they could spare a few of the guns for that side.

Our chaps were falling back up the slope. A few platoons, maybe a hundred men, went towards them to make some sort of stopline. A Bren-gunner firing from the hip dropped, joined by another and a few riflemen. He rushed another twenty yards, taking the others towards the wood.

Earthquake and volcanic eruption joined forces. A shell-burst riddled them with soil and chalk lumps. The bank flew up like a wall. He scrambled along, sight unfocused, a sharp deep itch in his arm. While scraping away grass and bits of sedge with the rim of his helmet, another explosion pushed him flat, the earth an anvil on which a hammer pounded.

He scuttled to where he'd been digging. The shape of the ground had changed. No sign of the man he'd been trying to dig out. A shattered hump of flesh and bone lay on the soil. Bullets were spitting close. His own part of the trench was unrecognisable. A runner lay dead in a hollow of new soil. Stretcher bearers took what wounded they could get to.

A whistle knife-bladed down the valley, ending an inexplicable silence. From his flattened position he saw German soldiers still pinned to the lower slopes. The barrage crashed from both sides. He tried to burrow, but there was nowhere to shelter. His puny guts imitated the rumbling earth.

The first shell must have twisted his sense of direction, for he'd gone the opposite way. He stumbled on the signaller by the radio and telephones. Atmospheric noises screamed out like a goose with its throat cut. He gave map references, sublime routine triumphing. The earth was a chaos of patterns. If you could take a full breath you were alive. He passed the test. The blood he saw wasn't his. Jettisoning his own deep tremors, he scanned fresh shellbursts at five hundred yards, his binoculars unable to hold still and let him see what was happening.

'It's worse in front of Messines,' Sergeant Weaver said.

'We'll hang on till our fingernails drop off.' His laugh was stopped dead by shells bursting at the head of the Roozebeek, obliterating his map reference. He marvelled at the speed with which his guns adjusted sights and began peppering anew. A line of cow-pats moved across the field towards new blown craters. The nearest hedge was on fire. An enormous shudder hid them with uprushing soil.

He put two of the runners busy with entrenching tools, digging shelter in the dry ditch bank a dozen yards away. The Germans were back in the wood, and up the spur beyond Roozebeek. His OP was a shambles: none of the neat sand-bagged dugouts you see on photographs, that you throw up in training. The littered ground didn't bear too close a look.

Be picking us off with rifles soon. But it was too good a vantage point to leave. If we stay they'll get round us. A few platoons were still dug in to hold them off. It would be sensible to get back beyond the road. FOO's weren't much good dead, though with dusk coming up they'd have a chance. The guns have never left the infantry in the lurch.

Mortar bombs fell on the Bren posts, and the foxholes between. 88 mm guns punched the hill behind and came back towards them. Take cover before the storm. He worked along the remains of the gully on his stomach. Shouts came from soldiers running out of the wood. A continual rivet-welding of machine-guns stitched the air, invisible except where men mysteriously dropped.

Bullets spattered along the top of their observation post. Soil hissed against his helmet. A man stood upright beside him. 'Bogger's nearly got me, sir.'

'Oxton! You came through that lot? You'll never see your old mother again if you aren't careful.'

Oxton's long anti-gas cape flapped from broad shoulders to ankles to keep off the drizzle, or the threat of it.

'Take that bloody thing off,' William said, thinking what a perfect target he made. 'In any case, it's for gas, not rain. Fold it up and put it away.'

'Yes, sir.'

'Good to see you, though.'

'I brought you some snap, sir. I'll see my mother in heaven, anyway.'

William laughed. 'If that's where gunners go.'

'*She* will, sir,' he said solemnly.

'Don't be so damned sanctimonious. What's this? Stew, and tinned pears?'

He smiled, as if glad to be back on his old familiar Belgian soil, showing his clean pair of false teeth that made him as vain as a budgerigar. 'And this tea, sir. Hot.'

It burned him. A miracle. Scorching and sweet.

'I had to run through a bit o' shit to get here, sir.'

He opened the dixie of stew and looked in. 'I hope you didn't bring any of it with you.'

'Not more than I could help, sir.'

'You old bugger. Get back now.'

He put the containers on the ground, then saluted, his eyes almost invisible under the rim of his tin hat. He went off singing 'Run, rabbit, run' over the noise of the shelling, so that it sounded like 'The Rock of Ages'.

He swallowed some of the tea, but before he could taste the food a column of earth went up, solid at the middle, ragged at the edges, synchronised to a grunt of the ground. Two fists hit his eardrums, and set him to face the other way. He was a rag doll, fell in the position of a foetus. Another drum of impacted earth blew like an abscess. A weird sound came to him, both arms bent over to protect himself after losing his helmet, his own deepest cry, an animal rage sawing into his head and stomach, a shout of both infinite relief and regret deep inside.

He brushed grit from his streaming eyes, and fought to release both legs from the soil-trap. Frantic yet systematic, his nails broken, stone chips cutting his hands, he scraped away. Unable to find his field glasses he kicked and burrowed. It would take all day. He crawled along. Another shell exploded fifty yards away. Bits of bloody flesh were under his hands, mangled, as if somebody had gone mad at a butcher's stall and scattered lights, lungs and chops everywhere, and had taken his clothes off to do it, and cut *them* up as well, mixing them in in his fury before cutting himself down – one shell.

Wounded were dragging themselves back from the posts. Dead were scattered, too many pieces of flesh to count. In brief silences, and even above machine-gun fire, he heard the unlucky maimed. Bits of the phone were littered around, bakelite and mica, glass and wire. A complete and undamaged radio valve was stuck in the soil like a silver tulip bulb. A piece of shell-tilled soil moved, and when an arm came out he dug round the body and recognised Brown his signaller who sat up, crazed and staring. His face was corpse-like. But he shook his head.

William kicked one of the unwounded runners out of his flattened pose. The other was playing with soil like a kid at the seaside. He considered what to do. 'There's nothing more for us here.'

Brown tried to stand.

'We'll get you back.'

'I'm not hurt, sir. It was a rum 'un, though.'

He lit cigarettes for them both.

'Keep down. They're still sending it over.'

The infantry were pulling back to the road so he scribbled one message – dated 28.5.40 – to the battalion commander saying that the guns would now consider all points east of it as held by the Germans, and one to his own guns saying they were reconnoitring to find a new post west of it.

They crossed a field. 'Can you run?'

'Think so,' Brown said.

'It's the only chance. We're a right couple of ragbags.'

'Still in one piece, sir.'

They moved quickly. The land was wide open, gentle and green, close to the sky and any eyes that chose to look down for the great game of housey-housey. Not many left. Bad time for farm buildings. Gunflashes came from the smoky haze of Gerryland. More shit for us. Some of our own shells were hitting them. Got them taped since morning, but they moved around to avoid it. Predicted shooting. He ranged them in, but it wasn't much good, though he sent a runner back and hoped he'd make it. Flatten 'em.

That wild fruity interior shout still pounded his aching gut. Its echo kept him company. He couldn't understand why he'd yelled such a thing at the last trump. Had death really sent for him, or had what he'd almost called out held it off? I suppose it's darkness we're afraid of. The word had been a stark and simple lightning flash at his roots: 'Father!' – as if he'd wanted his hand when walking away with him from his mother's funeral. He laughed at the idea of it. Suppose you'd shout anything when you were half blown up.

The wind of the sky was parted by a plane rushing down with

siren-fans shrilling, and three bombs fell. The blast was too far off for splinters. He imagined clutching a rugger ball, and zigzagged as if a whole team were after his garters. The Scotties in the last war dribbled a football across no-man's-land. The plane came low. He heard the thump of its guns, and didn't look for the soil spurting close. Chucked from pillar to post.

The hedge was on fire, more smoke than flame, but they got through, heat and ash blowing against them. The badly wounded lay in a lane: 'Don't leave us, sir!' a young soldier called. His cry grated, but he was forced to look, and the smile on his flour-white face irritated him even more. But he smiled back. His battledress was crimson down the left arm and shoulder: 'You'll be all right.'

Walking cases had been killed by the machine-gunning plane. It was a killpig of a ridge. Orderlies and an MO organised stretcher-bearers. Brown had been sent on, while he waited to make sure they came.

He steered by compass through pitted fields that looked different going back. The Germans had counter-batteried the guns. He caught Brown up, stooping slightly as they moved on. They took cover by a hedge from a few stray shells. When you lost men in a place you were reluctant to leave that land to an enemy. Wasn't much you could do about it. He stood from force of habit. His eyes felt as if they had been boiled and put back again. 'Come on, let's see what's left of us.'

The guns, moved further down the slope, were still clapping away. Trees were stripped and smouldering, underbrush burnt to powdered ash, sharp stumps as if gigantic pencils of differing heights had been stuck regularly in the earth. Trees had a hard time in these parts. Be difficult to find the path he and Oxton had reconnoitred this morning.

A makeshift cemetery had been dug in a field behind, stones and helmets marking the graves. Blood still showed. Most of the dead would stay out by the canal. Maybe the Gerries would bury them, or get the Belgians to dispose of another few thousand corpses in this corner of a bloody field. What junk hadn't been burned or buried was scattered around: axles, limbers, wheels, recoil gear, trunnions, buckled steel plate and shell cases, a rubbish tip wherever the eye looked.

He shivered with cold for the first time that day, his clothes plastered with sweat and grit and rain. A gun opened its loud mouth down the slope, and they walked towards the noise, skirting the burned-out wood. Absence of sleep was chipping at his brain. The first time he'd known real exhaustion was when he'd stayed a night with two girls picked up in Nottingham one Christmas. On the Ashfield train next morning his backbone felt like the proverbial string of conkers, and he'd been afraid of falling asleep in case he missed his stop.

He shared his last fags with the signallers. A machine-gun spat from a thousand yards off. They were up the hill. A platoon of infantry filed by: dead on their feet. The lieutenant saluted.

'Good luck.'

'Thank you, sir.'

Some smiled. They didn't look happy. Worn out. He watched them go on, hoping to deploy and hold the road. It was hard lines. There were more than five to one against. As long as we keep 'em off while the rest get to the coast.

Birds set up their evening whistle. The smell of burnt wood, hot ash and rained-on soil was everywhere. The last attack had been discouraged. Lorries drove slowly beyond the steep west side of the hill, joining the heavier engines of gun tractors and medium tanks going north. We'll do a moonlight flit. The Germans know what's happening, but it's driving them crazy because they can't get through and stop it.

Signallers were spooling wire back to the hot spots, and Captain Watkins was on his way out as FOO. 'They're waiting for you at headquarters, Scorty.'

'Where is it?'

'Down the slope a bit. We thought you'd gone over the bags to kingdom come! They're at 443648. You'll find it on your map,' he laughed.

'I don't have one – you comic.'

'I know. The BC will say bunkey-boo when he sees you all scratched up. It's a good thing you still have your revolver. Shoot yourself with it! Cheerio, old boy. Don't say bunkey-boo to a goose!'

Should be in a concert party. Yet he felt the loss of his map-case and binoculars, like a recruit who'd had his rifle stolen. He walked along the line of a hedge and into the field where four 25-pounders were in strict alignment, crews fallen in behind. Apart from full limbers he noted some fifty rounds stacked behind each, and surmised that to be the lot. The Number One saluted.

Through a hedge the adjutant stood by a map on an easel, surrounded by signallers who had set out telephones on a trestle-table. The BC, battledress off and sleeves rolled up, looked spruce and neat, as if on exercise and not in the middle of a free-for-all smash-up; though signs of it were on his face if you looked hard enough.

'Glad you've come, Scorty.'

'Thank you, sir.'

'Don't thank *me*. Rowlandson was killed, poor chap. Hansford and Cowper were wounded, so there aren't many of us left. Lot of letters to write when we get to where we're going.' He looked around: 'Where the hell is that infernal bloody char-wallah?'

Oxton lumbered over from the primus with two cups of steaming tea on a wooden tray with flowers painted on it. He was bent slightly, as if the load was too heavy, but in reality because he'd overfilled the cups and didn't want to get the saucers awash. 'Coming, sir.'

'You're a genius,' the BC said. 'Do you know, Scorty, he screed down the hill and went a mile across country till he found a farm where there was some milk to put in our tea. Told him not to go looting. What are the people going to say when they come back and find the British have thieved everything?'

Oxton always had an answer, but delivered it with such natural politeness that they had to accept it in the same spirit. 'I milked the cow myself, sir. Never done it before, but I pinned the beast against a wall. She followed me back halfway. Lovely, she was.'

There was much laughing. 'I don't suppose a female often falls in love with you, Oxton?' the adjutant said.

He was too proud of his achievement to be put off by

ridicule, as if it were something he'd be able to tell of in his next campaign. 'Wrote down what I took, sir, on a piece of paper. Sort of IOU for after the war.'

The BC was the first to stop laughing: 'Give a mug of your prime ulcer-producing tea to Captain Scorton. We can hardly recognise him in his rags and tatters.'

'I got blown around a bit,' William said.

'You'd better pay a flying visit to Burberry's when we get back. Look as good as new, strutting down the Haymarket.' William cursed life to hell, till the excellent tea got to his lips. The BC passed him a cigar from his leather case. Not such a bad old stick, after all.

'You get back to your troop, Scorty, and we'll think about the withdrawal.'

'Where are we going, sir?'

'The coast. We'll walk into the sea, towing our wooden guns behind us. The navy'll have some flat bottomed boats, and float us across to Blighty. We can't retreat into Germany, can we? I sometimes think you take the Strategy of Indirect Approach just a little bit too far!'

William looked at the trees, but not too many degrees aside for the BC to misconstrue it. The ridge felt more than home to him, as if he'd go blind should they have to move elsewhere. His world was of the faces surrounding him, bodies that knew the drill and loved fine guns – though he'd like more range to 'em. Thunderclapping fire was back at its height. If he left such sights and noises he'd be deaf as well as blind.

'Feeling up to it, Scorty?'

His mind swept itself clean. 'Yes, sir.'

'Got the hardest job tonight. Pulling out in good order will depend on us gunners. I think we've given the Hun enough of a pasting for 'em not to move, but if there's any sign of it, make 'em pay in blood and snot!'

He saluted, and went to his telephones and maps. The FOO signalled all was quiet. He looked at the sky. The clouds were heavier and it started to rain. Cotton gunpuffs, disintegrating birds of rust, appeared in it with the clatter of Bofors ripples boxing up from the plain. A dive-bomber dipped from its trio and screamed down at them.

The guns were letting off at one more German rush to cross the Warneton–St Eloi road. William kneeled with the phone piece to give orders to his Number Ones. The grey-blanket sky was full of rusty holes, AA shrapnel spitting like hail and joining the rubble from exploding bombs.

Before daylight dimmed, the BC smashed the last of their whisky supplies with a hammer, and when Oxton ventured to help, he shouted: 'Get off! Out, I say! This is a job for me!' – and Oxton stood with one hand knit into the other, a look of utter misery, as glass tinkled and the priceless fluid of thirty bottles ran into the earth, as if thinking that the only reason left to see his mother again would be to tell her of this awful waste.

Locked in his own work, and cradled by the drill and what already seemed the long normality of war, William felt it was immaterial whether he got away or stayed. Life went on, unless it did not. He gave orders to his remaining guns. Between fourteen years of age and now he'd felt like a troubled old man much of the time, but at this minute he was young and free of care, and hoped it would continue long into the future.

Darkness soaked its way through, and gunfire on both sides diminished at a sudden downpour of blinding rain. As a gunner he felt that God could see him more clearly at night, and that he put into him a feeling of guilt at taking part in this thing called war. But the thought didn't bother him, because war was, after all, a mere side-step from the greater reality of life itself. Such uneasiness was only a bird of passage through his mind, and didn't have a hope of staying when faced with the beautiful fact that he was still alive as a gunner.

The last of the infantry had trekked by in saturating dark, along busy roads towards the coast. Guns around them blasted off a final thundering to get rid of ammunition. Flashes lit their done-in faces. Of one infantry battalion, less than a hundred men were coming back out of six hundred.

In the circle of his own impenetrable lit-up piece of darkness he laboured diligently and forgot the past and future. There was no time to think, only to play the blacksmith till the hour came for smashing the precious gunsights and going downhill with the crews that were left.

In darkness the bloke up front steered his lorry by mistake off the road and into a farmyard. The blind gett. Luckily there was a large pond in the middle, with enough space simply to go round it and get out again the way they'd come. Dozey mare. But the entire convoy had to follow suit, because no one vehicle had room to turn. Pie-eyed fuckpig. He'd never heard so much livid swearing while the whole follow-my-leader snake unwound itself.

Not wanting to be wiped out by one big bladder of a bomb, the battery staff split up. William was jammed in a truck with fifty others. Everything was perfectly easy and soldier-like. For sleep, you snoozed standing up. For food, Oxton had filled packs with rations, so they'd eat for a while.

There was no panic in British pullbacks. We're good at sneaking off steadily when hard pressed because we know that sooner or later the Navy's going to pluck us from the coast and out to England, where we'll sit and thumb our noses at the enemy who, we assume, can no longer get at us.

He thought of his girlfriend left behind in Arras, recalled their walks in the evening countryside, finding a stone shelter of some Great War cemetery in which they sat for a bit of entente-cordialling till the moon came up over Vimy Ridge and made the wide and ever-rolling fields glimmer in its luminous light.

On lucky nights they'd go to the Hôtel de l'Univers and get a quiet room overlooking the courtyard, primed by a good dinner for bumping away on the soft bed. Mulling on it, the feeling between his legs was so intense he felt there'd be a mess if many more jolts shook the bloody truck.

In the last few days he'd forgotten such things, and fell to brooding on how many men and guns they'd lost, though even that didn't take away the image of Nicole stripping off her cotton step-ins in that dimly-lit bedroom with its walls of blue-flowered paper.

He stared beyond the narrow line at the first green water-streaked land of Flanders. The British always swore terribly here. Military police shunted them parallel to the main flux, and his gritty eyes stayed open by looking at the flowing grass and nondescript red roofed cottages. This is not me, he said to himself, trying to ease Oxton's boots from his feet. And then: this *is* me – before scrambling from the gharry to lie in a tadpole ditch till the Stukas had gone. They concentrated more on the coast – luckily – because the plain must have looked as if it were crawling with ants. There were too many to blast everybody. Visibility was fair over the flat land. It was dry and warm, and they were slowed by crowds the closer they got to the Channel.

The burning lorry was heaved off the road, bullying Redcaps cursing blue murder at the chaps till it was done. The wounded lay patiently enough. They'd have to wait till someone got them out of it. He felt his spirit wearing away as the truck pushed north. He'd been primed full to bursting by that last quick firing bout from his twenty-five pounders. He only wanted to be back on them with unlimited ammunition.

It blackened his heart to realise they had no more guns, not knowing where the next piece was coming from. Maybe they'd dish up a few obsolescent garrison shooters when they got to England, or send them off on some forlorn stunt as footsloggers. The back wheel kicked up a stone. A gunner would rather lose his life than his gun, but they'd been told to spike them and that was what they'd done.

He felt as if he'd been a whole lifetime married to those guns, and now he was exposed to any stray German who might come along in his tank or roar down from the sky in his deadly toy plane.

With the heat of the engine and so many bodies it was an effort to keep the eyes open and the back straight. He answered the chaps' questions as if he were God Almighty and knew all the answers, when really he was no wiser than a babe just born. Keep the brain clear for all queries, tactically mature, strategically adept. But he wasn't made for a retreat, having been trained and mentally built to stay behind those lovely guns till they blew up in his face, or he was shot dead by the first enemy to get close.

Better to die, but orders had to be gulped like acid. You

perished if you stayed. You rotted when you left. An artist cannoneer and master gunner couldn't give up his guns and be the same man ever again. Yes he could. In five minutes he could if he got another gun. But he half dreamed in the heat that he was still with the guns: flesh dissolving with their hot metal when all was split asunder in some final violence, and buried under the soil without apparent trace, staying till the sweet steel corroded, and his dead flesh twisted around it and rusted, and together they melted till nothing remained but God's clean soil.

When he shook himself, he was a mile closer to the sea, which he imagined he could smell above the odours of petrol and sweat. The superlative technical education on which he had prided himself, and in the glorious light of which his father would live for ever, hadn't prepared him for the fact that without his guns he'd feel as primitive as an ape.

He felt shame at registering such emotions, and wondered whether Watkins was equally clawed by their loss. Nobody could like what had happened but, as they'd often reminded him in a friendly or jocular fashion, *they* had different backgrounds and attitudes, and so took it in a more philosophical way. Perhaps they didn't think much about it, looked more towards the future than the past. But by pondering brutally on what had happened he might learn something. Certainly he would rather perish than lose his guns again. Such a thing couldn't be allowed to happen twice in a gunner's lifetime.

All kit and tackle had been chucked on to a heap, and blown up at the last minute. They had what they stood up in, and what was inside them. Oxton had amassed presents for his mother. 'Never mind,' William said.

'It's all right, sir. It's *me* she wants. I'll explain to her. But I've still got a French handkerchief. Bought it in Amiens. Real lace. It don't weight owt, and it takes no space up. Not much bigger than a stamp. So she'll get that. She loves things from France, sir. I had some beautiful stuff in that suitcase, though.'

They made their way towards rising heaps of smoke. He killed the future by letting each minute roll by under its own steam. He felt that they were driving into a holocaust, but he looked around calmly.

They queued by the East Mole. He could never understand why some were blown to pieces and he was all right. But a soldier stops craving to understand such things.

It takes too much time and concern. You'd never solve it, anyway. If you try to puzzle it out while the bombing is going on, you might destroy the sixth sense that seems to be protecting you. Question things, and you get killed. And if you wait to puzzle it through in safety, it's even more impossible because your senses have forgotten what it was like. So you end by calling it fate or Kismet, or just plain good luck. In any case, it takes too much time to figure things out. And time, as his father had always said, was of the essence.

At Dunkirk, he couldn't have been more right.

Part Three

CHAPTER SIX

He was back in England after a long year in Germany, on his way to a posting at Larkhill, and the Royal Artillery band played good nostalgic music in the mess, to a gathering in full-dress uniform, for the delectation of officers and their ladies. William walked through the groups and couples in the hall, and immediately noticed her because he had never seen a woman who was so tall and self-confident, and therefore easy to pick out of a crowd.

'You're a ladies' man,' Watkins said to him only last week – meaning there'd been so much competition for the right sort of woman during the war that he'd turned into such; in order to get his share of what was going. So he'd learned to recognise good qualities in a woman – if she had any at all – a skill which made him discerning, but at the same time easily influenced by whoever he won over to what he wanted. He wasn't exactly shy, but he knew how to show the necessary reticence during his scheme of operations.

After the post-war wilderness of Germany he felt that civilisation had restarted as he walked into the huge hall. To hell with austerity, rationing, and a Labour Government. Before the war he'd been a sergeant, and because of the impression this scene had on him, in some ways he still felt like one.

The war had become a normal part of life, a sort of haphazard jamboree in which you banged off your guns now and again, but entering this assembly as a lieutenant-colonel in full fig finally convinced him that he belonged to an invincible and disciplined brotherhood that nothing, certainly not time, could ever do away with.

He thought of his father and, while hoping it might be the

last recollection of him this evening, knew the pleasure old Charlie would have experienced if he'd seen him going with head high and back straight into such music and company.

And yet, God knows, certain aspects were normal and humdrum enough by now, though no one could deny he'd had full right to it from birth. On the other hand, he wanted to feel how extraordinary it was so that he could get the proper credit for having achieved so much since his boy-soldiering days.

His father was over seventy and, having retired from the post office, was again at the end of one of his many lives. On leave during the war he'd seen him with his corporal's stripes and chip-hat, and shabby Home Guard uniform that as a former soldier of the Queen he wouldn't have been seen dead in but which, according to Doris, he felt as proud of as a peacock. He stood up smart in boots and gaiters and creased trousers, and got that sparkle in his eyes before lifting his familiar rifle to set off on manoeuvres in Sherwood Forest.

Maybe Charlie in his proper soldiering days had glimpsed such gatherings as this. Then William felt almost angry, and glad that not even his few friends present could know he was occupying his mind with petty visions of his old father and where both of them had come from.

He hesitated in his walk towards the girl, in case his dead-set vector made her feel something was wrong, and that he wouldn't find her again if she moved to avoid him. The thick-lined co-ordinates of his life met and meshed. He felt carefree, and pleased there was nothing wrong with his dress or appearance, knowing now why he'd taken such care. He was lively and still young, though settled in his ideas. Feeling a certain emptiness at the middle of everything was only a sign that he hadn't yet lost his old sense of self-preservation.

She stood at the far end of the hall, close to the band in their blue uniforms playing some Gilbert and Sullivan knick-knack, listening to a tall fair-haired chap who'd have made her a good dining room chair to sit on if nothing else. It was amazing how many men weren't worthy of the woman they met up with. The only exception might have been when, early on, his mother and father were together, though even then he couldn't be sure. That was different, and impossible to fathom. Be that as it may, there were so many good women in the world, for mediocre men.

There was an illumination about her pale full face with its piercing, almost cold blue eyes. It was hard to break in. There must be no abruptness in his dealings. The idle vegetable brain can wait and wander as it likes. What other relaxation is there for a technically minded man? It's death though to be idle for long. Idleness is a sickness of the interacting brain and body, and the longer you laze in it the less likely you are to get out. A few hours' inactivity would make him feel he'd caught some kind of plague. There were many such times during the war, and would have been more if he hadn't contrived to keep his men busy to the hilt.

He couldn't deny that his six years of campaigning had been of the best. In one way the war hadn't lasted long enough to give him revenge for the loss of those guns in Flanders. He'd have pulled the world down for that. His actions had never been sufficiently hell-fire, though the others weren't dissatisfied. He'd driven through miles of scrap iron in the sand, charred planes on pitted runways, tanks arsed-up in the mud at river crossings, corpses fertilizing orchards and olive groves, but at such times he could never get out of his mind the failure to bring those beautiful guns back from Belgium in 1940. It was the one failure of his life that he thought he still had to make up for.

The war (or maybe it was only a combination of circumstances) had stopped him right-wheeling into wedlock till well after the last gun was silent. He'd had his chances, as they say, but what was the point of marrying while the war was on? It might be as snug as a scarf round your neck, but what woman could be expected to feel happy, with you in some outlandish part of the world doing your tiddly-bit for King and Country? You might be killed, and that was a fact. Or you'd get a letter one day saying it was all over because why should she ruin the best years of her youth waiting for you when she could have it big and sweet from another man? Such a thing became so common in the regiment that there'd been periodic parties in the mess for those who needed pulling out of their miseries.

Even the padre joined in, one night reciting from Psalm thirty-four holding a gin-fizz: '*The Lord is nigh unto them that are of a broken heart,*' which made 'em feel a lot more cheerful, you can bet.

Watkins stood ten feet from her, and William greeted him so as to stop his progress becoming too much of a rush: 'It's good to be in civilisation again.'

'Some damned attractive women,' Watkins agreed, his back to the one William was set on, which enabled him to keep part of her face in view. 'A far cry from the spoils of victory in Germany, what?'

He laughed. There'd been many of those: 'It's about time you settled down. The world's at peace now.'

'Can't hear myself think,' Watkins shouted, downing his champagne. 'I'd rather hear the noise of gunfire than loud music at a party. Damned sure I would, what? Shall have to hop-skip-and-a-dance in a bit.'

He'd put on weight, which didn't suit his two front teeth. In Normandy he'd flown over the handlebars of a motorbike after demanding a lift near Beny Bocage, but he'd got his dentist to fit two identical ones so that no one would tell the difference. We only see how old we are when we look at others, William thought, noting the lines of his friend's face. 'Do you good. They'll be playing the Lancers soon.'

Watkins took a laden glass from a passing tray, replacing the empty one: 'Must get treddled, Scorty.'

'It's early. You'll fall down.' He wouldn't. He'd put back another dozen yet stay on his feet. His continual swaying merely meant he was shaking the booze to lower levels.

'I hope you win her,' Watkins said, with a prodigious wink that folded his whole face into it.

'Win who?'

'I can see who your sights are focused on. Get the old smooth-bore working, eh?'

William was wondering how to get rid of him when, the real gentleman, he pushed off without a word to greet the adjutant.

Because of this lit-up aspect he thought she must be perfect in all other ways. His father once showed him a faded sepia photograph of a great grandmother on his mother's side as a young woman. She had features that in no way passed to the face of his own mother, as far as he remembered, but they reminded him, in the shape of the mouth, of the tall woman he was looking at.

When she set off to dance with the fair young captain he stood on the sidelines, content to watch her grey silk dress come into sight now and again. He wondered whether her face hadn't taken on this illumined aspect only when he stepped into the hall and started his moth-like progress towards her, and whether it wouldn't last only for as long as it took him to get to her. Others might also have seen it, but didn't act because it hadn't touched their spirits sufficiently. And if they were aware of this attractive quality in her face, maybe its very intensity put them off when they got too close. Still, now she was free, and he would find out.

'I'm Colonel Scorton. William, if you like. Some even call me Bill, after a while.'

She smiled. 'I know. I asked Watkins about you.'

Damn it! He hadn't seen that bit of crafty work.

'He wouldn't tell me much, except that you'd been in the same regiment during the war.'

'I'm glad he didn't give me away.'

'You stick together, I know that.'

'We're like brothers.'

She was tempted to laugh. He was good looking in a rugged sort of way, and with a self-confidence which she thought came by being overpleased with himself. She found it rather attractive when set against the inner despondency that she was determined to hide more from him than from any of the others she had so far spoken to. I suppose I like him, she thought. 'Watkins is a bit pissed. Told me something about you being the salt of the earth, whatever that means.'

'He has lots of pretty names for me. Don't know why.' He did, but there was no sense worrying about it.

'Anyway, I'm Georgina.'

She might have sounded too abrupt, if he hadn't lost his sense of self-preservation and fallen in love. But a certain amount of time had to pass before he knew whether he stood a chance. She'd used the word 'pissed' so he assumed he also could be direct. 'I suppose you're the General's daughter?'

'The Brigadier's actually. I'm Georgina Woods.'

He cursed himself for a fool, and added: 'Trust me to fall head over heels with a Brigadier's daugher.'

'You *are* funny.' She supposed a subaltern's girl wouldn't stand a chance. But she was taken with him. 'Maybe you'll be asking me to dance soon.'

'Will I have to marry you if I do?'

'Bloody right,' she laughed, 'though I suppose Mrs Scorton wouldn't like it.'

'She wouldn't. But there isn't one.'

She fell quiet and tried not to look at him. Not knowing what to say next, she hoped he'd be man enough to solve the problem, and save her being dragged into talk with someone else. As she'd finally said to the captain who'd been pestering her all evening, and who then ditched her because of it: 'Oh, please don't *bore* me with all that army stuff.'

'I saw you as soon as I came in,' William told her. 'Made a straight line for you. You looked splendid, standing on your own because no one was good enough for you!'

She smiled knowingly, as if to make him uneasy. Might do him good. 'I couldn't bear to talk to anyone. Don't know why.'

'You're the most stunning person in the place.'

'You only see what you want to see.'

She's talking to me, though. He took her arm: 'Come on, princess, let's spin. The only thing to do is get into the fray.'

She fell in love with him, she told him later, because of his easy and direct approach, and because he made it so obvious that he had fallen in love with her. Edison didn't make the lightbulb, he thought, I did. A filament lit up in a glass vacuum by a charge of electricity. Being generous herself – as well as tall, fair, and blue-eyed – she responded to it. Out of scores of people he'd gone only to her. His cultivated breeding of the last twenty years had been dropped the moment it suited him. He held her warm hand when they danced.

'Of course, I wasn't to know you were the Brigadier's daughter, was I?' he said during the waltz. 'But you're absolutely unique out of all the mob present.'

He knew she wouldn't mind if he repeated it. He had been the only one in whom that shine of her inner spirit brought out a confidence she could do nothing against. She admitted it to herself, and welcomed it as a sort of love and adoration which, being necessary, was not to be resisted.

She laughed, and got closer. His prattle was welcoming to her moods of self-denigration. She was used to people being courteous, or fawning, or even vulgar – the bastards – if they knew who she was and for some reason resented or were afraid of it, or didn't care one way or the other – which was worse – but here was someone who cut out all this mud-and-haystack stuff. He acted as if she belonged to him, which made her feel how sure and unassuming he was, but that he belonged to her – if she wanted him.

He told her that for some reason he saw things in her eyes which no one else could. And if anyone else did, they would only mix in the tawdry details of their own lives, so it was better left to him, who could see as far as the blue aquamarine of her soul. She took it as an act of primitive generosity that he had seen immediately into her, and so she believed whatever else he said, and held out a hand for him when he came back after they'd been separated by dancing with others.

As he took it he wondered whether in fact there *was* much generosity in him. He wasn't frightened of its lack, but by whether the attraction between them would last when she finally discovered that there wasn't. For he too would occasionally run himself down to a woman in a casual off-hand way because then she'd think he was being modest, and would appreciate the fact that he was merely trying to put her at ease. He'd learned something about the necessary give and take – 'even though I am a gunner,' he added, having told her this, and amused her by being so frank.

He remembered what they talked about that first evening, but it was as if they hadn't said much, thinking back, though they'd stayed most of the time with each other. He was no longer aware of being a middle-aged gunner, for it soon became apparent that being in love made you young again no matter what age you were: 'And you,' he said, 'you're much younger than me. About twenty-five, I'd say.'

'Twenty-eight.' He'd been accurate, instead of knocking a few years off her age. She was old enough to know that it was better for him to care than to flatter.

'When a woman falls in love she immediately gets younger, and more beautiful. That's fact, not fancy.'

Perhaps they danced too much, for after a while it took them further apart than they wanted to be. It was a tasting of life and death for the first time in both their lives, for him a swim into the blue aquamarine desert of her eyes, and for both of them a plunge into the ocean of their own life-ignorance. In military terms he despised the philosophy of unremitting attack as epitomised by some. More to his taste had been the subtler stratagems of the indirect approach, whereby you applied force economically and went for the nerve centres so as to paralyse the moral will to resist.

But this time he used no tactics, was completely unlimbered because he felt as if he'd known her all his life and was quite unable to decide where this marvellous sense of familiarity had come from. In other words he employed the most perfect tactics because he merely allowed himself to be used by his subconscious, which knew even better not only what he had always wanted but what he would eventually get.

It had to happen sooner or later. He'd often been in love, but when he met Georgina, he knew that he never had been. The other times were a laugh: calf-love, infatuation, the stitch, indigestion, cat-lust – anything but the way he felt now. Raw and full of fire at twenty, his desires later turned to pitch, boiling more subtly around his deepest innards. The older you get, he thought, going back afterwards to his quarters, the more stunning and all-crushing love becomes, but not less pleasant.

It was so sudden and cloying that he was convinced it would be for the last time. He'd waited long enough, he told himself while the uncharted lake of emotion got vaster on all sides till he could no longer survey its limits. A master-gunner of thirty-five doesn't make blunders when it comes to love.

CHAPTER SEVEN

Georgina had just broken off a two-year affair because the man wouldn't leave his wife and two children, get a divorce, and then marry her. Love justified everything, she said. If he loved her, there were no obstacles to their happiness. Aren't we happy already? he asked. Yes, but you know what I bloody-well mean. We can't go on with this hole-and-corner business. It was obvious that she loved him a thousand times more than he loved her, and by weighing up the pros and cons so coldly he was simply being craven, while she was jolly well ready to do anything to prove her love.

But finally, in spite of many half promises, he wouldn't move. She thought it was out of fear, weakness and treachery – a good war record went for nothing in such a situation – while he knew he was strong and cool-tempered enough not to push in the plunger. Something in Georgina held him back, though he maintained to the end that he loved her desperately, and would till the end of his life.

At the final meeting she screamed, punched, threatened to blow the whole thing wide open (his wife already knew, but he hadn't told Georgina that) and threw whisky into his face, while salt tears came up out of her soul.

But it was over now, all finished, and she would never make the same mistake again. The experience left her feeling shallow and vulnerable. She saw it as a failure on her part, which cut to the roots, so that for weeks she thought of killing herself, and it was the effort to fight off this maladroit craving for annihilation that made her seem so phosphorescent in aspect at the party. Only someone like William, who as well as having a certain sensibility towards women, had seen enough of death without being either coarsened or scarred, could pick it up so clearly.

When they met for a few hours at a hotel bar in Guildford she talked about her affair with the stockbroker in order – she said – that it need never be mentioned again. He held her hand in the darkened corner, and felt that she told her long and detailed story as much to be relieved of its burden as to be honest. He was touched by the fact that she confided in him, and felt that if he hadn't to be on duty early next morning, they would have taken a room at the hotel there and then.

She showed her affection openly, by touching and kissing him across the table, and he was pleased and surprised that she didn't care if anyone came in who knew her family. Her kisses were passionate and well-meant on the station platform, and he wondered why it had taken him so long to encounter such love as this.

The ending of the war had found him for the first time a fully integrated soldier in a career that might last another ten years, and would take him one more notch up the ladder. His choice of life had been dictated by his father's pushing, and now that such pressure was truly off, the emptiness could only be filled by those primal instincts which might have developed a quite different life in him had he been left more to himself when young. The lit-up tension that had come almost unnoticed was cushioned by the shock of love, and if it took the end of Georgina's affair to make her empty enough to meet him more than half way, then he could only be glad that fate was playing into their hands at last.

He was away for a fortnight explaining the use of mobility and firepower to those who, in spite of the war, seemed to have learned little. No wonder the Germans had made rings around some of them. All they wanted was to get back to the good life. Who could blame the soldiers for putting in a Labour Government? – though it would take much more than that to alter a country so dug in the grave. It had come to life a bit during the war, but had gone back to its old habits under a cloak of nationalisation. Still, that's not my business, though even my old dad wrote to say he'd voted Labour, and I know he's not done that before.

'A good soldier never looks back,' Charlie had always said,

but maybe he'd had to at last. Some of those whom William worked with seemed to live by doing nothing else but look back. In Queen Victoria's regiments maybe it had been a good principle, but he found that in his war, if you didn't look back as well as in every direction at once for the safety of your battery, you were just asking for that special kind of obliteration that the Germans always had in store for the unwary. He couldn't help thinking that if his father hadn't been so deadset against looking back he might have got to know himself a lot better than he had, though he supposed it was true that people rarely let on to others how much they twigged about themselves.

He took Georgina's letter from his tunic pocket, a bundle of pages covered back and front with large well-shaped handwriting, and read it for the dozenth time. She missed him, and adored him passionately because he'd made things worthwhile again. All her life she'd waited, knowing even at the worst and dullest moments that one day he would turn up.

I asked for it, he thought. His replies were written with similar affection, though only a fraction of the length because he hadn't the same amount of time. Her letters gave point and direction to his life, and he worked better with one in his pocket. They made him lighter in spirit, so that even Watkins and the other fellows in the mess noticed it.

Soon the exercise would be over and they'd meet for a weekend in Town. She was an independent woman of twenty-eight, though it had been no small fight to get free of her parents yet go on living in their comfortable Guildford home. Even at twenty-one Daddy had insisted that she come in no latter than eleven, and her mother had backed him up. Parents still keep the chains on as long as they can, he thought. Tetchy old Jacko, her brigadier father, was close to retirement, and he hadn't yet met him. The family flat at Knightsbridge, where Georgina stayed when she wanted a few days in town, was the place William had his eye on, knowing that love always found a way, especially when both parties were willing.

The long hut smelled of tea, and disinfectant. He rummaged about his large trestle-table covered with orders and lists of figures, and got out a map of southern England to see what surprises he could provide for Blue Force which was expected to move gainst Red Force in the morning.

It was late spring, and leaves were thick and heavy on the trees, the air fairly warm but with a mixing chill on the wind. In London you saw how grim the time still was, with coats of paint needed everywhere, and houses missing or with sides shored up. But he felt good, in spite of the dust and squalor.

She held out her hand as she came up the steps of the National Gallery. 'I kept thinking you wouldn't make it.'

He pressed her fingers. He was five minutes early, and it heartened him to see her so worried. 'You know what the trains are like.'

They stood by the balustrade. Her coat was well padded at the shoulders, and she carried a large handbag. 'I was sure something would stop you at the last minute.'

'The whole of Southern Command wouldn't have kept me away.' He'd felt a spirit of freedom and bravado rising in him during the last few months, and having drawn back each time only increased the confidence that might soon make it harder to resist.

'I told Daddy I had to see an old friend from boarding school.'

'What's wrong with the truth?'

'He'll know about us one day, my darling.'

She didn't know what Daddy would think of him, nor mummy, which was more important. In any case she wouldn't introduce him till she was *sure*. Must make certain that *that* doesn't happen again, even though she felt much tender concern towards him, and had waited eagerly to see him.

They stood a moment without speaking, as if to get over the fact that they had after all managed to meet. She was a big emotional girl and, glancing at her face, he recalled her letters full of love he could never get enough of.

'Shall we have lunch at the Savoy?' A child ran among the pigeons and scattered them to either side of the plinth. 'Or at Bertorelli's on Charlotte Street? It's hopeless trying to get in the Savoy without booking.'

He knew what her answer would be, for he could gauge her moods well. Both wanted to make each other happy in their separate ways, without imagining the other knew what they were about, and the jig-saw pieces fitted so well together they were light-headed as they walked by the dirty bookshops up Charing Cross Road. Because it was his first time in love, there was no sign of possible consequences that might take away the feeling of being alive at last. She held his arm, and London seemed a fresh and magic city to them both.

It was light and clean in the restaurant. They ate smoked fish, escalope Milanese, salad and cheese, and drank a bottle of Chianti. It was their first meal together. Georgina was hungry, but he was too fundamentally excited to relish his food. He talked, in order to please her, because in some way love seemed to separate them, and have little to do with the mutual regard they felt. But their instantaneous desire burned too bright to flee from, and any subdued wish to do so only increased their need to get closer and make each other happy.

He told her about his life as if that too was one of the obstacles to be cleared before they could get properly acquainted. Instead of hearing it as the drab story of a man who had pulled himself up by his own bootlaces, as Daddy might say, she thought it marvellous and inspiring, and couldn't wait – she interposed – to meet his dear old father whom he seemed to love so much. The constriction of the spirit, the elimination of the heart, and the crippling of all childish spontaneity didn't occur to her for a minute, so that he wondered whether he'd told it right – or whether something similar hadn't happened to her. She didn't see that such an upbringing couldn't possibly have made the person she thought him to be. But why go into it? You had to accept the good that God sent, not scare it off.

The main thing was to go on effortlessly amusing her so as to prove that her predilection for him was not displaced. He began to see mutual and reciprocated love as the most perfect form of spiritual machinery, but also that this was transcendentally better than mere love, and for that reason could not last. But what does last? Annoyed at the curious ins and outs of his mind, he beckoned the waitress and asked for coffee.

'Milk,' Georgina said.

He leaned his cigar on the ash tray. 'Black for me.'

They taxied to her parents' place in Knightsbridge, a large and elaborately furnished flat of some half dozen rooms. He took off his overcoat and cap, wondering if she intended springing her father on him. She turned with a faint smile from the living room doorway, her eyes so full of meaning that they were empty, opaque, aquamarine: 'A man lives in, sort of butler, but he's off for the weekend.'

Such good news settled his stomach, and he subsided onto the oversized settee. She scanned the tray: 'Oh damn, there's no soda.'

'Never mind. I'll survive.'

She poured whisky from a heavy decanter. 'I wanted my love to have soda with his whisky.'

'My insides have known hotter stuff than straight hooch.'

She sat in an armchair opposite. 'I'm sure they have.'

There was a smell of mothballs, and stale sweat which may only have been the lingering fumes of expensive decaying scents her father had brought back from France, where he'd been on a Battlefield Tour to Normandy, studying the various moves of Montgomery's 'Operation Deathride' near Caen. This was followed by a few days in Paris, and a stocking up on all the goodies he could find.

'I once had some liquor in Italy which almost sent me blind. Improved my gunnery no end. Got a tank that day.'

'Oh don't tell me a war story,' she pouted. 'I just want to sit and look at my love sipping his whisky like a hard man of the world!'

'Stop play-acting. You want me to be broody and sullen. Is that it?'

Her eyes shone. 'Yes.'

'Be careful my beauty. I *am* like that.'

'Good.'

'You won't like it.'

'I will.'

'I'm being honest with you.'

'I will like it,' she answered softly.

'Give me another drink, then, or I'll black your eye.'

She wanted to serve him. It came as a shock, because he'd never thought that any woman had come into the world to do that. It was a far cry from the raucous give-and-take of pub tarts a long time ago. She doesn't know what I'm like, no more that I know yet what runs in her. Do I even know what I'm like myself? There you've got me. We fall in love, and it blinds us to everything in the other person that we won't be able to stand in ten years – he'd heard it said in the mess recently and thought then how true it sounded. It made little difference to recall it now, set with a sort of drunken sanity along a road all his own. Only dull bastards ever learned by other people's experience.

No more polite conversation. Common parlance would only blight the atmosphere. He drank his whisky, a long look into it between sips, hoping his heart would in no way betray him. He strolled around the room, pausing before the heavy gold-framed pictures of mountain scenery from Kashmir. There was a portrait of Robert Clive, a battle-scene from the Crimea (Alma, it looked like) and in the library, a full-length tenth-rate oil painting of an infantry officer killed on the Somme. He looked about twenty, a slight smile on his lips, and eyes staring at his own present nothingness. The infantry still blamed the artillery for that killpig of a fiasco, for not cutting the wire properly, and for lifting the barrage too soon so that the Germans had time to come up out of their dugouts and get cracking with machine-guns.

There was a set of the Official History of the Great War in the library, red bound books, some with their spines faded to a salmon colour where they had caught the sun, as if the odd volumes her father had taken to read on holiday had been forgotten on the sand while he dozed off. There were copies of *Who's Who*, as well as almanacks, picture albums, the complete leatherbound works of Bulwer-Lytton, and manuals on tactics which ought to have gone out with Omdurman.

'Is my man brooding on all those deathly old books?'

He turned. Her eyes were close, a stare of soft incomprehension easy to meet. She was in love. She wanted to forget, and to start a new life. She waited for him to speak and break the look between them.

He didn't. They were holding and kissing, arms around each other. She was taller, and her lips pressed into him. He felt no need to speak. Like a real man, he'd let her do it, she thought, as the feeling between her legs pushed all the faint echoes out of her mind. 'I love you,' she said. 'I really do, my angel.'

He moved his lips to her warm forehead, then to her cheek, to show that he loved her, too. It was impossible to put the whisky down. Some spilled into his fingers. He held her with one hand but, realising that two were better than one, slid the glass on to the low table. She plucked at his top tunic button. His hand felt the softness of her delightfully ample breasts under the silk blouse. She couldn't undo his button, so squeezed him to her with trembling thighs.

The skirmishing went on, till she said, drawing back her head: 'Let's go into my bedroom' – as if to let herself know that she had given up all restraint in one vital second that was to dominate the rest of their lives, like in those trashy Paul Renin novels they used to read secretly at school.

The window of her room faced the back of the building, quieter as to traffic but not altogether silent regarding the clanging of dustbin lids, and a man's voice cursing in a whine of madness that he hoped she hadn't heard.

The three-quarter bed was covered by a flowered counterpane. She stood by it and, staring at him, rapidly undid her blouse, then took off her brassière by a deft movement of both hands behind her rib case so that it fell forward and on to the floor.

It was as if she couldn't wait to put some obstacle behind her, and he didn't object to such hurry because all he wanted was to lose himself in her body, so that they could know each other properly and decide where to go from there.

She arched her back, large breasts protruding, and didn't wait but threw off shoes, skirt, slip, stockings, knickers and suspender belt, bending so that her luscious pale bosom hung down. She stood stripped to the flesh, which was the only way he wanted her. You enter calm water, and suddenly you're heading for Niagara Falls.

He'd removed his tunic and tie. In his Boy Soldier days

they'd sometimes changed half a dozen times a day, but he wasn't speedy enough for Georgina, for she knelt at his feet and unfastened his trouser buttons with the same skill as in tackling the snappings of her own blouse. It was as well she was so quick, or he'd have exploded before reaching the air. Things calmed down. Such dexterity reminded him of his sweetheart in Arras, and he assumed that much had happened in the old country while he was away.

She ran a hand up the light curly hair from his groin, and said something which he didn't hear. They moved slowly to the bed. Like the end of the world, the first time came only once. She was a tough girl who had to be treated gently. He preferred to linger over it, but she called the tune, and it was a quick one. It wasn't, he thought, as if he worked for a living and had to get there on time or be sacked.

Even while set on his pleasures he felt that he would have to pay for it one day by hitting bottom and getting the bill. He'd always realised the value of what came to him, but the thought annoyed him now, and he decided that things would have to change.

They did. Eyes down: legs eleven. Two-and-six: bed and breakfast. He pushed all other voices away except silence. They fled like a pack of demons, so that what had been obstacles to total pleasure on other occasions now left him without defences when he needed them most, which convinced him more than ever that this was real love.

They held tight, and he poured into her.

'My love,' she said, 'my love.'

He couldn't tell whether they were words of despair or ecstasy, anger or even affection. He didn't know why he expected to know. She seemed to melt under her own hot breath, and they gripped each other like iron.

CHAPTER EIGHT

'Who is she, then?'

As if it mattered to the old bugger. But he'd have felt left out of life if it hadn't. At the same time it would have been better if he'd asked what she was like. You can't teach an old horse new tricks though; certainly not an old soldier. He ought to know that himself by now.

'She'll be twenty-nine next birthday. Daughter of a brigadier.'

'What's her name?'

'Woods – Georgina.'

'I've heard of *him*.'

'She's a good sort. We love each other very much.'

'Do you, by Guy? That's summat, in't it?'

There wasn't much approval in his voice, as if by marrying he was making a false move – to his own father first, to the army second, to himself third, and to the girl last of all. It was an uphill battle. He was ready to kick himself at getting into this tangle. 'We'll be happy enough. Don't you worry, dad.'

He'd borrowed Watkins' old Austin to motor up and see him. After saying hello to Doris he'd tipped out the last batch of his artillery maps saved for his father from the war. He had quite a collection, and enjoyed spreading them on the table to study the various moves and barrages in his spare time between digging the garden and doing odd repair jobs around the house.

Doris set down a cup of tea and a plate of apple-cake: 'Don't know what you want to bother with them owd maps for. War's over now, in't it?'

'If it weren't he wouldn't be here,' his father said; right, as usual.

'They're souvenirs,' William said. 'They'll be historical

relics some day.'

'Like me,' she laughed.

He drove his father the few miles to the Dukeries, and parked on Limetree Avenue because both wanted a walk. They strolled through the wood, along the lane towards Hardwick Grange. There was a strong wind, its noise rushing in the trees, and when two doves lifted into the air they seemed to move backwards before scooting up to the treetop for a perch.

'I'm not one for worrying,' he answered. 'I'm sure you'll be happy. It don't tek much to mek a woman content. It's sometimes what the world does to you as makes the trouble.'

It was hard to know what he meant. Life seemed too short at the moment to disentangle it. His father had insisted on coming out in his best clothes. He would not be seen with his son in anything except a dark suit, tie, boots, a grey overcoat, bowler hat and stick. His face was more lined, his short hair pure white under his hat, but he walked as erect as ever, and carried his seventy-three years well.

William didn't like being made to feel he'd said something wrong, especially when he couldn't fathom the reason. Even if there was a good one he wouldn't have taken any blame. Not any more. 'We used to come down here when I was a lad, do you remember? We must have mapped and compassed every part of this area.'

'Aye, I recall it. And do you know, it only seems like yesterday to me. A few years at most. Life's funny, though it's not been bad to us, has it?'

'We can't grumble.'

'No, not so far.'

He spoke as if he'd another seventy years to live or, William felt uneasily, as if life could yet be bad for them both, at a time when for himself he saw it as opening rosily and staying that way for ever. It was strange though to think he was getting married. Such a move seemed totally unnecessary to his needs. Like all soldiers, he had few friends and many acquaintances, and so could never feel cut off, never as lonely as he'd heard you could be. Only a lonely man married, they'd said, the sum total of their experience, reflecting the traditional voice of the mess; or a bored man, or a frightened man, or a man who's turning pansy, or missing his mother, or who's cracked up and lost his nerve – though he may call it love if he likes.

It was none of these things, and he could only put it down to the fact that he was a human being after all, as well as a gunner, and so would feel even better for the change. He'd always made the mistake of thinking that because he had never been attached to any woman for long he never would be. The clouds turned pink on the chocolate box when he met Georgina, and he didn't need anyone to take him inside and patiently explain why he was in love.

They walked in silence to the large stone houses of Hardwick Grange, the manor lower down set by an arm of Clumber Lake. 'You're right though, Bill,' his father said. 'You can't stay on Vinegar Hill for the rest of your life.'

'I suppose that's what I felt, if I'm to be honest with myself.'

From a saw-mill away to the right came the sound of spinning steel teeth biting cleanly through wood. 'That's the hardest thing to do,' his father put in, 'to be honest with yourself. I've allus found it so. What's hard as well is to know what's what. You can't even start to be honest till you've made up your mind what's what.'

William tapped the top of a gatepost with his stick: 'I suppose you're right.' But his father's simplistic homilies were beginning to catch in his throat. It's been my training, he thought, to weigh everything up accurately as a gunner, though only on the outside, never within where it matters most to me as a man. I have to start sooner or later, especially now everything's going to get complicated.

'I'm damned sure I'm right,' his father reiterated, pausing to drive home his point. They resumed their stroll. 'There's a lot of ups and downs between God and Man. I think of your mother more and more as I get older. I always did think of her, but now-a-days she seems closer to me than she was. We were only together ten years, and that was a good while ago. Passed like minutes. Twenty-four years in the army went like ten. And yet life feels hundreds of years long.'

They walked to the footbridge and looked into the stream. A car drove through a few inches of water across the ford. He wished his father had been as talkative as this when bringing him up, instead of the upright taciturn martinet instilling into him the gospel of Field Service Regulations and the sober ethic of learning and obedience. Not, he decided, gazing along the peaceful stream towards Clumber House, that he regretted it. The army had made a man of him, and given him a career, and he had his father to thank. He didn't know what he would have done, otherwise. And now he was happy because he'd found a woman he wanted to marry. The wood-cutting came in a high-pitched scream from the saw-mill.

His father stared into the water and said, without turning: 'Why didn't you bring her to see me?'

So that was it. 'She couldn't get away. She went off for the weekend with her parents, to some place in Wiltshire.'

She had offered to come with him. One positive word and she would have. But he hadn't insisted: 'I don't want to spoil your weekend.'

'Maybe you'll do quite the opposite.'

So why hadn't he said: 'Yes, come on, then. Let's motor to Ashfield and see the old man. He's a simple good-natured ex-soldier. You'll love him, I know.'

He hadn't. A gunner who'd seen all of it and more had lost his nerve, unable to bear her comments when they drove through the squalid landscape with its stunted copses, head-stocks, ruinous pit-buildings and dingy rows of houses. But it didn't seem like that to him, in spite of the places he'd been to and the life he'd led. He always liked coming back to the old town because it was where he'd been born and brought up. Doris would have made a fuss of her, and his father knew how to behave.

But perhaps he was too reticent about what formed a big part of him. Maybe because of his new life he'd kept it too much of a secret, something he felt slightly ashamed of and so never thought to share with anybody. But he would have to, now, though it was too early to show Georgina, for it would have meant a more total contact between them than he felt ready for.

'The right thing,' his father said, 'would be to bring her up with you. Don't think I'm only curious. I'm your father as well. If your mother were alive I'm sure you'd have brought her up to see us both.'

He felt crushed, blotted out with remorse. Then he smiled to himself: he only wants a good look at a young woman in his old age! But he checked himself, feeling it better to have stayed depressed than wallow in this sort of demeaning get-out. He was finding lately, however, that he had less and less control over his thoughts.

His father was right, and so he resented even more his parental ticking-off, no matter what underground flicker had sparked it. 'I'll bring her up next time,' he answered sharply. 'I should be able to get away in about a month.' If it hadn't been for him he might have become a teacher or a bank clerk and married a local girl. Such an amusing idea lightened his mood. He couldn't hold a grudge against his father. Doris once said he was more like his mother in that, with more of her easy-going temperament.

Charlie straightened. 'I don't see much to laugh at.'

He touched him on the shoulder. 'I'm tickled at my own daftness, that's all.' Two swans, necks extended, glided in white silhouette over green meadows and down towards Clumber Lake. He thought that of all the spots in the Dukeries, this was the most beautiful. It was a delectable place, redolent of peace. He would bring Georgina here.

'When's the wedding, did you say?'

'Three months. In the village she was born in.'

'Wiltshire?'

He nodded.

'Nice county, in places,' Charlie conceded, as they walked off the bridge and back through Hardwick. 'I expect you've money put by? Cost a lot, that sort of do.'

'I saved quite a bit during the war.'

'So did I. I've got a few hundred in hand.'

William knew he wanted him to ask for some, that he'd be happy to part with it for the wedding, feeling that his son would really love him if he popped that sort of question. But he didn't want to deprive him of the last anchor of his life. Neither had he the heart to turn down the offer that his father couldn't make directly.

'I'll see whether or not I'm going to be short.'

They left it at that, and walked in silence towards the car. Rain began gusting along the avenue, and the screech of the band-saw reached them in the wind. The smell of the trees rooted him comfortably back into his past.

Walking from the church door under an arch of drawn swords, garbed again in his dark-blue ceremonial rig with gold facings, he felt himself the happiest man in the world. But he recognised the smile on his face as a sudden craving for wide-open spaces. If it had been possible, reality would have dampened his delight. It wasn't, so he smiled again, and knew why he had been born, and wondered why he had waited so long for this sensation. There was a time and a place for everything, if you worked hand-in-glove with your fate.

Georgina, in white tulle (for a white lie, she'd joked), was by his side, and he felt neither gloom nor gladness coming from her, only a mere neutrality about their spiritual enlacing as if, like him, she wanted this part over and done with.

It had been a fight to get mummy to agree.

'Scorton? What's his family?'

'He's from Nottinghamshire, originally.'

The coalmines were being nationalised, but it was expected that those Labour rotters would make *some* compensation. 'What's his income, darling?'

'He has his pay.'

'Oh dear! A colonel won't afford you many frocks on that.'

Georgina won, because something told her that she had to stand against her mother. She had a now-or-never feeling, which wasn't difficult to maintain because she knew that her life was already decided, though not in the traditional getting-pregnant way. That hadn't happened yet, thank God.

Her mother saw that the stare in Georgina's eyes, and the flush of her cheeks, indicated that something worse might occur if she did not give in. And Georgina, standing by her wedding car, knew she had won a big battle indeed, a double victory in that she had also conquered her husband, not he her, and she hoped he'd never know it, but go on seeing himself as a knight in shining armour who had wooed a woman and gained a bride, and never realise that he had unknowingly blitzed her away from a past whose memory she could no longer stand.

Watkins, his old friend and best man, stood erect and forward-looking, as if it went against his principles to appear pleased on such a day. In reality his gut was bilious and his head tender from champagne and brandy soaked up last night in the mess to celebrate the departure to what he referred to in his tipsy speech as 'the last grazing field of life'.

The sky was blue, but with a ragged cloud lingering at the back end of the steeple. Standing by the cars, the brigadier kissed his daughter and shook William's hand again, nodding at him with only half a smile. Mrs Woods was almost as tall as her husband, a sensitive mouth on an otherwise pale and frosty face. William knew he wasn't much liked by the brigadier, though thought this was because the mother had taken against him from the beginning. Had it not been so he felt he would have got on well enough with Jacko.

'Don't you believe it,' Watkins had said when he mentioned it; and if he hadn't been drunk William would have split his skull, or broken his nose at least: 'The father never takes to the man who's going to rape his daughter.' But that was last night, so he could say what he liked. William had often come out with such things. But if the brigadier didn't like him, neither had he much time for that foot-slogger. If there was anything to him at all he'd have been a gunner, though he expected they'd soon clear the air between them. He even felt cheerful about it. Nothing could put the iron in today.

Charlie congratulated them, then stood apart because he had little to say after his nods and odd words before the service. With his medals he was the senior soldier of them all, a man of the Old Army whose only remaining grace lay in his pride. William wished he'd come out of it a bit and talk with more ease, since he knew their language.

Some crony of the brigadier's said: 'Who is that old sergeant-looking fellow there?'

'The bridegroom's father, I understand.'

'Good Lord!'

'Do keep your voice down, he's only over the way.'

William laughed to himself, feeling like the cock o' the walk with these infantrymen, not to mention the cat among the pigeons. One young major had a hand in his pocket, and it wasn't a cold morning. He'd noticed in the street these days how many men walked with hands in pockets. It didn't take long after leaving the army for the smartness to go. Bad time for the glove industry. Perhaps the major caught his stare, for he took it out.

In the car Georgina pressed herself against him.

'Feeling all right?'

Her 'yes' was like an echo of the one from church, which was chased by the touch of their cold dry lips in the brief press that followed: not like the mellow frenchified kisses they'd grown used to in the Knightsbridge flat, or the hotel they'd ensconced themselves in during a couple of weekends.

'Soon be over,' he said. 'Then we can take stock of the situation.'

'I'll feel happier.'

'A drink would do me good.'

'You had enough last night. Disgusting beast.' She turned and smiled, and he felt sorry for her through his gaiety. He didn't know why. 'Your father's got terrific dignity,' she said.

'My old dad was always strong on that. I hope he enjoys himself later. Seemed a bit sombre just now. It's funny how our parents look down-hearted when they realise we got married after all. I feel on top of the world.'

'You do look as if you've won a crossword puzzle.'

'Six down and two across,' he said. 'We'll do them in bed tonight.'

'Promise?'

'I do.'

The brigadier's head twitched. He sat in front with the chauffeur. You can't keep a gunner down, William thought, wanting only to get to the hotel with Georgina so that they could shut the door on the rest of the world and begin their junketings. He felt well charged with saltpetre, charcoal and sulphur, which needed only the smallest wandering spark to touch it off. But there were a few hours to go before the drumfire. She put a hand on his thigh, the reassuring pressure of complicity.

CHAPTER NINE

They stood at the door, dressed for the weather, rain hammering down the plate glass panels of this nobleman's pile turned hostelry, and William wondered whether it was worth setting out, merely to drop ten minutes later into another such place for morning coffee and soggy biscuits to avoid a further downpour. Water flowed from the hotel, falling along the lead and cast-iron gutters. He laughed at Georgina's gloom, unable to match her in it, as if being in love brought back his sense of humour: 'Tomorrow we'll stay in bed.'

He'd wanted to go to France and Belgium for their honeymoon but Georgina felt she ought not to travel so far because her grandmother was ill, and she loved her more than anyone except William, having seen more of her up to the age of eighteen than her own parents. An army daugher had little life beyond boarding school, and she had gone to her grandmother's for all exeats, half terms and most holidays.

So they went to Woodhurst in the New Forest, staying at a large dingy place that paid as much attention to their ration books as the hotels in Belgium would no doubt have given to their passports. The meals were bad and the wine was sour. 'The catering isn't exactly the best I've ever encountered,' he said at dinner.

'Oh I think it's rather enjoyable' – an opinion he put down to her boarding school days.

'Maybe you're right.'

'You've been spoiled,' she laughed. 'The artillery always were, so daddy said.'

By contrast, the breakfasts were sumptuous, and they ate their fill till half past nine, later smoking cigarettes in the lounge under the stare of the proprietor who maybe thought that instead of pounding his bed so much they should get out early into forest and glade with the rest of his half dozen guests.

The sour-faced maid looked on them as throwbacks to the days of Roman orgies. She would run in with their breakfast tray and nip quickly out, an additional glance at the hissing gasfire, which increased the smell of damp in the room and somehow heightened the sense of sin. Georgina was naked again, and fully awake beside him. They were in the gardens of the moon, locked in their own Alhambra.

Flesh to flesh, there were two hearts between them through which all unformed and as yet unconnected thoughts passed, his intercepting those from her, hers beating strongly so that he could feel its strength drawing his thoughts into the labyrinth of hers, from his sleep to her sleep, all through the night, so that they slept together in the furthest corners of each other.

And such sleep didn't refresh him. Its residue burned in his eyes, thinned down his flesh, and made him alive in every atom of himself. She told him twenty times a day how happy she was, and to believe her was simply another way of proving his love. After dinner, and a half hour sit-down in the cold lounge – it was too late in spring for fires, and too early in summer to be warm – they'd go upstairs and get into bed, lie awhile till, touching each other, he licked ears, nose, mouth and cunt before sliding in and, though hard for half an hour, came too soon and cried out at the silent thudding interior salvoes. Then it started again, probing, stroking, looking; feeling that with a mere two arms he could never reach enough places at the same time. And when he shot once more it was all too swift, though she had been up and over the bags three times already.

An elderly lady asked at breakfast if they couldn't be a little quieter at night because they disturbed her dog, so Georgina said to him later: 'Really, young Colonel, I do wish you wouldn't make such a terrible clatter with your young lady. Disgusting. You don't even *sound* married.' And she laughed as if it were necessary to some inner part of her spirit that he didn't yet know about. He'd laugh with her, glad at having married someone with a sense of humour.

When the rain stopped they went on to the single shopping street, then by the garage and into open country, walking without speech because neither of them could keep up the self-igniting prattle of a few days ago that had fed on the events of their marriage. In place of it she held his hand as if they were twenty, a public touch that made the difference in their ages seem like a whole generation.

They left the road and went into the wood. He opened the one-inch and militarily gridded map borrowed from the stores. 'There's a stretch of heath in half a mile. We'll see the horizon from there. I feel uneasy if there isn't a clear line stretching as far as the eye can see.'

'I like to walk in woods where you can't see fifty yards ahead,' she said. 'Perhaps that's what comes of living from day to day all my life.'

'You have a future now, my love.'

'I know it.'

He opened the gate which led into a lozenge-shaped clearing, and kept to the trees because the open part was patterned with islands of livid moss that looked treacherous to step on. He led her away from the mud. 'You're a brigadier's daughter, after all, from a long line of jungle-fighters. Both of us have been looked after by the army. It brought me up from the high chair.'

'I wonder what it's *done* to us?'

'Thrown us together.'

'Set us apart from others.'

'We'd have been separated from the mob, anyway. Watch that log, or you'll fall flat on your beautiful face.'

He stopped at the next fence to look at the compass, and she laughed at his steady concentration with the prism: 'Afraid of getting lost?'

'Gunners don't get lost.'

'Don't they?' There was irony in her voice. He was a man, after all, no matter what he felt. She loved him, it was true, but why must he seem so sure of himself? She supposed it was because he loved her, but why should that make it so easy for him?

'He might not be certain of his position from time to time,' he went on, 'but he never gets lost!' He held her by the shoulders: 'See those tall trees? We head for them. Then I'll get another bearing which takes us back to the road. From there we'll hike north two miles and reach Woodhurst in time for lunch.'

They climbed a stile. 'You make me feel safe,' she said. 'I've been looked after all my life in that way. Feels nice – sometimes.'

'Trust a gunner to look after you. A gunner is an independent person – by tradition. A German monk called Black Bert invented powder and cannon in the Middle Ages, and I suppose he must have been a bit of a lad, in spite of his habit. You don't concoct such things unless you've got Old Nick inside you. Gunners were always specialist people though. Let themselves out to the highest bidder. In the British Army they were civilians till the Royal Regiment of Artillery was formed in 1716. Even then it took 'em another thirty years to look like soldiers, and another forty before they were paid by the army instead of the 'civil establishment'. They were a wild undisciplined lot in those days. Got denounced in the seventeenth century for being bone idle and profligate. Couldn't be got at by military discipline. The earliest regarded themselves as artists, though I suppose it was such a hit and miss affair they couldn't do anything else. The rest of the army always went a bit in awe of them, like people do with blacksmiths.'

She kissed him: 'Isn't my man clever?'

'The gift of the gab. Liars and boozers all!'

'I hope you're trustworthy.'

'I reformed when I met you, my pet.'

'Time will tell.'

'It has already.'

They walked through an isolated grove of trees. 'I'm so happy to hear it.' She took off her gloves: 'My hands are chapped.'

'It's the wind.'

She stepped forward, and jerked back with a scream that burst into his heart and cut echoes out of the sky for miles around. A thrush lifted, flapped its wings from the bush she was close to. He fell against its small pointed leaves as if to push it down. 'What's the matter?'

Her panic was infectious, unlike that of a man, as if she were being burned from the inside. He looked for whatever horror it was, but the flight of the bird had left her with nothing but an unfathomable keening. Their marvellous life was buried under it. He tried to shake the undulating steely wail from her, but she was stiff and fixed, eyes set on the mud path a few feet ahead, an irrational possession that couldn't be cured by his art or science, or even love. Then he was angry with her for allowing the umbrella of his safety and protection to serve for nothing at the sight of a mere adder coiled on its very own piece of path in front.

He threw his stick and it burrowed under wet herbage and dead twigs. It had taken only a second or two, but she moaned as if it still twisted in her stomach. 'Come on, darling, it's gone now.'

He put an arm around her, but she was still in the dark of her shocked soul, shoulders heaving, all because of a damned snake, he thought, which wouldn't harm anybody unless you stomped right on it. And some good angel had saved her from that.

The mouldering smell of trees and undergrowth was no good, and he wanted to get her away, feeling guilty that he hadn't smashed out the snake's life to prove he took her distress seriously. She'd be frozen for ever if he didn't do something. It was a kind of shell-shock, and he'd seen enough of that to know what to do. Did he adore her, or did he not? There was no time for questions, only to do what his love had so far held him from. He opened his hand and gave a hard but controlled smack on her cheek. Then another.

She swayed away. 'What are you doing?'

'I'm sorry, my love. Had to.'

'Don't ever do that again.'

She covered her face, and tears seeped through her fingers. It was easier to comfort her now because she reached out and cried against him. But there was no one to ease the weight of his heart. She was trembling, so he took off his raincoat and put it over her.

They walked back the way they came. He cursed himself for being without his brandy flask, not having wanted its weight in his gabardine pocket, and for having brought the compass, which was almost as heavy. He wondered why so big and brave a girl was scared of a mere reptile; a heartless thought, though when they were back on the metalled road he felt she might be feeling embarrassed at her hysteria. 'Even if you step on one it isn't fatal,' he said. 'And they're the food of hedgehogs, which are the friend of the farmer!'

She had no intention of talking about the incident. 'I don't want ever to go into that wood again.'

At the hotel she had a second bath, as if what she had seen called for a thorough cleansing of her body. The bathroom door was usually left open, but now she closed it. Afterwards she stood at the mirror and put powder on, then dressed in a dark brown costume and a heavy woollen pullover.

'You don't need makeup,' he said. 'You're beautiful enough.'

'Not for long if I don't use it. Makes me feel better.'

He changed his boots, and got into a suit. Sitting at the table, he fixed on the advertisements in *The Times* before opening it, then tried a few clues of the crossword. During long waits at his guns he used to finish it, but today he only managed a couple of anagrams.

They drank several gins in the lounge before lunch. The colour came back under her powder. Her throat was flushed. 'I'm too warm.'

He touched her hand. 'I hope you're feeling better.'

She smiled. 'It was a horrible fright.'

He couldn't take the snake seriously, only her fear. 'I'd forgotten they were so common in the Forest.'

'Thank goodness we're going soon. I'd hate to stay too long. My period's started. I thought at least I'd be free till we got back.'

He cursed his luck. 'We had a good run, didn't we?'

A sudden smile showed how vulnerable she was, and he wondered what had happened to her; and therefore to him. The onset of her period might explain it for the time being.

'I'd like another drink,' she said.

'We'd better slow up. There'll be wine at lunch.'

She stood abruptly, and sent the last finger of his gin flying. The glass rolled across the floor. 'Let's eat, then. If I don't, I'll be sick – and I mean *vomit*. I'm starving. If you'd ordered me another gin I'd never have forgiven you.'

He drew his chair away so that she could pass. 'That would have given us something to remember the place by.'

'So you bloody say,' she cried. An elderly couple turned to look.

He took her arm. 'Come on, love, or the roast'll be cold.'

There was a hardness about her face, as well as painful uncertainty, and if they didn't get to the table he knew she'd drag him into an argument, and then she might get another crack across the chops. The idea of a quarrel was hateful, and he felt he'd knock her flat, big as she was, rather than take part in one. Such preposterous ideas made him smile. He loved her, so how could he let a notion like that come up from its lair?

He kissed her cheek. 'Take my arm, sweetheart, and let's walk out together.' He raised his voice: 'To show these inquisitive people that we really are in love, even though we've only been married eight days.'

She smiled now that he came into her wild game. 'You're a good sport,' she said loudly. 'Let's go and eat, then we can spend the afternoon in bed, doing you-know-what!' She turned towards the other arm chairs, and put her tongue out as far as it would go. 'Even though I am having my period.'

They walked away laughing, to murmurs of shock behind.

He congratulated himself on how he'd handled a high-explosive situation. He'd passed the tests she'd imposed on him; for that day at least. He loved her more at the end of it than at the beginning, because he thought he'd got the measure of her at last. What he didn't know was that she had got the measure of him, as well.

CHAPTER TEN

The lighter than paper tea cups were glazed with flowers, and with bees and ladybirds so accurately real he wanted to nudge them away with a finger before drinking. He was afraid to pick up his cup for fear of breaking it. Even the vast hotel at Bad Oeynhausen hadn't sported crocks like these.

He smiled at the idea of handing out such Minton cups laden with steaming char to the gun crews, heard the tinkle as one dropped from Oxton's nerveless fingers and hit the traversing lever. In fact it was he who, drinking brandy from the finest Bohemian glass after dinner in the Konigshof, bit too hard on the goblet because his lip flesh was dead from the liquor that had gone before. More liquid was dribbling down his chin than he'd ever let go of, and Watkins caught the tumbling glass bits, and passed a field dressing.

So at his mother-in-law's tea table when he drank too carefully she wanted to know in her sharp-eyed way what he was laughing at. It was impossible to tell her, even though the brigadier must have seen worse and might therefore be amused. And Georgina certainly would. It was better to be straightforward, though it was plain that he laughed from time to time without intending to. 'I was hoping I wouldn't be so clumsy as to break one of your marvellous cups.'

It seemed a normal gesture that whatever you admired in their house was generously given to you, which put a brake on his systems of praise. She presented them with the whole set six months later, a kindness they couldn't take full advantage of because the house they rented from two maiden ladies who'd gone to New Zealand for five years, was furnished in such full and chintzy style, that they had to store their own plate and linen in the spare garage at the brigadier's, where it was to stay in crates and trunks till they found the dreamhouse they planned to buy when they could afford it.

They lived meanwhile in their twenty guinea a month billet that stood away from the main road in its own small weeded-up garden. The traffic bothered Georgina, so they took over the back bedroom, even though the front one was bigger and had a more opulent fireplace. He was surprised she could be churned up by such a noise, though did his best to make life smooth, which wasn't difficult because she was the person he cared most for. If he could he'd switch his heart to the other side of his body to accommodate her wishes, which at his age might not distort the appearance of his face too much.

A clergyman uncle gave her seven hundred pounds and William turned down her offer to tip it into the expenses of running their lives. He refused out of generosity and pride, which are different sides of the same coin, for he knew later he should have accepted. She sensed straight away that he should, but under the cloud of loving it seemed no great matter, and she spent much time wandering the shops searching out items for their future home, and when she once persuaded him to go with her he noticed how pertinacious she was in finding the history of any defects or qualities in whatever object caught her fancy. He had never shopped in this way, and felt such methods would have sent him barmy; but the process put her into a good mood, though in the after dinner calm the distant barking of a dog would set her wishing she was in any other place and, he occasionally thought when it happened, with any other person, though he had a way of inwardly smiling about this.

He was close to her, and loved her skin as if it were his own, and her breath as if it were coming from his own mouth. He couldn't say fairer than that, and if he didn't it was only because he assumed she must know how deep his love was without too many words. But it took time to sense what it was that disturbed her, and when he congratulated himself on having done so, he saw so many confusions inside her that it seemed impossible to do anything except let her know as often as it came to him that he loved her. Because his love was at its height from the beginning he thought there was nothing more to receive or search for. When a love affair and marriage begins in a state of such passion there can only be a climb down to normality which neither of them knew how to live with.

He often stayed away for days reorganising training schedules on Salisbury Plain, and playing the old game of turning conscripts into gunners. Now that the war was over some of them no longer saw any cause to be in uniform, and made trouble just to break the monotony of their service. These matters often grew into something big, and wasted his time on courts-martial.

There wasn't much respect for discipline any more, and the regular soldiers felt it. The war was over, there was plenty of work in civvy street, and nobody liked being told what to do. It was their loss, because whatever they felt, the world was still like that. With too much ne'er-do-well carelessness in the regiment, he'd be glad if call-up stopped and they got back to a small professional army. The gunner today didn't give a bugger, he sometimes thought, was happy-go-lucky, and too full of fun and accidents. Frighten him with the glasshouse, and he'd get his wife or mother to write a letter to his MP. It wasn't the sort of life they'd plumped for, so all you could do was hope to frighten enough of them to keep the rest in order.

It took up time, when his deepest wish was to be with Georgina twenty-four hours a day. He knew this was soft and unrealistic, but he wanted it because he assumed she needed it.

She relaxed so much after their honeymoon that it was almost like a collapse. Her bouts of house-proud bustling quickly went, and more of the cleaning was left to the Irishwoman who worked for them. Georgina stayed in and read the novels she got from Harrod's library on her weekly trip to town.

Some days she didn't get out of her dressing-gown, and he laughed about it. Such a thing was impossible for him. When he stayed an extra hour in bed it put him in a bad temper for the rest of the day. The dreams he hadn't remembered had gone too far into his bloodstream. But Georgina liked to lie in, or wander around in her dressing-gown. Being free to do so was one of the advantages of being married. He wondered where she'd got such an idea. Having no prior notions of his own, he had to take hers as normal, which in his light-hearted ignorance he was quite willing to do.

But Georgina was almost equally bereft of the right sort of domestic influence. Her boarding school upbringing had taught her little enough, and what she had got from her grandmother during vacations hadn't amounted to much either. What she had never had, she created out of an indolent and wayward nature, and presented to him as traditional behaviourisms she'd been familiar with from birth. He became domestically polished not from handed-down experience and rules, as might have been hoped, but by someone else's temperament.

He was sharp enough to see this, though it didn't make him the least unhappy. In fact he touched wood many times, as a gunner should, that they were so engrossed in each other, so even-tempered, considerate, and fulsomely matched in bed.

He smiled at his recognition of these facts while he stared at himself in the mirror one morning. Out of bed early into a hot shallow bath and then an ice-cold shower he shaved afterwards so as to scrape away the slightly grey stubble before kissing Georgina awake. They were on a desert island, that place where all people meet when they fall in love. They were building up a relationship in marriage as if it were a lifeboat that would eventually get them back to a mainland of life, where they could live with normal affection and forget the desert island of being in love.

In the beginning neither had any problems as long as the other was free of them; and not knowing anything about each other gave them a clear field in which to be themselves.

CHAPTER ELEVEN

There was hardly standing room. What's more it was rough, and took five hours to Ostend, ploughing across the narrows and skirting the coast by Dunkirk, which churned his memories up.

Bottles and plates were sliding all over the place. The pissoirs were full of vomit. Luckily he'd seen the steward at Dover and got Georgina a cabin to lie down in. A bad beginning to a holiday, but maybe it would get better, in a place where there was no rationing, as there was in England even seven years after the war. But things were on the mend at last because the Tories were in again and pledged to end all that austerity stuff. Was that what we'd fought the war for? Even so, they'd dropped the travel allowance to twenty-five pounds, which wouldn't go far, though Jacko had given him another fifty quid in francs which would help a bit when he got it from the back pocket where it'd been since going through the customs.

He gave his seat to a middle-aged Belgian woman, and pushed his way on deck. The sea was grey metal, patched by mounds of heaving feathers, a great swell broken by high-dancing waves, not like the dead blue calm coming back from Dunkirk nearly twelve years ago. Just as well it had stayed flat when everything else was against them. He remembered the trip in a tug-boat packed so tight a small bomb would have killed them all. His mind had been elsewhere after bolting from the Messines Ridge, where he'd left more than his guns, and more of himself than he'd ever retrieve. Being pulled aboard the tug was a relief so overwhelming that he'd slept the whole six hours back. He looked through field glasses. Under the haze was a line of dark indigo, a few cranes and factories on the coast.

The boat docked and the mob surged to get off. He sat with Georgina in the saloon till the queue had shuffled out. Wearing her camel coat and headscarf, she looked pale, exhausted. He held her hand. 'We'll go straight to a hotel.'

She didn't care. 'It's only half an hour to Bruges. Do what you like.'

'We'll take it easy.'

Three months ago she'd had a miscarriage, and not long before that her mother had died of a heart attack. The experiences had deadened her. He didn't know how much. He only thought he did. But maybe they were deadening her into life, and wouldn't be so finally crushing, though it was hard to think so at the moment. She only knew that she wasn't over them yet, and all he could do was hope that a holiday would get her out of it.

'Did you sleep?'

'I dozed. But the stewardess brought me some tea. She was marvellous.' Her voice changed to irritable, for which he couldn't blame her. 'Let's get off. Don't like sitting here.'

A porter handled their cases. She seemed in a hurry to put the sea as far behind as possible before darkness. He wanted to stop in Ostend so that they could rest before moving on. Two small gunboats slid by the ship, a 75-mm cannon mounted on each, and headed into the dancing sea.

The taxi took them to an hotel on the front that wasn't shuttered and closed. Georgina sat in the lounge, reflecting that William had the smile of a man who didn't know himself. It's funny how a lot of men seem to have it. The thought that she only chose such men frightened her, so she scoffed and laughed it off. Stuff and nonsense. But the idea wouldn't leave her. There were too many like that nowadays. What man did know himself, anyway? What woman, for that matter. Did she know *her*self? Too damned-well she did – at times.

But a man had to *look* as if he knew himself, that was the crux of it. Her father always had – though had her mother thought so? Yes – she was sure of that. But these days William looked less and less as if he knew himself, and it disturbed her to think that maybe some change was coming in him. Bound to, sooner or later, but would it be for better or worse? The fact that she could see it coming made her doubt that it would be for the better.

William went up with the girl-receptionist to look at the room. He stepped out of the lift into a whiff of disinfectant. It was gloomy, but he didn't want to drag around looking for something better. Maybe it would brighten up as more people came in for the evening. A cat walked along the corridor and into a bedroom – no doubt to piss, he thought, wondering what he was doing in this place, at this time, in Belgium again.

The room looked big enough and clean, had a bathroom, wardrobe, Bible and dressing table. Any decision is better than no decision. 'I'll take it.'

He followed the girl out. I must be growing old to let such a thing shoot through my head. Maybe I'm getting a belly-ache from having looked back at Dunkirk. It'd be easier to billet the regiment than us at the moment. Easier to billet myself alone, which is no way to think.

'It's a reasonable room. You can have a bath and a rest before dinner,' he told her.

More lights came on to counter the dark sky. She reached for his hand, generous now that he'd done something for her: 'I feel all right now we're off that rotten boat.'

The next morning she fell asleep again after breakfast, as if she were in the hotel on her own. He looked at her face: a restful oblivion in which the anguish of her miscarriage might ease away. He thought how good it was to be out of England. The cloth and skin of it had dropped off, and given them a sort of peace.

He dressed and sat downstairs in the lounge to read his old 1930 Baedeker and plan trips on his map of Belgium. He smoked a pipe, and drank coffee, taking an occasional nip out of his old Arras brandy flask filled up duty free from the ship. The same waitress bustled around who had served them at dinner, so he got a smile when he remarked on the weather in French. She was about thirty, fair hair drawn tightly back from her forehead. Without the smile she was too severe, but he was in luck because despite his forty years she lit up nicely in

155

passing. If he'd been alone he could have fallen in love, but maybe she only smiled because his wife was upstairs. He didn't like to think so. It was easy to fall in love when nothing could come of it. Often, spending a pleasant hour in some strange town, he was so immediately drawn to it that in the flash of a minute he imagined a whole lifetime spent there: getting a humdrum but profitable job, courting, marriage, having children, and sampling the comfort of fitting in with local society. A hundred imaginary lives couldn't replace the one he'd never had, or fill out the single one he was lumbered with. He often felt that in spite of his adventures he hadn't yet started to live, and wondered whether he ever would, and whether the one he had wasn't in fact all there was to it.

Georgina lay in the same curled position facing the window. He entered like a burglar, and went around the bed to see her face. Her lips were pressed tight. Lines of anxiety showed on her forehead as if she were walking through a dream which might soon wake her. There were faint wrinkles under the pale shadows of her eyes, her fragile skin being easy for the blows of life to mark. It was unreasonable to look at her like this, because little of it was apparent when she was awake and her eyes pushed all small blemishes back behind the skin. The sheet anchor of their first tenderness and love was for ever with him.

The weather was fine and warm. He left his jacket behind, and she wore a flowered dress as they walked along the sands towards Blankenberghe. They passed an English family of man, wife and three kids in bathing shorts, standing silently at the water's edge and looking northwest as if they'd changed their minds about seeing the last of England. The man was tall, and thin as a stick, with a long straight pipe at his mouth. He suddenly jumped up and down, urging his feet into the curling cold water shouting: 'Come on, Daisy!'

Don't drown, William thought. We don't want another dead Englishman off the Belgian coast.

Georgina laughed. 'Don't *you* want to swim?'

He didn't fancy it from this side, remembering a ship blown out of the water with hundreds of men on board, bloody flesh, webbing, rifles, and bits of fouled khaki spewed everywhere. 'Not around here.'

They held hands, and had the dunes to themselves. 'Glad to be off the island?'

'What island?'

'England,' he said. 'John Bull's pattacake.'

'Oh yes.'

Who wouldn't be? They hadn't spent an uninterrupted fortnight together for years. They didn't know where they'd be tomorrow. He felt lightheaded, wanting to skip and run, pick up sand and throw it, chuck stones in the water, make castles for the tide to undermine. But he walked in the usual dignified way, as comical a straight-backed figure as the Englishman down the beach.

Talk to me, he thought. When she did it was never much, no more than he ever said to her. They communicated by short phrases, looks and pressures of the hand by which it was easy to show likes and dislikes, or the necessary measure of agreement that took them from one day to the next, but never the real sort of talk that told them things about each other.

She stepped out as if they had somewhere to go, and had to get there by a certain time. He was afraid of the silence between them, and didn't see how their destinations could ever coincide unless they began to talk. It hadn't always been this way, but now that communication was vital it seemed as if they had nothing left to say. She had suffered a lasting shock over the miscarriage, and in his grief and love he wanted to cherish her as at the time of their first meeting.

Maybe if you had nothing to say the only thing to do was act. Looking out to sea as the Dover ferry angled its way beyond the breakwater, the thought was a revelation.

'Why have we stopped?'

'The idea came to me,' he said, 'that I ought to love you more and more.'

'Silly! How can you?' She wanted to see how easy it was to make him angry, a simple but destructive test.

He'd act as if she hadn't made it: 'I want to look after you better. You know the sort of thing.'

'A soldier can never spend much time with his wife,' she said.

'Other careers are just as time-consuming.' He thought how often he'd stayed at the mess when he should have been at home with her.

'Anyway, don't try. You mean well, but I can't stand this earnest deadlock we slide into whenever you get serious. Let's walk. It's such a nice day.'

Perhaps she was right. What good was talk? He had to do something, and even though he had no idea what it would be, he felt that a solution would come if he pondered long enough.

The five years since her marriage had brought out the first grey hairs at her temples. Strange that the marks of getting old should come when for the first time she felt the stirrings of being really alive. She no longer saw William as that haven of safety she'd imagined he might be at the beginning. Any port in a storm is no port at all if waves get over the break-waters and pound you nonetheless.

As the Colonel's lady she went visiting the soldiers' wives in their married quarters, twice a week saying hello and may I come in and how are the children now? She liked the women for their patience and hard lives. They put up with their isolation at Larkhill, glad of a house which they might never have got outside, and all sorts of army care which, she saw too plainly, often only increased that expression of loss on their faces.

They didn't particularly like her. She wasn't such a fool as not to see it. But some in their sharply intuitive hearts saw that she too existed in that same vast bowl of loneliness.

And yet on the surface everything seemed all right. They were busy. There were gatherings for every rank – dances, cocktail parties, dinners, outings – a carefree life if you were relaxed and easy going enough to fit in.

It was her life, and she knew that outwardly there could be none better. But it wasn't enough, and William also sensed it, which she had to give him credit for.

She couldn't get used to the fact that the life she lived was life itself, and all there was to it. She was convinced it was not, which kept her in a perpetual state of discontent. The even rhythm of her days alarmed her because they allowed time to go so quickly. Even the soul-crushing event of her miscarriage had receded into the past.

Every morning she said to herself. 'This can't go on' – and every day it did. But she knew she couldn't be mistaken, that if things felt wrong then by God they were wrong. She didn't know how she'd lived with it so many years, but she had because there was also a generous and enduring side to her character, and one which said that not to endure such a situation till it changed of its own accord would be a loss of pride. And pride, finally, was everything.

They got on a train for Bruges, only fifteen minutes inland. He was glad to leave the noise of the sea, and look at the flat landscape that made the country seem bigger than it was. They'd made love the last night in Ostend, but Georgina had not enjoyed it. At other times afterwards there had been a look of distress on her face, which was the final confirmation of success, an expression broken by a smile. But not last night.

He'd done his best. When she wasn't dead to things she was unhappy. He thought he understood why, yet didn't altogether see what she'd got to be so miserable about. She had food, house, health back and, even, him. But it seemed as if the invisible middle of herself had gone smash. And if this was so, what was the reason? He was hardly powerful enough to put down such a forceful woman. He wondered if it hadn't been caused by something before they met, and he went back to that cosy conversation at an early meeting when she'd told him of the affair she'd recently broken off. That first real blow might ricochet through the rest of her life, a matter of first love not letting go, and the spirit being swept away because of what she'd lost. People could stay in thrall to an early loss for the rest of their lives. If you were unlucky, your morale could fester slowly to death over it. There was enough of it in him to point what was wrong with her, yet too much for him to be able to ease her out of it. And the more he did try to help her the more he came under the spell of what was crushing her.

When they went from the hotel for a walk before dinner it was raining, and difficult keeping away from traffic in the narrow streets. He took her hand to guide her, and followed his Baedeker plan to the main square. There was a heavy smell of frying chips everywhere. 'It's sickening,' she said. 'Let's go in here for a drink.'

If was a comfortable old-fashioned café which hadn't altered since his far-off brief stay in 1940. Dim lights, an ornate bar and heavy upholstery made it restful after the streets. At the next table three English youths were tipping out their pockets to see how many more drinks they could afford. From their talk he gathered they were sailors, whose boat was at Zeebrugge.

He ordered beer, and white wine for Georgina. 'You seem to have done a lot of brooding since we came on this trip.'

Both hands were round her glass. 'I suppose you could call it that.'

'What is it that's worrying you?'

'I don't know. Leave me alone.'

'Your brooding won't leave *me* alone. I'd like to help you.'

'I don't mean it to bother you. But it's all I've got.'

He couldn't feel as if it were the end of the world. 'Talk to me, instead of yourself. It might help.'

'Have *you* ever done it?'

He hadn't. 'I've never needed to.'

'Lucky man.'

He'd always been too busy to cripple himself with his own thoughts.

'I'll have another drink,' she said stiffly.

He called the waitress. She was trying to push the whole black load of herself on to him, but he knew there was no one else she could do it to. He didn't object if it helped her. They hadn't been so close for years, and he wondered why not. They were silent for a while, locked and trapped.

'There's a lot you don't tell me,' he said.

He winced inwardly at her bitter smile: 'You're always too busy. I don't want to bother you.'

He spoke before he could crush his tongue. 'If you loved me you would.'

It stung her. A blade of wine slashed into his face. The liquid flowed down his chin. The sailors at the next table had more money than they'd thought, and their laughter hemmed in their quarrel. She was in a bad way, but if he didn't say so maybe she'd come out of it. He unfolded his handkerchief: 'You'd better not do that too often on our twenty-five pound allowance.'

She too smiled, and reached for his free hand. 'Let's have another drink, then. I'll buy it.'

'Anybody'd think we were on our honeymoon.' He looked into her eyes, seeing that glowing aquamarine that had ensnared him from the first.

'Let's be,' she said, feeling carefree and suddenly happy. 'I've stopped brooding because my marvellous man has got me out of it with his special sort of magic.'

She leaned over to wipe his face. 'Let's pretend we were married yesterday.'

'This morning,' he responded.

'Don't spoil it.'

'At the British Consulate, in Brussels.'

'Yesterday's better.' She switched to her own handkerchief, and its perfume tantalised him. 'We've even got our first quarrel over with.'

'Yesterday, then, in the Cloth Hall at Calais. They gave us a bolt of serge as a present!'

She lifted her wine. 'And then we bolted!'

'Down the hatch this time. We'll go back for dinner, or there'll be nothing left but fried chips.'

Truce, he thought, as they stood up to go. The sailors' table was a flotilla of empty bottles. 'Have a good time, lads.'

'Thank you, sir.'

He gave the proprietress money to serve them more drinks. Georgina held his arm: 'My man's generous – and sentimental.'

The rain stopped, but the chip-mist still clung. 'They're good lads. Their fathers saved us.'

'You're happy in the army, aren't you?' she said at dinner.

He reached for the bread. 'This is damned good soup.'

'I asked a question.'

'I've never known anything else. It's my life. I'm neither happy nor unhappy.'

'Give me a straight answer for once, and then at least I *might* be happy.'

The inevitable tension was never far away, even after their tenderness upstairs. 'I don't live in a world of straight answers,' he said. 'Maybe I never will. I like being in the army though.' The only real answers were to questions of gunnery, but there ought to be proper answers in life as well. He said so, and added: 'Why do you ask?'

She parted her fish. 'I like to know what makes *you* happy.'

'Finally, only you. And that *is* a straight answer.'

'Do you mean that?'

'I do.'

She didn't believe him, though he hoped she would one day. How can I possibly make him happy, she wondered, when I'm so unhappy myself? Either it takes nothing at all to make him happy, or he's totally blind when he looks at me.

They left their luggage at the station in Ghent and went up the cobbled streets by tram to St Bavon's Abbey. She stood entranced at the Adoration of the Immaculate Lamb. The prophets and sibyls on the closed shutters were opened by the sacristan, and she held William's hand when the splendour and mysteries of the interior were revealed, showing Adam, Eve, Cain and Abel, and Old Testament heroes. He waited while she adored the Adoration and Redemption, feeling her sorrow and comfort when she looked at the image of a child which might have been born to them.

'The whole trip was worth coming just for that,' she said, when the shutters were closed to await the next group of tourists coming through.

He was drawn to the Rubens at the Tenth Chapel, of St Bavon renouncing his military career, kneeling in armour on the steps of a church to say that his soldiering was at an end. The mixture of purpose and bewilderment on Bavon's exhausted face went straight to his heart.

They travelled by train towards Courtrai and Ypres, crossing the Flanders plain through fertile meadows, drawing closer to the Messines Ridge faintly visible in the distance. They had cast the anchor loose and turned into wanderers in a strange country with no vital questions to be asked or answered, only each other to cling to, the one important issue being when they should eat and in what town they would look for somewhere to lay their heads.

At Ypres they put up at the Hotel Divan, a highly recommended place judging by the number of plaques and badges plastered on the walls outside. It faced the long sandy-coloured Cloth Hall rebuilt with the rest of the gutted town after 1918. Before dinner, while it was still light, they strolled along the narrow street to the Great War Memorial of the Menin Gate. On the pale concrete under the vast cold archway Georgina found the barely visible name of another uncle killed in the Salient, and who had not, as the phrase had it, 'any known grave'. The discovery excited her, and after dinner over coffee and brandy she wrote to tell her father.

Next morning they took the bus five miles to Wijtschaete. The land was flat for a while. Lush green fields on either side of the road looked sombre with their own fertility. They ascended the hill from the north, whereas in 1940 he had gone up from the south, so that it was like approaching his past by the back door. The road forked at St Eloi and, after a shallow dip, climbed steeply towards Wijtschaete. They got off the bus where a road branched into the village.

He felt lost, as if not knowing which way to turn. He wore his mackintosh, carried a haversack and stick, and field glasses. Georgina put the picnic basket at her feet and lit a cigarette. All it needed was the quick thunderous clap of a gun to bring everything clearly into place and show which way to walk. He soon caught on to the north and south of things. 'We go up this lane.'

She picked up the basket. 'Far ?'

His old artillery map had been coming to pieces at the seams, but he'd asked a regimental clerk to put it on cloth for him. He couldn't yet give this particular one to his father. 'Not very. I'll carry that, if you like.'

'No. I want to be of some help at least.'

He spied out the land, and no vivid flash returned. Soldiers shouldn't visit their old battlefields. He wondered whether they ought not to make for the nearest café and wait for the next bus back. Through glasses he saw that all the houses in

Wijtschaete were new. It wasn't that difficult to rebuild the past.

She was laughing. 'You are funny, with your maps and binoculars!'

'Come on,' he said, 'you big daft thing. Let's get going. Might as well have a look at the place now we're here.' He liked her carefree mood. Her refusal to take him seriously was good for him. If he'd been married to someone who respected his foibles he'd have been intolerable. Yet he did see himself, thanks to her flippancy, as a middle-aged man of fixed habits, a person of fussy unnecessary precision. He exaggerated the picture in the hope that it wasn't true, though he felt it must be.

A man more than twenty years in the service, who hadn't reached brigadier before the war ended, must seem a bit pompous and ossified to those younger men pushing from behind who created an atmosphere in which he wasn't at home any more.

Strange notions come on old battlefields. When he was there the first time they didn't get a look in because his life was on a razor's edge. The land was spread wide to the sky, and he wondered how any had survived out of such an open pitch. Gunners were a special breed, carefree, observant, astute, and tough. But, even so, they were taken with the rest when the time came. And were they, anyhow, so different?

He was beginning to see another side to his life, a primeval yearning to know more about the world and his relation to it. He had been through so much, but had taken in so little that might have enabled him to get closer in spirit to Georgina. They walked along the winding lane, brown earth and green patches of field on either side. Beyond Osttaverne were the same dark woods on which he had called down fire.

Leap-frogging back to when he was a youth of eighteen, he remembered how he had felt within his brain a mental area which could let him see the world many times clearer than he was capable of at that moment. He felt then that if he strove and perfected his powers of concentration, this blessed state of mind would soon take him over entirely.

And now, at forty, he realised that without any striving, and after having forgotten by the age of twenty that this clearer state of life had been revealed to him, it had in fact come about. But much had already gone again, as if it had been of no importance after all. This vague memory of how he had surmounted a certain barrier in his powers of perception now created an intense dissatisfaction as puzzling as that first intimation of mature life at eighteen.

The farm buildings had roofs and walls again. The fields and gullies his battery had pitted were scraped flat. Everything was mended as if nothing had happened. The nondescript ground raped of its sugar beet annoyed him by its understandable lack of remembrance. The deadness bit into his guts and made him want a car to drive away in. It was folly coming back. Even before leaving England he'd made up his mind not to give in to the temptation. And now that he was here he wondered if he'd done right, and knew that he wasn't used to being in the hands of fate, or doing something without having planned it.

Perhaps it was only a way of healing old wounds. The war that had taken place here had come to an end long ago, unlike the one he felt jarring inside him. The dead could not be brought back, but the living lived on, some of whom had yet to find out why they were on earth.

He stood by a gate, close to his old observation post, the heavy presence of a wood down to his right at four o'clock. Other woods to his left had been pummelled with high explosive, and shrapnel had peppered the space between. He recalled the noise of guns cutting grooves in the sky, opening pathways, making holes, creating pyramids of smoke, sending up columns of grit and grass and candlebulbs of flame. Such language of death was beautiful in its way, pulling back sharp smells, and showing these patches of field how man can pulverise the shapes that their own animals graze on for eventual meat. Shell tracks punctuate the mean point of impact, a rip of soil and smoke and air joining in a rigid geometrical cocked-hat that woe-betide any small part of you caught by it. It went on all day and much of the night, an ingoing-outgoing competition between one side and the other, each sending over their own ten thousand letters of the alphabet that made up pages of fear you couldn't admit to but felt your innards wilting under just the same, and that by night thrust sheets of gun letters and shell symbols into your dreams when you got your head down somewhere.

Gunners, trained to kill, made their own big chaos of sound, meaningless while their shells were in the sky, invisible on their precise trajectories, till they struck the soil like dirty grey flowers, the shortest lived blooms of all when they hit house or animal.

It was a language he'd been trained to love, to write scars on soil and flesh whose shapes you could never put down on paper. Artist-gunners poured alphabets through the sky, trying to destroy the blokes whose mother-tongue was different. So you clawed the other bastard's guts, worked till your braces were soaked with sweat, and your socks turned to the concrete you stood up in.

A cool east wind came along the valley. She looked at him from fifty yards off, and saw a lonely figure lost in his past. What will become of us? she wondered. Will we go on like this, getting older and older till we die? The idea sometimes horrified her, while at others it seemed quite pleasant. The map flapped as he caught it in both hands and pushed the folds together. Even at home, knowing the district well, he never went out without a map in his pocket. All her life she'd craved the contentment that he had been born with.

The sound of shots echoed from the other side of the hill, faint when the wind was against them, louder when it dropped. She strolled up to him with the basket. 'They laid it on especially for you.'

He turned towards the gunfire, which came from some party out on a pigeon shoot. Strange to hear such sounds on the day he had come back. 'You think so?'

'I phoned from the hotel, and told them to! Hungry?'

He took her arm. A car went along the narrow lane, and the driver looked at them with surprise. 'I'm starving.'

'Famished?'

'I love you.'

'Where shall we go?'

'We can eat in the wood over there.'

He'd pumped so many shells into it he felt he owned it. The

path was muddy in places, but the sun came through. 'Happy?'

'I am. We should roam around like this for ever. Makes us closer to each other.'

The wood was wired off, but he held up a strand. 'Pity I left my wirecutters at home.'

'They'd throw you in jail,' she said, getting through. 'I can see it in *The Times*. From our own correspondent: "Colonel Scorton, MC, RHA was locked up this morning for an outrageous act of vandalism on his old battlefield!" The chaps would have a horrible laugh about it in the mess.'

He wondered how thoroughly the wood had been cleared of unexploded shells, and decided they'd better keep to the rides. It was dull and shadowy, but they found a clearing that sunlight reached. She opened the basket. 'There's a bottle of wine, but they forgot the book of verse.'

'I expressly ordered it.'

She took off her jacket. 'Never mind, darling. We have each other.'

He passed the flask of brandy: 'Have a drink before lunch? Nice to find the world at peace.'

She put an arm around him. The warmth at her breasts, and the open cool air, made him randy. It had an effect on her, too. The ground was dry. 'I'm hungry for this.' She closed her eyes, then opened them wide as he kissed her. 'Come on, darling, don't mind my skirt.'

He wanted to savour it like the Caliph of Baghdad, but pulled down his trousers with a free hand. She guided him, so he had little say in the matter.

He decided to spend more time in the gym doing push-ups, because the arm he leaned on for his gentle thrusts began to ache. He took a hand from her breasts to steady himself, then put a hand under her, his lips on hers, letting himself go as close afterwards as he could get.

They went out of the wood, and back up the lane towards Wijtschaete. A young man looked as if he might own the land on which they were walking. 'Good afternoon,' he said in English.

William was annoyed at being accosted, but nodded. Georgina thought it would be pleasant to talk to someone who

167

wasn't a waiter, a shopkeeper or a hotel receptionist.

'Are you on vacation?' he asked from the other side of the lane.

'Looking around, you know.'

'We had a picnic in the woods,' she said.

'I hope the wire didn't hurt you. There might have been un-exploded shells from the war.'

William relaxed at the man's smile. 'I know. My guns put a few of them there.'

'Did they? I was in Brussels then. My father's house is near here, just beyond the village. He left when the fighting started, but returned after the English went.'

William winced at the recollection of defeat. 'We came back.'

'Thank goodness. Waiting was hard, but we knew you would. My father found a note on the table afterwards. When I translated it he said he'd always respect the British. He gave it to me, and I carry it around. He made me to go university to study English because of that.'

'I'm dying to know what's on the paper,' Georgina said. 'Unless it's a shaggy dog story.'

The young man searched fussily through his wallet, reached an inner compartment, and took out a piece of paper which he unfolded and passed to William. The Army Form B.250 was cut almost in four pieces by its creases, and said in fading pencil:

'IOU TO THE FARMER. I HAVE TAKEN UNE QUART OF MILK PLUS TWO LOAFS, 21 NEW LAID EGGS, AND SOME BEST BUTTER. I PROMISE TO PAY AFTER THE WAR WHEN WE'VE DONE THE GERRIES. SIGNED: HAROLD OXTON. GUNNER. RA. 28 MAY 1940.'

'Your face is like a beetroot, darling.'

'God! It's amazing.'

'Is it funny, or isn't it?'

He passed her the precious paper. 'Now I know how he fed us.'

'It must have been obvious at the time,' she said.

'You know him?' the Belgian asked.

'He was my batman. Went through the war with me.'

'Oxton?' said Georgina. 'What's he doing now?'

'Lives in Nottingham with his mother.'

'Isn't it strange?'

'I'll pay this bill,' William said, 'and charge it to battery accounts when I get back.'

The stranger was offended. 'Certainly not. We were happy to help. I keep the paper, for ever, as a souvenir.'

'It should be framed and put in the Artillery Museum,' Georgina said, enjoying the meeting.

'Let me have your card, at any rate.' William was sorry for his blunder. He would send a memento from England.

He shook William's hand firmly. 'This is my father's address. Come with me now. He'll be delighted.'

William took the card. 'We must be back in Ypres.'

They went on their way.

'I'm staggered,' he said.

When he turned for a last look over the ridge, she held his hand. 'So this is the place where the Germans tried to blow my darling to bits?'

'One of them.'

'I'm so glad they didn't.'

He could tell her now: 'I've made up my mind to leave the army.'

He wished his words would return and disappear. What's done is sickeningly done. He wouldn't want it otherwise. It was as if decisions were being made for him.

She squeezed his hand harder, for support though, not affection. 'What do you mean?'

'I'm resigning my commission.'

She felt he was being malign, or at best playing a sinister game of stepping aside from himself and seeing whether he could unnerve her, just when she'd reached a state of peace and relaxation. She couldn't find the proper words to counter him: 'For God's sake, what are you talking about?'

'Just what I say. I was born in the army, bred in barracks, forged and tempered on the battlefield – as the old song goes – but I'm leaving it.'

At whatever time he chose to tell her she'd no doubt have that same injured expression on her suddenly pallid face. Was it because he'd decided without a long course of painful consultation? Or because such a grave step threatened the basis of their lives?

'How long has it been on your mind?'

He'd be honest. 'Since we came on this trip.'

'The army's your life.'

'There's more than one life in a lifetime.'

'There jolly well isn't,' she snapped.

'That's up to us.'

'Don't be bloody ridiculous.'

It was for her sake that he was giving up the army, though he couldn't tell her that. But he would have broken it less clumsily if he'd known she'd take it so hard. He thought she'd jump at the idea.

She took off her headscarf, wrapped her hands in it, then unravelled them and drew the scarf across her face. He hoped the bus would come so that they could get back to dinner and, after a few drinks, a state in which the threatening storm would pass away.

Her voice was brittle. 'If you leave the army, I'll leave you.'

It sounded final. It was a vital issue, but *he* would have to make the change, not she. Her life was bound to be altered by it, but he'd assumed it would be for the better, and hadn't expected her to quibble.

She was afraid of change. It was like falling off a cliff, when you couldn't be sure of landing on your feet. If you knew you would, you might as well stay where you were. He imagined their laughter in the mess. What do you expect? Some stay on above forty, others don't. Those who leave want two lives for the price of one. Even three. 'Fraid of dying in harness.

'It'll break up our whole lives,' she said, having waited for him to end his cruel silence. 'I can't face it. I was just getting used to the one we have.'

He'd find it hard enough himself, but nothing could stop him. He'd keep explaining his point of view, so that eventually she might understand.

'Have you thought what this will mean to your father?'

It was one momentous decision of his life which he had no intention of talking to him about. 'It's my life,' he said calmly.

'It'll kill him.'

'Then it'll have to.' Maybe it wouldn't. Perhaps his father would see it as the final release, back into the light after more than fifty years service between them. It would make no difference, however he took it. 'He's seventy-seven. If he isn't old enough to understand it now, he never will be.'

She came close, and the surprising feel of her fingers on his wrist made him smile. 'It'll be a new life,' he said. 'Like going into an adventure.'

'For you.'

'For both of us. Otherwise I wouldn't dream of it.'

She'd complained of him being stuck in the mud and now she couldn't stand the idea of him trying to get out. Her inconsistency made her even more desolate. She was silent as they walked to the bus stop. His determination frightened her, as if he'd gone mad and was no longer the man she'd known.

'I love you,' he said. 'I'll see you're not hurt by it. The army phase of my life's ended. I want another to begin. I'm not the sort who rots away.'

'Why the hell did we come to this damned bloody place ?' she cried.

Her sense of calamity was catching. He felt that if he had a revolver he would shoot himself, to end his life and her misery. He fought to stop himself saying those words of easy surrender which would undo everything. He thanked God when the bus came down from the village.

CHAPTER TWELVE

'Come on, my love. That's it, my duck. It's not like it used to be, is it? I give you a hand now when you need it, don't I? Come on, my duck. It's the least I can do.'

Oxton's tone was halfway between cajoling and real affection, which anyone hearing would rightly have taken for the deepest concern. He wheeled his mother's chair to the lavatory door. 'There, now I'll help you to get up.'

At nearly ninety she was as fragile as an eggshell and weighed no more than a feather. Her wispy grey hair was combed back, and veins stood out on thin white wrists. He wanted her to live for ever, and maybe she would, for she had much strength in her hands when she held him while talking about something which had been bothering her during the long hours he had to be at work.

Her spirit was solid because its weight had been in him since he was born, a burden that he now carried happily and willingly, hoping to go on doing so till he died. How this would be possible since she was so much older faded into an irritating mist whenever his mind veered on to it. So all he could do was take the utmost care of her.

At such an age she slept little, woke at five in the morning and got up to wash from a bowl of water he put each evening on the stand. She took an hour to dress, an ageing fastidious lady who had to make herself presentable before her son came in at six to see her safely downstairs. He would ask if she slept well, whether or not she had dreamed, and if she had, about what. He'd make some comment on the weather as he swung open the curtains and glanced out.

The house was on the edge of Clifton estate, far-off from the two up and two down in St Ann's Well Road, where the walls had got wet in winter and where, whenever his mother wanted to go to the lavatory, she had to be pushed across a windswept cobbled yard. Thank God the council had got them out of that, or she'd have been dead by now.

He looked across the pasture and into the shallow valley of Fairham Brook, with Gotham and its humpy hill nudging up to the right when he turned his head. A good field of fire, he couldn't help thinking, in so far as any mob coming along that way would never get through the shell splinters if it was old Scorton's battery they were up against.

He'd been away from her twice in his life, for eleven years all told, when she sent him off to do his duty. Looking back, such gaps seemed only a few months, no more than vivid dreams. The First War often returned with its stench of cordite, the dead meat of your mates, and mud. It was a dream so real that it seemed as if it had never actually happened, but drifted in from a dark future he would get to after death. It was a terrible muddle he preferred not to think about, nor of being absent from his mother except to tell himself that it must never happen again.

'Don't fuss, Harold,' she said, a smile on her thin well-shaped lips. 'I can manage.'

She was modest, and would look after herself while there was breath in her body. She would stand and walk steadily enough, but she was slow, and tired easily. He'd often come home to find she had washed the pots and swept around the fireplace. 'I'm not *that* old,' she laughed, when he told her off about it. 'I can do my share.'

He had to laugh. She could, an' all. 'You'll tire yourself, though.'

She held the table edge. 'Don't be silly. I was going to set the tea things before you came in.'

'You're not as young as you were,' he wanted to say, but didn't like to mention her age, because last week she'd got so upset, it turned him upside down for the day. She'd looked as if she were lost, and disappointed in life, for those few brief minutes after breakfast.

He let her stand, then go by herself into the lavatory, while he mashed the tea and set the table. A few days ago he'd got a letter on army paper from his old Colonel to say he was leaving the army, to which message he added greetings to his mother and hoped she was well. He wrote once a year, and always mentioned his mother, which to Oxton seemed proper because he sorted out his real friends by this human and primitive politeness. The only real concern anyone could show was to ask after his mother. As he walked in to the 'Man o' Trent' on Saturday night for his few pints of the week his acquaintances and neighbours called:

'Hey up, 'Arold! 'Ow's yer mam?'

It was hard to see what a lifelong army man like Colonel Scorton would do in civvy-street, but he expected he'd get a post somewhere. There were always good jobs for blokes like that. From the cupboard above the dresser he took bread and butter, two eggs, a packet of lard and a pot of jam. She liked scrambled eggs and bread-and-butter.

A man couldn't stay in the army all his life, especially when he was getting on, but they'd lose a good gunner when Scorton went. He could go in again if there was another war, though. It's a poor spark who's too old for that. Any man should be fit enough to handle a rifle and fill sandbags.

Oxton worked all day shovelling mortar, pushing barrows, and hodding bricks at some new houses being slung up near Ruddington. Did more work than some of the twenty-year-olds, that was a fact, though the pay was better than in the good old days. What with his wage and his mother's pension, they weren't badly off. He earned twenty pounds a week and could have got thirty if he'd been willing to put in more overtime. But he had to get back to see his mother, and in any case too much of his money would go in tax. You had to watch 'em over that.

He heard water splash from the tap in the kitchen, and knew she was out, so poured her first cup of tea from the large brown pot. He went to her, holding eggs and lard: 'Come on in, my duck, and get some tea.'

He drew the chair to the table, then pushed the cup towards her, milk and sugar already stirred. 'Sit down, mother. Come on, my duck. This'll mek you feel better.'

'You are funny,' she said. 'Stop fussing. I can manage all right.'

He stood while she pulled her chair in. It was true she was quite capable. He picked a thread of cotton from the shoulder of her brown cardigan. 'I like to fuss,' he said, 'you know that. I've allus fussed over you, ain't I ?'

No other man had. The one who'd got her pregnant left before he was born. The great struggle she'd had to keep them both was to him an act of prolonged heroism which he must repay by looking after her. When she was asleep at night he would go softly into her room and get her glasses from the bedside table. Back downstairs by the desk lamp he took the soft cloth from his own case and breathed on the lens, polishing each one over and over as he listened to the news on the wireless, till they were so cleaned it seemed as if the frames had no glass in them. On the way to his own bedroom, next door to hers, he would put them soundlessly back on her table, then look at her face in the shadow of the dim nightlight for a longer or shorter time according to how many perturbations about her he'd gone through at work that day.

She slept so gently, as if there were no breath in her body, and he saw back to when she had been active and hard-working, getting him up for school and sending him off with a good breakfast before she set out for the factory. Such a past was a solid part of their lives, but thinking about it often put him into a state of dread because one day he might come into her room and find that she wasn't breathing at all. At such times he shrugged off this grim mood by bending his head close to take in more of her peaceful face, and putting a huge scarred hand so gently on her shoulder that she could not possibly have felt it except in a sleep that was dreamless. Then he touched her dry pale forehead with his lips, and said good-night under his breath. The moment his head lay on the pillow he was in oblivion, till the alarm went at six the next morning.

They ate breakfast together. While he bolted his own, his mother went on chewing slowly, looking now and again to-wards the window where the budgerigar's cage hung in the light. He buttered her a piece of sliced bread, and she used half with her egg, and the other part for strawberry jam.

He asked if she'd like another egg, or more bread: 'You don't eat enough, mother.' He shook his head. 'It's no more than our budgie would eat.'

She told him to mind his own business. 'I never did eat a sight, but I get all I need, and that's enough for me.'

He loved to hear her talk, to say things, to reminisce about the old days when he was a boy, because when she talked she was most alive. Then she was no longer an old lady, but became his mother of younger times, though he had to be careful not to make it seem as if he were goading her into speech, otherwise she might get angry or upset. 'I'm the one who eats every-thing,' he said, rustling the packet for another slice. 'But then, I need it, I expect.'

'You always were a big eater,' she said in her thin voice. 'As a lad you could never get enough.'

'I did, though,' he laughed. 'Let me pour you some more tea.'

'Yes, I like my tea.'

The Journal rustled through the letterbox, and he heard the newsboy pushing his squeaking bicycle to the next house. 'I'll get the paper for you.'

'Where are you going?'

'To get the newspaper.' He raised his voice, because over the last couple of years her deafness had become plain. Luckily her eyes were still good. While she settled herself to read he made cheese sandwiches and filled his flask.

'I should be doing that for you.'

'You have a good look at the news,' he said. 'Have a rest, my love.'

She laughed. 'I doze all day.'

'Ne' mind, my love. You need to.'

'You are a big daft thing.'

He was delighted when she said this. The morning was a good time. He wanted to sit with her all day, but had to go to work. Mrs Barnstone next door came in at twelve to give her a hot dinner. There wasn't much else he could do to make her comfortable. He took a bottle of brandy from the cupboard and put a few tots into a jug of lemonade so that she could have a sip of her favourite drink whenever she felt like it.

When he got home at six she'd be sleeping lightly in her

chair under the window in summer, or by the fire in winter, often with the photo album open on her knees. What her thoughts had been, or how she had kept herself occupied during his day-long absence, he did not know, but he'd have liked to sample those reminiscing pictures he was sure filled her mind every minute. Their faces in the album must have sent her from one phase of life to another, drifting not only into the past, but in all different directions.

In the last few months her memory had lost its sense of space and become confused, timeless and vivid. She talked of her school days in the 1870s as if she were still in them, or of seeing the melancholy convoy of ambulances coming up Derby Road one day from the disaster of Chilwell shell-filling factory in the Great War. Or she would talk about last Sunday's car ride as if it had been fifty years ago, thinking he'd taken her to Mansfield instead of Loughborough.

He stooped to pick up her photograph album that had slipped to the floor. She was a little confused. His movement woke her: 'Harold, you'll be late for work.'

'I shan't, mother. Unless you mean tomorrow. I've never been late so far. But I've just come in, duck. You was dreaming over your photos.' Her bottle was empty: 'You must have been thirsty today.'

She gave an alert smile. 'I was. It's hot out, isn't it?'

'We worked without our shirts on. I look as if I've been to Africa.'

'Don't catch cold. I don't want to lose you.'

'No fear o' that.' He went into the kitchen to put the kettle on. 'Any visitors?'

'Only Mrs Barnstone.'

'Did you eat all your dinner?' He struck a match and waited to hear from her before lighting the gas.

'Except the chop-bone!'

He put a hand behind her back and helped her to sit up straight. 'That's my duck. No visitors, eh? Are you sure a black man didn't pop in and say hello?'

'If he does I'll run off wi' 'im!'

'I expect you would, an' all.' He opened a tin of pineapple chunks. He'd stopped his old banger at the Co-op and run in for the shopping. He was proud of his car. It was one of his few pleasures, a big old Austin bought cheap, all spares borrowed or looted, and the whole assembly looked after like a favourite pet. It saved time getting to and from work sites, and helped his mother with an outing now and again.

'Maybe one day my old Colonel will come in for a visit. Remember him, mam? Drove up in his motor two years ago when he went to Ashfield to see his dad?'

'Nice man. Thought the world of you, I could see that.'

He spread a cloth, set cups and saucers noisily over it. 'We went through a lot together. France, Africa, Italy.'

'You did travel,' she said. 'More than I ever did.'

'They wanted to send me home because I was too old. At forty-eight! Would you believe it? He played hell till they let me stay on. He stood by me. I wanted to come home and see my old duck, but the war had to end first.'

'I was all right.'

'But I worried. Anybody would, with a mother like you.'

She nodded drowsily. 'Time you got married.'

He stood with the teapot in his hand. 'Plenty of time. I'm in no hurry.' Twice a year he made arrangements for her to be looked after while he went on a coach trip to London, to see a show and stay the night, taking enough cash in his money belt to walk around Soho till he found a woman to go off with. This section was dropped from the long description of his excursion to the big town.

'It's bad to hurry,' she said. 'That's what my teacher told me when I read the Bible too fast. I'm a good reader, at school.'

He looked at her hard. 'I think it's a long time since you was at school.'

'Course it is, silly. Pour me my tea.'

He reached across to the string bag hanging on the door-knob. 'Half a pound o' cooked beef for our tea. All lean, I said to the butcher. Not a scrap of fat, because it's for my mother's tea. I know Mrs Oxton, he said. Known her for years. How is she? A fine woman. We all know your mother around here. An owd Ruddingtonite *she* is! That's what he said. Scrimshaw's – you know who I mean, don't you, mother?'

She did. And she didn't. 'I knew everybody, at one time.

That looks nice. Lovely meat.'

He was delighted when she laid a slice over a piece of bread. 'You never lose your appetite do you, my duck?' Still, he had to be careful. The doctor said he wasn't to give her too much because her digestive tract was fragile, like paper. But she didn't need a lot of food, so there'd be no danger as long as he kept an eye on her. Poor love. The taste was delicious to her, and she made it twice so by eating slowly.

He was famished after work, in spite of eating a bag of toffees on the way back. 'Don't smack your lips like that,' she snapped, 'they'll hear you next door if you aren't careful.'

'Sorry, mother.' His mouth was full of food. He forgot himself when not attending to her and she slipped a few moments out of his presence. He'd drift across the continent of himself, thoughts spreading in all directions, till he was over the hills and far away, going back and forth in his life to the odd places he'd been to. Not that he had much time for it. You had to be sharp-eared and quick-eyed at work or you'd come to some mishap or other. The only thing he speculated on – and he did it more and more, whereas when young he never had – was what he would be doing in five or ten or twenty years' time. Where would he and his mother be? He craved to know what would happen tomorrow, but it was a blank impenetrable wall.

Having finished, he glanced at her eating, the centre of his pride and pleasure. Twenty years ago she'd had a stomach illness which almost carried her off, but now it seemed as if she would last for ever. He veered from such thoughts to pour more tea for them both.

'I'm going to scrub the kitchen tonight,' he told her, sounding like Sergeant Oxton. 'It's about time. Got to keep the place clean.'

'I'll help you.'

'It'll be all right, my duck. It'll only take a minute.' He continually fought her pride and independence, knowing she loathed being a helpless burden. But if he allowed her to clear the table or wash the tea things he must keep a good eye open to see that it wasn't too much for her bony hands and stick-thin wrists.

When her mind was sharp she seemed younger, and looked

at him as if to wonder what he really thought of her, and what he was able to make of her long life. But her thoughts did not stay clear. They mixed. They came and went. She got tired and had to sit down, and when she sat she often went to sleep when she'd hoped to stay awake. It was awkward for her, and not fair to Harold. When she dozed off, she felt she lost a bit of life. She missed something but didn't know what it was. Things drifted by. She was only as young as the strength in her legs. She loved it when her eyes were clear, when she could read, or see Harold properly. She liked to think about being wide awake and getting up to go to work.

Life was pleasant. She was looked after. There was no pain. She wasn't old, simply because she didn't feel old. It was only a tiredness. She couldn't imagine getting fully awake again, yet she wanted to, because without it she was no use to herself and even less help to her son. But she couldn't force herself to become as awake as he was when looking down at her. It didn't bother her too much. She was getting on, after all, just like he said.

She sat, she read, she ate, she slept, and the days flowed on in various stages of clarity. If she made an effort her mind filled up with sparks, and the room turned sharp and vivid. She could pull this delightful clearness to her but if she held on to it too long, her heart started to beat so soundly that it seemed as if her lips were turning blue. So she closed her eyes to rest till the drum stopped banging.

One day while Harold was at work it went on and on. She laughed gently to herself, as she had as a young child in the few moments given her to laugh, till the skin of the big drum burst under the pressure. Goodbye, Harold, she said faintly, right inside herself.

CHAPTER THIRTEEN

He came out of the mess at Woolwich and went with his characteristic quick walk between the cannon and across the Common towards the old RMA building where he'd left his car. The General had been sorry to see him go, and his farewell was marked by a party in that large hall where kings had dined and where he'd first met Georgina.

His car was stacked with a last sort-out of his belongings but he could still see through the back window. Down Academy Road he glanced quickly at his old college where he'd gone wet-eared though not wet-eyed from Ashfield as a boy, and recalled his father first laying down the plan for his career: 'It's not only a trade you'll have, Will, but you'll be a fully qualified artificer in the Royal Artillery. "Tiffies" they call 'em. You'll be remustered as a lance-bombardier straight away if you do well. And after serving a score-and-four like me, you'll be able to get a job anywhere with them qualifications.'

And then Sergeant Jones belabouring them with homely invective from his round pallid face, staring blue eyes and heavy moustache as they stood in gymshorts and plimsolls: 'All right, you *budmashers*, you four-foot-nothing imps, you limbs of Satan!' The pitch of his voice diminished. 'You're so small, Gibbons, we'll give you a box to stand on.' He came back to full range: 'You've been getting into mischief again, a thieving sort of mischief, like going over the wall of the CO's garden and nicking all the apples off his tree. Not even ripe. Green as the eyes of the little yellow god. Sour as its . . . piss, I expect. Now, come on, lads, own up to it. Who was it, eh?' His voice descended almost to a whimper so that he could work back to his shouting. A real voice-artist, William remembered. 'Sell 'em a penny a pound to buy Woodbines. I know. I *know*.

I *do* know, you *budmashers*. Half-inch your bootlaces while you're marking time, some of you would. Philips! Stop picking your nose or your 'ead'll cave in!' Seeing Captain Smith coming from the orderly room he began frenziedly shouting: 'Now then, come on, move. Up-down, up-down, up-down. Move to the right and run, run, RUN!'

Sergeant Jones had been through the mud at Third Ypres, and told them about it one winter's night near to passing-out time when they were roasting chestnuts in the potbellied stove and offered him a couple. 'I was king of the mud,' he said. 'King of the Bleeding Mud!'

That quick goodbye to his old college made William remember his bleak unhappiness on snapping his eyes open at the first wild communal shouting. After leaping to his feet, and seeing others in the room with arms swinging to snatch soap and towels, he felt alone, till he became anxious at being late, when his loneliness was killed stone dead by a quick reach at flannel or clothes.

In the sudden wide-open eye-ache of those mornings he wondered, before he set happily enough into action, where he had seen the look he felt on his face that must have presented itself momentarily to the boy in the next bed. Staring back into himself during those few seconds, which seemed to be illuminated with enough vision to last a lifetime, he remembered the same expression on another face from his past.

Being fed, clothed and given pocket money, life wasn't difficult, though the shock at leaving home made him wonder at times whether there'd been any need of it. But taking his father's adage to heart that a good soldier never looks back stopped the thought biting. Charlie's plan for him wasn't really broached till it had almost come to pass, and by that time William was too attached to him to be either surprised or angry.

At college he developed a single-minded energy for passing exams, and realised how this had been put into him by his father, so that he knew whose eyes he saw on first waking up in the morning long before the mixed blessing of their appearance died.

His father had tricked him into joining the army because he

hadn't wanted the responsibility of looking after a son any more, and William had collaborated in the mechanics of the trick in order to get out of his clutches. Like everything, it was both complicated and simple. As soon as he got used to his new life, he saw that everything had been for the best, but that his father, in a more diplomatic sense, had said the service of the dead over him as well.

Such thoughts tormented him to such a pitch when they took him over at the start of each day that they became his powerhouse, his electrical generator, the laminated armature-winding that created the electro-magnetic flux and gave him the force to work.

There was no other life, and once he got used to the speed and intensity his anxiety diminished. It was Sergeant Jones' single-minded delight to bully and drill them from reveille to lights out, which made them feel they belonged to something so big that nothing beyond the walls could have any meaning. On parade his shouts and those of other NCOs invariably ended in falsetto screams, as if their wind was finally strangled when it went on too long. Such a high pitch at the end of their orders was part of the pride they had in their drill-ground voice, and in a weird way suggested that if it brayed a second longer it would turn into a woman's.

He liked the rigid programme, because then he knew what there was to look forward to. Nobody complained at the discipline because they were in it together, and too stunned to sort out their responses. Being released from a long age of servitude with his father showed him that in fact his previous freedom had been subjection, and that what ought to have been a kind of imprisonment he now thoroughly enjoyed.

The tenseness that flooded him prior to a test made his blood run quicker, and he often looked forward as much to the next exam as to a promised seven-days' leave. He found more flexibility in himself – and even in the army – than he'd been led to expect from his father. There was no time to spare, nor energy to waste. That his industry came from a need to compete was something he'd rather have died than admit, but it made him all the harder to compete against. His comprehension of physics and maths gave him a sense of self-reliance no one could dent, and he made friends easily whenever he lost the need to feel superior.

His mixture of imprisonment and freedom proved there wasn't much of the experience he was missing, a feeling which increased his confidence by forming limits to his understanding. Within these limits the many demands only made him stronger, but he knew how to relax during the half hour spare after breakfast, the period following lunch, and the leisure before lights-out-much more than he'd ever been able to at home under the infinitely harder rule of his father.

The final common denominator was that of sticking together, and never snitching on your pals. Like when we came back in a gang, he laughed to himself, bawling songs and not caring whether we were kay-lied or not, and got a thousand days CB between us, which was even more than when we wrecked the billet after a pillow fight. The CO was almost grinning when he gave us that lot.

They developed a fine *esprit-de-corps*, which included a way of brewing alcohol in the lab, though they got barely a lip-burning sip each after giving a share to the scouts who kept conk in the corridors in case an instructor came in sight.

Strange, he thought, how I think about this rather than the rest of my army life. He drove south through Eltham, southeast to Chislehurst, and across the built-up valley of the Cray to intercept the A21 for Sevenoaks, glad to reach an expanse of restful green at last.

His reminiscing mood even went back to Ashfield, a puzzling and not altogether welcome plunge, unless early times always did turn vivid when you made a vital change in life, or reached the middle years. He couldn't go through the *Sunday Times* these days without getting stuck in the property columns to see what choice residences were on sale in Nottinghamshire. Not that he wanted to go there for anything more than a visit.

Threading Sevenoaks he felt like a young man set on his first adventure, as if his quarter-century of perils, uncertainties, stultifications and unforgettable times with the army had been no more than a rarified childhood. He wondered, now that it seemed he was getting a grip on it, what in fact his destiny would turn out to be.

'I'm useful to you, aren't I?' Georgina had said, and objecting very much to it. 'I'm the bridge you can walk over from one part of your life to the next.'

He didn't see things like that. Couldn't you change your style of living without it being regarded as significant? It was what you didn't do that was really important, or so he told himself, though he wasn't sure how much he believed it.

He would hand in his commission no matter what she felt, and so he didn't know whether he'd properly convinced her, or whether she finally agreed because she was too weary to do otherwise. In one way his solid purpose made it easier for her to resolve that from now on he would have to take full responsibility for whatever decisions he made. 'You're the sort of man who needs somebody's permission before he can act,' was her final shot. He thought she was wrong. The fact that henceforth he must do things without the supporting framework of the army would stimulate him, and release the necessary energy to launch him in whatever work he found.

He turned into the drive and put his car in the garage. The grass and turf were still botched and muddy from neglect. After so long moving from place to place they had collected all the bits and pieces left with Jacko and in various warehouses, and decked out their own sitting and dining rooms to see how the total accumulation harmonised within the four walls that belonged to them. They needed to sit among their knick-knacks and gew-gaws in a choice solidly-planted paid-up Home Counties residence surrounded by a couple of acres and plenty of trees, buffered by lawns, fruit bushes, a paddock, and the wreck of a vegetable garden which he'd one day get back into production.

There was work to do, both inside and out, and the thought gave him pleasure. It was their house, and they would live contentedly enough in the well-watered south-eastern countryside. To get a house in middle-age was as vital an act as getting married again. They felt it equally, and were drawn closer together. During the months of searching for it and buying it and moving in and sweating at all the preliminaries to make it more or less habitable, they had known moments of intense happiness, which alone made it worthwhile to him. The project had kept her busy while he was at Woolwich or Larkhill, and the house had certainly taken his mind off that sad time when he would leave his regiment for ever.

From an armchair in the lounge he looked through big windows to the green lawn deepening into shadow as a beneficial smoky rain came down. He could almost smell the air outside going faintly cool at its descent. It was June, and he'd light a fire tonight in the wide grate, having hauled in enough dead wood from under the trees for a few hours of comforting flame.

But the land around the village did not have that familiar homeliness of Nottinghamshire and the Dukeries. It lacked the mixture of forest and pasture growing on pebble beds and river gravel and soft sandstone all the way up from the Trent, a geological feeding of the atmosphere through grass and tree roots that permeated the gentle landscape in both summer and winter. But he'd travelled too far and wide to think you could have everything. As long as Georgina was happy, it was paradise enough, and the older she got, and the more years they were together, the more it seemed possible that she might become content.

He lit a cigarette. Two large wood pigeons with wings spread wide flew towards the roof, out of the rain. But she wasn't happy. Only a fool would say she was. She was tall, beautiful and calm. It was beyond him ever to make her happy. She took life as something to 'put up with'. She endured its smallness and disappointments with an erect head, and with what pride she could muster. He did not know why she was disappointed. As years went by the weight of her spirit gave no sign of lifting. She liked to talk about it, as if it were a problem they might share, but their moods rarely coincided. At such times he said she would grow to like life sooner or later, that she would become more relaxed, more tolerant towards herself, more attuned to what was good in the world. She would change without noticing it, and indeed was changing now. He suffered that she was so sombre, feeling his own spirit bludgeoned off-centre by it, seeing many things about himself that he might never have realised had he not been put into this crucible of another's suffering.

Even that fabulous aquamarine light occasionally went out of her eyes, and when it did his love became a steely unmitigated torment. He was glad he'd left the army, for he could not have gone on working with that concentrated self-possession a gunner and commanding officer must have if he were to do his job well. He loved her too much to mention this, knowing that no matter how bad it was for him, it was worse for her.

But he was convinced that it must break sooner or later. He didn't believe this simply to keep himself going. Change was contagious. It would happen. And though he felt a certain peculiar dread about it he also thought that whatever benefited her would ultimately be good for him also. But out of his own middle he couldn't help her. It was agony that there seemed nothing he could do. It was as if only fate could step in and help them both.

When he argued that things would improve, she only smiled and did not believe him. Why should she? How could he prove what hadn't yet happened? A gunner was nothing if not pragmatical, and now his life-long pragmatism was being eroded. Maybe this was necessary, and would steel him in his new way of life, but if so it was an advantage he could do without, since the cost was too high for Georgina.

Meanwhile there was work to be done on the cluttered jungle-like garden. He burned heaps of rubbish that the former owners had left in the garage and yards. He ripped ivy from the trees, chopping its thick roots with an axe. Such tenacious and parasitic stuff coiled around a trunk, sucking away and growing as stout as an arm till it destroyed the tree and pulled it down into a pile of rotten wood and dust. An apple tree was almost smothered, but he worked hard to clear the snaky limbs, climbed into the feebler branches to get the last sprigs out, and hoped that the tree would one day bear fruit again.

Certain rooms in the house needed redecorating, but he was no handyman as far as such fine work went. He was prepared to try but Georgina called in a firm from Moorfield to do it. She could see him doing the rough and mindless work, but any that needed finesse and skill she seemed to think beneath his dignity.

On some days he cycled around the district on a high sit-up-and-beg bicycle which the previous owner had discarded. It was enjoyable to live for the first time like one of the idle rich. But twenty-five years in the army did not entitle him to be slack for long, and after a month Georgina wondered one evening when he was going to look for a job. 'If you'd been thirty years down a coal mine, I could understand it,' she said, uneasy at seeing him so relaxed and unoccupied.

There were many possibilities. Retired Master Gunners sometimes went into the Ordnance Survey, but he didn't want to involve himself with the minutiae of topographical maps for the rest of his life, and become an unsung hero of British cartography. His father would be proud of him no doubt, but that side of life also was over and done with, and he didn't need anyone to live through him any more.

Ex-officers of middle-age could go to a teachers' training college, but Georgina would not hear of it. 'I refuse to socialise with schoolmasters' wives.'

Her remarks led him to think more favourably of the job than he might have done. 'It's useful work. I'd handle kids well.'

This hint that they'd no children of their own for him to play at daddy with irritated her. 'I'm sure you would. But when you think about it, it'd be so dull.'

He admitted that this was probably true. 'It wouldn't worry me. I've had my share of excitement.'

The reply was plain in her eyes: *You* may have had, but I haven't.

He let her see that she had won, and said no more. 'It'll be difficult to get some sort of management job, being over forty. I should have resigned my commission when the war ended.'

'Or not at all.'

'It's quite a tonic to know I've done the wrong thing.'

'You have your pension,' she said, ironically.

That was true. Financially they could coast along for awhile, but he felt that if his brain wasn't sharpened with some sort of responsibility he'd go sallow and bilious. However much the world was said to have changed, he told her, a man still had to justify the air he breathed by contributing something to it.

'That's because your family were working people,' she said. 'It's in your blood.'

It was a reminder that had been made more than once since he'd resigned his commission. Did she think that when he was out of a job he'd go on the dole, or join a hunger march? Such funny notions certainly spiked-up their conversation. 'I don't think it's a matter of what class you're from. Goes deeper than that.'

'I was only talking about your particular family.'

'They always worked,' he recalled, 'and that's a fact. Otherwise they starved. Except my father,' he added with a laugh, which she took as a barb aimed at her family. 'He was in the army. But even he set to when he came out.'

He realised that his feet were still sheet-anchored into a childhood which, though in no way hard, had been spartan enough. Looking back, he also saw how well-off he was now compared to those days.

He was more familiar with her background than she could ever be with his. Even though she had often been to Ashfield with him, she still imagined that his father and Doris lived quite comfortably. She saw their lives as being to a certain extent picturesque, which he did not hold against her, and looked upon his childhood in the same way. But when he used the word spartan in describing it she could only assume he was exaggerating as usual.

CHAPTER FOURTEEN

Old Jacko was tall and white-haired, bony and angular, the clumsiest person he'd ever known, the sort of man who moved in jerks, and often with amusing suddenness. When Georgina's mother died he had sold his London flat and bought a Queen Anne cottage near Leatherhead with a large garden and a good view south over wooded country. He was set to stay there for the rest of his life, reading war histories, nursing his plants and flowers, and helping the local Conservatives to increase the majority of their Government at the next election. He was a good old stick, William thought, always ripe for the bantering type of argument he'd never had from his own father – which was another advantage in being Georgina's husband.

Jacko had piercing and restless blue eyes, and a long solid jaw. The only thing that had ever been able to hold him perfectly still was his uniform. When he was in it – and he wasn't any more – he could stand immobile for hours. No parade was too tedious, but as soon as the battalions were dismissed and he went back to his office he was restless and angular and fidgety, unable to keep his hands still, or stay sat down for long.

He would stand, sway, not know what to do, then, taken with a bright idea, pace his office, as if intending to make a plan. He'd pick up books or straighten papers, place himself at the wall-maps, go back to his desk for a pencil, a dozen of which he had sharpened already, and with a few great strides return to the map, and draw a line around some city or along a river for no particular reason except that perhaps, deep in his mind, he wanted to obliterate that city, or cross the river and go marching away into some sort of freedom, his battalions fanning out behind. But he didn't. He'd range back to his desk and lift the telephone and call out some unnecessary orders or ask a few bothersome questions and, having put the receiver down, pick up an india-rubber, close in on the map again, and rub out the mark he'd made along the river and the circle he'd drawn around the city and instead make two straight lines through a range of hills – quickly and with great panache – then very painstakingly draw two neat arrowheads to point the direction of each.

Out in the field, or on manoeuvres, he was a good infantry officer, yet prone to interfere too far down the line. He was here there and everywhere, and seemed to need hardly any sleep. He'd be up at the weapon pits one minute, then back at the supply column, then over at the guns to pass the time of day, then at the signals wagon, then back at his Brigade HQ before they'd even missed him, or before their sighs of relief had died at his previous departure. He had the energy for twenty, as his battalion commanders said, and he wore adjutants out by the dozen.

He adapted quickly to change. The most sudden and complicated plan, whether sent down from Corps HQ, or formulated out of his own agile brain, did not faze him, though occasionally his tenacity and intelligence so outran the similar qualities in those above and below that chaotic situations developed. He was talented but volatile, energetic but unpredictable – which might be, William thought, why he had risen no higher than brigadier.

Retired to the country as a widower, he still had the same forceful dimension of restlessness. Why he hadn't driven his wife mad, William didn't know. She died before him, and that was a fact. But his wife had loved him, had looked after him in her cool and silent way.

For forty years from the day of their wedding he'd treated her with great deference and diffidence, as if eternal courtship were the only satisfactory way to treat a woman and run a marriage. Every day he reminded her how beautiful she was and, when conditions were right, took her out to dinner once a week, and came in with flowers whenever he passed a shop or stall. Given no reason to complain, she could only complain against herself and admit it to no one, and the only way to

avoid an inner destructive bewilderment was to become bitter –
but hide that too – so that it ended in icy stoicism which Jacko
appreciated because he dimly saw that life was like that for
everyone anyway. But he adored her, and never left off showing
his regard and respect. And William saw, while she was alive,
that she loved him too, and guarded him like a tigress. It was,
finally, their loyalty to each other which impressed him most.
And when she died he was surprised that Jacko hardly mourned
for her. She'd taken two steps backwards out of his life, and
one day he would do the same and join her. You couldn't
shed too many tears over that.

It was fortunate, William thought, that Georgina had her
mother's more solid qualities. But the restlessness of her father
was forever trying to break free, and because she didn't know
how to let it out in small enough doses for her to go on believing
she was a calm person, she lived a tense and troubled life.

When they drove over to see Jacko she became very much
like her mother, going around the house to see that every
knick-knack was in its accustomed spot. In fine weather
William and Jacko walked around the garden, William saying
that the army was no longer what it had been, not even for
him, that it was becoming more a question of science and
technique and individual know-how even quite low down the
ladder, and that there'd been a great increase in the live-and-
let-live spirit as far as old-fashioned discipline was concerned.

And while Jacko listened, and grunted, and put in his own
sharp comments, he leapt from side to side wielding a great
pair of shears to snap off the over-extended part of a bush, or
lop away a patrolling rose-sucker, or cut down some dead
alfalfa grass, or simply to shave off a single privet leaf that
stuck an inch from the hedge top. He wore a white canvas
blazer and a panama hat, and black lace-up boots for his large
feet.

'Way I see it, Billio' – all male names were made to end in
'O' because it cut the men down to size, hemmed in their
personalities, and rendered them as harmless as children
except when they were on the battlefield. Then the 'O'
between one order and the next slid out of sight and allowed
them finally to be themselves. 'You'll always need your

simple, hard, obedient infantryman. Gadgets fail, Billio, drop to bits, get knocked over, kicked in the dark, blown up, buried in error. Somebody gets drunk and stabs your tyres, puts sugar in your petrol tank instead of in their tea, staggers into your fancy dials and fuses everything, unclips your tank tracks by mistake. Then your good old infantryman comes back into his own. I'm not saying we don't need the artillery, mind you. Always need a bit of help from the guns, bless 'em!'

Georgina said they should stay a few days with Jacko because his daily help had given up her difficult job, and she wanted to get him a woman who would live in. At lunch William suggested that he get married again.

'Only to a young girl,' Jacko shouted, 'and no young girl will have me, though I'm keeping an eye open.'

Georgina laughed. 'It would be funny to have a step-mother younger than myself. She'd be like a sister.'

'Funny girl I've got.' Jacko poured himself and William half a tumblerful of brandy. 'Drink some o' this, Billio. But be careful. It'll make your toe-nails drop out while you're dreaming of green fields and woolly baa-lambs.'

She left the room, pretending to be busy. He winked, and nudged him hard on the knee with his elbow. 'Do you *manage* her?'

You couldn't be anything but straight with him, though he wished he'd mind his own bloody business. 'We do our best for each other.'

'Plenty of give and take, eh? She wants a lot of giving, I expect. Her mother did. *That*, especially.'

'Especially what?'

His head tilted and he laughed. Then he drank off his brandy as if it were cold weak tea. 'What every woman must have, young colonel. And what every man must provide.'

He pulled the band down from one of Jacko's Dutch cigars, stuck a spent match in the end, and lit it. 'We do all right, you know.'

'You're not a gunner for nothing.' He laughed again. 'Never thought I'd have one for a son-in-law, though. But beggars can't be choosers, can they?'

He seemed almost serious, and William wondered what he

was trying to say. There's none more subtle than those who haven't got things quite clear in their own mind.

'But that's what they want, Billio. Take my word for it. Plenty of *that*. More than half the battle. You RHA fellows are good at it, or so I hear. Almost as good as us foot sloggers.'

Next morning William set off on the forty-odd miles south-east towards home, leaving Georgina to interview a couple of women who might take on the job of looking after her father. He was glad to be in the car alone, which was his favourite situation for thinking things out. Jacko had put his finger on it. They hadn't made love much this last year or two, though things had improved since going into the house, as if the comfort and novelty of a new place were bringing them together again. But they quarrelled more, often over nothing, though there was no such thing as nothing when it came to making each other miserable.

He'd smoked his last cigarette, so pulled into a lay-by beyond Sevenoaks to get a new packet from his briefcase. At the other end, seemingly poised for going out, was a shining and opulent motor car. A short thin man wearing a light mackintosh and a thick cloth cap walked up and down beside it. The car must have been his, though William thought maybe he'd done a break from jail and stolen it. Otherwise where was his chauffeur? Or was he the chauffeur? He did ten yards one way and ten the other, looking so irritable that he'd do better to double the distance. William was curious to know what he was up to, and felt there was no harm in saying good morning.

The man turned sharply from his ten yard tether. 'I suppose I'll have to wait all bloody day.' He spoke well enough, but with a basic Thames Valley twang.

William walked up. 'What's wrong?'

He smiled sourly. 'Good morning!' – and turned contemptuously to his big car. 'Bloody caved in on me. Barely got it off the road. Britain can make it!'

'Doesn't sound too serious.'

'It doesn't move, though, and that *is* serious.'

There was nothing an artificer RA couldn't try his hand at. 'Happens to the best machines. Jump in and turn the engine.'

'You know something about cars?'

He was in a hurry to get home but you couldn't leave a chap stranded on one of the Queen's arterial lanes. 'I might.'

'I was thinking o' walking to the RAC phone, but it's a mile away.'

The engine didn't start. He looked at the ignition panel. 'Can you lift the bonnet?'

'I can, mate.' He released the catch. 'Where you going?'

'A village near Biddenstone.' William peered at the engine and spotted the fault. 'Fuel pipe's disconnected. If you have some pliers I'll fix it.'

The man rubbed his hands, and drew a luxurious leather pouch of tools from under a seat. 'You're a hero,' he said, when the engine sang. 'What's your line of business?'

William took a card from his wallet. There'd been no time to have new ones printed, so it showed his rank.

He reached into the glove box for one of his own. 'I like exchanging cards. Best idea man ever had. Pleased to meet you, Colonel.'

William glanced at it: 'Albert Monk, Managing Director, Entertainments Enterprises Ltd.'

'Going back to your regiment?'

'I resigned. I'm a free man now.'

He didn't know why he told this to a stranger, though it was true that having fixed the fellow's car put him in a commanding position.

Albert Monk laughed. 'You aren't looking for a job, by any chance? Still, I don't expect it would appeal to somebody like you.'

He was curious. 'If I knew what it was, I could tell you.'

'You'd be just the man. It'll pay two thousand a year, if that's the sort of sum you had in mind.'

It didn't seem feasible that he could be set up in work by a chap with the close-set eyes of a fifty-year-old lance-jack who knew every dodge. But there was something else about him, and William had the sense to realise that if he hadn't been in the army all his life he might have known what it was.

'There's a good restaurant at Bloatham,' Albert Monk said, chuffed with the idea of an artillery colonel running one of his centres. 'Will you do me the honour of having lunch with me, sir? Then we can really get down to my proposition. I've got a packet of Havanas in my car.'

William sensed his eagerness. It might be interesting to pass an hour and find out what sort of a man he was. You had to begin somewhere. 'I know the place you mean.'

'Follow me.'

CHAPTER FIFTEEN

It was ironic, or maybe typical, that the first job he tried for he should get, but Georgina didn't think it fit work for him. 'Something like a huckster?'

'You mean a fairground attendant? I wouldn't mind, even if it was. The army teaches you not to be fussy. Offer it to any of my contemporaries in Ashfield who'd been lucky enough to get office jobs and they'd sue you for defamation of character. But I've come up a bit since then.'

She tried to keep the scorn out of her voice. 'I suppose you see it as some sort of initiative test?'

'It'll pay well.' He poured more Burgundy. 'Two thousand is a good salary. And it'll go up when a bar, bingo hall, and billiard saloon are added to the bowling alley. Nothing wrong with being the manager of that lot. You need a capacity for organisation, diplomacy, honesty, presence of mind and the ability to deal with any rough house on the premises. I've been trained in those qualities, and most jobs in civvy street don't want 'em any more. It's too late for me to become a bank manager, and I've never fancied being on the board of some company or other, or turning into a probation officer, or a PT wallah, or getting a post as personnel manager in some big impersonal firm. Maybe I should never have resigned my commission, but I have and what's done is done, and I'm glad it is. Anyway, add the salary to my pension and we're going to be well off.'

The work might lack status, but what he did for a living had never been of such importance before that they had talked so long over it, which alone was a great step forward.

'I still don't think it's quite the thing for you.' She held out her glass to be filled. 'But if it makes you happy.'

'I'll give it a try. Let's drink to it.'

He was looking forward to the job with a lightness of spirit he hadn't even known as a child. She resented it, thinking it would take him further away than ever, in which case she would have to do something about her own life so as to survive the change in him that would affect them both. It was as if he'd got hold of a new toy that she could not share, and she'd never felt this way before simply because it was the first time he had changed his job. At the same time she was glad at his happiness, which seemed to hold some secret promise for her as well. She caught his mood. There was nothing else for her to do.

The tunnelling foliage of summer green, that had sprung up so intensely after a fortnight's rain, darkened the lane in places, even at midday, and he put headlights on so as not to slow down.

He drove into town and down the main street to a large red-brick building that had been put up as a picture house before the war, and converted to a bowling alley since. Between that and the department store next door was a narrow entry way leading to a car park at the back. Grass and weeds grew where the wall met the asphalt, and he decided to have that tidied up right away.

His office was a square small room which he marked off as his by a few books and photographs, and a framed town plan hung on the wall. His command was of four people: a cashier, a man in charge of the actual bowling, a bouncer (who looked as if he might be the first to get bounced) and a heavy middle-aged country woman with five children who blushed deeply (for reasons best known to herself) whenever he spoke to her during her mopping and polishing.

The cashier was a Scottish spinster who had been in the ATS Signals: 'It was a good life,' she said, in a well-trimmed Edinburgh accent. 'I'd like it all over again' – wanting him to know she was on his side, which he took almost as a warning against her till he realised that her goodwill and loyalty were genuine. She was also efficient during the busy nights of the week when no amount of noise at the pins, or the general nerve-wracking confusions of such a place, fazed her. She gave the money out, and her slightly forced smile was a fair measure of her sharp-eyed accuracy. Chief as he was, he knew he was only as good as those who worked under him, and with as reliable a cashier as Miss Callender half the battle was won.

The other half was in the hands of Jack Preston, an old friend of Albert Monk's who looked on his job as no more than a cushy billet. William wondered if he hadn't been Monk's cell mate at some faraway time in their lives. He was tall and well built, and half bald with strands of hair brilliantined back, and always wore a good suit. His rate of wages was high, but wouldn't pay for that sort of cloth. In prosperous times he must have put money by till after he'd made up to society for the way in which he'd got it. He could do without the present job anytime, he hinted. He had another, in fact, and was only doing this as a favour for Albert.

Overdressed for his part, he worked the machinery for dispensing bowls and bringing the skittles back to vertical. It was automated, but he stood by as if none of its intricacies were any secret to him, which made the players feel confident when they noticed him. He nodded to them like the lord of creation, and when he went beyond this and spoke a word or two it was very much appreciated by the working men and their wives who came in for a night's play. He was popular, and his seeming prosperity was a good influence on those who had money to spend. William wondered why Albert Monk hadn't put *him* in as manager, and thought it was because he didn't trust him. Every man in his place. Albert Monk thought it good and right to have a colonel at the top who'd keep a proper eye on things.

Jack Preston might cut a good figure as far as his personal self was concerned, but he didn't have an eye to the smaller details which were just as important. Keeping a shine on the establishment had a higher priority than Jack Preston's hair lying in place, or his perfume smelling right, or his bow tie being neatly tied. Albert Monk knew from his marrow that people liked to be in a clean and spotless place when they enjoyed themselves, so it was new, and modern, and well lit, and had vast sporting murals on the wall which were a disgrace to any artist, but looked pleasant and reassuring to the people who crowded in at the weekend. It needed a good man, of honesty, experience and discipline, to keep the place going.

William thought himself that sort of person. He could look after the whole caboodle, and get things done. He would see that they *were* done. He might not know anything about bowls or bowling alleys but that was beside the point. Within a month, on old artillery graph paper, he had drawn up a dozen schedules to be gone through during the working week. As long as he ticked off with chinograph pencils every job as it was done then the place functioned like a well-run battery of the RHA. All was laid down by note and rote: test doors for safety, check fire precautions, lights, cleaning work (a graph sheet to itself), machinery, drinks, food supply, finance, general inner and outer appearance, opening and closing times, meter readings at the end of each week.

Within three months the system was perfect. His first summer went full tilt because holidaymakers and day-trippers came down from London and many points north. He revelled in it. He walked unnoticed, he hoped, and unobtrusively, he thought, around the crush of people at the bar waiting for checks to have a go at the alleys.

It was his element to have people look up to him, just as at one time he'd considered his gunners to be in his own personal care, in as democratic a part of the army as it was possible to get. Now he was responsible for his patrons' safety, and for them having a good time in Albert Monk's lit-up rattle-trap that he wouldn't be seen dead in if he wasn't in charge. It wasn't his style, neither his class nor his inclination, though he couldn't condemn it because of that.

His patrons actually liked being in a crush, were not averse to queueing for a drink or waiting to get at the skittles. All year long many stood at a machine in a factory or served in a shop or hewed coal or maybe worked in a garage, and they hadn't saved up for their holiday to be quiet and sedate and cut-off, but to be in an ice-cream-eating, beer drinking, fish-and-chip scoffing, hey-up-Ted, and well-I'll-be-blowed-if-it-ain't-Bert-again good-natured crowd so that for a fortnight they could forget the self-and-boss-imposed loneliness. When they bumped into somebody or trod on each other's toes they could say: 'Sorry, mate' and 'That's all right, I've got ten of 'em' and 'it's a right old do, ain't it?' and talk talk talk about this year and last year and maybe the year to come, though next time perhaps they'd try Bournemouth or Llandudno or Scarborough or Blackpool where it might be less of a crush, but it'd be just the same there and if it weren't they'd never go there again and come back here complaining how dead the other dumps were.

He felt he knew their habits and wants. He'd not only grown up with them at school, served with them in the army up to 1939, but had been in charge of enough of them since, so that having slotted in at all stages gave him a deep sense of familiarity. Now and again he caught himself looking at a group as if he were one of them who'd worked all year in the same factory and travelled down in the same packed train, latched into the comforting and claustrophobic mix-up of their lives and families, trying to fight free perhaps, but caught just the same, as he sometimes thought he might have been if his life hadn't turned a sharp corner when his father pushed him into the army.

He didn't look too long. A quick turn of the eye showed how ridiculous it was. What you would or could or might have been had no meaning, because what you became and what you were was the reality and intention of your life. It was settled long before you were born, and the confused concoction of his outlandish picture soon vanished in self-esteem as he assessed himself and his past career, and his present position in life.

All the same, such inner disputations had their effect. Though he was the manager, there was something peculiar about his relationship with the clients. He was of them enough to understand them, yet not sufficiently one to be deprived of their respect. Not knowing how to take him, they deferred to him, and he never had any trouble with holidaymakers, whom he could tell a mile off. They had leisure, and were good natured because they had a better time by being so. They could be their own masters, as far as their wives allowed, and they had enough money to spend. They were in a strange place among other strangers, so the mixture of uncertainty and money created an atmosphere of tolerance and happy-go-luckiness he found easy to handle.

During the rest of the year local youths came from the town and country roundabout. At summer weekends they blended with the mood of the holidaymakers, not wanting to get into an argument with a steelworker from Sheffield, but after the two month holiday season was over they had the place more or less to themselves. Some were just tipping eighteen and waiting call up. Others were soldiers on leave in civvies; still more were spivs and lounge-abouts who'd never seen the inside of any army. Others were the twenty-one-year-old demobs who thought they had a right to boss the world because they could call themselves ex-servicemen. He wasn't overfond of them, but he wasn't afraid of them, and he didn't hate them. If they wanted a good game of nine-pins, or a quiet shot at billiards in the recently opened hall, that was all right, but if they got rowdy and bothered others, then he put them outside saying he never forgot a face and they'd better not show it in his place again.

Having been a soldier, he was not of the unforgiving sort, and if after a month he saw a youth back inside who'd once given him bother, he'd merely look at him till the fact registered, and let him stay as long as he behaved himself.

Albert Monk had done well by putting him in charge, and William saw how cunning and of this world he was, for to write Colonel Scorton MC on the application form as manager when applying to the local magistrates for extensions to the premises always got him what he wanted. But that was how the world went, and though the civvy part still at times seemed strange, he was beginning to enjoy himself in it.

A noisy gang came in one evening led by a well-built youth with wiry fair hair thick over his forehead, a swagger in his pin-striped Friday suit, and a badge on his tie – the king and back-bone of the awkward squad. Seeing him and his pals waiting peacefully at the bar ordering beer all round, William went away to his office.

Albert Monk had gone on and on about this problem: 'We don't want trouble with roughs. I'm frightened of it, and don't mind telling you. That's why I've got a big charmer like Jacky

Preston on the inside beat. But for God's sake, Colonel, no trouble. I can live without it, and so can you. War's over, eh?'

He nodded – an upstanding RHA man, forever curt and to the point. 'I'll see to things, Mr Monk.'

One or two situations had gone as far as the brink the first year, but it hadn't come to blows yet. It was always as well to sidestep that sort of thing, if you could. Send them elsewhere. You had your regulars to think about. You pampered them (or Jack Preston did) as if they were prize marrows. No use getting the place a reputation as a rough spot, or you'd soon be closed down in a town like this, with its vast old age pensioner population floating from a life of hard work and public service to the cemetery on the hill – as the local paper put it. Some of the young blokes were too high spirited because they missed a good gymnasium or sports team. Others were just bloody mean because they lacked a war to fight, though it wasn't up to him to oblige them with one. *They* were the ones you had to look out for. The more time that passed from the war the rougher it seemed to get. He often solved trouble by a strong look and a few hard words, finding that it had a good effect when he put on a bit of the old broad Nottinghamshire accent as if he'd spent the first thirty years of his working life down a coal mine instead of at a line of guns. A few fatherly no-bloody-messing words with the old Ashfield twang worked wonders, especially when combined with his straight-backed soldierly manner.

He often thought about his tactics in case of a rough house. There was no written manual, so he had to devise his own. He'd kept up boxing and jerk-work at a local gym, plus plenty of walking and cyling when he got the chance, so even at over forty he reckoned he wasn't a bad match if it came to a smack-and-tumble. He decided that if you'd got to do it, you should do it fast, not too hard unless you wanted a bill for a set of false teeth, and not too soft because you didn't want your own ivories knocked out either, but do it in the best and cleanest way possible. It was a good idea never to counterattack; by which he meant that if a whole gang was making trouble never go for the one that's letting fly. Make a set for one of his mates standing by egging him on. Then quick as lightning pound another who's giving the ring leader moral support, so that you put them against him, because by that time they think he's responsible for the injustice being perpetrated against them. This puts the element of surprise firmly on your side when you suddenly swing to the real target who thought he was safe because he'd seen you getting the wrong blokes.

The commotion and shouting were loud, and he heard it even before the cashier came in to say there was trouble.

'I'll be along,' he said, not standing up till she'd closed the door. Instead of going straight into the hall, which would be the expected direction of his approach, he walked along the corridor and out by a side door, making his way round to the main entrance, which he'd enter from the street. The doorman was absent. He'd have a word with him about that, even though he had gone in to help Preston.

Their policy, Albert Monk insisted, was to sort them out before any fool called the police, and he could see the sense of it. Solving their little domestic problems without outside help would save the taxpayers' money.

He walked in quickly, pushing through the ring of people who thought maybe he'd laid on a fight tonight as extra entertainment. A couple of bar stools had been upturned, and the big fair man he'd previously noted was sparring with the doorkeeper, a smile on his face at getting him so obviously at his mercy. Jack Preston lay on the floor and, though apparently undamaged, had two of the man's pals close by in attitudes of studied belligerence. They thought themselves kings of the situation, in spite of the noise and threats of the other customers who otherwise remained inactive, and imagined they could take their time about it.

William selected one of these, and hit him so hard he spun away from the bar and slid against the ring of people. The front onlookers, who had to move back quickly, trod on the feet of those behind. Then he hit the other, which merely pushed him clear, for he felt it important not to grapple but to keep his fists flying in the right direction because they seemed of a beefier stock than he. The main culprit looked surprised – it was too early to say uneasy – at the sudden despatch of his two mates, though he continued, for some stupid reason, trying to stir the doorman with his boots. When William pushed him off balance, he came out of it and hit back. But he wasn't a hundred per cent firm on his feet and, before he properly straightened, William let himself go a bit and sent a forceful hook to the chin.

He swung immediately round and hit the first man he had gone for who was coming back to help. Then he hit the ringleader again, and decided it was time to talk. He'd struck five blows, and the speed of his attack, dictated by his considered tactics on the matter, had calmed them down. A quick look told him there was no damage, so all he had to do was get rid of them and pull things to normal.

He tried to keep his breath quiet, though the hammers were going inside. Any hint of weakness might bring them back on to him. 'You've had your little game. Now get out. If you show your faces here again you'll end up at the copshop. You're lucky. Come on – out.'

They stood up. 'I'm sorry, sir,' one of them said.

He could afford to smile: 'So am I.'

At these moments – and such occupational hazards happened now and again, as they were bound to do – he felt most deeply himself. In a weird way he was part of them and their lives. Not that he relished scrapping. Nor did he particularly like that sort of customer, but it made him feel good for the rest of the evening because he'd met them on equal terms of strength and skill, and won. So he felt pleased with himself when he sat sipping a double whisky in his office writing a report on the incident in case anything further came of it.

He telephoned Albert to tell him what the week's takings had been, and when he mentioned the punch-up in a casual sort of way, Albert thought it so important that on Monday he was waiting at the office before he could get there himself.

'I was worried by your call, William. I haven't had an easy moment since you plugged it through.'

To be called by his first name unnerved him for a second. Then he was amused by the familiarity, and wondered why it hadn't come sooner. 'I had the situation under control in no time at all.'

'That's all right, then.'

Had he taken his life into his hands for this one to doubt that he could have done it quicker? They might have had razors, and slashed him. But they hadn't. In any case he had ways of dealing with that, too. If you reduce your tactics to an unthinking drill you have a ten to one advantage over them. They'd no doubt wondered at the gym why he was making those strange movements again and again.

Albert Monk stood up from the office chair, as if knowing he'd dropped a boo-boo. 'I'm not saying anything against you, Colonel. No fear. I'd give you another medal if I could for what you did. It's just that I'd like to have Jack Preston's guts for garters, for letting it get out of hand. Folded up like a bloody coward. Stopped me enjoying my Sunday dinner, and anybody as does that can go to the wall. The sooner the better.'

Preston had let the side down. It was remarkable how much he and Monk saw eye to eye.

'He can't ever be trusted,' Albert went on. 'You know what I'm saying?'

'He has to go.'

'You're a good manager, Colonel.'

He saw his game. 'You mean you want *me* to give him the push?'

'I haven't got time to hang around. Opening a place in Bolstead at the end of the week. So if you could pass on the news, and get another bloke in. It's no more than you're paid to do.'

'I'd like to dismiss the doorman, too.'

'Why, what's he done?'

'Left his post without permission. Came in to help in the scrimmage. Can't have that. I make my dispositions, and I expect them to be kept.'

He sat down again. 'I'd hate to have been a gunner in your platoon.'

'Battery.'

Albert Monk's eyes looked straight at him, and William knew that one false move on his part and he'd be out too. 'I've got complete confidence in you, Colonel.'

You'd bloody better have, he thought, angry at the un-

206

spoken threats sneaking around. 'I won't do it right away. I'll find a replacement first.'

'So you've got somebody else already?'

'It's more than my job's worth not to find a good man.' William took whisky and glasses from the cabinet behind his desk: 'I've always been a great believer in intelligent co-operation, and team-work. We'll have the perfect arrangement here before long.'

'Thanks to you.' Albert Monk lifted his glass, then leaned forward from his armchair and said in a confidential voice: 'You know, Colonel, I *was* in the army once, in the Pay Corps, but I got my papers because my health went to bits. I won't say what I got. Take too long. But I was turfed out, and then I had to make my own way in the world.'

'You made it very well.' William thought him healthy enough. Must have been drummed out via the glasshouse.

'I did.' He was proud of it. 'Worn't easy, though.'

'Nothing is.' He wondered how a master gunner came to be working for a foxy rogue like him. Yet there was something about him that he liked, perhaps because he also was a self-made man. Monk didn't know that William had come from a similar home as a boy, merely seeing him as the typical martinet army type – though a bit unusual for all that. Well, let him think so. You couldn't be too much of a mystery when involved with such a character.

Yet he found, in the village he lived in, that there were fewer respectable characters than he'd have thought, though the farmers were an industrious intelligent lot who worked the land more efficiently and with fewer men than practically any-where else in the world – so they told him. His nearest neighbour was Captain Wiggins who'd made a fortune taking guns to the Chinese Nationalists at the end of the war. All kinds of retired people lived there, and while some kept silent about their past, others jovially poured out tales as quickly as they could pour in the whisky.

Listening to them, William thought that far from being a nation of shopkeepers, the country was lapped around by a considerable fringe of ingenious and versatile freebooters, but marvellous people all the same, and such individuals that you could never tell which way they'd jump – unless they were in uniform.

There was, generally, a hard unambiguous gaze of loyalty and trust in their eyes, matched with a mouth that could always be relied on to do the unexpected. He'd seen it in all sorts of people and it had nothing to do with class because a person who came to mind in this respect was his one time batman Oxton. To think of him as a servant sounded too respectable and, somehow, demeaning. He was a lumbering, loyal, garrulous, brave king of the double makeshift who had allowed William to lead a tolerable life throughout the war.

The nearest Oxton had got to gunnery was gunpowder tea, though it wasn't by a long way the closest he'd been to danger. It was hard to say whether his steadiness under fire was because he had neither sense nor feeling, or whether his mother's photograph in his paybook had protected him from 'shot, shell and the pox'. It must have been a bit of each, and it slowly became clear during his talk with Albert Monk that a man with a long history of warfare and personal attachment to himself might not be a bad candidate for employment at the Entertainment Centre, if he could persuade him to shake Nottingham from his boots and come with his ageing mother down to Bingo-on-Sea.

CHAPTER SIXTEEN

Georgina's favourite occupation in the garden was dead-heading the roses. As long as it agreed with her he was grateful. He wasn't doing his share these days of helping to create that colourful harmony of lawns, flowers and fruits that must have been in her mind. She'd said: 'In a year or two we'll have it looking something *like*.' But he was so busy at the Rex Centre – as it was now called – that he couldn't put in more than an hour a week, and already the grass was needing another trim. Two acres was a lot to get looking something *like*, though the orchard and paddock could be left without spoiling the general appearance.

She stopped clipping. 'Home early today.'

It wasn't much after tea-time. 'I left things running smoothly. Like to get one evening off a week.'

She sat on the white-painted bench under the lounge window. 'Lovely to see you.'

He held her hand. It was amazing and marvellous how much more attractive she was than a few years ago. In her prime, as they say. Even better.

'Let's have a drink,' she said. 'I'm dying for one.'

'Whisky?'

'Hmm! Please, darling.'

He fetched the bottle, two glasses and a syphon. 'I'm going up to visit the old man this weekend. Feel like a run?'

It was three months since he'd seen him. Last year Charlie had been in hospital for an operation on the prostate gland, and he'd come out as if it had been his first superficial wound as a young soldier. He hadn't liked the hospital, and was tight-lipped about the fuss and babying, as if they'd made a concerted attack on his modesty.

While he hoped she'd have too much to do in the garden to say yes, he also wanted her company, because the atmosphere was less stiff when she came along. She liked his father's banter. Though never entirely at ease with her, Charlie behaved so well that she'd not so far perceived it. But William noticed it, as subtle as it was, not being his son for nothing. Also it was better having her with him because he was then able to maintain a certain distance from his father. And coming back they would leave late enough in the day to justify breaking the journey and booking into a hotel for the night – which situation she found so stimulating that in fact they got little rest.

But she didn't fancy going up to that dismal town and being a buffer zone for antagonisms flashing between William and his father. They thought they were being pious, filial and correct to each other, but after a couple of hours by the choky coal fire in the evening she felt like a worn out piece of rag.

There was another reason to stay behind. His nights away were rare since being at his bingo hall. In the army there'd been many, but they'd done her no good because she hadn't needed them. Now that she did, it was necessary to take advantage of any that came along. She didn't want to hurt him with the nights she spent in Town, and it was risky to say she was at her father's on the few occasions she'd done so. Not that Jacko would intentionally give her away.

'Do you mind if I *don't* go, darling?'

Take the A1 to Grantham, split northwest over the Trent towards Ashfield: a dullish journey, but maybe he'd pick up a hitch-hiker and chat a bit. 'Not at all. Stay here and take it easy.'

She smiled. 'I've so much to do, really.'

He was more uneasy at her decision to remain behind than on previous occasions. It was a flash of concern for them both that came and went, without reason. 'I'll go up Sunday, come back Monday. Only a couple of days.'

She pouted. 'I'll miss you. Always do when you go off like that.'

He was sorry he was going, and regretted having mentioned it, but he couldn't alter it now.

Beyond London, the worst of the journey was over. It was a hot summer's day and he drove steadily north. His jacket lay on the back seat and he enjoyed a carefree passage across the stretch of open land between the Thames and the Trent. His immaculate Rover had a clock in it, so he could time himself as he threaded towns and crossroads. A compass projected from the dashboard, but no matter how often it was compensated, the surrounding metal never let it read more than approximately correct, whereas he wanted to know his direction to the nearest degree, and test his skill at navigation. But unless he had a five mile run of straight road the needle hadn't time to settle down and give a bearing. And even then he knew he couldn't trust it. The only sure thing would be to shoot Polaris with a sextant at dusk like a sailor (he'd sometimes done it with a theodolite in the wastes of Libya), but having neither the instruments nor the necessity, since you couldn't get lost in England, it remained only a notion to help him along.

An altimeter recorded heights above sea level, a glorified barometer which wasn't much cop because it registered only to the nearest fifty feet, and there weren't sufficient heights to test it on outside the confines of Wales or the Peak – where he had no aim to go. Drifting, with the needle at a precise and steady sixty, along the quiet Sunday road, a long haul to Turkey or the Hindu Kush appealed to him. He thought it strange, to be drawn back to adventure after so long in the army, though it was only a daydream to keep him company on the lonely trip. He lit a cigarette, sunshine through the windscreen heating his face, eyes fixed on the tarmac, then flicking at the mirror to make sure his rear and flank were safeguarded before swinging to overtake some lorry or slow-coach in front.

At forty-odd life was halfway over, but he'd never felt better, young enough and strong enough and with sufficient experience to go with it. There was no reason why his health shouldn't stay good (touching wood from the match he'd lit his cigarette with) for another twenty or so years, which would make it a fine life and no mistake. His thick hair had a touch of grey at the sides, but having it cut short put most of it out of harm's way, and his teeth were holding firm, which all in all kept a spark in his eyes.

He stopped for petrol, and a woman whose car was pointing in the other direction looked at him in a way that seemed to make her feel good as well when he observed her with the same interested eye. She was in her early twenties, with long fine hair and a button nose, not pretty or beautiful, but young, and that was the crux of the matter. A woman of forty might not look at him twice, but he noticed these days how he often received a come-on from the younger sort – as if he'd got something a young man hadn't. In a way they were right, though he suspected they were drawn to the daddy in him. Not that he'd bother much about that if he got between their legs.

'Going far?'

'Only to Biggleswade.' She smiled. 'Just down the road.'

'Fine day for driving.'

She understood. 'Isn't it? Where are *you* going?'

He filled a pipe. 'Up north.'

'Cold there.'

'Not too much. I'll be on the loose when I get there.'

'Will you? I hope it keeps fine for you, then.'

He saw her ring. She was married.

'That'll be one pound eighteen, sir,' said the man who'd filled his tank.

There wasn't much point going beyond generalities, since she had a car of her own, and was going in the opposite direction, while he was set on a specific journey to see his father. If it weren't for the combination of these vital ifs, which made the difference between his heart being in it and not, things would have been on another level, and they might have started something which would have changed the world for them. They did a lot of smiling for such a short minute, and parted never to meet again, though he drove more cheerfully than for many a week.

By one o'clock he was sitting to lunch in the Angel and Royal at Grantham, two hundred miles from home with no more than forty to go. He'd always believed in the seven o'clock start. The more you did before midday the less there was to do in the afternoon. He was an early morning man because the night treated him kindly, and he thought maybe his dreams hadn't broken yet. He still had a few at night, and was never troubled going to sleep, nor getting up – though he'd done little but yawn since setting out. It was daydreams that plagued him, not those of the night.

The meal gave him energy. Oxtail soup, roast beef with potatoes and vegetables, and Yorkshire pudding, all of it smothered in rich gravy, then apple-pie and custard, with a large cup of pale black coffee. It cost the whole of ten bob with the tip, but it was worth it for the power of putting him back on his feet.

Or arse, he thought, crossing the Trent beyond Newark, feeling the smell of home again. It was an easy pull northwest to Ollerton, and then on to the Dukeries which he'd cycled in, mapped and explored on foot from almost as far back as he could remember, sometimes with his father pedalling beside him on his bike. He let down the windows and reduced speed so that he could get a whiff of the familiar air. As if to lay on a proper welcome a breeze blew clouds along and turned the green livid between the trees. Heavy summer vegetation was in full carpet. He felt like taking a room at the hotel in Edwinstowe, and staying a day or two on his own so that he could do a few walks in the Forest, coming back dog-tired at night to a meal, and as much ale as he could take before falling into a deep sleep.

But you couldn't sidestep into your dreams or yearnings. A soldier never looked back, at least not at anything he couldn't see. That which wasn't solid and obvious and movable was death, the end, nothingness. Or it was a brain without limits, the surrounding palisades suddenly down so that your faculties were free to spread in any of the six thousand four hundred ways of the circle. At which prospect you were frozen, staring while you rotted away. Or if you tried to act you only spun on your piece of tethering string.

The thought of it was like a vague but terrible dream that pushed its way back to him from somewhere or other. He was sweating and shaking, so stopped at a lay-by to smoke a cigarette till it went. He supposed all men were plagued with that sort of thing, and women too, though being a soldier it was easy to hold it off, or tear it away from yourself if it got a proper hold.

Having phoned his father to say he was on his way, he couldn't get out of it now. But even if his father and Doris no longer lived up here he'd have to make some excuse for a visit. In that sense he was giving in to his dreams. If you don't dream at night, you make bad ones that spin mischief in broad daylight.

Doris answered the door. 'Well, if it isn't our Billy himself! We thought you'd get here about now. Didn't we?'

Charlie came from the back porch with an inner tube on his arm. 'I was just mending this. Got to keep myself mobile, so the doctor says.'

I often feel older than he looks, and he's seventy-eight unless I've lost the power of calculation. In spite of his lined face he'd kept his height, which somewhat disguised the fact that he was so old. All his teeth were false, but filled his mouth in contrast to his slightly sunken cheeks. He wore glasses, and objected to them more than the teeth because whereas the teeth made him look younger, his glasses gave the game away that his sight wasn't good. Still, they allowed him to see fair distances again, so he felt they were worth it.

'A lot o' soldiers had glasses in the war,' William consoled him. 'One of my best gunners had horn-rims. Somebody sent the frames from home, and he got a pal from the signals to fit them in.'

'They feel strange, though,' his father said. 'But I expect I'll get used to 'em.'

He did, put them on as soon as he stepped out of bed in the morning, and didn't take them off till last thing at night. William handed Doris the bag containing whisky and cigars, and she put it by the coat stand, winking her thanks.

'Come in the parlour and see the tea she's laid. I'll finish my puncture later. Copped it on a thorn in the wood.'

It was the usual spread. He wasn't very hungry, though he wouldn't show himself unwilling at table. They'd think him either sick or sulky. She'd made a seed-cake, and opened a tin

214

of salmon, and they didn't do that every day. They watched him eat for a minute, before tucking in themselves, a sort of politeness that made him feel young again, and once more under their spell. He resented it, yet at the same time was glad he could still feel it.

Doris was a stocky old woman in glasses, her hair pure grey whereas Charlie's was white. She looked more worn, and he knew his father wasn't easy to live with.

'How are you getting on at that billiard hall?'

'Fine.'

He hadn't liked him resigning his commission. 'I never thought I'd still be alive when you came out of the army.'

'I wanted to live my own life for a change.'

He snorted because he'd no say in the matter. 'You can have your own life in the army. You could have stayed in till you was fifty with your rank. Longer, if you'd made brigadier. You're as restless as a blade o' grass. More than I was. I suppose it's just as well we aren't the same.'

William had taken a big step down in commanding a billiard hall, and Charlie was much more put out about it than Jacko. William was a nobody again, proved perhaps by his father writing 'Colonel Scorton' on the envelope of every letter he sent.

'We're expanding now – skittles, billards, bingo – and doing well, too!'

'As long as you're happy with it.'

Doris lifted the huge brown teapot with its rubber spout: 'He's got younger since he left the army. Took years off 'im, it has.'

'Happen so,' Charlie grumbled. 'Why didn't Georgina come up with you?'

'She wanted to, but she needed a rest from me more.'

'Is the marriage all right?' his father asked in his blunt way.

He found it hard to answer. 'We love each other as much as we ever did.'

'I'm glad to hear it.'

They sat in the parlour while Doris carried the tea things out to the kitchen. Charlie lit his pipe: 'I know you must make your own life, but there's no denying I was disappointed when you left the artillery.'

He said this every time he came for a visit. William was so used to it that it no longer bothered him. Nevertheless, there were occasional variations. 'You're a strong lad, and will have your own way, but I don't think I did wrong by getting you into the College o' Science. I had to find you a career, and I couldn't think of a better one. Even today it'd be hard to beat.

'Best thing you ever did,' he said, truthfully. 'I've a lot to thank you for.'

'Maybe you have. And don't think I didn't put a lot o' thought into it.'

William wondered why he was so solemn. His tone was vaguely upsetting.

'You were my only son, and you meant everything to me. I didn't want you to get any old job.' He held his hand tight, looked at him with his steady grey eyes. 'I didn't want you getting killed in a coal mine.'

'That wouldn't have happened to me.'

Charlie withdrew his hand, and sat upright. 'It did to some. A big lump o' rock pinned my mate to the floor. He couldn't move. We were cut off for four hours. He cried for help. I worked like a nigger, but the more I scraped the more it came down. They got him out alive, but he died in the ambulance. I joined the army, and my own father cut me off. Can a man do that to his own son? He did it to me. Maybe I'll meet him again one day, and there'll be an explanation. I sent you into the army because I didn't want you going down the pit, not even as an engineer. It cut me to the heart to send you off at fourteen, though I couldn't let you see it. You had your leaves and holidays though. You still stayed my son, so it was better for your generation than it was for mine.'

They went for a walk, and William noted that the town didn't look more worn than thirty years ago when he'd left it for the army. 'I expect they'll be pulling a lot of it down soon,' his father said, reading his thoughts. He walked with a stick, slower than usual. 'We'll go to the cemetery. It's not too far for us.'

William smiled at how he headed off the remark that such a trek might be too much for him. He'd have known better than to make it.

'Afternoon, Mr Scorton.' William recognised an elderly man who used to work at the grocer's his father shopped at.

'Afternoon.' He didn't stop, but touched his hat and passed on: 'Silly bugger. He drinks too much.'

'People have their little weaknesses.'

'They do,' Charlie said.

He was greeted by others along the street. There was no one in town who didn't know him. They nodded towards William as well, shy at acknowledging him. He would never have the same relationship to any town as his father had to Ashfield. He was almost at the age when his father settled there after the army. But he had made his home elsewhere and taken a different style of life. Yet how different was it, and how different was he? Maybe his father had felt just as alien when he came back. He'd stayed because he had to, and now he was known and respected as if he'd never been away. And he liked it, you could tell that. After twenty-odd years in the army he'd needed the protection of a small town like this. William could see that it had been the only place for him. The older you grew the more you understood your father. But he *was* different – he insisted to himself, without knowing why he needed to. He felt more fragile, more shattered than his father had been, yet in other ways stronger, more experienced. He'd spanned more. The fact that he had become a colonel had had more effect on him than he wanted to admit. He'd blown gaps into himself with his own guns. While still in the army it was all right. But now with no bounds to hold him, he didn't know where he belonged any more. You had to be a real man to live at ease while not knowing where you belonged. He liked it that way though, and treading the streets of old Ashfield with his father made him conscious of it for the first time.

They walked up the winding lane to the cemetery. 'Do you visit this place often, dad?'

'Once a month. I like getting out for some fresh air.'

That was his way of saying it was a duty which had to be done. 'I do sometimes come on the bike, but I have to push it up the hill a bit. Mind you, the ride's a treat going down, on a good day.'

He noticed how his father's walk quickened after passing the gates. 'This visit's impromptu like, for your sake. I'll come again on Wednesday with some flowers.' He refilled the vase at the tap and tried to revive the wilting roses. 'Do you remember when we came up here that raw day and made a compass survey?'

'What I do recall is the bag of cakes you took out of your haversack. I was frozen and starved.'

Charlie laughed, and a recently bereaved family looked disapprovingly in his direction. 'I tried to harden you in them days. But I took care you had your grub.'

William was glad to see him happy. It pleased him to observe how simple and good his father was. 'I remember the survey though. We were proud of that.' He could recall the smell of various inks when opened bottles were set on the parlour table, from which the cloth had been removed and carefully folded.

'I've still got that map,' his father said. 'We signed it in the bottom right hand corner as if we were *pukha* surveyors. Take it away with you, when you go.'

A desolate feeling came over him. He didn't want it. Yet he did want it. What was he trying to say by giving it to him? 'Are you sure?'

He grunted. 'Of course I am.' He would have to take it, whatever he felt. 'Pass it on to your own son.'

The willow tree by the corner almost overgrew the chapel. 'What did your mother say when your father cut you off from house and home?'

'When I went for a sowjer? She died too. She'd already died. But we met up a time or two. Your mother never cuts you off. I smashed the family to pieces when I joined the army, but it must have been smashed already if it only took that to do it. My father was already smashed as well, and he used me to finally smash him. I reckon he was just about ready to use anybody. So I didn't waste any regrets on him or the family when I joined up. I took care to see mother, and get the odd note to her through Doris. It was the only thing I could do, you see, and I was always glad I did it. I had too much to think about once I'd signed on, and it wasn't about the thing that got me there. I had my own life to lead, and I led it to the hilt like the rest of my comrades. All for one and one for all. If I had my life over again I wouldn't alter a minute of it. I hate people who belly-ache and regret things. Them as looks back and regrets all they've done haven't even got to the truth of things. We're born with the truth in our hearts, I'm sure of that. It's the only thing we've got to thank God for, as far as I can see.'

His father was open in what he said, but he was sad to hear him talking like this. Charlie leaned on his stick: 'Let's get back to the house. I'm developing the gift of the gab as I get older.'

William took his arm: 'I'm beginning to feel like a drink.'

He turned to the grave, stood stiffly, and gave his long dead wife a military salute. 'Time to go, Will.'

Why don't you wipe a tear away just for old times' sake? He smiled, but didn't care to say it out loud.

CHAPTER SEVENTEEN

Looking from the window, he found the simple mechanism of the dawn beautiful to behold. A swathing pathway of pale orange lifted under a lid of blue. The sun was a pinprick to the side of a tall tree, but instead of reaching straight up it shifted behind the copse, and a minute later came out the other side, to the right and south, and ascended in a slope to the dark grey horizon of the Pennines. Its light was so bright the eyes were dazzled, and he was forced to move away.

His father had already cooked him a breakfast of sausages and eggs. 'You can't drive south on nowt.' He busied himself with a huge pile of cheese and potted-meat sandwiches, and wrapped them in grease-proof paper. 'Have you got a flask?'

He fetched it from the car.

'I'll fill it with coffee.' It was liquid stuff, which Charlie liked because of the label on the bottle. It would taste good when stopping for a scoff in a lay by.

'Where's your knapsack?'

'I didn't bring one. Those days are over.'

'You never know,' Charlie said merrily. 'If there's a war, they'll have you back.'

He'd like to see me in for another four years because he thinks I might end as a brigadier.

'Happen they'd call me up as well. The world don't alter. It's got better since I was born, but it ain't changed in its basics. I'll put your stuff in a carrier-bag.'

He drove south at half past seven. After the red dawn the weather hadn't yet closed in, and it was open and fresh as he cruised through the tatty remnants of Sherwood Forest. He always wondered why he didn't stay at home for a week and really get the feel of it again. But, apart from his work, he couldn't get Georgina out of his mind.

It often seemed there was no love between them. When she wanted to make love, after they'd not done it for a while, she couldn't approach him through affection but only with a kind of hate. He felt her mood, and so couldn't relax to take her in his arms and soothe her, which was what she wanted. So she had to fight like a she-wolf and tear love from him, though when they ended up in bed it was a marvellous and mutual exploding of sex. He sometimes loathed her afterwards because she was only able to break down the barriers in this way, and with such dislike in the air, days might go by before they could make love again. His mood affected her and kept them apart so long that she was forced to go through her she-wolf act once more. But the rhythm was often broken, proving there was still a sense of collective self-preservation floating around. He smiled as he drove along. Sometimes he detested the life and wanted everything to be over and done with. But he was deeply in love, and when the mutual ripping to pieces was absent, as it mostly was, after all, they could laugh together and say that their violent quarrels were simply another way of making love.

He went over Red Hill and into Nottingham, via Arnold and Basford, picking his way through to the Market Square by instinct and memory, an easy process because traffic was mostly green double-deckers packed with people going to work. It certainly was better than before the war, with the factories working full-tilt and no grinding poverty any more. He parked his car so as to buy a *Times* and some cigarettes, then drove through the Meadows to Wilford toll bridge, over the Trent to Clifton.

At the housing estate, he knocked on Oxton's back door, hoping he hadn't set off for work. His luck was in because the blinds were drawn, though it was late for an old soldier like him to be still in bed. A neighbour emptying her teapot into a rose bush stared at him, and was about to say something helpful when bolts were heard being drawn from inside.

For a moment he did not recognise the man who stood before him, with a week's growth of black and grey stubble, sunken cheeks, and eyes like lollipops. He wore a filthy shirt, stained and baggy trousers and split carpet slippers.

'Oxton?'

'Yes, sir?'

He had trouble standing up. It was obvious that a disaster had hit him. He seemed shell-shocked. 'I called to see you.'

'Come in, sir.' He stood aside for him to pass into the kitchen. There was a stench of rotting clothes, decaying food, and a foulness he'd rather not give a name to. He certainly didn't fancy sitting down in the place.

'I hope you won't think I'm being nosy, Oxton, if I ask what's happened?'

He pushed some clothes off a chair. 'Please sit down, sir.'

He took up his offer.

'My mother died ten days ago.'

'I'm sorry. That's damned awful, Oxton.' It was bad to depend too much on somebody else and expect them to live for ever. But he felt Oxton's grief, and was silent till he spoke.

'It hit me hard.'

'Well, it would, wouldn't it? You were a good son.'

'She was a good mother, sir.'

'You've nothing to regret, or feel guilty about.'

It was a far cry from his unreal wish on the way up of staying a few days in Sherwood Forest. 'You can't live like this, you know.'

Oxton stood straight. He was well this side of sixty but the blow had put years on him. If he came back to life they would fall off just as easily. 'Don't seem worth living.'

'She was a very old lady,' William said. 'She wanted a rest. People do, you know. That's all it is.' He was surprised at himself for spouting such comfort.

There were tears in his eyes. 'But I miss her. It's hard, sir. She was my whole life.'

William passed the handkerchief that had been ironed last night by Doris. 'I'll stay a while, Oxton, and we'll talk. Is there any food in the house?'

'Nothing.'

'It's my turn to go foraging now. Sit down a while.'

He went to the car and came back with sandwiches, coffee, and the brandy flask halfway full. He cleared a space on the table. 'Let's get stuck into this. I've just had breakfast, but I'll take a taste of the coffee.'

He passed a sandwich. 'Come on, wolf it down as if the battery had been in action a day and you hadn't been able to loot anything. I know that would be impossible, but let's imagine it. We'll have a sip of this first, but only a sip.' He washed two glasses at the sink and poured brandy into them. 'We'll drink a toast to your mother, and to mine as well if you like, because she's dead too. Then you'll have something to eat.' He passed a glass: 'To your mother. She was a marvellous woman. And to you as well. You're a good chap, Oxton. Always were.'

'To my mother. And to yours, sir.' His hand shook, and more tears came to his eyes, but he knocked the brandy back in one gulp.

William poured coffee. 'And now this. Then eat your fill.'

'I don't deserve it, sir.'

'You deserve what you get, Oxton. You always get back what you give.'

He spoke such platitudes because he knew they were what Oxton needed to hear. But he also meant what he said. 'Now let's have no more nonsense.'

'All right, sir.'

He opened the curtains back and front. 'We want light.'

'I feel better already.'

'Without light we shrivel up. We're like the flowers. Even you, Oxton.'

'God must have sent you, sir.'

'Don't be bloody silly.' It was nice of him to say so. Maybe he had. 'If your mother knew you were letting yourself go like this she'd give you a piece of her mind.'

'You're right. She would.' He wiped more tears with the handkerchief and took a long drink of coffee. 'I couldn't help it.'

'I don't suppose I'd be able to, either. But that's the end of it. You can remember her without killing yourself. In fact if you died you wouldn't be able to remember her, would you? It's only the living who can remember the dead, as far as we know.'

He smiled – immense progress. 'I never thought of it like that.'

'Well, now you can.'

'I went a bit batchy, I suppose.'

He reached over and gripped his shoulder. 'Once a gunner, always a gunner. You remember that, Oxton?'

'Yes, sir.'

'When you've finished your early morning tiffin I have a proposition to make, but first I want you to wash, shave and change your clothes. You have a suit?'

'Yes, sir. Everything clean. Haven't touched it since the funeral.'

'Then we'll talk, because I have a job for you, if you'll come and live down south. So get scrubbed while I read my paper.'

Half an hour later Oxton came back wearing a navy-blue pin-striped suit, a clean shirt, a well-knotted tie and highly-polished shoes. William laid out the plan: 'And I can't say it clearer than that, not even with coloured inks and pencils on the best squared paper. It's an operations order, if you want to look at it that way. You must pack up here. Do you have any money?'

'I've got two hundred pounds in a mattress upstairs. And I haven't collected mother's insurance yet. Nearly a thousand. I paid it for years.'

'That's good then. You can get a flat if you like, and work for me as a doorman, and maybe later on something better. You're just the chap I've been looking for. Blokes like you are a bit scarce in this world, I'm finding out.'

'I'll need a week or two before I can wind things up.'

'Don't take too long. Once we move, we move. In the meantime, feed yourself three times a day. And clean up the mess. You'll need to get yourself fit.'

'That's no problem, sir. I'm already fit and strong. I'll walk a few miles a day. There's some lovely country around here.'

'I know you're in good shape, or I wouldn't have asked you. But tune yourself up for the job. Calibrate yourself. A couple of pints a day won't hurt you, either. Get your old build back.'

His father would have approved of his tone, though he

might have laughed at him behind his back. Oxton, with a sparkle in his eyes, would inwardly wink at it as well. He himself thought it time to shut up and go, leave him to fend on his own, and hope he would follow in a week or two. You couldn't tell. The world had been pulled from under him. But he sat a few hours more, to get him back into life.

'I want you to promise, though. I'm relying on you.'

'You have my word, sir,' Oxton said.

prick, then finished at him behind his back. Caton, with a
cane like his own, would throw the whole of it as well. He may
well dislike it then so much and go along like an old man for
once, and know he would follow in a week or two. You couldn't
tell. The wheel had been pulled from under him. But he was a
few hours away. He wrapped himself more.
A vast cold gnawing was working on him.
The past was vast, too. Caton had.

CHAPTER EIGHTEEN

Leaves fell like green snow. Those underfoot had an autumn
smell. They were dead, but scattering as he walked. You'll
soon be as dry and brown as these. He eyed the distant trees
behind. The idea brought down snow inside him. Why be in
such a hurry to get the years spinning? He was only forty-four.
Move, he thought, turning at an angle of ninety degrees and
setting across the park-like field towards the house whose
lights glowed in the lower windows.

She held his arm as they got near the gate, and breathed her
warm breath against him when they stopped. 'You know I love
you.'

He stepped away. 'But if you ever see him again I promise
I'll kill him, then I'll kill you, and afterwards I'll kill myself.
I mean it.'

What if he did? The poor fish had opened a love letter
addressed to her bank. They'd sent it on by mistake, and he'd
unlatched it with the bright new paperknife she'd given him
last birthday. He wished he hadn't. There were things it was
better not to know, for her sake, but mostly for his. He hadn't
time to worry about such rubbish and do his work efficiently.
With guts torn to pieces nothing was possible.

Her voice was hardened by his rejection when she'd tried to
make things up. 'You can have a divorce if you like.'

'We can go on as before, if you don't see him again.'

She was silent.

It'd be a hard fight, one way or another, working all hours at
the entertainments centre. It was boom time, years of expan-
sion and of never having had it so good. People might not have
too much money but they were willing enough to spend it on
bingo, billiards, booze and skittles, wanting to live easy and gay

after the grim decade since the war.

They went into the house. 'You've no idea what it means to me.'

'It means quite a bit to me, as well,' he answered.

She'd never expected such bitterness. 'I thought you were a worldly man.'

Laughter echoed from the mess: wife went off the rails, but there are plenty more women, don't you know? Yes, for other men. They sat in the lounge, and he poured two large glasses of sherry. Just as he was beginning to understand her, the balloon went up. 'I'm human like the rest of them.'

Her affair was with the same married chap she'd broken with when they first met. His wife had been dead two years and Georgina had encountered him in Leatherhead while shopping for her father. It had been going on more than a year. She came out with it when he tackled her about the letter. Maybe there'd been others, but he wasn't concerned with what he didn't know. She said there hadn't been, but who could tell? He laughed: maybe you weren't a man unless you went through this, only marvelling that it hadn't happened before. She'd always had time and opportunity, especially since he'd left the army and occupied himself with Albert Monk's entertainment empire.

'I know you're human,' she smiled, 'that's why I love you.'

'Everybody is. But you've been caught out.'

'That god-damn bloody awful little shit of a bank clerk!'

'Must have been his first day on the job. Can't you get him the sack? Australia's too good for him.'

They'd got back just in time from their heart to heart talk, for rain was teeming against the windows. She was cut by his mockery. 'You aren't going to ruin *my* life.'

'Nor you mine.' He hadn't wanted it to be like this. He felt the full push of black rage behind his eyes. His father had never hit a woman. But he couldn't believe it, otherwise where did he get this blind urge to punch her stupid head? The smell of powder and make-up tightened his will. He stood over her. Her blowsy tall beauty left her for a moment as she turned pale. Her lips thinned and hardened.

His hand spun the glass of sherry from her. If it was true

about his father never having been violent to his wife, then here was something he couldn't blame him for. His pure unalloyed hatred was responsible for the second movement which caught her face square on. He plunged into the maelstrom, and hit her again.

She didn't move, or cry out. There were tears on her cheeks. Then she walked quickly to the wide bay of the window. He picked up his drink and swallowed all of it. How had he got into this black dream? Found his wife knocking on with another bloke, and punched her about like a collier. He couldn't believe it. There was a terrible vein of achievement in it. He trembled at the shock.

She was like a statue, her big form facing away. The Siamese cat stalked in and brushed its tail against her stockings.

'Where does he live?' he demanded. His address was also care of a bank. Having no wife to hide it from, he was concealing it from his children. 'I'll find him, though.'

He'd look up the name in electoral registers and telephone books, launch a mad hunt to get him and bash his smug face in. He had a revolver and ammunition, and would take that. No he wouldn't. Is this how an officer and a gentleman behaves? He smiled, sharp enough to cut his throat. Ignore the whole thing, as if it hadn't happened. If she was in love there was nothing he could do. But if she made it too obvious he would leave, for to put up with it and to know about it was both demeaning and disgusting. He remembered all they had suffered together.

'I love *you*,' she wept, hands at her face.

'Like hell, you do.' How stupid to think she could love two men at the same time. She says it to stop me leaving, because if I did I expect the other bastard would drop her as well. Maybe that was what she wanted. Nobody would be the loser if they split three ways.

'I loved you,' he said.

She turned to him, hands down, as if interested in him again after a long indifference. He caught the genuine curiosity in her voice. 'You don't love me any more?'

He was amused at her sudden feeling for eternity. 'I don't feel anything for you at the present.'

'Well,' she cried, a defiant tone of hysterical regret, 'I'm not

228

having my life dominated by a worm like you.'

He sat down.

The door slammed, and slammed again as she crashed her way into the kitchen. Like a bloody rhinoceros. He wondered why a stupid thing like this had to bring the whole world on to them.

She came back along the corridor, went upstairs, pulled a precious Damascus plate from the wall – a present from her father – and sent it splintering on to a radiator. The bedroom door thumped. She'd gone in to pack. The end had come. Every sound cut into his ribs. The gravelling scrape of the wardrobe doors told him she was reaching in for dresses. He saw her arms stuffing them into a case, that lovable epitome of clumsiness trying to make them fit. Would she take the car? She'd go to her father's, then maybe to her fancyman's. What would it be like, living alone? Since this smash had obviously been on the cards he should have stayed in the army, where it would have been cushioned by a party in the mess. Now he had to face the flood alone. The worst mistakes come from what at first seems a wonderful thing to do. He'd be on his own for the first time in his life. The thought put him in awe and dread, but he was glad it had come so that he could get out of it as soon as possible. He liked the idea. Let the world fall on him. Life was a suffocating blanket. He'd rip everything to feel alive again. But his hand was shaking. It was the one he had hit her with, and his fingers ached.

She was coming downstairs, her tread so heavy that he pictured her with two weighty cases. He was wrong. The door burst open, and she stood before him, trembling from her words: 'This is my house as much as yours. If you think I'm going so that you can have it to yourself you're mistaken, you vile pig. Half the money came from my side, and I've worked just as hard to make it liveable. I'm not going to leave it to you. If you're such a little boy that you can't go on living with your whore of a wife then that's your problem. I'm staying put. *You* can do as you bloody well like. I thought I'd married a real man, not somebody who goes off his rocker at a little thing like this. Pack up and go whenever you like.'

Here was a different situation. The fact was he'd no intention of going. This was where he lived, and where he'd stay. He worked in the neighbourhood. After three years the entertainment centre was thriving. He'd built it into a business that ran on castors. And now she wanted to get rid of him, to smash up his life.

She was weeping, the great soft bitch. He felt the blunt knife of misery shifting around in his stomach. Would an age ever come when you didn't feel like howling at such a thing? 'We don't have to get so upset at it, do we?'

If he walked out he'd have to say goodbye to his job as well. What was the point of thinking about that, anyway? To get a flat in town would only prolong the misery. If the biggest item of his life went smash it was better to pull down the rest of it and bury everything. But he loved her – whatever that was – and couldn't move.

CHAPTER NINETEEN

She paced to the black frames of the uncurtained windows, then came and knelt at his feet, an arm along the arm of the chair he sat in. 'You look so miserable, my love.'

He laughed at her sense of melodrama, always based upon a broad appreciation of the obvious. 'You don't look the picture of happiness yourself.'

She had a wish to be free of it all, to step aside from the weighty torment, and having said as much to herself, the possibility of it seemed feasible – though she knew it would overpower her again at the next clash. But for the moment she was tired of it, and said: 'My make-up's all awash.'

He too was glad of the relief. 'Mop it off.'

'It's terrible to love someone, and not be loved back.' She wasn't entirely able to let go.

'We both know how it feels. That's a big step forward. We can wallow in it when we're living in our separate bolt-holes.'

'A nut in a bolt-hole,' she punned.

He groaned.

'Two,' she said.

He became flippant. 'When I'm there I'll surround myself by my army, a whole division for my self-defence.'

'Tell me a story,' she said.

'I will. And you'll join in. My division won't be the usual three brigades of four battalions, with a thousand infantry, plus guns and what-not. Oh no. I'll break up my division into twelve composite regiments with two battalions of nearly five hundred men in each. Each regiment (I've got to be precise, so you'll know what you're in for) will have a battery of five guns attached to blast your army when it comes out of its dugouts. Each one regiment of 1,300 men will have two machine-guns, ammunition column, cavalry detachment to keep me well-informed, signals to hold my units under firm control, commissariat to feed us, field company to dig us in, transport to shift us rapidly about, ambulances to pick up the bits – a whole division of twenty thousand, same as you, but twelve highly trained quick moving composite regiments, imbued with the hit and run spirit to attack lines of communication, fight at night, live off the land, melt away when the enemy comes on in strength, destroy his rearguards, and hit when he's over-extended. In reserve I've got an HQ battle group of over two thousand men with sixteen guns. Bump into any of this stuff and your out of date nit-witted battalions with their separate artillery brigades won't know what hit them – my pretty queen and commander in chief of the enemy forces.'

She stroked his trouser leg. 'I'll pick off your so-called composite regiments by superior manoeuvre. I'll close in on your guns till you've got nothing left and you run up the flag of surrender. I'll bring everything I've got against the weakest part of your forces, and roll up your demoralised units one by one. I'll make your whole army prisoners, and then capture *you*, and carry you off to my castle in the middle of my capital city.'

'Like hell you will. The war hasn't begun. You haven't even mobilised.'

'Yes I have. Annual manoeuvres have just finished and instead of the soldiers going home they're moving by devious and parallel routes towards your frontier.'

'You sly bitch!'

'You forget that my father taught me all about strategy and tactics when I was ten. Afterwards I crept into the library and read his books. You called me a bitch, so I break off diplomatic relations.' The leg bent underneath her was going to sleep, so she shifted it: 'My army's already on the frontier, moving on your capital.'

'I'll remind you,' he said, 'that I don't have a capital. Any town of my country will do. Communications are primitive. There's no nerve centre, which gives great advantages, because there's no place I can fall back on and take refuge in, and no place for you to make for. Come over the frontier if you like. You don't even know where my army is.'

'Do *you* know where it is ?'

'Its dispositions are secret. It's organised to harrass the enemy until he – or she – has lost both nerve and numbers. Then I go in for the great mopping-up and capture its fair commander. I'll take her to my secret lair and keep her a prisoner for the rest of her life.'

'While you're getting sentimental,' she said, 'my advanced brigade has captured the first town across your frontier.'

'I set fire to it,' he said, 'before I pulled out. And the bridge across the wide fast-flowing river was blown up by my sappers.'

She poured two glasses of sherry. 'Mine put out the fire. They're repairing the bridge. In fact they're building another because one was never enough anyway in your rotten tyranny.'

'My first composite regiment has its guns trained on it from the opposite hills. Its machine-guns mow down your sappers as they try to get pontoons into position.'

'You plan too much,' she smiled.

'The first quality of a good soldier.'

'You aren't a soldier any longer.'

'I am. War is too complicated a business to be left to your wife. My composite regiments are peppering your infantry crossing the river. They're suffering terrible casualties.'

She was exultant: 'All my seventy-two guns, plus four heavies, are blasting your so-called composite regiment to smithereens. Its five guns are gone.'

'Uncomfortable,' he admitted darkly. 'But if there's one thing my men can do, it's dig. Surprisingly few have become casualties. And my guns are intact because each one constantly changes position so that yours don't have a chance to register. One had its wheel broken, but it's been replaced.'

'All the same,' she said, 'I've a whole brigade of four thousand across. I'm on my white horse on Hill 231 Feet watching the field artillery go over, covered by the heavies and howitzers. My men are swarming up the hills on your side. I'll have you in a few more hours.'

'We'll see about that,' he said grimly. 'Don't you wonder

233

where my other eleven composite regiments are? I'll be the one to have you. Your troops are forming their bridgeheads but mine are falling back in good order. I can see them from my observation post on Hill 232 – Metres. Shot and shell is chucking soil around me, but that's no problem, because I always live as if I've nothing to lose.'

'Poor thing!' she mocked. 'My grandmother was a wise old dear who said that if you sleep on the floor you can't fall out of bed. She was the only person I ever loved, which explains why I'm in such a bad way. I can't even detach myself from her, never mind my own parents. I've yet to start on them, I suppose.'

'You'd better stop babbling,' he told her. 'While you're throwing your army across the river a couple of my regiments have nipped over to your side twenty miles upstream and are attacking you from the rear. They've captured the guns, and two of your battalions have panicked. You'd better get off your hill and high horse or I'll have your knickers yet!'

'What a vile enemy you are,' she said angrily. 'No chivalry. No finesse. No charm!'

'All's fair in love and war,' he grinned.

She walked across and drew the curtains, then turned off the light and left one table lamp shining. They sat on the floor and faced each other: 'My reserve brigade was expecting trouble from a cunning devil like you, so I sent them against your flank. They not only restored the situation but pushed you back. My guns were recaptured and we took some of yours. My sappers blew them up. We pursued your two regiments, pinned one against the river bank, and wiped it out. The communiqué is still coming in. A débâcle. I expect a few of your low-class scoundrels managed to swim to the other side. I'll strip you of everything if it goes on like this.'

A sixty-pounder shell burst in front of his dugout. His maps were in tatters. 'Your teeth are too big,' he said.

'Yours legs are too short,' she laughed. 'I'll beat you again and again till you come crawling to me on your hands and knees.'

'You're a whore.'

'You're a craven bastard.'

'I'll fight to the end,' he said. 'The remnants of my battalion got over the river. After a few days they'll be back in the fray. The other battalion is still on your side of it, so watch your communications. Meantime I've pulled my OP back a few miles. Two out of your three brigades are over, but before they reach the fertile central plain of my country they've got to cross a range of barren mountains.'

'Only ten miles wide. And there's a pass through them. The first brigade is already at the head of it and my pickets are crowning the heights on either side.'

'My scouts tell me that the four battalions of your brigade are at the narrowest point of the pass. Night falls quickly, and five of my composite regiments are in position – two to the north, two to the south, and one blocking to the east. That means twenty-five guns are firing onto your hemmed-in brigade and causing utter confusion. Those men crowning the heights were mine, not yours, wearing your uniforms and signalling the all-clear. You ran into my trap.'

Her face was rigid and pale at his trick.

'The carnage is indescribable,' he went on in a matter-of-fact tone. 'The night is filled with gunflashes and a smothering rattle of small-arms fire. You're locked in the ravine and we're dislodging boulders with dynamite. My sappers planned it in peacetime. I've sent two other regiments to the river to stop you reinforcing your trapped brigade or trying to break through and relieve them.'

She pulled herself together. This wouldn't do. He was talking stuff and nonsense. Her entire brigade might be trapped, and seven hundred men lost, but many were rallying on higher ground where they weren't so exposed, and which gave them a better field of fire. In fact a counterattack had driven so many of his men off the heights that at one place *he* was in a fix.

Dawn glowed over the battlefield. Things weren't so bad as they had been, but her brigade was still trapped.

'*Your* losses aren't small,' she said. 'The two units you sent towards the bridge were mauled. My second brigade is moving along the heights to the north and south.'

He still had the situation under control, but thought it

prudent to pull his seven investing regiments from the battle and send them in different directions over the plain. In spite of his well-planned ambush she had broken through to the heart of his country.

It was difficult to disengage in daylight. One false move could mean total defeat. It was hazardous to break off fighting without being pursued and overwhelmed. While the first battalion of each regiment stood as a rearguard, the second battalion retreated a mile or so in good order, then stopped and prepared its defences while the first battalion retreated through it. When darkness came his force had dispersed in safety.

He sat by his camp fire: she had kept up the offensive so far, forcing him across the river and breaking through the mountains in spite of the fact that their forces were equal.

'So much for your composite regiments,' she scoffed.

It was her tradition versus his improvisation, and the time had come to show what he could do. Both armies were now in the wide open spaces, with no more rivers nor mountains to cross, a rolling land of small streams, occasional woods, well built villages and towns, and hills of no more than a few hundred metres.

She took off her blouse. 'It's so damned hot. I send three hundred mounted infantry in all directions and can't find any part of you. Your country's empty. Hollow. There's nothing there. That's why you pack in at the first blow. My three brigades move twelve miles a day on parallel lines, and meet nothing. The population is sullen, and unhelpful. What sort of a war is this? It's a poor general who leaves me high and dry. That's the story of my life. I was born and built to be in the midst of battles where I could do my stuff. You bloody well know what I mean!'

'While you're raving,' he said, 'you've had the brigade wiped out that was guarding your lines of communication. My ten composite regiments with fifty guns obliterated it. My reserves are at the pass blocking the route back to your country. Even to reach the mountains you have to fight through all my regiments, and you've only got eight battalions. You might as well surrender to save further bloodshed.'

He drew a map on a large sheet of paper to emphasise the gravity of her situation, while she went to the kitchen for a tray of food and a bottle of champagne. 'You're trying to demoralise me,' she pouted when she came back. 'You think you're a master of psychological warfare, but you're not. When a teacher tried to humiliate me in front of the others at school, I didn't let it upset me. In fact I was able to think more clearly after the effort of staying calm. Then I turned out my best work, because I'd been given something to fight against.' She passed him a sandwich: 'That pounding of my communications brigade cost you a lot of casualties. In fact you lost a whole regiment!'

He opened the champagne. They drank a toast to victory, and he took off his shirt: 'One of my regiments at the western end of the pass has sent its guns to shell your two bridges over the river. Three regiments are over it and moving on your supply dumps beyond. One of them is already raiding into your country.'

She took off her brassière. Her bosom was magnificent, and he couldn't wait for peace to break out. 'During the night I force-marched one brigade north, and another south,' she told him, 'then fought a rearguard action in daylight. Caught you napping. They avoided the pass and crossed the river at two points, then closed the pincers on one of your composite what-nots and wiped it out. My remaining six battalions are now safely back on my own frontier.'

His trousers slid from under him. The champagne was half gone. Only his underpants were left. 'That won't save you. I'll pursue you relentlessly. My HQ group is bombarding your frontier fortress, and my regiments have now entered *your* country.'

It was a lovely country, ripe at harvest time, extensive, with beautiful soft tints, temperatures, indolence and fleshy undulations. It was a land of peace, its people only wanting to work and enjoy the passing years. He must capture her before winter.

'What's wrong with your arm?' she exclaimed. 'Why is that bandage around your head?'

'A couple of shell splinters got me. Couldn't resist being up front with my men. I often think I'd rather be a private soldier, going into danger with friends I've had so long I know I can rely on them to the end.'

'You're getting past it,' she laughed. 'The responsibility's wearing you down. Why don't you go into hospital, and let a younger man take over?'

'You mean a less experienced, less astute person? No bloody fear. Anyway, they're in a bit of a flap down at your HQ. I'm closing in on your capital from all directions.'

There were tears in her eyes. 'The decrepit but faithful garrison is preparing to defend it, till I arrive on my white horse, riding with the vanguard, stiff-lipped, fatigued, my guns and wagons throwing up dust as they race along the roads and through the fields.'

'I'm impatient,' he said, 'but I've learned to wait. My binoculars see the pennants of your palace still flying, and puffs of smoke from an antique cannon. Its shell blows up a peasant's barn in front of me. The heavy guns of my HQ group are unlimbering left and right. I send messages to my regiments to attack the city. Others will rush to hold you up on the road. I face both ways.'

She was lying naked across the carpet, an Afghan specimen that daddy's punitive column had brought back from the North West Frontier. 'You're a bullying hypocrite,' she said. 'I'll never surrender. My guns reply to yours. My cavalry are bravely fighting in front. My whole brigade is going forward over the ridge, down into the valley, and up the long green slope towards your earthworks halfway to the skyline. I'm leading my last eight thousand, and if we don't break through, I'll die with my brave army.'

'Your city fell without a shot, and the regiment that took it is being sent to reinforce my line against your last attack. I went into your palace, found your private apartments, pressed your silk pillows to my face. I handled your underwear, and ran my sword through two score of underskirts hanging on a rack. I lingered for a moment at your dressing table.'

She screamed and clutched him. 'A man in front of me was blown up. His blood splashed over me. Horrible. Warm. My men went down from your artillery.' She drew away, a smile of triumph: 'But we broke through! It's a rout. Your soldiers are running. We cut them down. It was marvellous to see them run!'

He took off his pants, and reached out to her. She pushed him away: 'There was open land in front. We were exhausted but exultant, and marched towards my capital. Then we saw your fresh regiments spread over the horizon and coming towards our depleted brigades, your front longer than ours, and guns already firing. We were outflanked.'

'It was the end,' he said. 'Your army knew it. They made a final charge. It was magnificent, but it wasn't love.'

He kissed her tears away. 'You lose today, I lose tomorrow. As soon as I saw you and fell in love I knew it was war to the death.'

'Don't let's kill each other.' Her hands were touching him in every place, kissing him as he entered her palace, which proved much easier in the wake of blood and slaughter.

CHAPTER TWENTY

Business was good even in winter months, because people would drive from twenty or thirty miles away to spend an evening at the Rex Centre. William had advertised in local papers, and word of mouth had done the rest. His best move had been to make Oxton his chief doorman. He would discreetly push any rowdy gang on to the street with minimum fuss, saying; 'Come on, lads, let's have no bother, or I shall have to take you in hand,' so that even the hardest of them went.

If Oxton had been provided with camp bed and sentry box he would have kept the place under observation twenty-four hours a day. But at midnight he locked up and drove to his flat on the outskirts of town where his landlady, he told William, looked after him to the fullest possible extent. Now a middle-aged woman, she had come to England as a refugee from Germany before the war and, Oxton added with a wink, was a wonderful sort who hinted now and again that she wouldn't be too shocked if he asked her to marry him. Lucky Oxton! A simple man of all the virtues who demanded nothing of life, but who nevertheless got back what he'd put into it. Asking no questions, he received no self-destroying answers.

Oxton was hardly able to believe his luck. 'You mean that when you're not here I'm to be completely in charge?'

'Even when I am, you're my second-in-command.'

It was a big responsibility and he'd have to be careful:

'It's like having a commission, sir.'

Oxton stood in front of his desk as if he'd brought a report to the orderly room. William checked a smile, keeping his face squared-up to the weight of his words. 'It's not a cushy billet, Oxton. I want somebody I can rely on a hundred per cent.

You'll have to see that we open and close on time, that the doormen are in their places, and that Miss Callender isn't bothered by rowdies. It's most important to keep things in order.'

With his smart suit, well-ironed shirt, tie fixed in place with an old regimental pin, and shining boots just big enough to make him appear aggressive and steady as he kept the various halls and alleys of entertainment under constant watch, and with thin hair stranded back over his impressive head, Oxton was a different person to the man William had found wrecked with grief in Nottingham a few years before. He stood up straight, his formidable appearance sobered by a heavy opal ring on his left index finger and a watch-chain decorating his waistcoat.

'I'm familiar with the drill, sir.'

'I know you are.'

The long-ago life with his mother, still the bedrock of his being, had dimmed. Memory replaced grief. She'd been cremated, and the urn was on top of the television in his flat. Its shape connected him to her, a worn out autumn leaf that had melted away.

Back from work after midnight, he would put on a dressing gown before going in to see his widow across the corridor, pause to look at the urn and sigh in memory of that long life which had vanished all too quickly for his sense of loyalty and love. At odd moments he'd wonder when he would pack up and go home, till he got back to immediate reality and knew that he was at home. It felt a strange place he lived in, and a sense of dream-like isolation would permeate him as it often had in the army moving to a place whose name he might not know till they were on the march again.

Seeing him so silent and thoughtful William reached into the cupboard. 'Have a splash of whisky to chase you out of the doldrums.'

'I'm not in 'em, sir. Life's a funny thing. Who'd have thought I'd be working for you again after I left the gunners ?'

He poured good measures. There was a busy night ahead. 'A good deal of what happens to us is pre-ordained, Oxton. We don't have much say in the matter. Half of our will is

Man's but a good half is God's!'

'Cheers, sir! My old mother – may she rest in peace – used to say that God helped only them as was good to others. Don't know where she got that from, but there's truth in it, because you're good to me.'

He didn't like to see Oxton in such a mood. But he was a man with his own mind. 'How is Mrs Hamling?'

'Very well, sir. She's a nice woman. Lovely cook. Imagine me eating that Gerry stuff! The Germans made her leave in 1938. She don't like 'em much for that. Whenever I drink whisky it reminds me of us pulling out that night near Wipers, when the BC went mad with the hammer and smashed all them bottles of it. I cried like a baby. The taste allus brings it back.'

'Didn't want the Germans to get it.'

'They'd only have drunk it, sir.'

He put his glass on the table: 'Come on, must get the place open.'

Oxton did look as if he'd had a commission in the army. William was amazed at the change in him. Maybe it was due to his release from the loving servitude of looking after his mother, as well as living down here and having some responsibility, not to mention the influence of Mrs Hamling. His life was happy and well-ordered compared to his own.

Driving home he was filled with a desolation not new to him during the last year or two. The senseless scrapping with Georgina went on. The mock war was a real war, an endless campaign of attrition grinding them into invisibility for each other. When the hours of their quarrel dragged by, he'd feel he was going mad, that his heart was out of control in its agony, that he would murder her, begin to smash till she was dead. She would go away for one or two nights, and he wouldn't ask questions when she came back, and so felt himself choking on his own bile. She would return in a calm and loving mood and, after a fabulous night in bed with her, he would appear happy and say nothing.

It was impossible to do his work properly. Instead of seeing that things were running as they should he'd sit in his office and dissect the mechanism of his past with Georgina, and try putting it back into a coherent pattern, hoping by a feat of clarity and decision to do good for them both.

Days would pass before he went to check the various departments. Sooner or later he'd have to give up his work. Something would go wrong and, understandably Albert Monk would throw him out, so he was training Oxton to take his place. He knew the job well, and was perfect for it – as Albert Monk would see when he came on his rounds.

Driving along the unlit gullet of the road late at night, half blinded by the wide flash of an occasional car from the opposite direction, and already feeling the soul-tearing welcome waiting at home, he thought maybe if the prospect got intolerable he'd drive to Dover or Newhaven and take a boat to France on the first stage of his disappearance from her life. Or was it better to go north to Scotland? Or west to Wales? He'd get a job somewhere, change his name, pulp his brain to that of another person, escape from this long stupid dream and get back to reality. Start all over again. He'd had other lives in his life already, each one different, so why should he regard the present one as so fixed and permanent? He could go to Canada, marry again and have children, so that looking back, this life would be like a dream, as Oxton's had. But he wondered if he had the stamina to make that clean mechanical break. It seemed to need more gut-strength than he had.

He couldn't do it because this present life had to be fought out to the end – till death parted them, or God decided one way or the other. It would be cheating to cut fate off in its prime, even if it were possible. He couldn't even swing the steering wheel and hit some tall strong permanent tree by the roadside because he had a horror of botching it, of surviving and living the rest of his life as a cabbage in a wheelchair. He hadn't come through his soldiering for that.

He let himself in with the key. She was asleep. So were the birds. A word would have been nice, but he listened to music on some German station and made tea.

She wasn't asleep. She stood in the doorway in her long grey dressing gown. 'I heard you come in.'

He had wanted to be alone. 'Tea?'

'How long is this going to go on?'

'Till we both drop dead.'

'I can't wait that long.'

'Until you clear out, then.' Why waste words? Why choose them? The time for care had gone. There's nothing more beneficial and relaxing than saying what you think when you know you're quite capable of measuring every word.

'You're absolutely inexcusable.'

He couldn't look at her.

'So you want me to go?'

He sensed her agony, even through his own. 'No, I don't, since you ask.'

'Do *you* want to go?'

He was tired, but he smiled. 'I'm here, aren't I?'

'Sometimes I wonder.'

It was the same pattern. They'd gone through it a thousand times already. He tried to deflect her from it. 'How did it go today?'

She had been to Conservative party headquarters, helping to check the electoral roll for canvassing. 'There were so many of us that we finished by five. I went back for a drink with Mrs Matthews.'

'Others go?'

'Half a dozen. Lady Tressall drove me home. I had something to eat, read for what seemed like hours, then went to bed. I couldn't sleep.'

'I'm sorry life's so dull for you.' He meant it.

'Are you?' The hard edge was back in her voice. It's every woman for herself where he's concerned, she thought. It's no use thinking what *he* wants. Only what I want.

'There's not much I can do about it.'

'You mean you don't want to. You can change your job.'

'That's not so easy.'

She sat facing him at the table. 'Tell me after you've tried. We could give up the house and go to Dorking or Guildford.'

'You want to be nearer the scene of action,' he said caustically.

'No, bastard. I'd be closer to my father. He needs me. He's getting on.'

'A poor excuse. I'm tired.'

'You always are when I want to talk.'

'You only want to talk when I'm dead in my tracks.'

'Is my poor boy tired?' Mockery was the only way to get through to him, but she was ready to dodge if he leapt at her.

He wasn't tired. At his guns in action he would go for days without sleep, and this domestic battlefield was a cure for any man's insomnia. 'We've been through it all before.'

'And nothing gets done. Nothing. Ever. You don't realise how hard my life is.'

Now she wanted pity. A lady of leisure. 'This house is easy enough to run,' he said in a level voice, steering away from the quarrel. How hard was her life? The word was misused. To have a brood of kids, and go out to work as well, and come home deadbeat in the evening to a back-to-back, and a husband who wanted his dinner – that was hard. Well, it was neither here nor there. She meant something quite different.

He couldn't see what she was getting at, thought himself less of a man for trying to understand. But he knew he had to, whether or not she tried to do the same for him. It was useless and hopeless. They had started off on the wrong foot, not only when they had first met, but from the day they were born in their separate corners of the universe.

'Get a housekeeper. We can afford one.'

'It isn't that either,' she snapped. 'You bring everything down to money. No wonder you can't see what's going on in front of your nose. I'm sick and tired of living like a goldfish in a bowl. We might fuck from time to time but we don't share anything any more.'

Such accusations turned him silent. She wanted a nursery world of total openness, complete contact, an age of innocence that, because he had his own confusions as well as a living to earn, he could never take her back to. The only thing to do was abandon ship.

'I've failed you,' he said icily. 'Try someone else. It's never too late.'

'I love you,' she said. 'But if it can't work with us, I don't see myself setting out on the adventure of life with any other man.'

'Thank you, for nothing.'

'For nothing? You call that *for nothing*?'

245

She swept her arm across the table, knocking his teacup, the sugar and a jug of milk onto the floor: 'You can sleep outside like a dog if you like. I'm going to bed.'

And so it went on, one quarrel merging into the next, no difference, no effort. Instead of the calm beauty of understanding saturating their lucky lives, the passions became worse, the hatreds more intense.

She expected him to follow her upstairs, to say something, to apologise maybe, even to broach a subject so entirely different that they'd have a chance to forget how stupid they'd been by arguing over nothing.

What did she want? Whatever it was, he couldn't give it. When you ask that question it's finished anyway. He'd given her everything – his life and his spirit. What do two human beings finally want of each other? The world was sitting on his neck. Don't ask questions. It's a sign of defeat. Two walls face each other, hands and feet bricked in, unable to move. They can only stay solid, strong and still, to look but never to meet, and finally crumble towards each other at death when their putrefactions had rotted the cement.

He wanted to laugh. It didn't matter. He wouldn't go up to her. He'd drink more tea and smoke another packet of cigarettes, and sit half dead to the monkey-music on the radio. For some reason unknown to either, they were playing a game. It was unreal. It wasn't a proper life. Was it a pastime because they were bored? Instead of going mad, or killing, they tried to destroy each other's spirit, and so their own.

She had already turned off the light when he went up. He should have gone to her sooner. She had lost patience, hoping he would come. But he could sense she wasn't asleep. She was waiting for him to say something.

The weight of the world fell from him. 'We *are* a couple of bloody fools,' he laughed. 'What have two people like us to argue for?'

She sprang up, the crease marks of the sheet showing down her face. She leaned forward as if in agony, her breasts bulging against her night-dress, hair swept untidily back. Now he wanted her to play the big mother and comfort him. I'm not made for that sort of swooning perception. Let him try getting through to me as well. 'You don't know,' she hissed, 'and you'll never know because you don't want to. You could know, but you're too mean to ask questions. You're too arid to find out.'

He stood by the tall heavy mahogany wardrobe with its two long mirrors. He felt the strength in him to heave it over so that it smashed to pieces against the floor and the bed. She was right: 'There's nothing I can do. I love you with all my soul – but I don't know what you mean.'

'You haven't kissed me since you came in,' she accused. 'You haven't touched me. You haven't comforted me.'

She was right again. But how could he go up and kiss her tenderly when she was tearing his guts out? You could, though. You should. To kiss her now would kill his pride. It would even humiliate her.

He went out, tried to shut the door so that she wouldn't think he was slamming it. It was childish. It would go on tomorrow, would continue the day after. It would poison the day after that. A bed in the spare room was made up. He got into it. Exhaustion was blinding him. He put out the light and drifted into sleep. Marvellous oblivion – down into the warmth and dark.

The door burst open.

He wanted to sleep, to be alone, to die. He knew he ought not to feel any of this, but his fibres were pulling apart.

She put the light on. 'You can't even say goodnight, to prove we're still civilised. This is low-class behaviour. It's bad form. Even savages wouldn't carry on like this.'

The foulest verbal spew was ready to fly loose. He'd say nothing, rather than risk letting it out.

She came closer. 'You don't usually sleep facing the wall.'

He didn't answer.

'Sulking, eh?'

A fist spun. She didn't wheel back in time. Wetness ran from her nose. 'You dog,' she cried. 'You stinking coward.' She had come with love in her heart, intending to get into his bed and comfort him. You couldn't live with an animal. She ran back to her room.

It was cold, and he sweated with misery, his chest wet with the smell of self-loathing. He pitied Georgina. He put the light out and pulled the clothes over his head.

Sleep was impossible. He didn't deserve it. Sleep was for the angels, or for those with no conscience. Was this life? There must be a purpose in it. When he put the light on it was three o'clock. He couldn't sleep in tomorrow, because Albert Monk was coming for his monthly look-over.

He went to the bathroom. On his way back he saw a thread of light under Georgina's door. He didn't want to go in, but he knew he must. His first love for her came rushing back. He would go in. She'd throw him out as he deserved, but he'd go in, nevertheless, and be tender.

She sat at the dressing table, a swab of cotton wool at her face.

'I'm sorry,' he said, kissing the warm of her neck. 'I really am.'

'I feel a lot better already,' she said sarcastically.

'I'll put a key down your back. That'll stop the bleeding.'

She shuddered. 'None of your working class remedies on me. Not any more. If you don't mind.'

'They're as good as any others,' he said, 'though I don't think they're especially working class.'

'They are. And they're the only ones you know. It's stopped, in any case.'

He kissed her again. 'What about the other remedy?'

'Which one is that?'

'The universal one.'

She wiped her face clean and turned for another kiss: 'We can try it, if you like.'

'Let's get into bed and call a truce.'

She smiled. 'I thought you were tired?'

He embraced her, feeling the old hard force of his penis rising up. Why do we need to go through such agony to get to this? she wondered. She didn't believe it was necessary. The agony was real but it would soon end, in spite of the animal pull that still kept them together. She drew off her nightdress and got into bed.

248

He followed her, fragmented with exhaustion and bewilderment, able to do his duty before they sloped away into troubled sleep.

CHAPTER TWENTY-ONE

Georgina was up already, and came into the room with tea and orange juice on a tray. Mrs Smithers was busy with the vacuum cleaner in the living room downstairs. The noise disturbed him. 'Time to move, my love,' she said, rattling the tray down.

He felt as if he'd been blown up, and just crawled back together again, each piece having lain doggo till the joints healed. 'What time is it?'

'Ten. Your breakfast is ready.'

He swallowed the orange juice, then jumped out of bed. 'I'll be down in five minutes. But let's have a kiss first.'

It was brief and neutral, but maybe the truce would last.

Breakfast waited for him in the kitchen: 'What about yours?'

'I've had it.' It would be nice to eat together for a change. But he didn't say it. She lit a cigarette: 'We have a dinner party tonight, so I hope you can get home early.'

'Albert Monk's coming. He doesn't leave before nine, so I won't be back till ten.'

'You knew we were having people in,' she said. 'I saw you put it in your diary when I told you last week.'

He touched her wrist affectionately. 'Can't be helped. They're your friends, so it won't matter if I'm not in till afterwards. Save me some coffee, though.'

They were people of the district she'd met through the Conservative Party. There was a doctor who drank too much; a young hard-working farmer and his wife; a retired major, and his brother who'd been a tin miner in Malaya (some people said they weren't brothers, ha-ha); a young couple who sold antiques; and the headmaster and his wife from a nearby prep school. There was Dora Thrush, a pretty little dark woman of about forty who lived in a cottage on the edge of the village and painted landscapes (as well as female nudes, some said), and whose eighteen-year-old son had just gone up to Cambridge.

She poured more coffee. 'It's difficult being married to someone who runs a circus.'

He opened the back door onto the lawn. 'Albert Monk changed the date of his visit.'

'You could have told me.'

He could have. Failed again.

'You knew what you were doing. I don't stand a chance where you're concerned.'

He turned. 'I'll be back on time. Even if I lose my job.'

'Why be so dramatic? You know that won't happen.'

He walked onto the lawn. Housemartins flitted to and from their mud nests under the eaves. Their young were beginning to come out, fat little pale-breasted birds swooping down to feed on the wing, then making many attempts before getting back into the narrow opening of their nests. They were locked in the tyranny of their lives just as he was surely clamped into his. Their nests, made from bits of mud and straw, stuck delicately but precariously under the eaves – so fragile that one false nudge on the return approach would cause them to crumble and fall. The birds would then die in the night from cold.

He went back inside. 'I can't be other than I am,' he said, as if it were a statement of policy. 'I suppose the trouble is that you didn't really know what I was like when we met.'

'I was in love,' she said.

'So was I,' he smiled.

'I don't mean with you.'

He overtook every car ahead on twists and bends. So she never got over her six-foot-five lollipop head. Let her have him. Better the old flame than fresh fields and pastures new. O God our help in ages past. Vomit will out. No padre can say the service of the dead over my heart. Ashes to ashes and dust to dust. Fullstop to an old sentence. It's gone on for over ten years. I take a long time to learn. The cistern is empty. Time to do something. He felt like a groggy boxer. Should he turn into the man who went out after dinner to buy a packet of fags and was never seen again? There's no going to India for me, but if I stay I'll be broken-spirited for the rest of my life. If I leave I'll still be smashed, but I'll be myself again some day. It's gone on too long. A pack of skittles going down. She'd struck at the root and basis of his love. But she can never do it a second time. Somebody else might, but never her. If you can't win, pull out, get your guns off the field before the sky opens up. So foul a sky clears not without a storm. Wake me when the rain stops. He pulled up sweating at a traffic light. What is love, anyway? She could have her boyfriend as long as she goes on loving me. She hates my guts, though. I'm the cause of all her sorrows. Every day is different, so tomorrow might be better.

'You look pleased with yourself,' he said, as Oxton came into the office. 'Ask Miss Callender to bring some coffee.'

'I'll get it, sir.'

He felt calmer in his own ordered domain. What did it matter if the sky fell? Another one would spread. I'm sorry for her. I love her. It's like wrestling with a thousand anacondas to try and quell her turmoil. It isn't a full moon. She's not even expecting her period. Oxton came back with his pot of coffee. 'You haven't stopped smiling this morning,' William said. 'That's not like you. What is it?'

'I'm on top of the world, sir!'

'Take a seat, then.'

'We're getting married, sir. We talked it over last night.'

He stifled a laugh – of joy, envy and congratulation. Oxton in his prime was unobtrusively sliding into domesticity and affection, released at last by his long-living mother into another kind of real world. William remembered the shabbily dressed ragbag of a batman-soldier staggering through shellfire in the Belgian countryside, and saw him now as a confident smart man of the marrying class.

'We're very happy, sir.'

'Like a drink? Or later?'

He hesitated. 'Would you be my best man?'

'I'd be delighted.'

'It can't be at a church. In the registry office, next month.'

Albert Monk went through the books and was satisfied. It

was a warm day but he didn't take off his overcoat, silk scarf and trilby hat. William got him to swear-in Oxton as able to run the place any time he decided to take a holiday.

'If you say so, Colonel. I can see he's an A1 man. Anybody works for me, and I stand by 'em. But I'm not well these days. Ulcers, I expect. Knives in my guts. The doctors don't know anything, so I don't bother with 'em. If you can't trust somebody with your life, don't let their shadow cross your path.'

'I'd still see a medico, though. They've always got some tricks up their sleeves.'

'I'm like a cat. Cure myself. Depends what you put in your mouth. My old woman knows a few tricks. I trust her, you see.'

An easy visit, but he was still half an hour late for Georgina's party. It was dusk and, while walking from the garage to the front door, he noticed a pale three-quarter moon pressing itself into the sky. The dull rattle of conversation came from the living room as he took off his coat in the hall. He couldn't face its part humorous, part earnest tone. They seemed to have something important to say to each other, even though as individuals they met often enough. A sudden gust of laughter from Georgina swept over all.

He recalled those words from the morning that had cut him to the liver because they signified she had never loved him. To use one of the old phrases that he hated but were always true: he'd caught her on the rebound. She'd drifted in from the storm, latched onto him so as to get her own back on the man who had jilted her, but had proceeded to work it out on him, and now that it had taken its full effect she would go back with a clean heart and a clear conscience to the one who had first hurt her. It was not very consoling to see it like this.

Launched into life on his father's lie, he'd lived the follow-up part on Georgina's. A foulness crept into him. He went upstairs for a shower and to change. Then he'd go down with his well-developed stiff upper lip, and show himself as Georgina's loving husband before her friends. The one glad feeling of the day had been Oxton's news about his happy change of life. He deserved it, having spent most of his time serving others. Locked in his own giving and generous ways, his full reward was coming at last.

He stepped under the shower, cold water pouring down forcefully to refresh him, till his flesh was numb, and then turned warm. He set the jet against his face. Towelling himself, he wondered what he had ever given so as to deserve love and peace in his life. He couldn't draw up a profit and loss account, for it wasn't his way any more, but he wasn't aware that he had ever been ungenerous, or unloving.

It was a problem to know which of his several suits to put on. The statement 'I don't mean with *you*' so matter of factly made, hammered him again. Her underwear was scattered over the bed, and he thought to open the window and throw it out. He loathed the idea of being forced to smile and chat and play the host to people he had nothing to say to. That single phrase of hers had exhausted him. Yet why did the fact that she'd never had any love for him bite so deep ? He'd loved her and got ever-renewing life from it, so what did it matter ? If he loved her still, wouldn't it be kinder for him to think – and maybe it was true – that she'd only made her devastating admission in order to hurt him, to jolt him into life because she'd seen him as dead except at those times when he'd wanted to savage her ? And if it were really true that she'd never loved him shouldn't he – if he loved her – be sorry that she'd lost so much ?

He wanted to get into bed, fall asleep between cool sheets, and never wake up again. He held her underpants so that the light shone through their pinkery. They were silken in his fingers. He had no will to choose a suit. His consoling reflections broke bitterly over him when he realised that she'd no doubt already forgotten what she'd said that morning. If he reminded her of it she'd laugh and say: 'What the hell are you talking about, darling ?'

He didn't want to go down. There was only one thing to do. He threaded her pants over his feet till they covered his arse and bollocks. He looked at himself in the full length mirror. I may as well go all the way.

He sat on the edge of the bed and smoked a cigarette, hearing the noise downstairs. In the room he used for a study his old service revolver was locked in a drawer of his desk.

Should he take that down, give them a shocking and noisy show?

Laughter was the only answer. His mind was empty, but its light had enough candlepower to work his limbs. He clipped the brassière across his chest and stepped into her blue carpet slippers. This is the end. This is what she wants, and what she'll get, and what I want her to get.

The stairs creaked. There was no time to lose. The Siamese cat ran towards the kitchen. Cigarette smoke puffed from his lips as he opened the lounge door.

Georgina had never been one for the softened tints of oil lamps or candles, had always been suspicious of a dimmed and intimate atmosphere, so that every gathering of people was illuminated by a full wattage of the room. Their talk stopped.

He smiled at the look on their faces. 'Do go on enjoying yourselves,' he said, in a friendly and ordinary tone. 'I only came in to say hello to my wife.'

Georgina's eyes were big and wide, her face dead pale under her make up. 'What are you dressed like that for?'

'I know you didn't mean me,' he said. 'I've always known it.'

'Get out,' she screamed.

The sixty-year-old doctor took her arm, but she pushed it off. Her underwear ludicrously covering his hairy chest and loins filled her with bewilderment and rage. When her sort were faced with such uncertainty, they killed. She picked up a heavy glass ashtray, cigarette ends running down her arm. The doctor took it away from her.

'Poor thing,' someone said, but who did they mean?

He walked out of the room and closed the door.

Laughing on his way upstairs, he thought how he'd tell the joke to any old friend he met. He took her underwear off, rolled it into a ball and threw it where he'd found it. Then he dressed in his dark suit back from the cleaners.

He removed the rest of his stuff from the common wardrobe, took his clothes out of the chest of drawers, and carried all of it to the spare room by his study. The party got going again downstairs, but with a less intense pitch than before. They had something to talk about now.

CHAPTER TWENTY-TWO

Two people passed silently on the stairs. Beyond the window, trees ached in the wind. The wind ached as well. It wasn't the sound of the wind that put them into this state of madness. The sight of the trees was likewise not to blame.

When Georgina went into her room she was no longer mad. He felt sure of it. When he went out of the house he was himself again, neither one thing nor the other. That was certain. Whatever they felt like when apart they could not blame each other for, though they nearly always did because there was no one else important enough to put the burden on.

At work he added up figures, juggled with income tax and expenditure and insurance stamps, inputs and outputs, profit and loss, and the various problems of Albert Monk's prospering island of pleasure. By the end of the month or quarter, figures might lie in a state of perfect balance. Or nothing came out right, whether adding was done by eye and hand or a machine, or even a third person's brain. So how could it be said that man did not have a soul, when even figures lacked a certainty of resolution?

The house had a large garden, and when he had been mowing the lawn for an hour she wished he would stop, or that it would pour with rain and drive him inside. But if he came in how would she manage him? It was no use living in quiet countryside if a machine went all summer long.

When we were courting I drove up to her house in a tank, and Jacko roared me off because he wanted tranquillity while writing his war memoirs. It was our joke for a long time, but it didn't change her idea of me as I drove away and let Jacko get back to his mournful chapters on Third Ypres.

The overgrown ground needed clearing. Everything had

been neglected. Around the lawn the jungle lay, brambles and thickets, and nettles as tall as himself. A zone of trees separated the garden from the paddock which was also knee-deep in grass. The hedges were twice as broad as they should have been and the back path leading in could not be found.

The garden had been his delight at the end of May when the heavy summer days opened out. The grass of the large lawn had grown into patches of daisies and buttercups, yellow heads slightly taller than the white, and all buttressed by the thick green of up and coming grass that nothing could stop.

He walked along its borders of bushes and trees, and brambles overburdened by the weight of new shoots pushing into the garden as if to slyly conquer it. The heavy, predatory green would sooner or later come in by the windows and strangle them both. So he'd get the lawnmower, clippers, axe and handsaw and shave the lot off till the land was flatter than Napoleon's head.

She looked at the full red roses whose petals blew in the wind like a new sort of vivid butterfly, and wished she could bring them in, protect and comfort them. It was not in her nature, yet how did she know it wasn't? She'd always been told, that's why, but maybe it was and they were wrong, and perhaps even she herself was wrong.

A gaudy and satisfying future made a picture beyond this misery. But rose petals and butterflies were never still, and disturbed her. It was a high wind that nothing could stand against. The lawn was covered with petals, except where he was fanatically mowing.

When he saw her face at the window he knew she was thinking about the roses, and that she wished he would stop cutting the grass and come in. Only a few patches of lawn surrounding the house had yet been cleared. He always knew what she was thinking, and that she knew what he was thinking. How else could he assume they were both mad when they passed each other on the stairs? A soldier never takes anything for granted. It was an easy and murderous law.

At that particular point they stopped thinking about each other, and saw steel glass when they looked at the faces they were passing, each with its own image occasionally reflected, while at other times a complete blank greeted them.

The grass was smooth and rich because there had been rain in the last fortnight to keep it moist. He surveyed its clarity from the back door. The only blemish was a tawny overgrown bush at the far end forming a small salient into the lawn, which he decided to get rid of so as to make the symmetry perfect. Both knew that madness was in the eye of the beholder.

It was harder work than he'd expected. The roots under the bush went in all directions. They were well packed in, and a fair area of lawn was ruined as he snapped each one from its centre with a pick-axe. When the vegetation was heaped into a fire at the far corner of the property, he did not feel a sense of victory at what he had done.

The line of the lawn made a dent in the opposite direction. The eroding of the salient revealed a re-entrant into the area overgrown by nettles and bushes, so he got a scythe and cut the long grass as far as the outer hedge. The brambles were so high, and the grass so thick, that he was surprised to uncover young apple trees and currant bushes. It disturbed him that anything should remain upright within his field of fire.

The poison of madness left by the passing of Georgina on the stairs made it difficult to fasten one thought to another. When the dark grey sea is pouring into the brain, do something, drive yourself to the last measure of your strength. They faced each other in silence, each fighting back the same ocean. After a quick meal of bread-and-cheese, he returned to clearing more weeds and long grass.

Relax, enjoy it, be happy, he'd told Oxton after the Town Hall wedding, advice it was easy to give someone else. And Oxton would take it because he didn't need it. He embodied it.

That smartly dressed sixty-year-old had acted the fool for the first time in his life. But then, he'd never been so happy before. During the ceremony he mimed that he was being forced into marriage because not he but somebody else had got Mrs Hamling into trouble. She was a patient, wry, plump, competent woman who'd deal with him afterwards and therefore make him happy. They'd both suffered in their lives, and so were created equal.

William was able to run Albert Monk's bingoville and

skittledrome while Oxton spent his month's honeymoon in Israel, where Mrs Hamling's one surviving brother lived with his family. And Oxton came back as solidly impressed with the place as he was in love with his wife.

William still had energy for the garden. His time in the army had not been wasted where keeping fit was concerned. The only thing free in this world was the sweat of your brow, his father had said, and you ought to be grateful when you get paid for it – thinking no doubt of time spent furiously digging like a rabbit when under fire. With bullets hissing around it was common sense, after all.

During the slaughter of nettles a pleasant thought slipped away before he could recite it to himself in the sort of plain language which would enable him to get comfort from it. He swung at the nettles, consoled by the fact that the garden was being inexorably cleared. He could already see from one fence to the other, along the front of the house.

The thought that had got lost left a spiritual pain. Absence increased the importance that he felt it might have had for him by staying. Yet in vanishing it had become insignificant. Why had it deserted him? He didn't know. He knew nothing except the swing of his arm and the ache in his shoulders. In the wilderness thought was meaningless. Colonel Scorton would not be treated in this way, either by stray and no doubt ridiculous words, or by his wife. He raked up heaps of nettles and carried them to the bonfire.

The thought, that he knew would drift back sooner or later, and which did, was that they had been united in madness on the stairs, and that he didn't doubt it had also entered Georgina as they passed, joining them with the same madness, a pleasant reminder that whatever remained of mutual love was at an end – a cool and desolating notion. In the meantime he had uprooted an entire thorn bush, and scythed away the surrounding barrier of nettles.

He felled small trees from the lawn so that they wouldn't block his progress when he walked in a straight line. A wire fence marking off the paddock was rolled up to free him from going through the allotted gap if he wanted to change direction and head for the farthest corner of his land.

Rubbing away sweat which dripped from his bushy brows and stung his eyes, he wondered if Georgina was alarmed at these new extensions of space around the house. She hadn't mentioned it, for a sort of normal life still seemed to go on between them. In wondering who would break first he was unable to see that he had already done so.

The fence had been taken up, but a line of trees still marked its course. He couldn't level the whole world. Or couldn't he? The trees obstructed his free will when walking. The bushes growing between them formed a barrier almost as impenetrable as the fence. He thinned out the bushes, and a continual pall of smoke hung over the garden.

His pain was held at bay. While working he stayed strong enough to bear it. He would never break down. He did not know what it meant. There were no limits. He hectored himself with lucid thoughts as he opened tracks between the line of trees. The more space the better.

She also must be clearing her spaces, and if she isn't, then God help her. She's been doing it ever since we met and married. We were novelties for each other. Because of our different families there wasn't that total joining into love there should have been. Or maybe there had been too much of it because they were so different. When you get this far down, every force and perversity cancels out another, leaving a morass. We met on such a narrow front in the beginning that when the rest of it became apparent we found it impossible to exist side by side. There was too much about each other that we hated. Two people in an equal union shouldn't need such hatred to sustain them, or to tear them finally apart.

The remaining trees did not impede his walking but they blocked his line of vision. He wanted to stand at one corner of his land (it was hers as well, but all his now that he was devastating it) and see to the other far angle with nothing in the way. Distance had to melt like butter, space to taste like pollen or honeysuckle through sixty-four hundred gradations of a circle.

He hated the trees that were eating up his soil. When he rested it was so silent that a single bone-dry sycamore leaf sounded distinctly as it blew across the lawn. We aren't similar enough to keep each other sane. He picked up an axe to drown the sound of the leaf. Maybe we've become similar by living so long together.

He assumed that they had got married so as to spare two other people from torment. But who were they? As a colonel and gunner he'd been a man at the height of his powers. He felt again at his peak, but in a different way. The first small tree came splintering down.

When he was young he used to believe that things would improve as you got older. Now he knew that everything gets worse. I'm wrong. It gets better and worse at the same time. The more trees he sent cracking the wider grew the sky when he looked up, and this alone made life worthwhile. To do the very worst thing of all was better than not acting. But action was only action if it was to do some good. He told himself that at least he'd been a good soldier, especially in the tight spot at Sidi Rezegh, when he zig-zagged his guns forward and pounded those eighty-eights for a change. But who cares about that now? With so much wood he made bonfires every day, revelling in heat and smoke as his garden became a wilderness. The roots of all trees, both his and Georgina's, were wrenching apart. The sun was snake-yellow through the smoke screen, and there was so much ash from the previous fires that he spread it over the waste land with a shovel.

Except for the house, everything within the irregular borders of his property was flat. It had been ripped up, chopped down, mown smooth, burned and scattered. A small aeroplane could have landed there.

CHAPTER TWENTY-THREE

He didn't know how long he had lain in bed. Even the taint of the sheets, which at first had served to prolong his sense of identity, no longer bothered him.

If you leave your wife, the first seventy-two hours are the worst. If she leaves you, it might take a week. In a mutual scattering you don't know you've done it till you've done it, but that's the worst of all.

In his mind he'd done all three. Each one had happened many times over. Formerly it had been in the mind, but now it was real.

If you make your own bed you have to lie on it. He saw what it meant. Such tremendous truth hid the real truth. Whoever made such remarks had no idea of the truth because they were always on the self-righteous end of it. Lying in bed was never comfortable. You were a prey to psychic devastation. He had turned his garden into a desert so that he would be able to see things clearly, but a garden within was growing up in its place.

His bed wasn't uncomfortable, because it was narrower, and only one person could be in it at a time. He could nurse his agony all on his own. You cannot share your wounds with anyone else. Every soldier knows that. No one can share your wound if they haven't shared your fate. His father, quick to recognise the twists of his spirit, steered him into a profession where you weren't expected to share your wounds. William was unable to tolerate his wound without questioning life itself. Charlie Scorton, that debonair sergeant of the Queen's army who'd marched, prayed, and drank his way through life with the colours and never a care in the world, hadn't told him what to expect when he got out of its shelter.

Sublime patterns create themselves. Nature's way weaves

with Man's so that you don't know where one ends and the other starts. We are all animals, part of nature, no different when it came to a marriage smashed like so many others. Is a quick sharp suicide the only honourable way out? The world is swarming with people who got themselves free of a similar plight by mutual commiseration and renewed link-ups as dubious and ill-fated as the first marriage they'd made.

The only thing is to set off into the world. I'm already in it, have been since I was born. My head fills with words. I have been in the world too long to be able to see what it can offer me, or what I am able to offer it. I've been behind the mask so long that it's grown more real than my face. If I try to bring my real face back to life, the mask resists. It's a more vicious and deadly battle than any real one I've been in. Smoke, noise, and a splinter in the shoulder is nothing compared to it – though being close to death makes a man of you.

If I get up will I start off another twenty year cycle, begin it all over again and land myself back in the same place as now? Better starve to death, a holy man in the wilderness. The soldier and the priest are a back-to-back beast, as we used to sing in the mess: bred in barracks and on the battlefield, forged and tempered in the shifting sky. Good riddance to the spark of life. He dreaded that it should drive him back among the living. The tickertape in my brain falls as dry bracken. It's dangerous to act. I can't hold back the words. My brain always made do with what few I allowed it, even as a boy, though it never complained.

A blank mind is the bliss of life, emptiness without sleep. If I *try* to push all words out, to attain the peace of emptiness, I can't do it. I sweat with exasperation because I'm a human being. The dam breaks and the words flood in: generators creating a brilliance that lights up my brain.

Then, suddenly, the peace that I struggled for comes without effort. Words vanish. My mind is at peace. Something bigger than my spirit is able to manipulate me whenever it likes. It can help me or torment. I have no say in the matter.

When the first words assemble at the windows of my mind prior to swarming in, I try all sorts of tricks to hold them off. I force my eyes onto empty landscape, focus my attention on squares and circles, go back to a schoolroom blackboard of geometry at the apprentices' barracks (already a defeat because I need words to recall the picture) but finally I begin to count, deliberately and slowly, to hold back the word-forming sentences about to take me over once more.

I never succeed in keeping my mind empty, because I am not in control. The only way to stop words swarming in would be to kill myself.

I took to my bed because the vertical position was not possible any more. Standing up, you see towards other people. Lying flat you see into yourself. My body rebelled against staying on its feet. When I have to get out of bed, as I must several times a day, I go on all fours, like an animal.

I lie and stare at the ceiling, and because I can't look through and see heaven I'm left with the only alternative of having to look into myself. The more I fix on that plain white ceiling the more I penetrate layers of myself. I've seen the sky often enough not to weep when it isn't there.

You look for God, and never see him, so begin searching for him in youself. But it is difficult to get into your soul with open eyes. Lying in bed, an inexhaustible army lays siege to what you do not want to reveal. Getting inside yourself would mean giving up your defences.

I can't get into the unity of my own spirit without hardship or difficulty, which proves I am not in control of myself. And if I'm not, then who is? Whoever controls my own inner workings has taken my will away.

If I could decide why this was so I might make the first step towards knowing myself. I'm cautious where I was decisive. I'm slow, perhaps sly at last. I'm not in control of my own spirit. I go to sleep and have beautiful dreams, then weep because I have woken up and seen that nothing could last. Why weep at the thought of death? Only a real man weeps, cooks or goes mad – and considers himself normal. When I walk again I will carry a shield, like Hector running around the walls of Troy – as I saw in a picture-book on first going to school when I was five.

CHAPTER TWENTY-FOUR

She came back. She won't leave me alone. Then he remembered he'd sent for her.

'Why don't you get up, instead of lying there like a pig?'

'I like it here.'

'It's disgusting. You've gone to pieces.'

He tried to smile. He leaned on one elbow but it was too much for him. He couldn't easily pull his old strength back. 'I wallow in it.'

'You *are* a pig.'

He grunted.

'Pig!'

'Leave me alone.'

It was true that she loved him. She also hated him for hiding behind the stockade of his own collapse. But she still didn't want the final smash to take place, to get caught by separation and divorce when they could make some perfectly civilised arrangement. 'I drove here thinking how much I loved you. I hoped we might make it up. But you have no respect for me, lying in such squalor.'

He didn't need her. 'Leave me.'

'You've no respect for yourself, and that's worse. You're not a man any more.'

'Isn't that what you wanted?'

'Poor self-pitying fish. Next time don't phone *me*. Call your father.'

'I phoned Oxton.'

'Call anybody, but not me.'

He looked at her, as if through two round holes in a concrete wall. 'Don't go. You're the only person I've ever loved.'

'I doubt that.' She lit a cigarette. 'You've never loved anybody.'

'I loved you.'

'What a lot of nonsense!'

He loathed the inflexion of her voice. His father had been a soldier. He had become a soldier. He'd even married a soldier – and told her so.

Maybe he was coming back to his senses, since he made her laugh.

'You're not a soldier any more,' she said.

It was as isolating as battle. Beyond the ring of their conflict nothing else existed. But there were no big guns in this war, no splashed entrails or limbs sundered. But your spirit went, in the quiet premeditated hiss of the fight.

He held her warm hand. 'I'm still in love with you.' He had to say things he didn't believe if they were to get back to a normal life. Give it another go. Stitch up the rips. He began to feel that the voice of sanity was the voice of destruction.

'Get up and have a bath, then maybe we can talk.' She opened the windows, seeing a long way over the green and wooded countryside, so clean, so distant from him lying in his stinking bed. Cold air rushed against her, and she hoped it reached his face. It was set for rain.

'I'm going to make a meal. Come down in about an hour.'

He bathed, shaved and dressed, not groggy, but pale and full of bile. Why was he on earth? The only excuse for being on earth was to find God, otherwise you were a mean-spirited idler. In trying he knew that nothing and everything was within himself, that there was only the vast emptiness of a spirit not yet born. Its faintest stirrings tore him apart. Every scrap of himself was painfully divided.

Georgina managed to hold the sea back because there was no point letting it in. She had all she wanted – him, her lover – everything. But he could see the pain in her, nevertheless. Like him, she hated this life and didn't know how to get free of it.

She made a good meal – soup, steaks, salad, dessert. He ate it, sitting stiffly, freshly cleaned, revived after his rest, pure, ethereal, and empty. She loved him – at the moment. Did she have to love him all the time, every minute of every day?

What sort of life was that? Is the world *that* small? Is life *that* dull? Why did he insist on trying to kill her?

It was a mistake to bring out the Minton porcelain, those exquisite plates and flimsy teacups. They'd been in her family a long time. They were beautiful and defenceless, hardly the objects to have on the table in such an atmosphere of spoliation.

In the argument he couldn't find words, and hers tore into him like steel splinters, so he turned the dinner service, coffee cups and saucers, into his vocabulary, a rabid flying concatenation smashing at the wall.

She wept. How lucky she was. She had tears in her. It was finished. He was on his feet, and saying to himself: Why wait so long? Life was too short for this.

SMASH MATRIMONY, he wrote on a white wall of the spare room, dipping his two inch sable brush in a tin of red paint. If mine is smashed my heart explodes. The field is free for me.

The paint began to run, his exhortation bleeding its fourteen letters copiously down the white loony-bin wall. They bled as if the wrists of each letter had been slashed. The words, with a life of their own, were oozing their lives away, getting back at him for writing them, by an open and determined suicide. Wanting the last word, he wasn't getting it, even now. He slopped excess paint from the brush, leaving only sufficient to make a dry letter that would not run.

She came in. 'My God, what are you doing?'

The wardrobe was heavy as he dragged it free: 'I'm writing on the walls.'

'You're mad. Oh, what can I do?'

He smiled like a child expecting to be praised. '*Your* walls. *Our* walls. Four times. Two for you and two for me. Fair's fair. Let's wallow in equality – the communism of despair born out of blood-red love!'

She smiled. He wasn't without spirit, after all. 'You expect me to say I'm going home to father, don't you? Well, I won't, not until you've gone back to yours. That'll be your first move if you're serious in writing that stuff.'

He smiled, and she wondered why he'd turned so pale, why he wanted to die. Let him, let him. If he was trying to frighten her he wouldn't succeed. He took an old-fashioned jack-razor from his pocket. Pouring the rest of the paint over the opened piano got him nowhere.

The first deep longitudinal cut in his fleshy wrist brought out his own paint, and he held it to the last clear wall. The letters lost the majuscule precision that had been possible with a brush, but attained a flowing hand-writing that raced to freedom from his veins.

She laughed as he sat on the floor. She wanted to weep. But she called to him on her way out that he could clear up his own mess. He could die, if that was how he felt. She was off, and she'd damn well never come back. Didn't like it here. He'd been bullying her too long, and this was the last straw.

CHAPTER TWENTY-FIVE

O'Grady says: Night-firing. Tongues of flame. Oh God. One gun rested every hour. The swish of shells, whing and booom! The cannoneers at Waterloo fell dead-beat and slept under their guns at the height of the battle. Flashes from gun muzzles. Some were so exhausted they never woke up again. Cats' eyes exploding in the dark. The crack of shrapnel. Red flashes through smoke. Applebread Farm goes up, then Quick Lime Corner, taking Thieves' Kitchen with it. Forlorn Copse burst into flame. Map names. Lover's Lane goes west. Chikers' Wood and Random Hill. A thousand field guns in the Ypres Salient wheel to wheel pumping shells into the mud. Two-way traffic sent the same tonnage coming back, pulverising sky to make more rain. A deluge after every battle washes the dead, and drenches the wounded. Wagon lines, tractors, lorries, trailers, trucks, stores, dumps, and that ever-present faint glow from illuminating mechanism over the dial sights where guns are laid on new targets. Spots German battery-flashes over the Canal. Get a fix and smother them with all you've got. They spot you and try the same. Wounded dressed by RAMC. Head cut off by ammunition box. Red. A pall of smoke from Armentières. No smoking in vehicles. A pitiful moaning of unmilked cows. Gas mask and waterbottle; tin hat and pistol; lanyard and whistle.

Never say never. Defend it if you have to, but don't counter-attack. Make a new one somewhere else and call it surprise. Label it shock. If your enemy is waiting for the un-expected, shake him with the *expected*. Paralyse the will. The moral is to the physical as three unto one. Never counter-attack: it always puts you at a disadvantage. Pull out. Use space. Make speed. Create time. Confuse. Be patient. Disappear fast out of hell, then reappear, full of strength. Do something, and do it now. It's never too late. Never say never. A peculiar treasure. Precious stones from sardius to jasper, all twelve blown into the sky for near two thousand years and down again into their own solid soil that belongs to me and all of us. Oxton in Israel. Pass the salt, pass the tears. Spatchcock Tower for observing fire. The bow in the cloud brings rain and pain. Chimney Manor. Gloomy Fen. Sweatbread Farm. Never say never.

Get up, O'Grady said. Get up. The fire blazed beautifully, a lot of wood thrown on. The officer's Burberry. The scurring rain. The screech-block of his rifle. Leave me under the trees. Don't move me. Bay rose, the sad flower of summer that dies in autumn: he sat by the roadside and smoked his short pipe. Bell tents by the side of the wood down Shottermill Lane.

Leave me alone. Don't lift me up. Let it flow. The earth hears gunfire, bombs falling, someone under the soil hammering with fist and feet, so many buried demons hitting frantically to get out. A thousand-fold great crack of a gun, impossible to tell about, a thousand-score a day creating death and weather. All's fair in love and war. 'A gunner I was, a gunner I am, a gunner for evermore.'

O'Grady says: Don't laugh. You're dead. A shrapnel gut and a jellied head. Fix your life by survey, observed fire, or open sights. Love to everybody. Rats paradise. Water fills the wooden ship. Shandy and vodka. Energy where art thou? Travelling by train he saw a configuration of farm buildings, a canal going along the front of it, a road over the railway followed by a footpath bridge, and later at the camp he found its name on the relevant map sheet. North of Bedford, a farm with courtyard, thatched roof, horse-and-cart, farmer's men, peace, work, bread and meat, ale and sleep. Eighteen: up and coming Master Gunner.

Noise of heavy firing from the south. Gunfire tea. Noise like thunder claps. Thunder box. Tinder sparks far off in the night. Owls killed in trees. Not quick enough to fly. The last match struck. Leave me alone, he said aloud, lips not moving. Sounds shouting in his stomach. Number each paragraph in your reports. Count the words on all signals. Very Lights, flares, heliograph. White Sheet. Messines. Plug Street. One-in-forty-thousand. He couldn't remember her name, nor ever forget her face. The fall from grace is swift and sudden. Limber up, and if too late, spike 'em while there's time. Patience and brute force was a subtle combination that boiled his eyes and put them back. Don't move me. Leave me alone. Fuck you, O'Grady. I'm lingering in my own free will for the first time. Smoke and pestilence. Drumfire on four horizons. Degrees or mils, it's all the same.

Flash spotting. It spun, rolled into a wider light. Better to go before *he* does, though he'll catch me up if there is such a thing. Sent me forth on this one-way trip. Vomiting in the Channel from Dunkirk, sick at the thought of my smashed guns, and from that oily rum the good matelot gave. But it was the last time. Nothing happens twice. Phoned my father at the post office in Ashfield to say I'd got back safe. Took four hours to get through.

The blinding light sent every pain to its point. Leave me. Don't move me. The coalstone dead. You're not, sir. . . . Retreat. Pull out. No beetle is too small to be crushed. The Volume of Fire. Better to be a fool than feel guilty. Devouring angel. Knocked through the sound barrier. A thin white skin of dismal snow. Once is enough to last for ever. Each white spume-top of the boiling sea is the collapsing fist of a dead sailor. Ostend ahoy! Bright red. Two eyes moved closer and became one. What's left except a few red shreds of spirit and flesh? One battery firing. The rats of paradise. The half-section breaks new ground.

'We'll see what we can do, sir. But the guns aren't here any more. More's the pity, I suppose. But you lost a lot of blood. Good job I came. You'd have been a goner.'

White pain at his temples. Emptiness. Open my eyes. Take a chisel to the lids. Swore something awful. Smashed the whisky. The light's like fire. Don't open them, then. My eyes are in the muzzles of the guns. Dark, flash. Dark, flash. No noise except a river rushing from ear to ear. Legs move. Flag-wag. Lamp. Runner. No more pigeons. Wireless. Arm dead, an anchor to it, a blanket round it, pressing in. Couldn't even manage that.

'I was thinking of coming, anyway. Good job it was Sunday. Told the wife I'd take a run in the motor to see how you were. Found you in a right state. Must have had an accident. Good job it wasn't too deep. You lost a lot o' blood, though. Had a field dressing in my car. Always come in handy.'

He'd moved him to the main bedroom – cool, calm, unsullied, old stuff. Like flowers, grow more. Fallow. Life's long. Drink life. Get more. Revive. Warm tea. Sweet.

'How many lives have you saved, Oxton?'

He tried to smile, but his lips shook. There was light on his glasses. 'Only my own, sir.'

CHAPTER TWENTY-SIX

He stood in the middle of the space he had created. He was tired, but the world was not. He had seen those stars before, from desert and through jungle clearings, and from country-side he'd walked through happily with Georgina. He had noted them cycling with his pals as a boy from the grammar school at Cuckford into the long straight rides of the Dukeries in summer, or camping by the Trent when the moon was full and they couldn't get to sleep so he'd walked outside to look. The stars were the studs of an iron door opening onto infinity. If he could get the strength to push hard enough, he would go through, was what he'd thought then.

Wherever he was he asked: what am I doing here? It was a question the stars never asked. When the full moon came up he sat in the garden at midnight and howled like a dog. His sounds carried in the still air and maybe frightened the vicar down the lane, who was just going to bed after writing his weekly sermon.

He had great visions, lying in bed with his own oblivion, or when at the end of the garden looking over the single thin railing and across the deep imaginary gorge which was made real by the fixed intensity of his eyes. Without the dynamite of drugs to blast open these membranes leading to his deepest inner cases, without any apparent sickness to let him down into the profoundest depths of his stomach, without even desiring to curl up like a foetus at the back of his own brain, he took in the enormous view of his vastly expanded self across the wide deep gorge of his own making at the end of the garden.

His hands were calmly latched onto the thin protective railing to steady himself but mostly to gauge the horizon with neatness and accuracy. Across the gap, enormous battles took place. He stood in the morning to watch the spectacle beyond the rimline of rocks on the opposite side.

Between the horizon and the altocumulus cloud cover squadrons of pterodactyls flew in from the line of steaming forest. He strained his eyes and regretted he had no compass to gauge the angle of their approach, and wondered whether they had seen him before he saw them. As they got nearer, more light came into the sky, and he was grateful for this because it was better that he saw them in vivid light rather than wait for them to attack him in their specially contrived twilight of midday.

The first squadron came within range. With his trained observing eyes he saw several other squadrons manoeuvring in the hazy air above their own jungles on the horizon, unsure that they would come in his direction. But the rapid approach of the first squadron took attention from the further mustering of their reserves, as a clear pattern of thirteen soared above his head with long necks craning, wide black wings beating the wind, one in front and four ranks of three ponderously rowing the air, leathery hides glistening as if they had taken off from under water.

The noise of their slowly fanning wings passed. The worst dreams come while we are awake, because we know we cannot open our eyes from them. His whole life had been a dream, when he considered it from such a dream as this.

The first squadron wheeled in the sky behind, passing over again higher up and going back in the direction from which it had come. In perfect formation, their rush of air was drowned by three other squadrons approaching at low altitude. Because of their noise the first squadron appeared to travel back, graceful and beautiful, in silence.

The three squadrons came on, and his head felt open to the sky, which seemed wholly filled with slow wings, shut beaks, leathery skins, and soulless eyes, as if each of their stone-dead spirits had been created to menace his fragile living one that would never have wings to cross the gorge and find out what great chaos of material gave them birth on the other side.

The whole two-score came over, so that he was able to glimpse those ossified vegetable eyes as they gave a slight dip and climbed with the utmost grace to gain height before flying back, mouths clamped as if invisible ropes were around each jaw. No longer afraid, he calmly watched their manoeuvres, and because he had kept his eyes open he no longer felt threatened.

The air increased its temperature as each squadron flew over. He stood by the rail. Sweat saturated his clothes to a salty stench. Such sweating protected him from the pterodactyls, and though the loss of salt and liquid was weakening it would help him to face whatever might attack from across the gorge.

The leading squadrons returned, formation changed into a single file angling from the right. He tried to estimate the height, but couldn't decide because it didn't seem important. His will had gone. The line descended as it got closer, and his instinct told him to get onto the earth and dig with bare hands. He resisted, fought blindly against all sense and reason, and stayed on his feet to watch despite the danger.

The leader lagged so far behind that it seemed to be alone, and he was fixed by its beauty and menace as it flew silently along. An itching spread over his hair, but he was too engrossed to claw it away, standing straight-backed, eyes fixed, arms down, seeing the jaws of the pterodactyl open, with a large white egg inside.

A thousand voices were telling him to run, far and wide in a thousand fragments, so that at least a part of himself might escape, but by their insistent power he knew them to be snares that he must ignore if the already shattered pieces of his spirit were ever to come together again. As the pterodactyl dipped and turned, the egg rolled silently from its jaws, weighing so much that the body soared almost vertically towards the sun. The second also released its white dot over the stubbled rocks of the plain.

Before the first egg struck he resisted a last impulse to flee. He heard the thump as it hit the earth, then the roar that created an enormous upshooting of orange flame. Each egg fell, and the clockwork regularity of their descent engulfed the plain with searing flowers of boiling fire, until all connected to make a wall of heat that reached from the earth to the sky, blotting out the horizon without which he could not live.

The thousand voices kept telling him to run, but he knew he must not, even though as each egg burst his heart exploded. He died and lived again, disintegrated with every impact. His brain shattered and entrails split, and came together before the next fragmentation. His body burned to ash, and reassembled. His spirit shattered each time to the outermost limits. He was alive in the ash, and his eyes witnessed it.

He had to cross the gorge, and walk through the wall of fire in order to become one person and live at peace in the world. Only the wall of flame was left. The gorge closed itself, nothing between him and the heat. He made sure his boot laces were fastened, to be certain he'd be truly shod when he walked into the fire which held him back from a region of secrets. His impulse was to run away, because he couldn't see how the human body, with its thin and sensitive skin, could walk into a wall of searing heat.

Flames hissed as each nucleus fought for ascendancy over those around, which could only end in one of them retaining power. If that happened, where would the losers go? Visible trees of flame intent on destroying each other presented a red barrier to stop him walking across the plain.

He moved over the stones till his clothes and skin smouldered. Standing still was more painful, so he went on, against reason and hope. He knew that to discover something fundamental about yourself meant pushing against what seems an impossible tide. You do the opposite of flowing downhill like water, that takes the easiest course and finds its own level. There comes a time when a way is shown which appears to be insane and painful. It happens once in a lifetime, but its very impossibility convinces you that it is the only thing to do.

The heat forced his eyes shut. He had a terrible fear of being blinded. He felt his hair burning. The gorge had been less of an obstacle. He would have found a way of getting over, a knowledge of trigonometry enabling him to land a fallen tree exactly across by judicious leverage and the application of ropes.

Voices telling him to run back were so loud that he was impelled towards the flame to get out of range. Their braying made an intolerable ache at his dead centre, and in order to escape it, he moved towards the heart of the fire. The flame lost its searing heat, became supportable though kept its awesomeness. He entered it with limbs of white ash.

If he stopped moving he would fall on the baking impacted soil till both he and the flames vanished together. He walked quickly, regretting that he couldn't observe the colours and patterns at his leisure. The flames shifted and changed, swirled from the yellow of saffron to the deep-blood colour of liver. Steely beheading axes swept rigid flower petals up in fire and smoke.

The flame that surrounded him held back its final weapon so that he could walk through unharmed.

CHAPTER TWENTY-SEVEN

All he owned could be moved in the car, boot full and trunk roped on to the luggage rack. When you finally departed, it was surprising how little you needed. His training as a soldier would always come in handy. He sold the house, sent half the money to Georgina, and banked his share of three thousand. All surplus furniture had gone under the hammer.

As he walked to his car he felt free for the first time in his life. The sky looked and smelled the same as it had when running home from school as a boy. For once in his life there was no future, which he felt was how it should be. He thought it a pity he'd waited so long to get to it, but he had no patience with vain regrets.

Ashfield had a sort of glamorous calm as he drove into the awful red brick of the place. A late October sunlight gave dimension and colour. On the way in was a filling-station with gleaming pumps, and at another place a new arcade of shops. But the middle of the town with its ancient market cross was close enough to the hills on one side, and woods on the other, to spike the nostrils when the wind brought fresh air in.

He parked the car and walked. Having neither job, prospects, nor future didn't make him in any way uneasy. He went into a café and took a cup of tea – its overfill slopping into the saucer – to an empty table. He pushed sauce bottles and a plate of pie crusts aside. A man at the next table was reading the *Football Post*. Two bus drivers were talking about chrysanthemums.

'You can bring me one, when they come up,' the girl behind the counter called. 'I love chrysanthemums.' She was slim, with large breasts, bright paint-rimmed eyes, and a black tooth showing at the laugh she gave on being so cheeky as to

278

call out. They obviously weren't strangers to each other.

One of the men smiled slyly. 'I'll bring you two if you'll come out wi' me tonight, duck.'

'Yer wife wouldn't like it.'

'She wain't know.'

'What? Round 'ere?'

'We'll goo up Newstead.'

'Bring me the blooms, first.'

Chaffing was all it was. He was home, and not just visiting. But it wasn't the end of the road for a man of fifty who hadn't yet started to live. It made him young again. He fitted in. They didn't stare at him 'gone out', even though he wasn't in working clothes. A pair of flannels, shirt and no tie, and a jacket, made him ordinary enough: a well-built grey haired man of middle height, face slightly lined but sharp at the eyes. He could even do without a car, but Georgina hadn't wanted it. They were generous in the division of the spoils. At the moment of parting they were finding similarities, which made the good-byes amiable. She'd already bought a smart Italian car, a green blaze for the twisting arterial lanes. Be careful though, he told her, yet knowing she was a woman with fine reflexes when it came to action. Only love made disasters for her. He hoped she'd suffered the last one and would be happy from now on. He had a strange feeling she was pregnant when he'd said farewell, though she hadn't told him anything.

He drank his fourpenny cup of tea and went outside. Dusk was coming in, coal dust, iron smoke, frosty mist. England seemed big: twenty countries wide, forty subtle sceneries long, layers of generations, seams of accents. He wouldn't worry about Georgina and her adventures. To have lost her, and still to bear the weight of anxiety over what was happening to her, was too much. She'd be all right. Leave her in peace.

The town centre was alive with buses and light. People spoke the old comfortable twang. There were more cars than he'd seen before. Chicken and chips, hash and curry. He suddenly realised that he wanted to get home.

'I'm glad you've come,' Doris whispered in the hall. 'Doctor were up just now. He's poorly.'

She was grey, worn out, an old woman of seventy. But when

279

she smiled the spark came back. 'He's been asking for you. I made him some broth, and he enjoyed it.'

He hung up his overcoat. 'I got here as soon as I could.' The place had the same smell of carbolic soap, stewed tea, soil from the plant pots, and a human smell of coal-gas and sweat. 'I'm sorry he's not well.'

'It's his age.' She shook her head. 'He's eighty-three.'

'I *am* well,' he called from the parlour. 'Don't listen to her, Bill.'

His voice was clear. He sounded in his prime still. But he wasn't, and never would be again. 'I thought he was in bed?'

She looked hard, which he took to signify that going to bed during the day at his age would mean only one thing, and he wasn't having that.

Charlie sat upright in a high-backed chair, fully dressed with a blanket over his knees, a tie on, and cleanly shaven. There was a slight nick to one side of his chin. His hair was milk white, slightly longer than it had been. He held out a hand: 'Kiss your old dad, William.'

The spark in his eyes had beaten a rearguard action. 'I'm for India in't morning. Glad you've come to see me off. The train to Chatham, and then down the Medway. The band playing us out as we stand to attention on deck. Keeps the horses quiet. The buggers start up though when the sea chops us about.'

He shook his hand. There was nothing to say for the moment.

'My mind's not wandering,' Charlie said sharply. 'I was only thinking back.'

William laughed. 'I know it wasn't.' But it had been. He was fighting hard for clarity. That's how old soldiers fade out. He held his hand, and there was no snapping it away any more.

'I wanted to go again at the time of Suez. Good time. Tried to go for a sowjer and get sent out. At your age? they said. Can't fight on two sticks, grandad. Just like that – to me! But I got talking to that sergeant. Had a laugh about it, then a pint together in the pub.'

William sat by him. 'I thought about going back myself, but they had enough men.'

'They've always got good men. It's the other thing they sometimes lack. But I was hoping you'd stop by. Where's Georgina?'

Should he tell him? He wouldn't lie. 'We don't live together any more.'

His hand stiffened.

'We separated.'

'Fought like cat and dog, I suppose? Me and your mother did. But God brought us together. No staying power today.'

'It didn't work out.'

'Whatever did?'

Let it drop.

But Charlie wouldn't. Not that sort of bloke. 'Might get married myself,' he winked.

Doris came in with a tray loaded with tea things. 'You never did, after your Alice died, did you? You ran around plenty, though.'

Veins of rage stood out on his temples. 'Shut your mouth, woman, in front of my son!'

That was what his trips to Nottingham were about when I was a kid. 'Nothing wrong with that, dad.'

She poured their tea. 'One of 'em came round the other day to ask how he was. Sat here a couple of hours. Don't know what they was talking about, but they were going at it hammer-and-tongs.'

It was no good trying to stop her. 'I'll tell him about *your* antics in a bit,' Charlie said.

She blushed. 'Get some of this nice seed-cake.'

'I would have gone to Suez,' he said, 'like a shot. Terrible for a sowjer who's too old. Wouldn't take me. I'd a gone up them beaches like a three-bellied snake. Even now. Pump the palm trees full o' bullets. Covering fire. See 'em tumble down. Then single shot. Thirty aimed rounds a minute. Shorncliffe used to rattle like a bag o' peas!'

'War's over, dad.'

'It's never over. Got to keep our heads above water. The Navy fired a salute as we passed Gibraltar. Heaved my guts up all the way to Malta and the Canal. Most of us first-timers did. Fine old ship. Didn't like it, though. Hit a monsoon in the

Indian Ocean. A chap likes dry land.'

'A soldier always did.'

He drank his tea. 'Even Waziristan. Damned place. Hated it so much we fought like lions. We were lords o' creation in India, though. No place like it. Swagger, we could, private, trooper, lance-jack and gunner. The sergeant-major might frighten you, but by God you could swagger when you got out of camp. The Germans didn't break *us* at First Ypres.'

It was nearly forty years since he'd been in the real army, yet he'd never got over it, and who could blame him? He insisted on going out for a walk. 'You'll catch your death o' cold,' Doris said, though knowing she couldn't put him off.

'It's good to see you, Bill. Makes an old man young again to see his son.' He got into his overcoat, but wouldn't take William's arm. They went to the end of the street. It was dark and windy. 'I like to feel the air on my face,' he said, looking more like his old self when they got back.

They sat at the kitchen table for a supper of bread-and-cheese and coffee, and it made William feel old to see him.

'She was a fine lass, Georgina, but you'll have to get wed again, thee knows. You'll get kids next time.'

He was going to say: 'I'm fifty, for God's sake,' but it struck him as impolite in front of a man of eighty-odd who still didn't consider himself old. 'You never know,' he said, for the joke of the thing.

'You'll have kids yet. And bring 'em to see me. It wouldn't surprise me if Georgina didn't tek up with another feller and have a kid, either. You didn't hit it off in that way. I've heard of such.'

There were so many things he could tell him. But he let him talk. His age and honour demanded it. He was an old soldier. Like I might have been. Sitting with his father he felt isolated, inefficient, yet impacted with all the memories of him as a stern parent full of concern to give him a proper start in life. He was glad there was so much love left.

'I've got secrets, Bill,' he said to him.

Don't tell me. Leave me alone. We all have something to hide, he thought, though mine have already blown the lid off my life. 'What are they?'

'There's no point in telling 'em this late in the day,' Doris said.

Charlie laughed, then paused as he lit his pipe. 'It's funny when I think about it. I tried to kill myself as a young feller. I wouldn't a bin here now if it worn't for Doris. I'm allus sorry your mam and me didn't have a girl, William. A sister would have been good for you.'

'You talk tripe-and-onions,' Doris said, going to get some coal in.

Charlie grasped his wrist: 'It's true enough. I hanged myself, but she came in sooner than I'd expected and cut me down. That was before I went for a sowjer. I was in a pit accident.'

'You told me.' For God's sake, stop. Why did old men always go out backwards through the door of their youth?

'Not all of it. I loved this pal of mine. We was at the same school. Never apart. Went out together. Even chased young girls together. When you lose somebody you love you don't want to live any more. If you do you're not human. He died by my side in the dark. But you never get over it. You never forget. Why should you? If you forget things like that there ain't no God. And I never forgot. The only thing wrong I've done in my life was trying to kill myself. It was a death worse than death that Doris saved me from. That's what I've got to thank her for. She never likes to hear me say it. Upsets her. But don't ever forget anything, Bill, then God'll look after you. If I know you'll never forget anything, then I'll know I've always done right by you.'

For once in his life William made a decision that was all his own, in applying for a three-year course at a teachers' training college in nearby Yorkshire. He wouldn't be the only man of his age because it was allowed for those who'd spent twenty years in the Colonies and such places and were no longer needed there, to retrain as teachers. He was, it seemed, ideal for it. His years at the Bingo paradise had been a waste, though nothing was barren of fruit. They only looked on his army time as important, and at the interview he sensed that he needn't worry about the result. They'd even pay him for three years, and give various allowances. It never ceased to surprise him how generous the world could be.

'Well I bloody never!' his father exclaimed. 'A sowjer turning school teacher. Happen you'll be headmaster one day.'

'I start too late for that ambition. There's a job for me, that's all.'

'And what can you teach 'em?' he asked sharply.

'Mathematics. A gunner knows his trigonometry and algebra.'

'Aye, teach 'em some sense. Kids 'ave no sense nowadays.'

'They might have a bit more than we had. But I'll watch 'em. I think they'll listen to me.'

'Aye.'

It was a discouraging note, but he understood it.

There was a summer to wait. He bought a new Raleigh and filled the saddlebag with lunch, set off with map and field glasses on fine mornings to traverse the lanes as far as Southwell or Newark, Buxton or Matlock, to get breath in his lungs and strength back into his legs. He glanced over the hedges at rising fields, copses and cottages, and went bowling along like a youth.

He felt an inner light without age or measurable brilliance that would show him the way strongly enough to illuminate the broad path for others. The forests in his mind were as burned out as those trees on the Messines Ridge many years ago, and as brutally as those he had torn up from the garden by his own personal explosion. Both burnings had scorched and fretted into ash, but from the earth inside him – to which he was more firmly latched than he'd ever imagined he could be – some wisdom had grown in the flowering silence, creating a patience he could draw on and teach others how to use. The universe of himself, even the tiniest corner of it, didn't frighten him any more.

Things had changed from his father's day, and even during his own, and he was still changing because he had gone through such ups and twists since being born. Time was a snake eating its own tail, but the ground shifted under it just the same, in earthquakes.

The weather was dry with a smell of growing wheat, of

apple orchards and rich pastures. There was no monotony in pedalling, as if the wheels worked a well to draw up thoughts from underground.

Times had altered. People often felt this when they got older, but he had entered a state of calm beneficial chaos where regimentation of the spirit no longer had any place. People were more on their own than they used to be. They had more freedom. But what is freedom? One had to make sure it was not simply the act of changing one slavery for another. Yet we're leaving something behind. Nothing is certain or stable. We're left with our own devices, with which to fill up our own emptinesses. The young people feel it, so I can't be wrong. We're also going towards something. The pull of both is so mixed we must find something to go towards and be sure to try and reach it. Out of order came chaos, and out of chaos must come some sort of order. Nothing stays still – even my bicycle when I'm not thinking of pedalling. Chaos mustn't get the upper hand, though we don't want to get back to the brainless and soulless sort of order we had before. People can't live without organisation, no matter how loose and continually threatened it might be, so we have to get used to a state in which we can protect one and all under heaven without being crushed.

Let's hope we reach a time when we'll feel settled enough to hope the world will go on living. Heaven and Hell play hide-and-seek inside us, and if only they'd call a truce and not continually burn us with their rivalry, maybe we could settle down to achieving harmony with each other.

He cycled beyond Southwell, having seen the Minster often enough. It was only ten o'clock so he went south towards the Trent, pushing his bike along the riverside near Bleasby, where he could sit on the grass. But jet bombers came over the high wooded banks from Syerston airfield across the river.

Cycling back, he felt more exhausted than the score of miles should have made him. It began to rain. He passed the miners' houses at Blidworth. At the next hill he got off his bike and pushed, feeling refreshed on getting to the top.

When he free-wheeled down the slope he sensed that something was wrong at home and knew he should get back there as soon as possible. The grey clouds dish-ragged about. A coal lorry threw up muddy water when it swerved to avoid him. It was all part of cycling. When he left that morning Charlie had breakfasted already, and talked about clearing a few weeds from the rows of broad beans in the garden. He looked frail, and even his back wasn't straight any more, though he fought hard to keep it so. Doris wouldn't let him tire himself too much.

He stopped in a lay-by and ate a sandwich, took a few swigs of unsweetened tea from his flask. The huge overgrown hedge between him and the field was sprinkled with drops, and smelled sweet. After all these years, he'd come home again. But when he started teaching he'd find some other part of the country to work in, moving to a fresh place every few years.

He set off through the drizzle without feeling tired. An hour later he removed his clips by the back door, and put the bike in its shed, having already seen the doctor's car on the road outside.

His father was sprawled in the armchair, and he watched him go, a helpless but stubborn old man who would not be carried up to bed because he regarded it as shameful to die in such a place.

CHAPTER TWENTY-EIGHT

What will we do now? Doris wondered, on the drive home from the cemetery, where Charlie had been put to rest next to his long-departed wife. Her cheeks were wet with tears, and William held her hands. She'd lost everything. Not even her brother was left.

'My college is less than an hour's drive,' he said, 'so I'll see you every week.'

'He shouldn't have gone,' she said – for form's sake, feeling an agonising tiredness from the years spent looking after him. She wished only to be alone for a while. Without putting words to it, she'd desired it often, and knew it plainly. So she felt guilty, and wept.

'He was tired, well above his three-score-and-ten.' Form perhaps demanded that he weep too, but he didn't. At the house Doris took out the side of beef, as well as sandwiches, cake and drink for those half dozen mourners who came back, men who'd worked with Charlie in his post office days twenty years ago. There might have been others, but in his tenacity he had outlived them.

'Maybe you *will* find a young woman and get married,' she said later. '*And* have children.'

He checked himself. Never say never. 'Perhaps I will. Life begins whenever you want it to.'

'It's a shame you couldn't have had any sooner. Charlie would have loved that. He did mention it to me a time or two.'

He'd disappointed him in that, though he hoped not in everything. In me he'd tried to create a better image of himself. He'd both succeeded, and failed.

He bought a house at Scarcliffe, near the college, one of a

row on the way to the colliery. It was worth it for three years, rather than pay rent, for he intended to sell it afterwards and move on. Mobility was still the spice of life.

After the first year he married a teacher at the college, who at twenty had said she'd never get married, but who seemed ready to do so now she was thirty. A son was born to them six months later, and after another year, they had a daughter.

They moved to Northumberland and taught there. Doris visited them. So did Oxton with his wife. He took the children walking in the hills, and told young David Scorton where he'd place his guns if he had a battery of his own. The boy was thrilled to hear him, but he was interested in science more than anything else.

A man can look younger than his age, but if he knows he does there's something wrong with him. At sixty William had short greyish hair, was strong in build, and fit from plenty of physical exercise in which he had always believed. He'd been in the army and, after a lifetime of it, through the army. His father had pushed him into it but he forgave him for that: we have to forgive our parents if we want our children to forgive us. There'd been nothing to hold against him, but looking back on it, with no vain regrets, he realised that he hadn't really been cut out to be a soldier.

He was nearly ten years into another marriage, and they had two children. Now that he seemed beyond everything he was most into himself, which was where he should have been before he got into anything at all. But whose life ever worked out like that? Maybe more than you imagine, he said to himself, though it was hard to think so.

April 2nd 1976